To Have And To Hold

HELEN LACEY
MYRNA MACKENZIE
CATHY GILLEN THACKER

MILLS & BOON

First Published in Great Britain 2018
by Mills & Boon, an imprint of HarperCollins*Publishers*
1 London Bridge Street, London, SE1 9GF

TO HAVE AND TO HOLD © 2018 Harlequin Books S. A.

Made For Marriage © 2012 Helen Lacey
To Wed A Rancher © 2011 Myrna Topol
The Mummy Proposal © 2010 Cathy Gillen Thacker

ISBN: 978-0-263-26717-4

05-0518

MIX
Paper from
responsible sources
FSC™ C007454

This book is produced from independently certified FSC™
paper to ensure responsible forest management.

For more information visit: www.harpercollins.co.uk/green

Printed and bound in Spain
by CPI, Barcelona

MADE FOR MARRIAGE

HELEN LACEY

For Robert
Emphatically, Undeniably, Categorically.

Chapter One

Callie Jones knew trouble when she came upon it. And the thirteen-year-old who stood defiantly in front of her looked like more trouble than she wanted on a Saturday morning. For one thing, Callie liked to sleep later on the weekend, and the teenager with the impudent expression had banged on her door at an indecently early 6:00 a.m. And for another, the girl wasn't anything like she'd expected. Her long black hair was tied up in an untidy ponytail revealing at least half a dozen piercings in her ears, plus another in both her brow and nose. And the dark kohl smudged around her eyes was heavier than any acceptable trend Callie had ever seen.

"I'm Lily," the girl said, crossing her thin arms. "I'm here for my lesson."

Callie opened the front door fractionally, grateful she'd had the sense to wrap herself in an old dressing gown before she'd come to the door. It was chilly outside. "You're early," she said, spotting a bicycle at the bottom of the steps.

The teenager shrugged her shoulders. "So what? I'm here now."

Callie hung on to her patience. "I told your father eight o'clock."

Lily shrugged again, without any apology in her expression. "Then I guess he told me the wrong time." The girl looked her over, and Callie felt the burning scrutiny right down to her toes.

Callie took a deep breath and glanced over the girl's head. Dawn was just breaking on the horizon. Another hour of sleep would have been nice, but she wasn't about to send Lily home.

"Okay, Lily. Give me a few minutes to get ready." Callie pointed to the wicker love seat on the porch. "Wait here. I'll be right back."

The girl shrugged. "Whatever."

Callie locked the security mesh screen as discreetly as she could and turned quickly on her heels. She didn't want an unsupervised teenager wandering around her house while she changed her clothes. Dashing into the bathroom, she washed her face and brushed her teeth and hair before slipping into jeans and a T-shirt.

She skipped coffee, grabbed a cereal bar and shoved it into her back pocket. She really needed to do some grocery shopping. But she was too busy. Busy with her students, busy trying to ensure the utilities were paid, busy not thinking about why a recently turned thirty ex-California girl worked twelve-hour days trying to make a success of a small horse-riding school situated a few miles from the eastern edge of the Australian coastline.

Callie grabbed her sweater from the back of the kitchen chair and headed for the front door. Once she'd locked up she pulled her muddy riding boots off the shoe rack, quickly tucked her feet into them, snatched up her battered cowboy hat and placed it on her head. She turned around to find no sign of her visitor. Or the expensive-looking bicycle.

Obviously the teenager wasn't keen on following instructions.

She put the keys into her pocket and headed for the stables. The large stable complex, round yard and dressage arena were impressive. Callie had spent nearly every penny she had on Sandhills Farm to ensure it became a workable and viable business.

Okay kid—where are you?

Tessa rushed from around the back of the house. Still a pup, the Labrador/cattle dog cross bounded on lanky legs and yapped excitedly. Obviously no kid was back there, or Tessa would have hung around for attention.

So, where was she? Callie's intuition and instincts surged into overdrive. Miss Too-Many-Piercings was clearly looking for trouble. She called the girl's name. No answer.

When Callie opened the stable doors and flicked the lock mechanism into place, a few long heads immediately poked over the stalls. She looked around and found no sign of Lily.

Great—the kid had gone AWOL.

And where on earth was Joe, her farmhand? She checked her watch. Six-twenty-five. He was late and she'd have to attend to the feeding before she could start the lesson with her missing student.

First things first—find Lily…um…whatever-her-last-name-is. She clicked her fingers together. Hah—Preston. That's right. Lily Preston.

She's got the father with the sexy telephone voice, remember?

Callie shook some sense into her silly head when she heard a vehicle coming down the driveway. Joe…good. She swiveled on her heel and circumnavigated the stables, stopping abruptly, mid-stride, too stunned to move.

Indiana—her beautiful, precious and irreplaceable Hanoverian gelding—stood by the fence, wearing only an ill-fitting bridle. Lily Preston was straddled between the fence post and trough as she attempted to climb onto his back.

Think...and think quickly.

Callie willed her legs to move and raced toward the girl and horse, but it was too late. The teenager had mounted, collected the reins and clicked the gelding into a trot Callie knew she would have no hope of sustaining.

She's going to fall. And before Callie had a chance to move, Lily Preston lost control, tumbled off the horse and landed squarely on her behind.

She was gone. Ditto for her bike. Noah Preston cursed and headed back into the house. The last thing he'd told his angry daughter the night before, just as she'd slammed her bedroom door in his face, was that he'd take her to Sandhills Farm at seven-forty-five in the morning. She hadn't wanted him to take her. She wanted to go alone. Without him. He should have taken more notice. The time was now six-thirty-three and Lily had skipped. In typical Lily style.

"Daddy, I'm hungry."

Noah turned his head. His eight-year-old son, Jamie, as uncomplicated and placid a child as Lily was not, stood in the doorway.

"Okay," he said. "I'll make breakfast soon. But we have to go find Lily first."

Jamie rolled his big eyes. "Again?"

Noah smiled. "I know, mate, but I have to make sure she's safe."

"She is," Jamie assured him in a very grown-up fashion. "She's gone to see the horse lady."

"She told you that?"

His son nodded. "Yep. Told me this morning. She rode her bike. I told her not to."

The horse lady? *Callie Jones.* Recommended as the best equestrian instructor in the district. He'd called her a week ago, inquiring about setting Lily up with some lessons. Her soft, American accent had intrigued him and he'd quickly made arrangements to bring Lily out to her riding school.

So, at least he knew where she'd gone and why. To make a point. To show him he had no control, no say, and that she could do whatever she pleased.

Noah spent the following minutes waking the twins and making sure the three kids were clothed, washed and ready to leave. Jamie grumbled a bit about being hungry, so Noah grabbed a few apples and a box of cereal bars for the trip. He found his keys, led his family outside, bundled the children into his dual-cab utility vehicle and buckled them up.

He lived just out from Crystal Point and the trip took barely ten minutes. Sandhills Farm was set back from the road and gravel crunched beneath the wheels when he turned off down the long driveway. He followed the line of white-washed fencing until he reached the house, a rundown, big, typical Queenslander with a wraparound veranda and hat-box roof. Shabby but redeemable.

So where was Lily?

He put Jamie in charge of four-year-old Hayley and Matthew, took the keys from the ignition and stepped out of the vehicle. A dog came bounding toward him, a happy-looking pup that promptly dropped to Noah's feet and pleaded for attention. Noah patted the dog for a moment, flipped off his sunglasses and looked around. The house looked deserted. An old Ford truck lay idle near the stables and he headed for it. The keys hanging in the ignition suggested someone was around. He spotted Lily's bicycle propped against the wall of the stable. So she *was* here.

But where? And where was Callie Jones? He couldn't see a sign of anyone in the yards or the stables or in the covered sand arena to the left of the building. The stable doors were open and he took a few steps inside, instantly impressed by the setup. A couple of horses tipped their heads over the top of their stalls and watched him as he made his way through. He found the tack room and small office at the end of the row of stalls. The door was ajar and he tapped on the jamb. No one answered. But he could see inside. There were pictures on the wall—all of horses in varying competitive poses. The rider in each shot was female. Perhaps Callie Jones?

Noah lingered for another few seconds before he returned outside. The friendly dog bounded to his feet again, demanding notice. The animal stayed for just a moment before darting past him and heading off around the side of the building. Noah instructed the kids to get out of the truck and told them to follow him. As he walked with the three children in a straight line behind him, he heard the sound of voices that got louder with every step. When he turned another corner he stopped. The breath kicked from his chest.

A woman stood by the fence.

Was this Callie Jones? Not too tall, not too thin. Curves every place a woman ought to have them. Her jeans, riding low, looked molded onto her hips and legs. Long brown hair hung down her back in a ponytail and his fingers itched with the thought of threading them through it. Noah's heart suddenly knocked against his ribs. *Lightning,* he thought. *Is this what it feels like to be struck by lightning?*

Noah probably would have taken a little more time to observe her if he hadn't spotted his daughter sitting on the ground, her clothes covered in dust and a big brown horse looming over her.

* * *

"What's going on here?"

Callie jumped and turned around on her heels.

A man glared at her from about twenty feet away.

"Hey, Dad," called Lily.

Uh-oh. The father? He looked *very* unhappy. Callie switched her attention back to the girl sitting on the ground. She was sure Lily's butt would be sore for a day or so. And she was thankful Indiana had stopped once he'd realized his inexperienced rider was in trouble. Which meant all that had really happened was Lily had slipped off the side. It wasn't a serious fall. And she intended to tell him so.

Callie wiped her hands down her jeans. "Hi, I'm—"

"Lily," he barked out, interrupting her and bridging the space between them with a few strides. "What happened?"

She made a face. "I fell off."

"She's okay," Callie said quickly.

"I think I'll decide that for myself," he said and helped his daughter to her feet.

Lily dusted off her clothes and crossed her thin arms. "I'm fine, Dad."

Indiana moved toward Callie and nuzzled her elbow. "Good boy," she said softly, patting his nose.

"You're rewarding him for throwing my daughter?"

Heat prickled up her spine. "He didn't throw her."

Silence stretched like elastic between them as he looked at her with the greenest eyes Callie had ever seen. It took precisely two seconds to register he was attractive. It didn't matter that he scowled at her. She still had enough of a pulse to recognize an absolutely gorgeous man when faced with one. If she were looking. Which she wasn't.

Then she saw children behind him. A lot of children. Three. All blond.

A familiar pain pierced behind her rib cage.

"Lily, take the kids and go and wait by the truck."

"But, Dad—"

"Go," he instructed.

Callie clutched Indiana's reins tightly. Gorgeous, maybe. Friendly, not one bit.

His daughter went to say something else but stopped. She shrugged her shoulders and told the smaller children to follow her. Once Lily and the children were out of sight the man turned to her. "What exactly do you think you were doing?"

"I was—"

"My daughter gets thrown off a horse and you just left her lying in the dirt. What if she'd been seriously injured?"

Callie held her ground. She'd handled parents before. "She wasn't, though."

"Did you even check? I'll see your license revoked," he said. "You're not fit to work with children."

That got her mouth moving. "Just wait one minute," she said, planting her hands on her hips for dramatic effect. "You don't have the right—"

"I do," he said quickly. "What kind of nut are you?"

Callie's face burned. "I'm not a—"

"Of all the irresponsible things I've—"

"Would you stop interrupting me," she said, cutting him off right back. It did the trick because he clammed up instantly. He really was remarkably handsome. Callie took a deep breath. "Your daughter took my horse without permission."

"So this is Lily's fault?"

"I didn't say that."

He stepped closer and Callie was suddenly struck by how tall he was and how broad his shoulders were. "Then it's your fault?" He raised his hands. "Your property, your horse...it's not hard to figure out who's to blame."

"She took the horse without my permission," Callie said

again, firmer this time, making a point and refusing to be verbally outmaneuvered by a gorgeous man with a sexy voice.

His green eyes glittered. "So she was wandering around unsupervised, Ms. Jones?"

Annoyance weaved up her spine. *Ms. Jones? Nothing friendly about that.*

She took a deep breath and willed herself to keep her cool. "I understand how this looks and how you must feel, but I think—"

"Are you a parent?" he asked quickly.

"No."

"Then you don't know how I feel."

He was right—she didn't have a clue. She wasn't a parent. She'd never be a parent. Silence stretched. She looked at him. He looked at her. Something flickered between them. An undercurrent. Not of anger—this was something else.

He's looking at me. He's angry. He's downright furious. But he's checking me out.

Callie couldn't remember the last time she'd registered that kind of look. Or the last time she'd wanted to look back. But she knew she shouldn't. He had children. He was obviously married. She glanced at his left hand. *No wedding ring.* Her belly dipped nonsensically.

His eyes narrowed. "Have you any qualifications?"

She stared at him. "I have an instructor's ticket from the Equestrian Federation of—"

"I meant qualifications to work with kids?" he said, cutting off her ramble. "Like teaching credentials? Or a degree in child psychology? Come to think of it, do you have any qualifications other than the fact you can ride a horse?"

Outraged, Callie opened her mouth to speak but quickly stopped. She was suddenly tongue-tied, stripped of her usual ability to speak her mind. Her cheeks flamed and thankfully her silence didn't last long. "Are you always so...so rude?"

He smiled as though he found her anger amusing. "And do you always allow your students to walk around unsupervised?"

"No," she replied, burning up. "But you're not in possession of all the facts."

He watched her for a moment, every gorgeous inch of him focused on her, and she experienced a strange dip in the pit of her stomach, like she was riding a roller coaster way too fast.

"Then please...enlighten me," he said quietly.

Callie bit her temper back. "When Lily arrived early I told her to wait for me. She didn't."

"And that's when she took your horse?"

"Yes."

"Why didn't you tell her to get off?"

"I did," Callie replied. "Although I've discovered that sometimes its better practice to let people find out just how—"

"You mean the hard way?" he asked, cutting her off again.

Callie nodded. "But she wasn't in any danger. Indiana wouldn't have hurt her."

"Just for the record," he said quietly—so quietly Callie knew he was holding himself in control—"Lily knows all about hard life lessons."

She's not the only one.

Good sense thankfully prevailed and she kept her cool. "I'm sorry you had a reason to be concerned about her safety," she said quietly. "I had no idea she would do something like that."

"Did it occur to you to call me?" he asked. "I did leave you my cell number when I first phoned you. Lily arrived two hours early—didn't that set off some kind of alarm bell?"

"She said you'd told her the wrong time."

"Does that seem likely? This arrangement won't work

out," he said before she could respond. "I'll find another instructor for Lily—one who can act responsibly."

His words stung. But Callie had no illusions about Lily Preston. The girl was trouble. And she certainly didn't want to have anything more to do with the man in front of her. Despite the fact her dormant libido had suddenly resurfaced and seemed to be singing, *pick me, pick me!*

She wanted to challenge him there and then to who was the responsible one—her for taking her eyes off Lily for a matter of minutes or him for clearly having little control over his daughter. But she didn't. *Think about the business. Think about the horses.* The last run-in she had with a parent had cost her nearly a quarter of her students and she was still struggling to recoup her losses. Three months earlier Callie had caught two students breaking the rules and had quickly cancelled all lessons with the troublesome sisters. But the girls' mother had other ideas, and she'd threatened to lodge a formal complaint with the Equestrian Federation. It could have led to the suspension of her instructor's license. Of course Callie could still teach without it, but her credentials were important to her. And she didn't want that kind of trouble again.

"That's your decision."

He didn't say another word. He just turned on his heels and walked away.

Callie slumped back against a fence post. Moments later she heard the rumble of an engine and didn't take a breath until the sound of tires crunching over gravel faded into nothing.

She looked at Indiana. She'd brought the horse with her from California—just Indy and three suitcases containing her most treasured belongings. Indiana had remained quarantined for some time after her arrival. Long enough for Callie to hunt through real estate lists until she'd found the perfect place to start her riding school.

Callie loved Sandhills Farm. Indiana and the rest of her nine horses were her life…her babies. *The only babies I'll have.* It made her think of *that man* and his four children.

A strange sensation uncurled in her chest, reminding her of an old pain—of old wishes and old regrets.

She took Indy's reins and led him toward the stables. Once he was back in the stall Callie headed for the office. She liked to call it an office, even though it essentially served as a tack room. She'd added a desk, a filing cabinet and a modest computer setup.

Joe, her part-time farmhand, had arrived and began the feeding schedule. Callie looked at her appointment book and struck Lily Preston's name off her daily list. There would be no Lily in her life…and no Lily's gorgeous father.

She looked around at her ego wall and at the framed photographs she'd hung up in no particular order. Pictures from her past, pictures of herself and Indiana at some of the events they'd competed in.

But not one of Craig.

Because she didn't want the inevitable inquisition. She didn't talk about Craig Baxter. Or her past. She'd moved halfway across the world to start her new life. Crystal Point had been an easy choice. Her father had been born in the nearby town of Bellandale and Callie remembered the many happy holidays she'd spent there when she was young. It made her feel connected to her Australian roots to make her home in the place where he'd been raised and lived until he was a young man. And although she missed California, this was home now. And she wasn't about to let that life be derailed by a gorgeous man with sexy green eyes. No chance.

Callie loved yard sales. Late Sunday morning, after her last student left, she snatched a few twenty dollar bills from her desk drawer and whistled Tessa to come to heel as she headed for her truck. The dog quickly leapt into the passenger seat.

The drive into Crystal Point took exactly six minutes. The small beachside community boasted a population of just eight hundred residents and sat at the mouth of the Bellan River, one of the most pristine waterways in the state. On the third Sunday of every month the small community hosted a "trunk and treasure" sale, where anyone who had something to sell could pull up their car, open the trunk and offer their wares to the dozens of potential buyers who rolled up.

The sale was in full swing and Callie parked a hundred yards up the road outside the local grocery store. She opened a window for Tessa then headed inside to grab a soda before she trawled for bargains. The bell dinged as she stepped across the threshold. The shop was small, but crammed with everything from fishing tackle to beach towels and grocery items. There was also an ATM and a pair of ancient fuel pumps outside that clearly hadn't pumped fuel for years.

"Good morning, Callie."

"Hi, Linda," she greeted the fifty-something woman behind the counter, who was hidden from view by a tall glass cabinet housing fried food, pre-packaged sandwiches and cheese-slathered hot dogs.

She picked out a soda and headed for the counter.

Linda smiled. "I hear you had a run-in with Noah Preston yesterday."

Noah? Was that his name? He'd probably told her when he'd made arrangements for his daughter's lessons, but Callie had appalling recall for names. *Noah.* Warmth pooled low in her belly. *I don't have any interest in that awful man.* And she wasn't about to admit she'd spent the past twenty-four hours thinking about him.

"Good news travels fast," she said and passed over a twenty dollar note.

Linda took the money and cranked the register. "In this place news is news. I only heard because my daughter volunteers as a guard at the surf beach."

Callie took the bait and her change. "The surf beach?"

"Well, Cameron was there. He told her all about it."

He did? "Who's Cameron?"

Linda tutted as though Callie should know exactly who he was. "Cameron Jakowski. He and Noah are best friends."

Callie couldn't imagine anyone wanting to be friends with Noah Preston.

"Cameron volunteers there, too," she said, and Callie listened, trying to not lose track of the conversation. "Noah used to, but he's too busy with all his kids now."

"So this Cameron told your daughter what happened?"

"Yep. He said you and Noah had an all-out brawl. Something to do with that eldest terror of his."

"It wasn't exactly a brawl," Callie explained. "More like a disagreement."

"I heard he thinks you should be shut down," Linda said odiously, her voice dropping an octave.

Callie's spine stiffened. Not again. When she'd caught the Trent sisters smoking in the stables, Sonya Trent had threatened the same thing. "What?"

"Mmm," Linda said. "And it only takes one thing to go wrong to ruin a business, believe me. One whiff of you being careless around the kids and you can kiss the place goodbye."

Callie felt like throwing up. Her business meant everything to her. Her horses, her home. "I didn't do anything," she protested.

Linda made a sympathetic face. "Of course you didn't, love. But I wouldn't blame you one bit if you had because of that little hellion." Linda sighed. "That girl's been nothing but trouble since her—"

The conversation stopped abruptly when the bell pealed

and a woman, dressed in a pair of jeans and a vivid orange gauze blouse, walked into the shop. Black hair curled wildly around her face and bright green eyes regarded Callie for a brief moment.

"Hello, Linda," she said and grabbed a bottle of water from one of the fridges.

"Evie, good to see you. Are you selling at the trunk sale today?" Linda asked.

Her dancing green eyes grew wide. "For sure," she said and paid her money. "My usual stuff. But if you hear of anyone wanting a big brass bed, let me know. I'm renovating one of the upstairs rooms and it needs to go. Catch you later."

She hurried from the shop and Linda turned her attention back to Callie.

"That's Evie Dunn," Linda explained. "She runs a bed and breakfast along the waterfront. You can't miss it. It's the big A-frame place with the monstrous Norfolk pines out the front. She's an artist and sells all kinds of crafting supplies, too. You should check it out."

Callie grimaced and then smiled. "I'm not really into handicrafts."

Linda's silvery brows shot up. "Noah Preston is her brother."

Of course. No wonder those green eyes had looked so familiar. Okay, maybe now she *was* a little interested. Callie grabbed her soda and left the shop. So, he wanted her shut down, did he?

She drove the truck in the car park and leashed Tessa. There were more than thirty cars and stalls set up, and the park was teeming with browsers and buyers. It took Callie about three minutes to find Evie Dunn. The pretty brunette had a small table laid out with craft wares and costume jewelry. She wandered past once and then navigated around for another look.

"Are you interested in scrapbooking?" Evie Dunn asked on her third walk by.

Callie stalled and eased Tessa to heel. She took a step toward the table and shrugged. "Not particularly."

Black brows rose sharply. "Are you interested in a big brass bed?"

Callie shook her head. "Ah, I don't think so."

Evie planted her hands on her hips. "Then I guess you must be interested in my brother?"

Callie almost hyperventilated. "What do you—"

"You're Callie, right?" The other woman asked and thrust out her hand. "I saw the name of your riding school on the side of your truck. I'm Evie. Lily told me all about you. You made quite an impression on my niece, which is not an easy feat. From what she told me, I'm certain she still wants you as her riding instructor."

There was no chance that was going to happen. "I don't think it's up to Lily."

"Made you mad, did he?"

Callie took a step forward and shook her hand. "You could say that."

Evie, whose face was an amazing mix of vivid color—green eyes and bright cherry lips—stared at her with a thoughtful expression that said she was being thoroughly summed up. "So, about the brass bed?" she asked and smiled. "Would you like to see it?"

Brass bed? Callie shook her head. Hadn't she already said she wasn't interested? "I don't think—"

"You'll love it," Evie insisted. "I can take you to look at it now if you like. Help me pack up and we can get going."

Callie began to protest and then stopped. She was pretty sure they weren't really talking about a bed. This was Noah

Preston's sister. And because he had quickly become enemy number one, if she had a lick of sense she'd find out everything she could about him and use it to her advantage. If Noah thought she would simply sit back and allow him to ruin her reputation, he could certainly think again. Sandhills Farm was her life. If he wanted a war, she'd give him one.

Chapter Two

Noah didn't know how to reach out to his angry daughter. He hurt for her. A deep, soul-wrenching hurt that transcended right through to his bones. But what could he do? Her sullen, uncommunicative moods were impossible to read. She skulked around the house with her eyes to the floor, hiding behind her makeup, saying little, determined to disassociate herself from the family he tried so frantically to keep together.

And she pined for the mother who'd abandoned her without a backward glance.

She'd deny it, of course. But Noah knew. It had been more than four years ago. Four and a half long years and they all needed to move on.

Yeah, right...like I've moved on?

He liked to think so. Perhaps not the way his parents or sisters thought he should have. But he'd managed to pull together the fractured pieces of the life his ex-wife discarded.

He had Preston Marine, the business his grandfather created and which he now ran, his kids, his family and friends. It was enough. More than enough.

Most of the time.

Except for the past twenty-four hours.

Because as much as he tried not to, he couldn't stop thinking about the extraordinarily beautiful Callie Jones and her glittering blue eyes. And the way she'd planted her hands on her hips. And the sinful way she'd filled out her jeans. For the first time in forever he felt a spark of attraction. More than a spark. It felt like a damned raging inferno, consuming him with its heat.

Noah stacked the dishes he'd washed and dried his hands, then checked his watch. He was due at Evie's around two o'clock; he'd promised her he'd help shift some furniture. Evie loved rearranging furniture.

Within ten minutes they were on their way. Hayley and Matthew, secured in their booster seats, chatted happily to each other while Jamie sat in the front beside Noah. His one-hundred-and-forty acre farm was only minutes out of Crystal Point and was still considered part of the small town. He'd bought the place a couple of years earlier, for a song of a price, from an elderly couple wanting to retire after farming sugar cane for close to fifty years. The cane was all but gone now, and Noah leased the land to a local farmer who ran cattle.

He dropped speed along The Parade, the long road separating the houses from the shore, and pulled up outside his sister's home. There was a truck parked across the road, a beat-up blue Ford that looked familiar. He hauled Hayley into his arms, grabbed Matty's hand and allowed Jamie to seize the knapsack from the backseat and then race on ahead. The kids loved Evie's garden, with its pond and stone paved walkways, which wound in tracks to a stone wishing well. And Noah kind of liked it, too.

"Look, Daddy...it's that dog," Jamie said excitedly, running toward a happy-looking pup tied to a railing near the front veranda.

The dog looked as familiar to him as the truck parked outside. His stomach did a stupid leap.

She's here? What connection did Callie Jones have to Evie? Before he could protest, Jamie was up the steps, opening the front door and calling his aunt's name.

Noah found them in the kitchen. Evie was cutting up pineapple and *she* was sitting at the long scrubbed table, cradling a mug in her hands. She looked up when he entered the room and smiled. A killer smile. A smile with enough kick to knock the breath from his chest. He wondered if she knew she had it, if she were aware how flawless her skin looked or how red and perfectly bowed her lips were. The hat was gone and her brown hair hung over one shoulder in a long braid.

Discomfort raced through him. Noah shifted Hayley on his hip and hung on tightly to Matty's hand. She looked him over, he looked her over. Something stirred, rumbling through his blood, taunting him a little.

Evie cleared her throat and broke the silence. "Well," she said. "How about I take the kids outside and you two can... talk?"

Noah didn't want to talk with her. He also knew he wouldn't be able to drag himself away.

Callie Jones had walked into his life. And he was screwed.

Callie couldn't speak. They were twins. *Twins.* Who looked to be about...four years old?

The same age as Ryan would have been...

She smiled—she wasn't sure how—and watched him hold the twins with delightful affection. He looked like Father of the Year. And he was, according to his sister. A single dad raising four children. A good man. The best.

A heavy feeling grew in her chest, filling her blood, sharpening her breath.

The children disappeared with Evie, and once they were alone she stood and flicked her braid down her back. He watched every movement, studying her with such open regard she couldn't stop a flush from rising over her skin.

I shouldn't want him to look at me like that.

Not this man who had quickly become the enemy.

"I didn't expect to see you…" he said, then paused. "So soon."

She inhaled deeply. "I guess you didn't. Frankly, I didn't *want* to see you."

His green eyes held her captive. "And yet you're here in my sister's house?"

Callie tilted her chin. "I'm looking at a bed."

The word *bed* quickly stirred up a whole lot of awareness between them. It was bad enough she thought the man was gorgeous—her blasted body had to keep reminding her of the fact!

"A bed?"

"Yes." Callie took another breath. Longer this time because she needed it. "You know, one of those things to sleep on."

That got him thinking. "I know what a bed is," he said quietly. "And what it's used for."

I'll just bet you do!

Callie turned red from her braid to her boots. "But now that I am here, perhaps you'd like to apologize?"

"For what?" He looked stunned.

For being a gorgeous jerk. "For being rude yesterday."

"Wait just a—"

"And for telling people my school should be closed down."

"What?"

"Are you denying it? I mean, you threatened me," she said, and as soon as the words left her mouth she felt ridiculous.

"I did what?"

She didn't miss the quiet, controlled tone in his voice. Maddeningly in control, she thought. Almost too controlled, as if he was purposefully holding himself together in some calm, collected way to prove he would not, and could not, be provoked.

"You said you'd see that I lost my license," she explained herself.

He looked at her. "And because of that you think I've been saying your school needs to be closed down?"

"Yes, I do."

"And who did you hear this from?"

Callie felt foolish then. Was she being paranoid listening to small-town gossip? *Have I jumped to conclusions?* When she didn't reply he spoke again.

"Local tongues, no doubt. I haven't said a word to anyone, despite my better judgment." He cocked a brow. "Perhaps you've pissed off someone else."

Retaliation burned on the end of her tongue. The infamous Callie Jones temper rose up like bile, strangling her throat. "You're such a jerk!"

He smiled. *Smiled.* As if he found her incredibly amusing. Callie longed to wipe the grin from his handsome face, to slap her hand across his smooth skin. To touch. To feel. And then, without explanation, something altered inside her. Something altered *between them*. In an unfathomable moment, everything changed.

He sees me...

She wasn't sure why she thought it. Why she felt it through to the blood pumping in her veins. But she experienced a strange tightening in her chest, constricting her breath, her movements. Callie didn't want anyone to see her. Not this man. Especially not this man. This stranger.

But he did. She was sure of it. *He sees that I'm a fraud. I can talk a tough line. But I live alone. I work alone. I am alone.*

And Noah Preston somehow knew it.

Bells rang in her head. Warning her, telling her to leave and break the incredible eye contact that shimmered like light between them.

"You need to keep a better handle on your daughter."

"I do?" he said, still smiling.

"She broke the rules," Callie said pointedly. "And as her parent, that's your fault, not mine."

"She broke the rules because you lacked good judgment," he replied.

Callie scowled, grabbed her keys and headed for the door. "Tell your sister thank you for the coffee."

He raised an eyebrow. "Did I hit a nerve?"

She rounded her shoulders back and turned around. "I'm well aware of my faults. I may not be all wisdom regarding the behavior of teenage girls, but I certainly know plenty about men who are arrogant bullies. You can point as much blame in my direction as you like—but that doesn't change the facts."

"I *did* hit a nerve."

"I wouldn't give you the satisfaction."

As she left the house and collected Tessa, Callie wasn't sure she took a breath until she drove off down The Parade.

Noah waited until the front door clicked shut and then inhaled deeply, filling his lungs with air. A jerk? Is that what he'd sounded like? He didn't like that one bit. A protective father, yes. But a jerk? He felt like chasing after her to set her straight.

Evie returned to the kitchen in record time, minus the kids. "They're watching a DVD," she said and refilled the kettle. Evie thought caffeine was a sure cure for anything. "So, that went well, did it?"

"Like a root canal."

"Ouch." She made a face. "She called you a jerk. And a bully."

"Eavesdropping, huh?"

She shrugged. "Only a bit. So, who won that battle in this war?" she asked, smiling.

He recognized his sister's look. "It's not exactly a war."

Evie raised a brow. "But you were mad at her, right?"

"Sure." He let out an impatient breath.

"Well." Evie stopped her task of making coffee. "You don't usually get mad at people."

Noah frowned. "Of course I do."

"No, you don't," Evie said. "Not even your pesky three sisters."

He shrugged. "Does this conversation have a point?"

"I was just wondering what she did to make you so...uptight?"

"I'm sure she told you what happened," Noah said, trying to look disinterested and failing.

Evie's eyes sparkled. "Well...yes, she did. But I want to hear it from you."

"Why?"

"So I can see if you get the same look on your face that she did."

"What look?" he asked stupidly.

Evie stopped what she was doing. A tiny smile curved her lips. "*That* look."

He shook his head. "You're imagining things."

Evie chuckled. "I don't think so. Anyway, I thought she was...nice."

Yeah, like a stick of dynamite. "You like everyone."

Evie laughed out loud. "Ha—you're not fooling me. You *like* her."

"I don't know her."

Noah dismissed his sister's suspicions. If he gave an inch, if he even slightly indicated he had thoughts of Callie Jones in any kind of romantic capacity, she'd be on the telephone to their mother and two other sisters within a heartbeat.

Romance...yeah, right. With four kids, a mortgage and a business to run—women weren't exactly lining up to take part in his complicated life.

He couldn't remember the last time he'd had a date. Eight months ago, he thought, vaguely remembering a quiet spoken, divorced mother of two who'd spent the entire evening complaining about her no-good, layabout ex. One date was all they'd had. He'd barely touched her hand. *I live like a monk.* That wasn't surprising, though—the fallout from his divorce would have sent any man running to the monastery.

Besides, he didn't want a hot-tempered, irresponsible woman in his life, did he? No matter how sexy she looked in her jeans. "So, where's this furniture you want me to move?" he asked, clapping his hands together as he stood.

Evie took the hint that the subject was closed. "One of the upstairs bedrooms," she said. "I want to paint the walls. I just need the armoire taken out into the hall."

"Oh, the antique cupboard that weighs a ton? Lucky me. At least this time I'm spared the stairs. Do you remember when Gordon and I first got the thing upstairs?"

Evie smiled, clearly reminiscing, thinking of the husband she'd lost ten years earlier. "And Cameron," she said. "You were all acting like a bunch of wusses that day, huffing and puffing over one little armoire."

Noah grunted as they took the stairs. "Damn thing's made of lead."

"Wuss," she teased.

They laughed some more and spent twenty minutes shifting the heaviest piece of furniture on the planet. When he was done, Noah wanted a cold drink and a back rub.

And that idea made him think of Callie Jones and her lovely blue eyes all over again.

"Feel like staying for dinner?" Evie asked once they were back downstairs. "Trevor's at a study group tonight," she said of her fifteen-year-old son.

"On a Sunday? The kid's keen."

"The kid's smart," Evie corrected. "He wants to be an engineer like his favorite uncle."

Noah smiled. "Not tonight, but thanks. I've gotta pick Lily up from the surf club at four. And it's a school day tomorrow."

Evie groaned. "God, we're a boring lot."

Noah wasn't going to argue with that. He grabbed the kids' things and rounded up the twins and Jamie. The kids hugged Evie and she waved them off from the front step.

"And don't forget the parents are back from their trip on Wednesday," she reminded him.

"I won't," he promised.

"And don't forget I'll need your help to move the armoire back into the bedroom in a few days. I'll call to remind you."

He smiled. "I won't forget."

"And don't forget to think about why you're refusing to admit that you're hot for a certain riding instructor."

Noah shook his head. "Goodbye, Evie."

She was still laughing minutes later when he drove off.

Noah headed straight for the surf club. Lily was outside when he pulled up, talking to Cameron. She scowled when she saw him and quickly got into the backseat, squeezing between the twins' booster seats. Normally, she would have resigned Jamie to the back. But not today. She was clearly still mad with him. Mad that *he'd* made it impossible for her to go back to Sandhills Farm, at least in her mind.

Noah got out of the pickup and turned his attention to his best friend. "So, Hot Tub, what have you been up to?"

Cameron half-punched him in the shoulder. "Would you stop calling me that?"

Noah grinned at his playboy friend and the unflattering nickname he'd coined years earlier.

"I'll do my best." He changed the subject. "Did Lily say anything to you about what happened yesterday?"

Cameron nodded. "You know Lily. I hear the horse lady's real cute."

Cute? That's not how Noah would describe Callie. Cute was a bland word meant for puppies and little girls with pink ribbons in their hair. Beautiful better described Callie Jones, and even that didn't seem to do her justice. Not textbook pretty, like Margaret, his ex, had been. Callie had a warm, rich kind of beauty. She looked like…the taste of a full-bodied Bordeaux. Or the scent of jasmine on a sultry summer's evening.

Get a grip. Noah coughed. "I have to get going."

Minutes later he was back on the road and heading home. By the time they reached the house Noah knew he wanted the truth from Lily. Callie Jones had called him a jerk. If he'd misjudged her like she said, he wanted to know. Lily tried her usual tactic of skipping straight to her bedroom, but he cut her off by the front door, just after the twins and Jamie had made it inside.

"Lily," he said quietly. "I want to talk to you."

She pulled her knapsack onto her shoulder and shrugged. "Don't you mean talk *at* me?"

He took a deep breath. "Did you ride that horse without permission yesterday?"

She rolled her eyes. "I told you what happened."

"Was it the truth?"

Lily shrugged. "Sort of." Her head shot up and she stared at him with eyes outlined in dark, smudgy makeup. "Is she blaming me?"

No, she's blaming me. And probably rightly so if the look on his daughter's face was anything to go by. Noah knew instantly that he'd overreacted. *Clearly. Stupidly.*

Noah suddenly felt like he'd been slapped over the back of the head. *I never overreact.* So, why her? Evie's words came back to haunt him.

You like her.

And he did. *She's beautiful, sassy and sexy as hellfire.*

But that wasn't really Callie Jones. It was an act—Noah knew it as surely as he breathed. How he knew he wasn't sure. Instinct maybe. Something about her reached him, drew him and made him want to *know* her.

Lily's eyes grew wider and suspicious. "You've seen her again, right?"

He wondered how she'd know that and thought it might be some fledgling female intuition kicking in. "Yes, I have."

She huffed, a childish sound that reminded him she was just thirteen. "Is she going to give me lessons?"

"I said we'd find you another instructor."

Lily's expression was hollow and she flicked her black hair from her eyes. "So, she won't?"

"I don't think so."

"Couldn't you ask her?"

Good question. He could ask her. Lily wanted her. Lily never wanted anything, never asked him for anything. But she wanted Callie Jones.

"Why is it so important to you to learn from Callie? There are other instructors in town."

She cast him a scowl. "Yeah, at the big training school

in town. It's full of rich stuck-ups with their push-button ponies."

"How do you know that?"

She chewed at her bottom lip for a moment and then said, "From school. The *Pony Girls* all go there."

Pony girls? Noah felt completely out of touch. "And?"

"The Trents," Lily explained. "Lisa and *Melanieeee*. They used to go to her school. *She* kicked them out a couple of months ago."

Melanie Trent. Lily's ex-best friend. And now her nemesis. "Why?"

"They were caught smoking in the stables," Lily supplied. "Big mistake. Anyway, I know that she lost some of her other students because of it. You know what the Trents are like. They don't like *anyone* telling them what to do."

Noah did know. Sonja Trent, the girls' mother, had worked reception for him a year earlier. He'd given her the post as a favor when her husband was laid off from his job at the local sugar mill. Two weeks later she left when Noah had made it clear he wasn't interested in having an affair with her. Sonja was married and unhappy—two good reasons to steer clear of any kind of involvement.

"Did you know *she* was some big-time rider?" Lily said, bringing Noah back to the present. "Like, I mean, really big time. Like she could have gone to the Olympics or something."

He tried not to think about the way his heart skipped a beat. "No, I didn't know that."

"If *she* teaches me then I'll be good at it, too. Better than *Melanie*. Way better. And maybe then she won't be so stuck-up and mean to Maddy all the time."

Maddy Spears was Lily's new/old best friend. Friends before Melanie had arrived on the scene and broken apart because Maddy was a quiet, sweet kid and not interested in flouting her parents' wishes by covering her face in make-up or wearing inappropriate clothes.

"I could apologize," Lily suggested and shrugged her bony shoulders.

That would be a first. Noah nodded slowly. "You could," he said, although he wasn't sure it would make any difference to the situation.

"I really want Callie, Dad," Lily said desperately.

You're not the only one. He cleared his throat. "I don't know, Lily…."

Noah wasn't sure how to feel about Lily's desperation to get lessons from Callie. Other than his sisters and mother, Lily hadn't let another woman into her life since Margaret had walked out.

Neither have I.

Lily didn't trust easily.

Neither do I.

"We'll see. Go and get washed up," he told her. "And maybe later you could help me with dinner?"

She grabbed the screen door and flung it open. "Maybe."

Her feet had barely crossed the threshold when Noah called her name. She stopped and pivoted on her Doc Martens. "What now?"

"Whoever you have lessons from, you have to follow the rules, okay?"

Her lips curled in a shadow of a smile. "Sure thing, Dad."

Noah watched his daughter sprint down the hall and disappear into her room with a resounding bang of the door. *Okay…now what?* But he knew what he had to do. He had to see Callie again. More to the point, he *wanted* to see her again. And he wondered if they made bigger fools than him.

Callie unhitched the tailgate and took most of the weight as it folded down. Indiana and Titan snorted restlessly, sensing the presence of other horses being unloaded and prepared for the Bellandale Horse Club show that day. Bellandale was a regional city of more than sixty thousand people and the event attracted competitors from many of the smaller surrounding townships.

Fiona Walsh, her friend and student, led both horses off the trailer, and Callie took the geldings in turn and hitched them to the side.

"I'm nervous," Fiona admitted as she ran her hands down her ivory riding breeches.

Callie unclipped Indiana's travel rug. "You'll be fine. This is your first competition—just enjoy the day. You and Titan have worked hard for this."

Fiona's carefully secured red hair didn't budge as she nodded enthusiastically. "Thanks for the pep talk. I'll go and get our stalls sorted."

Callie organized their gear once Fiona disappeared. Both horses were already groomed, braided and ready for tack, and by the time Fiona returned Callie had saddles and bridles adjusted and set. It took thirty minutes to find their allocated stalls, shovel in a layer of fresh sawdust, turn the horses into them and change into their jackets and long riding boots.

Callie's first event was third on the agenda and once she was dressed and had her competitors number pinned to her jacket she swung into the saddle and headed for the warm-up area. The show grounds were teaming with horses and riders and more spectators than usual, which she put down to the mild October weather. She warmed Indiana up with a few laps around the ring at a slow trot and then a collected canter. She worked through her transitions and practiced simple and flying changes. When she was done she walked Indy toward the main arena and waited for her name to be called.

The dressage test was a relatively simple one, but she gave it her full concentration. This was only her third show in as many months and she wanted to perform well. Indiana, as usual, displayed the skill and proficiency in his movements that had seen him revered by followers of the show circuit when she had been competing years before.

Before it all went wrong.

Before Craig Baxter.

Handsome, charming and successful and twelve years her senior, Craig had been a gifted rider. So gifted, in fact, that Callie often overlooked his moodiness and extreme perfectionism. Because underneath the charm and success, it had always only been about the competition. About results. About being the best.

And nearly four years after his death she still hurt.

It's better to have loved and lost...

Yeah...sure it was. Callie didn't believe that for one minute.

Love hurts. And it was off her agenda. Permanently.

What about sex? Is that off the agenda, too?

She'd thought so. But...in the last week she *had* been thinking about sex. Lots of sex. And all of it with Noah Preston. The kind of sex that had somehow invaded her normally G-rated life and made her have X-rated thoughts. Well, maybe not X-rated—she was still a little too homecoming queen for that. But certainly R-rated...

The announcement of her score startled her out of her erotic thoughts. She bowed her head to acknowledge the judges and left the dressage arena. As she cornered past three other riders waiting for their turn Callie eased Indiana to a halt. Because right there, in front of her, stood the object of all her recent fantasies.

Chapter Three

Dressed in jeans, a black chambray shirt and boots Noah looked so damned sexy it literally made her gasp. He held keys in one hand and a pair of sunglasses in the other.

She stared at him, determined to hold his gaze. Finally, curiosity got the better of her and she clicked Indiana forward. "What do you want?"

He moved toward her and touched Indy's neck. "Nice-looking horse."

"Thank you," she said stiffly, hoping he couldn't see the color rising over her cheeks. Callie collected the reins and swung herself out of the saddle. "Did you want something?" she asked again once both feet were planted on the ground.

"I did."

So tell me what it is and go away so I can stop thinking about how totally gorgeous you are and how much you make me think about wanting all the things I never thought I'd want again.

"How did you know I was here?"

"Your apprentice told me where to find you."

Joe? Callie wanted to ring his neck. "So you've found me. And?"

"I'd like to talk to you."

Callie tilted her chin. "What have I done now?" she asked, clutching the reins tightly so he wouldn't notice her hands were shaking.

He half smiled and Callie's stomach did a silly leap. "I guess I deserve that," he said.

She moved Indiana forward. She wouldn't fall for any lines, no matter how nicely he said them. She wouldn't be tempted to feel again. She couldn't. It hurt too much. "Oh, I see—today you come in peace?"

"I wanted to apologize."

"You're a week too late," she said stiffly and led the horse away. Callie felt him behind her as she walked—felt his eyes looking her over as he followed her past the rows of small stables until she reached their allocated stall.

Fiona came out from the adjoining stall. "Hi, Noah," Fiona greeted with a cheek-splitting grin. Callie didn't miss how the other woman's hand fleetingly touched his arm.

Clearly, no introductions were required. Fiona saw her look and explained that she taught his son at the local primary school and took an art class with his sister, Evie.

"So you two know each other?" Fiona asked.

"Yes," he replied. "We do."

"I'd better go," Fiona said quickly and began leading Titan from his stall. "My event is up next. Wish me luck."

Callie watched her friend lead the big chestnut gelding away and then turned her attention to the man in front of her.

"Okay," she said. "You can apologize now."

He laughed and the rich, warm sound dipped her stomach

like a rolling wave. Callie felt like smiling, but she wouldn't. She *wanted* to be mad at him—it made her feel safe.

"I overreacted last week," he said. "I know Lily took your horse without permission."

Her chin came up. "Bravo. I'll bet saying that was like chewing glass," she said as she opened the stall and ushered Indiana inside. Then she clicked the bottom door in place. "So," she said, "was there something else you wanted to discuss?"

"First, that you reconsider and give Lily riding lessons."

Callie didn't try to disguise her astonishment. "I thought you were going to find her another instructor."

"Apparently you're the best around."

"Yes," she replied, fighting the rapid thump of her heart. He was close now. Too close. "I am."

"And I want the best for my daughter."

"You should have thought about that before you called me an irresponsible nutcase."

His green eyes looked her over. "Is that what I said?"

Callie unbuttoned her jacket. "Words to that effect," she said, feeling suddenly hot and sweaty in the fine-gauge wool coat she'd had tailored to fit like a glove. She longed to strip off her hat, but the idea of him seeing the very unattractive hairnet she wore to keep her thick hair secure under the helmet stopped her.

He smiled. "Then I owe you an apology for that, as well."

"Yes, you do. So, anything else?"

"That you give me another chance," he said quietly. "I might be a jerk on occasion…but I'm not such a bad guy."

She snorted and that made him smile again. God, her hormones were running riot. Did this man know how earth-shatteringly gorgeous he was? She had to pull herself together. He leaned back against the stall and Callie watched, suddenly mesmerized as the cotton shirt stretched across his chest as he moved. *One step and I could touch him. One tiny step and I could place my hands over his broad shoulders.*

"So, do we have an arrangement?"

His voice jerked her thoughts back. "No, we don't."

"Are you going to play hard to get?"

The double meaning of his words could not be denied and Callie blushed wildly. She looked at her feet, thinking that any minute she was going to plant one of her size nines into her mouth and say something she'd regret. And typically, she did exactly that.

"I'm not playing anything with you," she said hotly. "As you pointed out so clearly last weekend, I don't have the skills required to handle your daughter. What I do have is a business to run…a business that means everything to me. I work hard and I won't do anything that could tarnish my reputation."

His gaze narrowed. "And you think teaching Lily would?"

"I think…" She stopped. It wasn't about Lily. It was about him. She only hoped he didn't realize it. "I think…another teacher would be better for her. Someone she would actually listen to."

"And if I promised that she would listen to you, Callie?"

She drew in a breath. It was the first time he'd said her name. It sounded personal. Intimate almost. "You can't promise something like that."

"She'll do what I ask."

Yeah…like putty in his hands. That's how Callie felt at the moment. "Look," she said pointedly. "All I want to do is run my school and care for my horses and try to fix up my house, which is crumbling around my ears. I just don't want any drama."

It sounded lame. Callie knew it. *He* knew it.

Something passed between them. Awareness? Recognition? A look between two people who hardly knew one another…and yet, strangely, on some primal level, had a deep connection. More than merely man to woman. More…*everything*. It scared the breath out of her. Thinking about him was one thing. *Feeling* something for him was another altogether.

"And there's nothing I can offer you that might make you change your mind?"

Callie's temperature rose and launched off her usual, well-controlled sensible-gauge. It was ridiculous. She couldn't imagine everything he said to her had some kind of sexual innuendo attached to it.

"Nothing."

"Even though you say you need the cash?"

It sounded foolish put like that. But she wasn't going to give in. "Exactly."

"That doesn't make a lot of sense."

"Well, you know me—all bad judgment and recklessness." She picked up the pitch fork. "Now, if you don't mind, I have to go and watch Fiona."

He half shrugged, looked at the pitch fork as though she might consider running him through with it, then took a small card from his pocket and passed it to her. "If you change your mind—"

"I won't." Callie folded the small business card between her fingers and opened the door to Indiana's stall. She slipped inside and waited a full five minutes before emerging—and only when she was certain Noah Preston had left.

Noah usually let the kids stay up a little later on Saturday nights. But by eight-thirty the twins were falling asleep on the sofa and Jamie took himself off to bed just after Hayley and Matthew were tucked beneath the covers.

Lily, however, decided to loiter in the kitchen, flicking through cupboards as she complained about the lack of potato chips. She made do with an opened box of salted crackers.

"So," she said as she sat. "Did you ask her?"

Noah stopped packing the dishwasher and looked at his daughter. The makeup and piercings and black clothes seemed more out of place than usual in the ordinariness of the timber kitchen. He wished she'd ditch the gothic act, but he'd learned fast that barking out ultimatums only fueled her rebelliousness.

"Yes."

Lily looked hopeful and Noah's heart sank. How did he tell his kid the truth? "She's thinking about it," he said, stretching the facts.

His daughter's expression changed quickly. "She's still mad at me?" Lily dropped the box of crackers and stood. "She's the best, Dad. And learning from the best is important. It means I might get to be the best at something, too."

She looked painfully disappointed and Noah felt every ounce of her frustration. If she'd followed Callie's rules, it wouldn't have been a problem.

"Lily, whoever you get lessons from, you'll have to follow the rules."

Lily's dramatic brows rose. "I'm not the one who shouted at her."

Noah stiffened. "I didn't shout. We had a conversation."

"Yeah, and after that she said she wouldn't teach me."

He had to admit his daughter had a point. If he hadn't acted so irrationally and lost his cool with Callie, he figured Lily would have been able to stay at the school. Lily had messed up, but so had *he*.

"'Night, Dad," she said unhappily and left the room.

Noah looked at the clock. He was weary but not tired. He left the dishwasher and headed for the living room. The big sofa welcomed him as he sat and grabbed the remote.

Another long Saturday night loomed ahead. He flicked

channels absently and settled for a movie he'd seen before. It didn't hold his attention for long. He kept thinking of Callie. She was a real dynamo. All feisty and argumentative, high octane. But underneath, he saw something else…something more. He wasn't sure how he knew—but he did. Whatever was going on with her, she wore it like a suit of armor. And he was interested in knowing what lay underneath all that fire and spirit. Hell, he was more than interested. Way more. The way she'd glared at him from beneath her hat, the way she'd filled out her riding jodhpurs… His skin burned thinking about it.

He flicked channels again, but it was no use. Television wouldn't hold his attention tonight. More so than usual, he felt alone and…lonely. Absurd when he lived in a house filled with children. And when he considered how great his family was. He loved his kids. His parents were exceptional, and his sisters were the best he could ask for.

But right now he wanted more than that. He needed more than that.

But what?

Company? Someone to talk with?

Sex?

Perhaps it was more about sex than he was prepared to admit. Up until a week ago he'd been in a kind of sexual hibernation. But Callie had him thinking about it. And got him hard *just* thinking about it. And not the vague, almost indistinct inclination that usually stirred him. This was different. Way different.

Maybe I should ask her out?

That was crazy. That would be like standing in front of a bulldozer.

She can't stand you, he reminded himself. *Okay, maybe I'll just ask her to reconsider about Lily again?*

Despite his brain telling him to forget the idea, Noah

picked up the telephone and dialed the number he couldn't recall memorizing but somehow had. She answered on the fourth ring.

"Callie, it's Noah Preston."

Silence screeched like static. Finally she spoke. "Oh—hello."

"Sorry to call so late."

A pause. "That's okay—I'm not in bed yet."

His body tightened. He had a startling image in his head and shook himself. *Maybe I will ask her out.* "I was wondering if you—"

"I haven't reconsidered," she said, cutting him off.

"What?"

"About Lily," she said on a soft breath.

All he could think about was that same breath against his skin. "I was actually—"

"Janelle Evans," she said quickly, cutting him off again.

Noah paused. "What?" he asked again.

"She's an instructor just out of town. She has a good reputation. She breeds quarter horses. I have her number if you're interested."

Oh, I'm interested all right. But not in Janelle Evans.

She was talking fast and Noah knew she was eager to end the call. *Bulldozer,* he reminded himself. "Ah—sure."

He took the number she rattled off and had to ask her to repeat the last few digits because she spoke so quickly.

"Well—goodbye."

He hesitated, feeling the sting of her reluctance to engage in conversation. "Yeah, okay—goodbye."

She hung up and he dropped the telephone on the sofa. He needed a shower—as cold as he could stand. Then he'd go to bed and sleep off the idea that he wanted to make love to Callie Jones more than he'd wanted to do anything for a long time.

* * *

On Sunday morning Callie woke at seven, after spending a restless night fighting with the bedsheets.

It was all Noah Preston's fault. She didn't ask for his late-night call. She didn't want to hear his sexy voice just before she went to bed. She didn't want to spend the night thinking about him.

She dressed and made short work of a bowl of cereal topped with fruit, then grabbed her hat and headed outside. The sun was up, already warming the early October morning air. She fed Tessa then headed for the stables, where Joe waited outside Indiana's stall.

"Are you taking the big fella out this morning?"

Callie shook her head. "Not today." Indy's long head swung over the top of the door and she ran her hands down his face. "'Morning, my darling boy." She turned back to Joe. "He did well yesterday, two firsts and a third, so he gets a day off. Give him a feed, will you, and then tack up Kirra. The English saddle please."

Joe made a face. "What do I tell the kid?"

Callie frowned. "What kid?"

"The one who's here for a lesson."

Callie shook her head. "I don't have anyone booked until eleven."

"I know," Joe said. "I checked the booking sheet. But she's here." Joe pointed to the office. "I put her in there," he said, then more seriously, "and told her not to touch anything."

Callie strode the twenty meters to the office and swung the half-opened door back on its hinges. She stood in the threshold and looked at the young girl sitting at her desk.

"What are you doing here?"

Lily Preston swiveled in the chair and got to her feet. "Um…I'm here for my lesson."

Callie inhaled deeply. "You're not having a lesson."

"But I thought—"

Callie placed her hands on her hips. "You have to go home, Lily." She turned on her heels and went to walk away but stopped when the teenager spoke.

"Please."

She turned back and looked at the teenager, whose green eyes were wide open, their expression sincere. Lily *was* sorry. Callie could feel it. Something tugged at her heartstrings.

Callie took a deep breath. "Indiana is my horse, Lily. And as quiet as he is, you could have been badly hurt. And I would have been responsible."

Lily's chin lifted, half defiant. "But I can ride a bit."

"A bit isn't good enough for a horse like Indiana, especially in an ill-fitting bridle and without a saddle."

Lily looked shame-faced beneath her makeup. "I really didn't mean to cause any trouble," she said. "I just…sometimes I just *do* things. I don't know why. I do things I know are stupid, but I can't help myself."

The tug on Callie's heart grew stronger. She knew exactly what Lily meant. Kindred spirits, she thought. But, oh, God…what should she do? Say yes to this girl who looked at her with such raw intensity. A girl, she suspected, who rarely showed that side of herself to anyone. But a girl whose father she couldn't stop thinking about. Who, without even trying, was making Callie feel, imagine.

"I'll do whatever you want," Lily said quickly, almost desperately. "Please teach me."

Before Callie could reply Joe stuck his head around the door to tell her Kirra was ready. She thanked him, then returned her attention to the teenager. "I'll tell you what— you stay out of trouble while I work my horse and we'll talk after." She stood aside for Lily to pass. "No promises, just talk."

Callie led Lily from the stables and told her to stay put

near the dressage arena. She gave her an old soda crate to sit on and then took the red bay mare into the arena. She worked her for twenty minutes, trying to concentrate on the maneuvers and transitions from trot to canter. But her mind wasn't really on the job. Lily sat on the sidelines, watching her, masked behind her makeup.

Ten minutes later Noah Preston's silver utility vehicle pulled up outside the stables. Callie continued with her ride, watching as he got out and opened the back door of the truck. The children stepped out. The older boy grabbed the hands of the twins and listened as his father spoke to them. Then he headed for Lily. He had a great walk, she thought. And he looked so good in jeans and a black T-shirt. Way too good.

Callie watched as the kids followed behind him. And again it stirred something inside her. An old longing. And it gave her a snapshot of a life she'd never have.

Ryan...

The longing turned into a pain—a piercing, incredible hurt that always took root behind her ribs when she thought about the beautiful baby boy she'd lost when he was just two days old.

I miss you Ryan...I miss holding you...I miss watching you grow up and become the person you could have been.

Kirra sensed her distraction and started prancing sideways at a trot. Callie got her quickly under control and eased her to a halt in the center of the arena. And she watched as Noah began talking with his daughter. Lily nodded, he shook his head. Lily said something, he replied. The conversation lasted for some minutes and the three younger Preston children stood quietly behind their father. Finally, Lily waved her arms about and stomped off toward the truck. He said something to the three kids and they sat on the soda crate. Then he headed through the gate and into the arena.

Callie dismounted and pulled the reins over Kirra's head,

collecting them in her left hand. She fought the ridiculous impulse to take off her safety hat and smooth out her hair or rub her hands down her breeches.

He stopped about two feet in front of her. "Hello," he said

Callie swallowed. "Hi."

He went to say something but then stopped. He patted the horse instead. He had nice hands, she noticed. Tanned and strong looking. She quickly snapped herself out of her silly female fantasy. "I was going to call you," she said. "You beat me to it."

"I knew she'd be here."

"You did? How?"

"Because you were the last thing we talked about last night. And I know Lily—when she gets her mind stuck on something, she can be impossible to deal with."

Callie raised her brows. "Looks like you're surrounded by impossible women."

My God, am I flirting? That's what it sounds like.

And he smiled. As though he liked it. "I could think of worse things."

Everything around her suddenly felt hot—the air in her lungs, the sand beneath her boots. "Anyway—she didn't do any harm while she was here."

"She's changed since her mother left."

Not what he wanted to say, Callie was sure of it. It was too familiar, too personal, too everything. And Callie wanted to clamp her hands over her ears. She didn't want to hear any more. She didn't want to know him. She didn't want to know *more* of him.

"No problem." It was a pitiful attempt at sounding indifferent.

"She used to be…sweet. A real sweet kid. And then she changed almost overnight."

Callie felt another surge of feeling for Lily. She knew all

about change. She knew what grief and hurt could do to a person. "Is that the reason for the makeup and black clothes?"

He shrugged. "Something to hide behind, I guess. She still wants riding lessons."

Callie clicked Kirra forward and began to walk from the arena. "Well, Janelle Evans is a good instructor."

He stepped in beside her. "She's asked for you."

"She can't...you can't...I just..."

Something happened then. Her legs stopped moving. Her lungs stopped breathing as she turned and their eyes locked. For one extraordinary moment Callie knew that whatever she was feeling, he was feeling it, too. It was crazy, heady and blindingly powerful.

He spoke first. "Lily rarely asks for anything."

Callie continued walking. "Which means?"

"Which means I'm inclined to do whatever I can to see that she gets what she wants."

They got to the gate. Callie tied Kirra to the railing, took a deep breath. "I'm not sure I—"

"Callie," he said "Please, reconsider." He placed his hand on her arm. A light touch, but the electricity coursing between their skin could not be denied. He looked at his hand but didn't remove it. Callie stood still, held in place by his touch, by the mere wisp of space that lay between them. "Lily needs you." He paused, watching her. "And I...and I need you."

Chapter Four

Callie moved her arm. Away from his touch. Away from temptation. Away from the realization that she liked how his hand felt against her skin.

I need you...

There was something startlingly intimate about the way he spoke the words. She couldn't remember the last time a man had said that to her. Maybe never. Craig hadn't needed her. And Noah Preston didn't need her, either...not really. He just wanted her to teach his daughter to ride a horse.

"I can't."

He smiled. "Yes, you can."

God, he was relentless. Callie lifted her chin. "I said I can't."

"She'll be on her best behavior," he said.

Callie expelled a heavy breath. "Even if she is, I'm not—"

"Is your unwillingness actually about Lily?" he interrupted her. "Or something else?"

Her heart quickened. "Like what?"

He looked at her. Really looked. Callie felt compelled to turn her gaze away, but she didn't. *Couldn't.* She'd never felt this kind of intensity with anyone before. She'd spent years convincing herself she didn't want it.

"I thought that perhaps you and…" He stopped, hesitated and sort of half smiled. "I think we…I think *we* might have started off on the wrong foot."

He wasn't kidding. But she wasn't about to admit it. She wasn't about to admit to anything. Instead, she thought about the practical. "Why this sudden confidence in my abilities?"

"Because Lily believes in you."

Callie didn't break their eye contact. "Even though you don't?"

"And if I said I did? Would you reconsider teaching Lily? If I apologized again for being a jerk and asked you to do this for my daughter?"

Her insides quivered. *Don't be nice to me.* "You don't give up easily."

He shook his head. "Not when I want something." He looked around. "I heard you'd lost some students recently."

She stared at him. "How did you know that?"

He grinned. "Local gossip."

Callie's skin prickled. Just like the local gossip she'd listened to last weekend. "Yes, I did."

He looked around, to the house, then back to her. "So, it looks like you're not doing well financially."

More prickles. "I'm not filing for bankruptcy just yet."

A full smile this time. "I didn't mean to imply you were," he said carefully. "But I thought perhaps we could strike a deal."

Cautious, Callie's interest spiked. "What kind of deal?"

"Your usual fee—plus I'll help prevent your house from 'crumbling around your ears.'"

She stilled. "And how exactly will you do that?"

"I'll do whatever maintenance needs to be done while Lily's having her lessons."

Callie looked at him suspiciously. "Do you work construction?"

"No," he replied. "But I know my way around a toolbox."

I'll bet you do. Suddenly she was tempted. Very tempted. She *did* need the money. And as for his offer to help repair her house…that idea dangled like a juicy carrot in front of her nose. With windows that wouldn't open, doors needing repair, fence palings hanging loose and the knowledge she needed to chase the entire house with a paintbrush, the lure of his offer teased her. Refusing would be impulsive. And foolish.

And Lily…she wanted to help Lily. Helping Lily was suddenly important to her.

Oh, hell.

"Okay," she said quickly, before she had time to think about what it might mean to have him hanging around her house every Sunday morning. Him and his adorable kids.

Noah looked instantly pleased. "Good. Will you start today?"

She shook her head. "No. Next week. Sunday, nine o'clock."

He stepped back, finally, and she dipped underneath Kirra's neck, feeling safer with the horse between them. "Thank you, Callie. You won't regret it."

Too late…she already did.

He walked off without another word, collecting his kids along the way. Once his truck had disappeared down the driveway, Callie took off Kirra's tack and led her to the washing bay.

Joe appeared, his hair spotted with straw from the bales he'd been lugging off the truck and into the feed room.

"So, what's the deal with Vampira?" he asked, grimacing as he passed Callie an old towel. "Scary." He shuddered. "Do you reckon she's got tattoos, as well?"

Callie wasn't about to admit that she had one herself. "That's not nice."

He shrugged his lanky shoulders. "If my little sister went around looking like that my parents would go ballistic." He made a disagreeable face. "Was that her dad—Noah Preston?"

Callie stopped rubbing the towel over Kirra's flanks. "Do you know him?"

"I met him last weekend when he was looking for you. My Uncle Frank bought one of his boats last year."

Her interest increased tenfold. "He sells boats?"

Joe shook his head. "He designs boats," he replied. "And builds them. Top-of-the-range stuff. He's got a big factory in town. Uncle Frank reckons his boats are the best around."

Noah was a boat builder. And a single dad. And too gorgeous for her peace of mind.

As she led Kirra back to her stall, Callie couldn't stop thinking about how deeply he affected her. And how much she wished he didn't.

The Crystal Point Twilight Fair was an annual event that raised funds for the local elementary school and volunteer Rural Fire Brigade. Callie had been invited to provide horse rides for a small fee. The money collected would go directly back to the organizing committee, but it gave her an opportunity to promote her riding school. Sunshine and Peanuts, her two quietest geldings, loved the attention and happily walked around the makeshift yard she'd put together with a little help from Joe. There was also a jumping castle, a small carousel, a baby animal pen and a variety of stalls selling homemade cakes and candies and assorted handicrafts.

"So, are you staying for the dance later?" Fiona asked as she navigated Peanuts past her.

Callie checked the child clinging to Sunshine's saddle and smiled at her friend as they passed one another. "In this outfit?" she said, motioning a hand gesture to her worn jeans, thin sweater and riding boots. "I'll skip it. I have to get the horses back anyhow."

On their next passing Fiona spoke again. "I could use the company."

"Maybe another time.'

Callie didn't socialize much. Or at all. There seemed to be little time in her life for anything other than work. And she wasn't exactly in the right frame of mind to be thinking about dating.

Dating? Where did that come from?

She maneuvered the pony toward the entrance and helped the child dismount. The queue had grown and about six kids were waiting in line. She took the next one in turn.

An older woman came forward with two small children. They looked familiar and she glanced at the woman, taking in her attractive features, dark hair and deep green eyes.

Noah's children.

Callie's breath caught in her throat. The blond-haired pair were unmistakable. They were Noah's twins. And she was certain the striking-looking older woman was his mother.

"Is something wrong?" the woman asked.

Callie shook her head. "Of course not… It's just that I know your…Evie," she said quietly, suddenly self-conscious. "And Lily," she explained. "I'll be teaching Lily."

The other woman smiled. "Yes, I know. My son told me."

Callie's skin heated. She stopped herself from looking around to see if he was close by. "Let's get the kids up on the pony."

"Can they go together?"

"Yes." Callie took the little girl's hand and helped her into the saddle. She was such a pretty child and had an adorable smile. Something uncurled inside her with a sharp, ripping intensity. She'd become so adept at covering her feelings that children didn't normally do this to her...didn't make her think about Ryan. But this little girl did. With her bright eyes and rosy cheeks, Noah's daughter made her remember all she had lost.

Callie managed a smile, fought against the lump suddenly forming in her throat and helped the little boy aboard the pony. He was quieter than his sister and didn't say a word, while the little girl chatted for the entire duration of the pony ride.

She walked the perimeter of the arena a few times and learned that the girl's name was Hayley and her brother was Matthew. They were four and a half and couldn't wait to start school soon. They loved their grandma and Aunt Evie and didn't like green vegetables all that much.

By the time the ride was over Callie had a strange pain wedged behind her rib cage.

She headed for the gate, passing Fiona on another round, and was surprised to find the children's grandmother gone.

And Noah stood in her place.

"Daddy!" Hayley exclaimed. "Look at me."

He was smiling that mega-watt smile and Callie's stomach rolled over. "Hello."

She swallowed hard and tried not to think about how good he looked in jeans and a navy golf shirt. "Hi." She glanced into his eyes, saw awareness, felt that familiar jolt of attraction. "Your mother?"

He nodded. "She's gone back to trawling the craft stalls." He gestured to the kids. "Did they behave themselves?"

"They were perfect little angels."

He laughed out loud. "Angels? That doesn't sound like my kids."

Callie smiled back. "She's a natural. So is Matthew."

Both children looked pleased as could be with the praise. He hauled Hayley into his arms and then placed her onto the ground. Matthew followed soon after. The kids moved around to the front of Sunshine and began stroking his nose.

"So, can you take a break from this gig?"

"A break?" she echoed. "What for?"

He smiled. "To talk. You could let me buy you a soda."

"I really don't think—"

"I'd like to get to know you better."

There it was, right out in the open. "Why—"

"You know why, Callie."

Without anything to hide behind, Callie felt so raw, so completely exposed, she could barely draw breath. She stared at him for a moment and then looked toward the now queue of one waiting for a turn on a pony. "Um…I probably shouldn't," she said on a whisper. "There's someone still—"

"We'll wait."

We'll wait. Him and the children she wanted so desperately to avoid—but somehow couldn't.

Fiona chose that moment to come up behind her and announced she'd happily take charge of the remaining child and then volunteered Joe to help with Sunshine. Before she had a chance to protest, Joe had taken the gelding and Callie found herself leaving the arena with Noah and his children.

"That was fun, Daddy," Hayley said excitedly.

"Was it, poppet?" He looked at Callie as they walked. "Maybe the twins could have riding lessons, too."

"Maybe," Callie replied and almost jumped from her skin when Hayley grasped her hand. She stopped walking immediately and looked down. The little girl tugged her forward, giggled and acted as though holding her hand was the most natural thing in the world.

Instinct kicked in and she went to pull her hand away... but something stopped her. Maybe it was the lovely, infectious laugh coming from the little girl. Or perhaps it was that Noah was watching her with such blistering intensity she knew that if she moved, if she rejected the child's hand, he'd see it. And he'd see more than that. He'd see through her and into the parts of herself she kept so fiercely guarded.

"Anything wrong, Callie?"

Already suspicious, she thought. Already figuring her out. "Not a thing," she lied and allowed herself to be led toward a refreshments stall.

He bought drinks all round and Callie had just cranked the cap off her soda when Hayley announced she wanted her face painted.

"Can we, Daddy, please?" she pleaded and skipped toward the face-painting tent.

He nodded and they all followed. He passed the colorfully decorated painter a couple of notes from his wallet. Hayley insisted on going first while Matthew waited patiently behind his more flamboyant sister.

Callie stood to the side. "Where's your other son?" she asked. "And Lily?"

"Jamie's with Evie. And Lily doesn't do fairs."

Callie half smiled. "Too cool, huh?"

"Or stubborn."

"She's headstrong," Callie said. "And there's nothing wrong with that."

He crossed his arms and she couldn't help looking at his chest. He was remarkably fit and broad shouldered and her awareness of him spiked. It had been eons since she'd been this attracted to someone. Maybe never. She'd been with Craig for so many years, and any true desire they'd felt for one another had faded long before his death. But Noah had kickstarted her libido with a resounding thud.

"Speaking from experience?" he asked quietly while keeping a watch on his kids.

Callie got her feelings back on track. "I'm sure my parents thought me willful. I liked to do things my own way."

"And still do, I imagine."

She wasn't about to deny it. "She'll come around," Callie assured him, sensing it was true, although she had no idea why she thought so. "Raising a teenage girl wouldn't be easy—especially alone."

"Sometimes...no. But they're all pretty well behaved most of the time. Even Lily."

"Do they see their mother much?" she asked before she could stop herself. She wondered why on earth she was so interested in this man and his children. She wasn't usually so inquisitive. Who was she kidding? She was *never* inquisitive.

"No," he replied. "They don't."

Callie's tongue tingled with another question, but she held back. The more she knew about him, the more *he'd* want to know about her...and she wasn't ready for that. She wasn't sure she ever would be. But despite her reticence, she suddenly had the image of his four motherless children burned deep in her heart.

Heaven help me...I'm actually in danger of falling for this man.

Noah felt her pain. She'd done a great job of building a big wall around whatever it was that haunted the depths of her blue eyes. *But not quite good enough.*

"Will I see you tonight?" he asked, determined to keep her talking.

"For the dance?" She shook her head. "No. I have to take the horses back home."

He pressed on. "You could come later."

She stepped back. "I don't...I don't...it's just that I don't..."

"You don't what?" he asked, picking up her trailing words.

"I don't date," she said bluntly.

Noah half smiled. So they had something in common. "Neither do I," he admitted and when she looked surprised, he explained what he meant. "Four kids make dating... difficult." He raised his brows. "What's your excuse?"

She shrugged and took a deep breath. "I don't have one."

Not exactly the truth and they both knew it. "Are you nursing a broken heart?"

She crossed her arms and dangled the soda bottle between her fingertips. "Not the kind you might be imagining," she said softly.

Noah's curiosity soared. He wanted to know all about her. Everything. She'd been hurt in the past, that much was obvious. But by whom? "Want to talk about it?"

She shook her head again and stepped back fractionally, as if she was looking for an escape. "I should go." She tapped the soda bottle. "Thank you for the drink."

She said goodbye to the kids and walked away, leaving him staring after her.

Callie sat on the edge of her bed and examined the contents of her open wardrobe.

She'd arrived home an hour earlier. The horses were fed, the dog was asleep in the kitchen and she was left wondering why she was actually considering dressing up and heading back to the fair. But Fiona had called and begged her to go. So, her friend needed her. That was as good a reason as any. It wasn't because there was a band playing and that there would be dancing. It wasn't because Noah would be there.

She knew getting involved with him was out of the question.

He has four children.

He had what she would never have. Her heart felt so heavy in her chest when she thought about it. She'd kept a lid on her feelings for more than four years and had accepted she could never have another child because of complications during Ryan's birth. Ryan was her child…and he was gone. But in a matter of days, and without warning, the lid had lifted off and suddenly she was *all* feelings…*all* memory…*all* want.

Noah makes me want.

Desiring him was one thing. She hadn't expected to *like* him. She hadn't expected to like anyone ever again.

Forty minutes later she'd dressed and drove back to the fair.

It was well past eight o'clock by the time she arrived. The stalls and kiddie games had been replaced by a large dance floor and clusters of tables and chairs. The whole scene had been decorated with hundreds of tiny lights, and food and drink vendors were on hand to satisfy appetites. The turnout was impressive. People had dressed up and were clearly enjoying themselves. The band was good and the dance floor was busy. Callie spotted Fiona standing near a tent where drinks were being served and quickly headed for her friend.

"You're here!" Fiona squealed and hugged her close. "Thank goodness."

"You said you could use the company."

"I could. Great dress—aren't you glad I insisted you buy it?"

It *was* a great dress—a flimsy chiffon concoction of muted caramel shades with a halter top. The skirt fell just above her knees. "Of course."

"Fiona!"

They both turned at the sound of the pleasantly pitched female voice. A dark haired woman with the most amazing green eyes came toward them, buffering against a few people in her stride.

"M.J.," Fiona greeted. "Good to see you."

Fiona introduced them and the green-eyed beauty made a startled sound. "*You're* Callie? Lily's riding instructor?"

Callie bristled. "You know Lily?"

M.J. laughed delightfully. "She's my niece," she explained. "I'm Noah's sister."

Of course. The resemblance to Evie was unmistakable. And those eyes were all Preston. "I didn't realize he had more than one."

"There are three of us girls."

"Is Evie here?" she asked, acutely conscious that Noah would be nearby.

I'm not here for him. I'm not. I can't be.

"Nah—she's looking after the kids," M.J. said. "It's just me and Noah tonight."

And then, as if drawn by some inexplicable force, Callie turned her neck and met his gaze head-on.

Noah knew the exact moment Callie arrived. It was as if some internal radar, attuned to only her, had taken hold of him. The area seemed smaller, the air heavy, and the noise of glasses clinking and people speaking faded into a barely audible sound. She looked incredible. The dress, the hair tumbling down her back, the heels that showed off her amazing legs—he wondered if any of the half a dozen people around him heard the strangled sound that formed in his throat. She must have felt him staring at her because she turned her head and looked right at him.

A blinding and electrical visual contact hit him from his

feet to his fingertips. His best friend, Cameron Jakowski, jabbed him in the ribs with an elbow and gave a low whistle of appreciation. Noah didn't like that one bit. With three sisters and an independent working mother, he'd learned at an early age not to objectify women.

"Who is that?" Cameron asked.

"Fiona."

Cameron raised his brows. "I meant her friend with the great legs."

"Callie Jones," Noah replied quietly.

Cameron chuckled. "The horse lady? Very nice. No wonder you've been keeping her to yourself."

"That's not what I've been doing."

"Sure it is." Cameron smiled. "Shall we go over so you can introduce me?"

"No."

"I just wanna talk to her."

Noah stood perfectly still. "Hard to talk without teeth."

Cameron laughed loudly and began walking toward them. "Okay, I get the message," he said once Noah caught up. "But introduce me anyway."

He did so begrudgingly. Cameron liked women and women usually reciprocated. He was stupidly relieved when Callie seemed oblivious to his friend's brand of charm.

Once the introductions were over Fiona dragged Cameron onto the dance floor. Noah bought a round of drinks and they sat down at a table way back from the noise of the playing band. It wasn't long before M.J. went off in search of the man she'd arrived with and he and Callie were alone.

She looked nervous. And beautiful. He'd never seen her hair loose before. It was longer than he'd imagined and hung way past her bare shoulders. He felt like running his hands through it and tilting her head back so he could kiss her throat.

"You came back," he heard himself say.

She glanced at him. "Yes."

"I'm glad you did."

"It's still not a date."

Her words made him smile, and Noah's whole body thrummed with awareness. Being around her, sharing molecules of space with her, undid him on so many levels. "Of course not. *We* don't date, remember?"

Her blue eyes sparkled. "Do you have to be so agreeable?" she asked quietly.

"Do you have to keep looking for a fight?"

One brow rose sharply. "You like provoking me. It's probably because you were surrounded by women growing up. You know, the spoiled only son, indulged by his mother and adoring sisters, given license to say whatever he wants."

He laughed. "I'm sure my mother would disagree with you."

"Ha—I'd like to talk to your mother," she said and he saw her flush.

"I'm sure she'd enjoy that, too. So where's your family?"

She hesitated for a moment, like she was working out how much to reveal. "California," she replied finally. "My mom lives in Santa Barbara. My brother Scott has a place in L.A," she added. "He works for the fire department."

"And your father?"

"He died ten years ago."

Noah pushed his beer aside. "So why Crystal Point?"

"My dad was born in Bellandale and I vacationed here many times when I was young. After my—" She stopped for a moment. "After I finished professional competition I wanted to do something…else. I'd always wanted to have my own riding school and secured Sandhills Farm for a good price."

"It was a courageous move," he said. "I mean, without family support."

"I had that. I still do."

"Do you miss it?"

"California? Sometimes," she admitted. "But I needed to... to get away."

She'd said too much. He felt it with every fiber inside him. "Get away or run away?"

"Both," she admitted.

"Have you been back?"

She nodded. "I try to get back every year to see my family."

"You're close to them?" he asked.

Callie nodded. "Very."

"But you wouldn't move back to California for good, would you?"

She looked into her glass. "I'm not sure. For the moment this is home."

"That's...good news. For Lily," he clarified. "And the rest of your students." He paused, looking at her. "How many students do you have?"

"Not nearly enough," she replied. "I lost a few a while back. An unhappy client," she explained. "Or an unhappy parent, to be precise."

"Sonja Trent?"

Callie stilled. "You know her?"

"I know her." He took a drink and looked at her over the rim of his glass. "How many more students do you need?"

"To stay afloat?" He could see her doing a quick calculation in her head. "About a dozen or so. I could advertise— but of course that takes money. If I hike up my tuition fees, I risk losing the students I have to one of the bigger equestrian clubs in town who do a group rate. And with insurance costs and the price of feed sometimes I feel like I'm..."

"You feel like what?"

"Like I'm pushing a barrow of manure uphill with a faulty wheel."

He smiled, thinking how he knew that feeling. "I don't think you should dismiss the idea of raising your prices," he said after a moment. "Cheap doesn't necessarily mean value. Sure, your clients could go to the bigger establishment—but would they get what you can give them? Probably not. One-on-one lessons with someone who has your experience is what customers will pay for. Your skills and knowledge make your time valuable, Callie—you've earned the right to be rewarded for it."

Her eyes shone bright with tears, and in that moment Noah wished he knew her better. He saw vulnerability and pain and fought the instinctive urge to reach for her. Now wasn't the time. But soon, he thought. *Soon.*

The compliment went straight to Callie's heart and she fought the sting behind her eyes. Silly, but his words made her feel taller, stronger. Her defenses were down. He broke them down. No, not broke...something else. Somehow he took the barricade around her apart, piece by piece, holding each one of those pieces in his hand, showing her what he had in his palm, drawing her out, making her want and making her feel.

Making me unafraid.

She was momentarily stunned by the intensity of her feelings. What she'd first thought was just attraction suddenly seemed so much more.

She liked him.... She really liked him.

This is a good man, a tiny voice inside of her said. A good man with a dazzling smile and integrity oozing from every pore. A man who made her feel safe when she'd believed no man would ever make her feel that again.

How did she resist? She wasn't sure she could. She wasn't sure she wanted to.

But…to feel again? Where did she find the courage to do that? If she let herself care for him…she would also have to let herself care for his children. She had to allow them inside and into her heart. Into her heart that was only barely glued together these days.

"Callie?"

She realized she'd been staring at him and dropped her gaze. "Yes?"

"Would you like to dance?"

Instinct screamed no. "I can't."

"Yes, you can. It's just a dance."

It wasn't *just* anything…she knew it as surely as she breathed.

"I really—"

"Come on," he urged and took hold of her hand. Before she could protest further he'd pulled her gently from her seat and led her toward the dance floor.

She'd always liked the idea of dancing but had never been all that good at it. Craig had complained it was a precious waste of time when there were horses to train and competitions to prepare for.

The band played covers of popular tunes, and just as they reached the dance floor the beat changed to a much slower number. Callie didn't move at first. At over six feet Noah was considerably taller than her, and she tilted her head back to look at him. Everything about him drew her in. The white collared shirt he wore emphasized his broad-shouldered strength and as she curled her fingers into the soft fabric and felt the hard muscle beneath, every ounce of blood in her veins surged. She hadn't been this close to a man for so long…and never one who'd affected her so powerfully.

The music was slow and they moved well together. One

hand lay gently against her hip and he held her free hand in his. She felt the intimacy right down to her toes.

She took a deep breath. "Noah ..." Saying his name set off a surge of feelings inside her. Her body tensed and she knew he felt the sudden shift.

"Yes, Callie."

"Don't expect too much."

He looked at her oddly. "Are we talking about your dancing skills or something else?"

"Something else," she admitted on a sigh and wasn't sure where the words came from. And she wasn't sure she wanted to know. She felt like the worst kind of fraud by denying the obvious and refusing to admit to the feelings running through her.

She was suddenly paralyzed by the realization. It was impossible. She had no room in her heart for anyone. Not him. Not his children. "I have to go," she said a moment later as she dropped her hand from his shoulder.

"I'll drive you home," he said quietly.

Callie stepped back, oblivious to the music, oblivious to everything other than Noah and her furiously beating heart. "I have my truck."

"Then I'll walk you to your truck."

"That's not necessary."

"Yes, it is," he said and continued to hold her hand.

By the time they'd left the dance floor their palms were pressed intimately together. Callie didn't pull away. Deep down, in that place she'd switched off and never imagined she'd switch on again, she found she liked the sensation of his fingers linked with hers. She liked it a lot.

Her truck was parked midway down the car lot and the walk took a few minutes. It was dark and there were a few couples hanging by their vehicles. Callie spotted one pair kissing madly, another simply holding each other. The entire scene screamed of the kind of intimacy she hadn't felt in a long time.

The kind of intimacy she suddenly craved.

She knew it was foolish to want it. She had nothing to offer him other than the fractured pieces of her heart. And for a man like Noah, she knew that would never be enough. He'd want the *whole* Callie. The Callie she'd been before her world had been shattered...before *she'd* been shattered.

And that woman simply didn't exist anymore.

Once they reached her truck she twisted her fingers from his. "Well, good night," she managed to say and shoved a hand into her small bag for her keys.

She found the keys, pulled them out and accidentally dropped them at her feet.

Noah quickly picked the keys up and pressed them into her palm. "Good night, Callie."

She looked at him and saw desire burning in his eyes.

He wants to kiss me...

The power of him drew Callie closer, until they were barely a foot apart. She felt her lips part, felt herself move and felt her skin come alive with anticipation. He leaned in and kissed her cheek so softly all she really felt was breath.

Not enough ...

Callie instinctively reached up, grasped his shoulders and pulled him toward her with all her strength. Driven by instinct, she planted her lips on his mouth and thrust her tongue against his. He tasted good. He felt good.

No...more than that. He tasted...*divine*. And her lips, denied for so long, acted intuitively. She felt her blood heat, felt her skin come alive, felt desire uncurl way down, igniting the female part of her that had lain dormant since forever.

Callie felt his rush of breath as he started to kiss her back. She got the barest touch of his mouth, the barest taste of his tongue. She waited for more. She longed for more. But then he stopped. He pulled away, kissed her cheek again and straightened. Callie released him and stepped back on unsteady feet.

Air crashed into her lungs, making her breathless. She looked at him, felt the burning red-hot gaze. *I know he wants me...*

She knew it, felt it and tasted it in the brevity of his kiss.

"Good night, Callie," he said. "I'll see you Sunday."

Callie got into the truck and started the engine. She wasn't sure how she drove home. All she could feel was the tingle on her lips, the heat in her blood. All she could think was how she had just kissed Noah Preston.

And how her life would never be the same.

Chapter Five

Noah was thinking.

About kisses. About perfect lips and sweet breath.

"What's up with you?" Lily asked, shifting in her seat, looking incredibly young in riding breeches and a dark T-shirt.

Noah looked directly ahead. She'd become way too astute for his liking. "Nothing."

"Yeah…right." She crossed her arms. "I hope you're not gonna hang around while I have my lesson."

"I've got some work to do at the house."

Lily turned her head. "Yeah—that's right. Her place is a real dump." She huffed. "I think you just want to see *her* again. I'm not a little kid, you know. I saw exactly how you were watching her last weekend." Lily rolled her eyes wide. "And she's not bad looking, I suppose, if you go for that type. She's not like my mother."

No one was like Margaret—thank God. But he wouldn't be telling Lily that.

"Do you think you'll ever get married again?"

That was a first. He looked at his daughter. She stared straight ahead, but Noah wasn't fooled. She looked just a little afraid. And Lily never looked afraid.

Married? How could he explain his feelings to his daughter? Noah was pretty sure the younger kids would welcome a new mother into their life. And he...he truly wanted someone to share them with. He longed for a wife and a friend and a lover and all that corny stuff he knew made up a healthy marriage. He wanted what his parents had...years of trust and love. But it was a big deal, expecting a woman to take on four children. And he had no intention of bringing someone temporary into their lives. Noah didn't want temporary. If he got involved again, he wanted permanence. He wanted...forever. He wanted promises that wouldn't be broken. For the kids' sake.

And mine.

His train-wreck marriage lingered like a bad taste he couldn't get out of his mouth.

Is that why I didn't kiss her back...when all I wanted to do was haul her into my arms?

The truth rocked Noah. He'd spent thirty-six hours wondering what kind of fool didn't kiss a beautiful, desirable, passionate woman back when she'd made it so clear she wanted to be kissed. But he knew why. It wound up his spine. It filled his lungs. *Fear.* Fear that he'd want more. Oh, not sex...because he was pretty sure kissing Callie would quickly lead to making love to Callie. He wanted more of *her*. The more of her Noah suspected she wouldn't want to give. To him. To anyone. He didn't want to feel her, taste her and then have the door slammed in his face. He didn't want to be rejected...*left*.

And she'd left before, hadn't she? She'd moved across an ocean to change her life—to get away. From what, he didn't know. What if she wanted to change it back? Noah wasn't going to put his kids or himself through the risk of being wreckage in her wake.

It was best that he hadn't kissed her back. Best that he stopped thinking about kissing her at all.

"So, would you?"

Lily again. Noah got his thoughts back on track. Marriage. Right. "Maybe one day."

She scowled and *harrumphed.* "Do *we* have any say in it?" she asked, using the collective, but Noah sensed she was asking about herself. "I mean, if you're going to shack up with someone, shouldn't we at least be able to have an opinion about it?"

"Marriage is a little more than shacking up, Lily."

She shrugged, looked straight ahead and remained quiet for about twenty seconds. Lily had something on her mind. "Did you know that fifty percent of all second marriages fail?"

He almost choked. *Where the hell did she come up with this stuff?* "That's an interesting statistic, Lily. Where did you get it?"

"Social Studies," she replied. "We're studying human relationships this semester. There's a boy in my grade who's had two stepfathers—can you imagine? And Maddy told me that when her stepdad moved out last year it really sucked. She liked him a lot."

Noah got his daughter's point, delivered with all the subtlety of a sledgehammer. "I have no intention of jumping into anything, Lily," he told her.

"But if you do get married again, how do you know she won't run out like my mother did?"

I don't.

And Callie…she seemed as fragile and unpredictable as the wind.

Lily didn't say anything else, and when they arrived at Sandhills Farm she jumped out of the truck. It took him about ten seconds to find Callie. She stood near the house, in jeans and a flame-red T-shirt, one hand on her hip and the other held a cell phone to her ear.

She spun on her heels and looked at him. His heart pounded behind his ribs. That kiss…how did he forget about it? How could he not want to feel that again? Noah took a long breath and headed toward her. Lily reached her first and jumped around on impatient toes while Callie continued her telephone conversation.

She was frowning and clearly not happy with the caller. When she disconnected a few moments later he pushed aside his lingering thoughts about kissing her and immediately asked what was wrong.

"Just another irresponsible horse owner getting away with neglect," she said hotly.

He frowned. "What?"

"I volunteer with an organization that saves abused and neglected horses," she explained. "A couple of weeks ago I got word that there are three horses somewhere on the other side of town that are stuck in a bare paddock and need veterinary care. We've only had sketchy reports on their whereabouts so far. The owner moves them around to avoid impoundment."

"That's terrible. What can you do?" Lily asked in a shrill voice.

"Seize them, hopefully."

His ever-astute daughter picked up on the obvious. "Isn't that stealing?"

"Not when the owners are breaking animal protection laws."

Lily nodded. "If you need any help, I'll—"

"Leave it to the experts," Noah said. "I'm sure Callie has it under control."

"Your dad's right," Callie assured Lily. "But you can help me nurse them back to health when we finally find them. Joe's saddled Samson for you," she said as she pointed toward the sand arena.

Once Lily headed off, Callie turned to face him. Her eyes were blue and luminous. "I have a list," she said quickly. She pulled a small piece of paper from her pocket and held it toward him. "Of things for you to do." She made a dismissive gesture. "Of course, if you've changed your mind I'll—"

"We had a deal," he said, sensing she was mentally backing out from talking to him as fast as she could. She half shrugged and took a breath, trying to look causal, but Noah wasn't fooled. The tiny pulse at the base of her throat beat like a wild thing. And the promises he'd made to himself only minutes before vanished. All he wanted to do was take her in his arms and kiss her…properly.

"It's only small stuff," she said. "A couple of windows that won't lock right and the back fence—"

"No problem," he said quietly and took the list.

"I'll be about an hour with Lily," she said and pivoted on her heels.

Noah watched her walk into the arena, back rigid, arms held tight to her side. He lingered for a few minutes and observed Callie's interaction with his daughter. Lily looked unusually cheerful and he knew she was excited to finally be in the saddle. The lesson started with Callie laying down a firm set of rules and Lily agreeing to every single one.

Lily respected Callie. Somehow, Callie understood what Lily needed.

Noah experienced a strange pang in his chest, dismissed it and headed for his truck to unload the toolbox. He had a lot of work to do.

* * *

Callie was wound like a spring. She'd barely slept the night before and had struggled to concentrate during a lesson earlier that morning with Maddy Spears, her newest student.

She knew she had to concentrate on Lily...and ignore the fact that Noah was only a couple of hundred meters away.

I kissed him. And he didn't exactly kiss me back.

She wasn't sure whether she should feel relieved or insulted.

"How's this?" Lily asked Callie, interrupting her reverie.

Callie focused her attention on the teenager. She was impressed with Lily. The girl had a natural seat and good hands. Once the lesson had concluded she eased on the long reining lead and called Samson to a halt in front of her.

"That was good. Well done."

Lily raised her brows. "Do I get to ride off the lunge rein next week?"

Callie unclipped the lead. "No."

Lily dismounted and landed on her heels. "Why not?"

"Balance," Callie replied and handed the reins to her.

Lily frowned. "Huh?"

Callie began walking from the arena. "Every rider needs to start with balance. Once I know you've aced it, the lead comes off."

Lily clicked the horse forward and followed. "And what if I don't?"

"You will," Callie said. "You have a good seat and soft hands, essential for a successful rider. Take Samson to the wash-bay and Joe will help you strap him down."

Lily buried her face into the animal's neck and smiled. "I can do it by myself."

Callie raised her brows. "What was rule number five?"

Lily exhaled heavily. "Don't question the four other rules."

"Exactly. Go and get Samson sorted. I'll see you when you're done."

When Lily was out of sight Callie considered her options. Hang around the ménage or show some guts and see what *he* was up to. Her boots made their way across the yard until she reached the house. She stood at the bottom of the steps. Noah had his back to her and she watched him maneuver an old window off its track, make a few adjustments and then replace it. Her heart raced. No man should look that good in jeans. He raised his arms and she got a quick glimpse of smooth skin beneath the hem of his T-shirt. *Oh, sweet heaven.* Suddenly, he stopped what he was doing, turned and looked at her.

"How was it?" he asked.

She gulped. "Huh?"

"Lily—how'd she do?"

Callie put the image of skin out of her mind. "Very good. She's a natural."

He smiled at her and she felt the power of it through her entire body.

"Are you okay?"

It's just skin. I've seen skin before. "Yes," she replied and swallowed. "I'm fine."

He stepped away from the door. "She behaved herself?"

"She did," Callie replied. "She's quite sweet, actually."

He grinned. "Well, I'm pleased the two of you are getting along." He leaned back against the balustrade. "Seeing as that's out the way, are we going to talk about *us* now?"

Callie took a quick breath. *Here we go.* "There's nothing to talk about."

"Yeah, there is."

"It was just a kiss," she said, and the moment she'd said the word *kiss,* she regretted it immediately.

"It wasn't *just* anything, Callie."

He was right. Callie felt it down through to her bones. "Okay," she admitted. "It wasn't."

"So, what shall we do about it?"

Her heart raced. *Do?* "I don't know if we…I don't think we should do anything." She took a deep breath and inhaled a burst of bravado. "We just won't kiss again."

There's that word again… When the word should probably be bliss. Because she suspected that's what really being kissed by Noah would feel like.

He smiled and came down the steps. "I don't think I can make that promise to you, Callie."

Stupidly, she smiled back for a second. "You didn't kiss me back." The words popped out of her mouth. "I figured you weren't interested."

He took another step toward her. "Would you like me to prove to you that I am?"

Callie almost swallowed her tongue. *He is interested…he wants me.* "Right here?" she asked, wondering what kind of madness had taken hold of her.

He shrugged. "Why not?"

Callie took a step backward. He wouldn't, would he? Kiss her out in the open, where anyone could see? Possibly in front of his daughter? She warmed from head to toe. But no…she looked at him and saw he was smiling. "Are you teasing me?"

"Just a bit."

Callie didn't quite know how to react. Teasing and flirting were almost an alien concept to her. Craig had never teased, never flirted. It was always business, always work, always pushing toward being better, being the best. Only now, years later, did Callie realize how little laughter there'd been in their relationship. But Noah had a relaxed sense of humor, a relaxed sense of *self*. She was sure he worked hard—but he didn't live to work. He lived for other things. Like his kids. It would be hard alone, raising four children single-handedly.

Craig hadn't wanted one child.

In the end Craig hadn't lived to see his son born. And Callie had buried them both within days of one another—her tiny son and the man who was supposed to have loved her but instead betrayed her.

The worst week of her life. Excruciating. Soul-destroying. Heartbreaking.

"Where are the rest of your kids today?" she asked, shifting her thoughts from Ryan. And, for some reason, she wanted to know where his children were and who was caring for them.

"With Evie," he replied. "I didn't think you'd want them underfoot while you're working."

"You're right, I don't," she said quickly. Too quickly.

He'd heard the tremor in her voice because his brows slanted together for a brief second. "You don't like kids?"

You don't like my kids...that's what his question sounded like.

Callie shrugged again. *I adore kids,* she wanted to say. *If I had my way I'd have a dozen of my own and love them with every fiber inside me.*

But that was a pipe dream. Ryan was the only child she would ever have. *And I can't replace him. I won't let myself love like that again.*

"I like kids," she said softly.

"Me, too," he said, smiling again. "Can I call you sometime this week?"

Callie was startled. "For what?" she asked, her heart beating wildly.

"Don't look so suspicious," he said quietly. "Nothing sinister."

Callie felt foolish then. "Sorry," she said on a breath.

"I thought you might like to go out sometime."

Like a date? She should run as fast as she could. The idea

of going out with him was terrifying. Because she sensed it was something she could get used to. "I don't…it's just that I'm…I'm better with horses than I am with people."

"And yet you became a teacher?"

She shrugged. He had a point. She could have turned her skills toward training horses for the show circuit. But teaching the kids…that's where she found real happiness.

"Speaking of which, I have to get back to work," she said. "I have a new student starting in fifteen minutes."

His green eyes scanned her face. "Business looking up?"

"Yes," she said quickly. "Much better. I had a new student start this morning, plus three calls yesterday and now four new students starting over the next two weeks."

"That's good news for you."

"I know," she said, a little breathlessly because she always felt as if she didn't have quite enough air in her lungs when talking with him. "When I lost clients following the incident with the Trent girls I wasn't sure I'd be able to recoup. Sonja Trent accused me of discriminating against her daughters and threatened to lodge a complaint with the equestrian federation. Nothing came of it, of course, except she managed to persuade half-a-dozen parents to pull their kids out."

"And then some jerk says he wants to see you lose your license?"

Callie smiled fractionally. "Ah—well, that was a bit of a red flag for me."

"Rightly so, considering the circumstances. I would never have done it, you know?"

"I know," she said, softer this time, feeling like their worlds were moving closer. "I lost my temper. When I called you a jerk I didn't know you." She paused, searching for the words. "I didn't like you. But I know you now. I…like you now."

I more than like you…

"I like you too, Callie."

Her heart beat like a freight train and it was so loud she wondered if he could hear it.

Minutes later he took Lily and left, leaving Callie standing by the porch with a smile on her face so deep her jaw ached.

Lily arrived unexpectedly at Sandhills Farm on Wednesday afternoon, riding her bicycle. She wore her school uniform, sensible leather shoes and her black hair tied back in a ponytail. The uniform looked oddly out of place with her full makeup. "I've come to see Samson," Lily told her when Callie approached her.

"Does your father know you're here?" Callie asked.

She crossed her arms over her chest. "Sure."

Callie began her next lesson with Maddy Spears and Lily began chatting with Maddy's mother, Angela. They seemed to know one another quite well. Her suspicions were confirmed a little later, once Maddy's lesson had finished and Lily came forward with a kind of indulgent authority and steered Maddy and Sunshine toward the washing bay, flipping Callie an assurance that the gelding would be looked after.

Callie gave the girls an opportunity to do the right thing and headed over to speak with Angela Spears.

"You know Lily?" Callie asked, slipping through the fence.

"Everyone knows Lily," she replied. "Another marvelous lesson," the other woman said before Callie could open her mouth. "You are a genius," she said. "Maddy's talked of nothing else but you for days now."

"I'm flattered."

Angela Spears's perfectly bowed mouth beamed at her. Callie couldn't help noticing how immaculately groomed she was. Riding breeches and grass-stained T-shirts had become her usual garb. Too bad—she looked pretty good in a dress.

She hadn't forgotten Noah's reaction the night of the Twilight Fair dance. He'd looked at her dress, and her legs and her mouth…

"Noah was right about you."

Angela's words instantly grabbed Callie's attention. For a crazy second she wondered if she'd inadvertently said his name without realizing it. "What do you mean?"

"He told me you were an amazing instructor."

Her curiosity surged into overdrive. "He did?"

Angela nodded. "And he said I'd be foolish to let Maddy miss the opportunity to learn from you and that she couldn't be in safer hands. Of course, I completely agree now," she said. "And Maddy's so looking forward to getting her own pony." She let out an animated gasp. "Oh, you must help us select the perfect pony when the time comes—I insist. And I'll pay you a finder's fee, of course."

By the time Callie had waved Angela and her daughter goodbye, Lily had disappeared. But she wasn't hard to find. Callie headed for the paddock behind the house and found her sneaking morsels of carrot to Samson.

"So, Maddy's your friend?"

Lily nodded. "My best friend." She gave the gelding another treat.

Callie thought about the three new students she acquired that week. "And what about Jacinta and Skye Burrows and Chrissie Drew—are they friends, too?"

"Nope," Lily replied. "But I think my dad knows Mr. Burrows."

Callie's heart skipped a beat. *He's looking out for me*. It felt like forever since anyone had done that.

Normally she would have resisted the gratitude that coursed through her. On some level she should probably have resented it. Because interference meant involvement. It meant…intimacy. It meant she had cracks in her armor.

But she experienced none of those feelings. Only a deep-rooted appreciation.

And an overwhelming longing to see him again and tell him so.

Callie headed into Bellandale the following morning. She found the address for Preston Marine via the business card Noah had given her and parked outside the large building situated in the center of the town's newest industrial estate. She got out of her truck and ran her hands down her jeans.

She was impressed the moment she walked into the showroom. A long and luxurious-looking cruiser was to her left and three smaller boats, including a catamaran with full sails, sat to her right. Printed designs on easels flanked each of the boats and more designs were framed on the walls. A circular reception area greeted her as she stepped onto the tiled floor and a fifty-something man came toward her. He wore pressed trousers and a shirt with Preston Marine logo sewn onto the breast pocket.

"How can I help you?" he asked politely.

Callie hung on to her nerve. "I'd like to see Noah Preston. Is he here?"

The man, whose name badge read Len, nodded. "He's out back in the workshop."

"Oh," she shrugged. "If he's busy I can—"

"You can wait in his office," Len suggested and walked ahead, motioning her through a door on the left. "I'll call him."

Callie followed with unusual obedience, passing a small, efficient-looking woman who sat behind the reception desk, tapping on computer keys and wearing the same style shirt as Len. When she entered the office Len quickly excused himself, and Callie sat on a long black leather lounge. As far as offices went, this appeared better than most. And it was as neat as a pin.

She didn't have to wait long.

"Callie?"

Noah stood in the doorway, dressed in chinos and the same corporate shirt as his staff. He stared at her with such raw intensity she was relieved she'd been sitting. Her knees would surely have given way if she'd been standing. "Hi."

"Is everything all right?" he asked as he closed the door.

"Oh, yes. I just wanted to speak with you." Callie felt absurdly self-conscious beneath his penetrating stare. "This is a nice office," she said, desperate to fill the silence rapidly smothering the space between them.

"Do you think?" One hand moved in an arc, motioning to the chrome and glass furnishings. "I'm not sure. I've only had this place for about six months. Grace did the decorating. It's a bit too modern for me"

And just who was *that?* "Grace?" she asked as she stood.

"My other sister," he explained.

Stupidly relieved, Callie scanned the room again. "It is modern but appropriate, I think." She relaxed a bit. "You said you'd just moved here?"

He nodded. "I've kept the original workshop down by the Port, but the business needed larger premises."

"And a showroom?"

"Buyers are keen to see the finished product," he replied. "Would you like a tour?"

"Maybe after we've talked."

He closed the door and walked farther into the room. "Okay, let's talk."

Callie clutched her hands together. "I just wanted to…to thank you."

Noah tilted his head. "For what?"

"For Maddy Spears, and Jacinta and Skye Burrows and

Chrissie Drew," she said. "And as of this morning I have another two students starting next month."

He shrugged. "It was only a couple of phone calls."

Callie knew it was way more than that. "It means so much to me," she admitted. "My business…" She paused, and then shook her head. "My horses…"

"They're important to you?"

"They're everything," she breathed.

Noah saw the emotion in her eyes and his chest tightened. "Because they don't let you down?"

She took a shaky breath. "I…I…"

"Someone did," he said and figured there was no point in holding back. "Husband? Boyfriend? Lover?"

"Fiancé," she confessed on a sigh.

"What did he do?" Noah asked, preparing himself for the worst.

She hesitated for a moment. "He lied to me."

Lies and deception went hand in hand—Noah knew that from experience. The fallout from his ex-wife's infidelity had broken his world apart. "Then he wasn't worthy of you."

The emotion in her eyes shined brighter and Noah fought the impulse to reach for her. Everything about Callie affected him on some primal level. He wanted to hold her, soothe her and protect her. He'd never felt such a blinding need before.

She nodded and the gesture spoke volumes. "The horses… they make it simple, you know—uncomplicated." Her hands came together. "Anyway, I just wanted to say thank you for helping me. I guess I'll see you Sunday."

"How about Friday?"

"What?"

"Friday," he said again. "Tomorrow night. Dinner and a movie?"

Callie stilled. "I don't really think a date is—"

He smiled. "Oh, believe me, this wouldn't be a date. Just

you, me, a DVD and the kids squabbling over a bowl of spaghetti."

"Noah, I can't."

"Sure you can," he said easily. "You wanted to thank me—so, thank me." His voice faded for a moment, and then he spoke again. "Dinner, movie, simple."

Silence stretched between them. He expected another refusal and waited for it.

Instead, she nodded and said softly. "Dinner. Yes, okay."

Chapter Six

Noah picked the kids up from Evie's that afternoon. He found his sister and three youngest children in her pottery/art studio, all four of them cutting up cardboard and crepe paper. Pots of glue and an assortment of other hobby equipment lay on the big table in the middle of the room.

They all cheered a round of hellos when he walked into the room and perched on a stool near the kitchenette to the right of the door. Evie left the kids to their crafting and joined him.

"Coffee?" she asked and grabbed a couple of mugs. He nodded and she poured from the pot of filtered brew. "You're early today."

Noah glanced at his watch. "Not by much."

His sister raised her brows. "Bad day at the office?"

"Not particularly." An unusual day. A day filled with thoughts of Callie. Like most of his days lately.

"Trevor has a video-game party planned for tomorrow

night," she said of her fifteen-year-old son. "Do you feel like coming round for dinner? M.J.'s coming over, too."

"I have plans," he said and drank some coffee.

Evie's eyes widened instantly. "A date?"

Noah didn't know what to call it. "Sort of."

"Anyone I know?"

Like a dog with a bone, Noah knew his sister wouldn't let up. Besides, he had nothing to hide about his relationship with Callie. *Relationship?* Is that what it was? It felt…he didn't know what the hell it felt like. Something. Everything. Like she was the air inside his lungs and he couldn't draw in enough breath. His desire for Callie burned a hole through him. *And I haven't even really kissed her.* He'd thought about it, though. He'd imagined it. Dreamed about it. Wanted it so much he could barely think about anything else.

"Callie."

Evie didn't bat a lash. "No surprise there."

"I suppose not." He finished his coffee and stood. "I should get going."

"Sometimes you have to try people on," Evie said quietly. "To see if they fit."

Noah looked at his sister. "That's not the problem."

"So there is a problem?" she asked.

He shrugged and felt like spilling his guts, but he didn't. Because what he felt, what he knew was that beneath the sassy, quick temper and barriers she'd erected around herself was an incredibly fragile woman. A woman who'd been hurt.

I'm going to get my heart kicked in…

That's what he felt deep down. That she was all risk. Like the wildest ride at a theme park. Like parachuting without a chute. But…despite feeling that way, Noah was unbelievably drawn to her. He wanted her, even with the threat of losing himself. And knowing he was prepared to take that chance turned him inside out. Because Noah never risked himself emotionally. He couldn't afford to. The kids needed stability—they needed a parent who could be relied upon to always do the right thing by them. And if he was to bring another woman into their life, that woman had to do the right thing by them also. They needed unreserved love.

Could Callie do that? Could he trust her to love them? He just didn't know.

"There's no problem," he said to his sister. "Thanks for watching them. I'll see you soon."

As Callie zipped up her favorite sundress—the white one with sprigs of tiny blue flowers—and stepped into a pair of silver sandals, she could hear Fiona's voice calling from the kitchen. Her friend had arrived to work her horse and had stayed for a coffee and chat.

"So, you're going on a date with Noah?"

"It's not a date," Callie insisted as she headed from the bedroom. "It's just dinner."

When Callie reached the kitchen Fiona was standing by the sink. "At his home? With his kids?" Her friend raised both brows. "That's a date."

Of course it's a date. I like him. I'm attracted to him.

Just because they weren't going out dining and dancing alone didn't mean it was anything other than a real date.

I shouldn't go. I should keep to my plan and not get involved.

But Callie knew it was too late for that.

She arrived at the Preston home at exactly six o'clock. She grabbed her tote, locked the truck and headed toward the front porch. At the top of the few steps lay a sleepy-looking golden retriever who barely lifted its head at her presence. It made her smile, thinking of Tessa and her boundless energy.

"That's Harry," said a small voice. A young boy stood

behind the screen door. He opened it and stepped in front of her. "He's very lazy."

She smiled "So I see. Not much of a guard dog, then?"

Jamie giggled. "Nope. And he snores really loud." He opened the door and stood to the side. "I'm Jamie—are you coming inside?"

Callie filled her lungs with air and stepped across the threshold.

The polished timber floors, brick-faced walls and warm textures of the furnishings appealed to her immediately. She caught sight of a huge stone fireplace and headed for it, settling her sandaled feet on a thick hearth rug in the middle of the room. The two sofas were covered in a soft caramel color, and a large stone lamp was nudged between them on a round coffee table. The sideboard along one wall was dotted with an assortment of bric-a-brac, most of it obviously created by young, eager hands. The warmth radiating in the room was undeniable and she experienced a deep longing behind her ribs.

"This is the living room," Jamie informed her. "And my TV."

"*Your* TV?" she asked, noticing the huge flat screen and shelving either side showcasing a few hundred movie titles.

"Well, Dad's, really. Do you like spiders?"

"Well, I…"

The sound of feet on floorboards caught her attention, and Callie turned as Noah came down a staircase at the rear of the living room.

He stopped on the bottom step. "Hello."

She hadn't realized the home had more than one level and he must have caught her look.

"The loft," he explained. "The previous owners used it for storage but it seemed a shame not to make use of the view up there, so I had it turned into a master bedroom."

"And bathroom," Jamie supplied.

Noah's bedroom…where he slept. Callie was suddenly rooted to the spot, absorbed by the way he looked in worn jeans and a soft white T-shirt. His feet were bare and it seemed incredibly intimate somehow. His hair was damp, too, and she figured he'd just showered. Which made her think of soap and skin and water cascading over strong muscles. Before Callie could say anything the twins scrambled into the room on fast little feet and planted themselves in front of her.

The little girl touched the hem of her dress. "Callie's here!" she announced excitedly. "You look really pretty. Daddy won't let me wear nail polish."

Callie smiled, amused despite the fierce pounding of her heart. "I wasn't allowed to wear it either until I was…" She paused, looked at Noah and took a gamble. "Sixteen."

Noah smiled. "Good answer." He dropped off the step and took a few paces toward her, his eyes not leaving hers. "You do look lovely."

Eaten up with nerves, she almost told him that he looked lovely, too. But didn't. Because lovely wasn't the word. He looked…hot. And so incredibly sexy in his jeans and bare feet that she had to swallow a few times to regain her composure.

"Okay, guys—give Callie some room to breathe." He moved forward and took Matthew's hand. "I have to get these two in the bathtub. I won't be long. Make yourself at home."

"Where's Lily tonight?"

"At a sleepover at Maddy's," he replied as the trio padded off down the hall.

Callie relaxed fractionally. Until Jamie repeated his question about liking spiders. She had an awful thought he might have one in a jar for her to inspect. Within seconds he was off down the hallway. Callie dropped her tote by the sofa and moved toward the mantel. About a dozen framed photographs caught her attention. Most of them were of the children, and one was of three women. Callie recognized Evie and could see the resemblance in the striking woman beside her with dark hair and perfectly symmetrical features. The other woman, clearly younger, looked familiar, and Callie remembered M.J. from the Twilight Fair. An older couple, his parents for sure because she recognized his mother, filled another shot and then there was a picture of Noah with Cameron, both holding up a fish on a hook and both laughing in a way that only best friends could.

There were no pictures of his ex-wife and she wondered why she thought there might be. Perhaps she just wanted to get a look at the woman who had borne his children and the woman he had loved.

Callie looked at the picture of the twins again and a familiar ache filled her heart.

But she wouldn't think about Ryan tonight…she wouldn't make comparisons. And she wouldn't envy Noah his beautiful, perfect children.

Jamie returned with a heavy book and patted a spot on the sofa. Callie sat down and spent ten minutes listening to him talk about and show pictures of the most hideous-looking arachnids she felt certain would give her nightmares for weeks. But he was a charming boy, polite and very smart and quite mature for his age.

Noah came back into the room without the twins. "They're playing in their bedroom until dinner," he said. He looked at Jamie and smiled. "Hey, mate, how about you go and join Hayley and Matthew?"

"But, Callie has—"

"Seen enough crawlies for one night. Off you go."

Jamie disappeared without another protest and the air thickened between them almost instantly.

"I hope he didn't freak you out too much."

"A little." she said, shuddering. "He's a lovely child. You should be proud of him."

"I am," he replied. "Join me in the kitchen?"

Callie stood and followed him down a short hallway.

The Tasmanian oak kitchen impressed her as much as the rest of the house. She walked to the window and glanced outside. Beyond the patio there was a pool, a hot tub and a gloriously lush garden.

"Would you like a drink?" he asked and grabbed two bottles from a rack above the refrigerator. "Red or white?"

She chose the Merlot and watched as he pulled the cork and poured two glasses.

"Thanks." She took the glass and leaned against the granite countertop. She sipped her wine. "You have a lovely home."

"Thank you. We've only been here a couple of years." He drank some wine, then grabbed a pot and filled it with water. "I bought the place after my divorce."

So his ex had never lived here? She was instantly curious. "Did you have a bitter breakup?"

Surprisingly, he answered. "I guess you could call it that." He flicked on the gas.

Still curious, she asked another question. "Why doesn't she see the children?"

He pulled out a few items and dumped them on the counter. "She lives in Paris with her elderly mother. When she's not in rehab."

Callie gasped.

"Prescription meds," he explained. "Or at least that's how it started for Margaret."

She had a name. "Is that why she left?" Callie asked.

Noah stopped what he was doing and turned toward her. "She left because she didn't want to be married to me anymore." He smiled then but without humor. "Hard to imagine, eh? The addiction started afterward."

Callie allowed herself to hold his gaze.

She felt a strong surge of compassion and deep feeling. But before she could say anything he passed her a paring knife. "Can you make the salad?"

Callie took the knife. "I...I guess. But I should warn you, I'm not much of a cook."

He laughed. "It's salad, Callie—it doesn't need cooking."

"I could still mess it up," she said, trying to push back the color tinting her cheeks.

"Watch and learn."

They worked in silence for a while. Callie chopped and diced vegetables while Noah stirred the sauce simmering in a large saucepan and popped linguini into boiling water.

"That smells good," she said and sipped her wine.

He replaced the lid on the same container. "I can't take the credit, I'm afraid."

She placed a hand to her mouth in mock horror. "Store-bought? I'm devastated."

"Evie," he corrected. "She often doubles up on portions when she has guests staying at the B and B. She takes pity on my single-father status. Actually, I'm pretty sure she thinks I feed the kids macaroni and cheese five nights a week."

"And you don't?"

"Only three nights. Gotta squeeze the frozen pizzas in, too."

Callie chuckled. "Please tell me you're not serious?"

Noah put up one hand in a Boy Scout salute. "I'm not serious. They eat vegetables—even those horrible slimy green ones."

As if on cue, the children returned to the kitchen. Callie remained by the countertop, working on her salad but also watching as Jamie set the table, so serious in his task, his

little tongue clicking in his mouth as he straightened cut-
lery and placed paper napkins beside each place setting. The
twins hovered, one each side of her, stepping back and forth
on small feet, as though wanting her attention.

She smiled and asked them about their daycare teachers,
and Hayley immediately began to tell her everything about
a usual day in the classroom. Callie listened, still chopping.

"Can I have some of that?" Hayley asked as Callie cut a
carrot.

She nodded and gave them each a little piece of vegetable,
which they took with eager fingers and ate just as quickly.
A few moments later she did the same with a couple of snow
peas. And again with a sliver of cucumber. Their infectious
giggles echoed around the kitchen.

"I like having a grown-up girl here, Daddy," Hayley announced and Matthew nodded in agreement.

Callie stopped chopping and stood still. She glanced
toward Noah and saw he'd stopped his task also. He was
staring at her, a deeply smoldering stare that made her knees
weak.

"So do I," he said quietly.

And then, without warning, Hayley hugged her, gripping Callie's leg as hard as her small arms would allow.
Callie stilled her task, rooted to the spot. Her heart surged
in her chest. Suddenly she was *all* feelings. All anguish. All
memory. All hurt. The little girl lingered, waiting, and Callie
instinctively knew what the child wanted.

She placed the knife on the counter. *I can't do this. I can't.*

But she did. She reached down and touched Hayley's head,
without looking anywhere but directly at the wall in front of
her. Her fingertips felt the soft, little-girl hair and her womb
contracted instantly, rolling like a wave. Hayley lifted her
chin and Callie's hand touched her face.

Oh, God...help me here. Help me not want this. Help me not feel this.

Her throat felt suddenly thick, burning with emotion. All her fears, all her longings bubbled to the surface. She looked at Noah again and sighed. How could she possibly explain what she felt? To explain would mean to be exposed, to be vulnerable, naked in front of him.

Hayley giggled and Callie patted her head gently a couple of times before removing her hand. Once she'd broken the connection her womb flipped again, but differently this time. She felt empty, bereft.

She looked at Noah then and saw he was watching her with such searing intensity she had to lean against the counter for support. But to have his child? An adorable child like Hayley. What a dream that would be.

Not a dream. A fantasy.

"Hayley, take your seat," Noah said quietly. "Dinner will be ready soon."

The kids all whooped and raced for their favorite spot at the table.

"This is done," Callie said and grabbed the bowl.

Meals were usually a quiet affair for Callie. She ate alone most of the time, unless Fiona was around or she offered to make lunch for Joe. But this was something else. The kind of meal she remembered from her childhood, when the kitchen had been the centerpiece of the home. Lots of laughter, lots of spillage and wipe-ups and grubby faces.

Family...

Another woman's family, she reminded herself.

But I'm here...and I feel such a part of them. Like somehow...I was made for this.

Callie's salad was a success, with Jamie kindly telling her it was the best he'd tasted—even better than his Aunt Evie's.

Afterward, she volunteered to load the dishwasher while

Noah put the twins to bed with a story. Jamie chatted to her as she worked, telling her about school and how Fiona was his favorite teacher and how he liked to make things and that he wanted to learn to play the trumpet. Then he told her he would choose a movie to watch and disappeared down the hallway. By the time Noah returned, the kitchen sparkled and the coffeemaker gurgled.

"I helped myself," she said. "Although I can't find any cups."

He opened a high cupboard, extracted a pair of matching mugs and placed them on the counter. "Milk, no sugar."

The way she liked hers, too.

Jamie reappeared, clutching Madagascar in one hand and a Harry Potter sequel in the other. They unanimously chose Madagascar. Callie took her coffee into the living room and sat down in the corner of the long sofa. She placed her coffee on the side table. Jamie said something secretly to his father, then excused himself and raced down the hall.

"He likes you," Noah said quietly as he set up the DVD player.

"How do you know that?"

He turned his head and smiled. "You'll see."

Jamie returned a few minutes later. He asked her to hold out her hand and dropped something onto her palm. She stared at the thin leather strip threaded with dark, shiny stones.

"It's a bracelet," he said, pointing to the stones. "They're hematites."

Callie touched the smooth stones. "It's lovely."

"I made it," he announced proudly. "You can have it."

"You made this?" she held it up. "You're very clever. But I couldn't possibly take it."

He looked so disappointed she longed to snatch the words back. "You don't like it?"

Callie rubbed the stones again. "Of course I do. I just thought that if you made something this pretty you might want to give it to someone...like a girl."

Jamie frowned. "You're a girl."

"Smart kid," Noah said as he sat at the other end of the sofa. "My sister Mary-Jayne makes jewelry," he explained. "She lets the kids craft pieces when they stay with her." He looked at his son. "He doesn't part with them easily."

Noah watched her reaction. She looked increasingly uncomfortable. Jamie was a warm, generous child and incredibly easy to love. And although she'd interacted appropriately all evening, he sensed something else was happening to her.

His suspicions were elevated. Was it him making her nervous? Noah couldn't be sure. In the kitchen she'd been relaxed and chatty. When it was just the two of them she usually looked fired up and ready for anything. But then Hayley had hugged her, and Noah had witnessed reluctance in her response to his daughter. The realization landed on his shoulders.

The kids...it was the kids. He felt sure of it.

How can she not like my kids? They're unbelievable. Everyone likes my kids.

Finally, she spoke. "In that case, I would love to keep this. Thank you."

That settled, he flicked the play button and sank back into the sofa. With Jamie between them she seemed light years away from him. Which was probably exactly how she wanted it.

Jamie fell asleep after about twenty minutes. Noah gathered him up and carried him to his bedroom. He tucked him in bed, kissed his forehead and returned to the living room. She hadn't moved. He flipped the DVD to a CD and

waited until the music filtered around the room before head
ing back to the sofa.

"Would you like some more wine?" he asked before he sa

She shook her head. "I should probably go home."

Noah glanced at the clock on the wall. It was barely nin
o'clock. He didn't want her to go. He had to say what was o
his mind. "I'm not a threat to you, Callie."

She looked into her lap. "I know that."

"So why do you want to leave?"

She expelled an unsteady breath. "Because being here
feel…involved." She stopped, looked away. "I feel involve
with you."

Suddenly there was something very raw about her. "Woul
that be so bad?"

She looked back toward him. "No," she said on a breath
"Yes…I can't—"

"I'm not your ex, Callie," he said bluntly. "And if yo
screwed up, and if you chose the wrong person to give you
heart to, don't feel alone. Just get in line."

"Did *you* screw up?" she asked.

"With Margaret?" he nodded. "For sure. But I should neve
have married her in the first place." He shrugged. "She wa
pregnant with Lily," he explained. Not, *I loved her.* To say
he'd truly loved Margaret would have been a lie. "We had a
baby coming. It seemed the right thing to do."

She smiled fractionally. "It was the right thing to do."

In the beginning he'd believed so. Especially the day he'd
held his newborn in his hands. But later he'd wondered i
they should have considered a shared custody arrangemen
of their daughter instead of a marriage between two people
who were never suited to one another.

She looked at him, hesitated, and then took a steadying
breath. "My fiancé wasn't who I thought he was."

"Was he unfaithful?"

She shrugged. "I don't think so." She dropped her gaze for moment, then turned back to look at him. "He was killed n a car wreck four years ago."

It wasn't what he'd been expecting and Noah saw the walls lose around her as if they were made from stone. A cheating, dishonest spouse was a whole lot easier to compete with han a ghost. "And you're still grieving?"

She gave him an odd look. "Most of the time I'm simply... umb."

He reached across and took her hand. "Can you feel that?" e asked as he stroked her forefinger with his thumb.

She looked to where their hands lay linked. "Yes."

"Then you're not numb, Callie." Noah fought the impulse o drag her into his lap. He wanted her so badly he could arely breathe. "You just fell in love with the wrong man."

She closed her eyes briefly. "I know."

"So maybe we'll both get it right next time."

For a moment she looked like she wanted to be hauled into is arms. He was tempted. Very tempted. But the look lasted nly a moment.

She grabbed her tote. He could see her walls closing in, ould see her shutting down. "I should go."

He knew the evening was over. "I'll walk you out." Noah tood and followed her wordlessly to the front door. Even vith music playing in the background, the house seemed uncommonly quiet. Harry lifted his head when Noah opened he front door, then dropped it disinterestedly.

"Well, thank you for dinner," she said, clutching her bag. "And for part of a movie."

Noah prepared himself for her hasty departure, but she topped at the bottom step and turned. "I know what you vant, Noah. And part of me wants that, too."

The air stuck in his throat. "But?"

"Right now I just…I just don't have room inside myse
for any more…feelings."

The raw honesty in her voice was undeniable. He wasn
sure how the brash, argumentative woman he'd first met ha
morphed into this exposed, vulnerable creature he couldn
take his eyes off. His insides churned. *Don't be afraid of me
Don't be afraid of what's happening between us.* He didn'
say it. He couldn't. He wanted to kiss sense into her…to mak
her really see him, really feel him. But she wanted to run an
that annoyed him. *God, this woman's undoing me.*

"Will you ever have room?" he asked quietly.

She looked at him. Through him. "I…don't…I *can't.*"

Moments later he watched her drive away and waited o
the porch until the taillights disappeared at the end of th
driveway. And he knew he was falling for a woman who'
just admitted she didn't want to feel anything. For anyone
Ever.

Chapter Seven

The familiar sight of Noah's truck arrived at exactly eight fifty-five Sunday morning. Callie was coming out of the stables when she saw him retrieving his toolbox from the tray. She said hello and he said the same, but he quickly headed for the house and began repairing the screen door.

While she was left wondering if he was angry with her, she was also left facing Lily. And Lily was in a dark mood. The grunted when Callie clipped the long lead rein onto the halter secured beneath the bridle. And then again when Callie knotted the reins in the middle of the gelding's neck and instructed Lily to do arm raises.

Lily muttered a "this sucks" under her breath and began her lesson.

It became a long fifty minutes, with Callie acutely conscious of Noah's presence at the house. She wished she knew his moods better. *Was* he angry with her? He worked without breaking; he didn't even appear to look in their direction.

She hadn't heard from him since Friday night. She'd thought he might call. But he hadn't called…and as tempted as she'd been to pick up the telephone herself so she could hear his voice, she hadn't.

"What's up with *you* today?"

Lily's accusing voice vaulted her back to the present. "Nothing," she said.

"You're not paying attention to me," the teenager complained.

Callie switched her mind into instructor mode. "Of course I am. You're doing great." She grabbed a neutral subject. "How did your sleepover go at Maddy's?"

Lily's gaze snapped at her suspiciously as she trotted Samson in a circle, skillfully rising from the saddle in between beats. "How did yours go with my Dad?"

Maybe not such a neutral subject after all!

Callie's face burned. She called Samson to a halt and waited until he slowed before roping him in. Once horse and rider were in front of her she spoke. "It wasn't like that."

Lily's expression remained skeptical. "Yeah, sure."

"I stayed for dinner," she explained. "And then I went home."

Lily didn't like that, either. Her look became as black as her mood. "So you guys are friends now?"

Callie thought about how to answer. "I…suppose."

Lily dismounted. "I thought you were *my* friend?"

Uh-oh. Callie chose her words carefully. "I am, Lily. I have all different kinds of friends."

"Well, *he* doesn't look at you like he wants you to be his friend. He looks at you as if he wants you to be his *girlfriend*."

Callie grabbed the reins and tried to squash the sudden heavy thump of her heart. *He's not looking at me like anything at the moment.*

"We're *just* friends," she said firmly, unclipping the reigning lead and handing Samson to Lily. "Give him a brush down and ask Joe to get a small feed for him." She caught Lily's scowl. "Horsemanship includes ground work and is all part of learning to ride."

Lily started to move then stopped and swiveled on her boot. "I just don't want things to change, that's all. I like coming here. I like learning how to do stuff."

"Nothing's going to change," Callie assured her, sensing that it was what Lily needed to hear. "I promise."

"So you're like, not moving back to California or anything?"

California? "No."

Lily shrugged. "Because people do move. People…leave."

Like her mother. Callie took about two seconds to figure it out. "Not all people," she said gently. "Not your dad."

Lily didn't look convinced. "Yeah, I guess," she said. "It's not like I don't want him to date or anything…I mean, as long as whoever he dates is not some old witch who hates kids. But you're *my* instructor…and if you went out for a while and then stopped going out, I wouldn't be able to come here anymore. When adults break up that's what always happens."

Callie drew in a deep breath. "We're not dating. We're friends."

Lily nodded but clearly wasn't convinced. Callie remained in the arena until Lily had led the horse into the stables. She wiped her hands down her jeans, tightened the hat on her head and walked toward the house. He wasn't on the porch. The side gate was open and she headed around the back. Noah was by the fence, pulling off a couple of loose palings, while Tessa bounced around his feet.

"Lesson finished?" He spoke before she even made it twenty feet from him.

"Yes. She did a great job. A few more lessons and she'll be ready for her own horse."

He kept pulling at the palings. "I'm nearly done here."

Callie took a long breath and stepped forward. "I was talking with Lily," she said, watching as he kept working. "She knows…I mean, she thinks there's something going on between us," she blurted.

"I'm sure you set her straight."

He *was* angry.

"I said we were just friends."

He glanced at her but didn't respond. Callie took another step and called the pup to heel. But Tessa, the traitor, remained by Noah's side. He popped the palings in place with a few deft swings of the hammer.

"Sure, whatever." He started walking past her but Callie reached out and touched his shoulder to stop him. He looked at her hand and then into her eyes. "What?"

"Exactly," she said, digging her fingers into his solid flesh. "What's wrong?"

He didn't move. "Nothing."

A big fat whopping lie—and they both knew it. "Are you mad or something?"

"No." He still hadn't moved.

"So, we're…okay?"

He shrugged. "Sure."

Callie dropped her hand and felt the loss of touch immediately. He looked tense. More than that…he looked as wound up as a coil.

"Noah," she breathed his name on a sigh. "If you—"

"Just drop it, Callie," he said quietly. "I have to get going. See you later."

She stared after him and watched his tight-shouldered walk with a heavy feeling in her chest. She almost called after him. *Almost.* Tessa followed before she turned back and at at Callie's boots. She touched the dog's head and the pup whined.

"Yeah…I know what you mean, girl," she said and waited until his truck started up and headed down the driveway.

She lingered for a moment, staring at the dust cloud from the wheels. Once the dust settled she headed back to the tables and prepared for her next student. Fiona called after lunch and made arrangements to drop over later that afternoon. Her final student left at four o'clock and once Joe took off for the day Callie grabbed her best show bridle and began cleaning the leather. Cleaning her gear had always settled her nerves, and she undid the nose band and cheek strap, set them aside and dipped an old cloth into the pot of saddle soap.

It wasn't much of a diversion, though. Because Callie had a lump in her throat so big, so constricting, she could barely swallow. For two years she'd had focus. The farm. The horses. Her students.

And now there was Noah. And Lily. And the rest of his children.

Deep down, in that place she kept for her pain and grief and thoughts of her baby son, Callie realized something that shocked her to the core. *If I reach out, I know in my heart I can make them my own.* She wasn't sure how it had happened so quickly. Feelings hadn't been on her agenda for so long. Now, faced with them, Callie could feel herself retreating.

She wondered if she should have told him about Ryan. Would he understand? He'd had his own disappointments, but he didn't appear to be weighed down with regret and grief. Maybe people *could* move on? Perhaps hearts did mend.

Right then, Callie wanted to believe that more than anything.

But to feel again? Where did she get the strength? Ryan's death had zapped all her resilience. Before that she'd been strong, unafraid, almost invincible.

She was glad when she heard Fiona's car pull up outside and called for her to join her in the tack room. Only it wasn' her friend who stood in the doorway a few moments later. I was Noah.

He was back. And he clearly had something on his mind Callie got to her feet quickly. Her heart pumped. "Did you.. did you forget something?"

He stood in the doorway, his eyes locked with hers. "Do yo still love him?"

She was poleaxed. "What?"

Noah was in front of her in three steps. "Your fiancé. Do you still love him?"

"He's dead," she whispered.

"I know. But that wasn't the question." He reached for her, slid one arm around her waist and drew her against him "The thing is," he said, holding her firm. "If you still love him, I'll do my best to stop…to stop wanting you." His other hand cupped her cheek, gently, carefully. "But if you don' love him, then I'd really like to kiss you right now."

Her insides contracted. "No," she said on a breath.

"No?"

"I don't love him."

His green eyes darkened as he traced his thumb along her jaw. "Good," he said softly.

And then he kissed her.

Callie let herself float into the warmth of his mouth against her own. It was a gentle possession, as if he knew her, as if he'd been kissing her forever. Only one other man had kissed her before this, and as she allowed Noah's lips to part hers, any recollection of that faded and then disappeared. He didn't do anything else—he just kissed her, like he couldn't get enough of her mouth, her taste, her tongue.

Instinctively, Callie's hands moved along his arms and to his shoulders. She touched his hair, felt the silky strands beneath her fingertips and slanted her mouth against his. Finally, when he lifted his head Callie felt so much a part of him she swayed toward his chest. Noah held her still, one hand on her shoulder while the other splayed on her hip and she lifted her chin higher to look into his eyes.

"Noah—I think…" Callie willed herself to move, but found such incredible comfort in his arms she simply *couldn't*.

He didn't let her go, either. "You think too much. How about you stop thinking and just feel?"

Oh, how she wanted to. But her doubts tormented her, taunting around the edges of her mind in a little dance, telling her that taking meant giving. And giving was…giving felt as far out of reach to her as the stars from some distant planet.

He leaned into her, like he knew her fears. "I'd never hurt you, Callie."

In her heart she knew that. "But…but I might hurt you."

"I'll take that risk." He kissed her again, long and slow and deliciously provocative.

Heat radiated through him, scorching her, and Callie wondered if she might melt. Kissing had never felt like this before. Nothing had ever come close to this. He was strong and safe—a haven for her shattered heart.

When the kiss was over she spoke. "But earlier today you were angry with me."

"Yes. No. Not angry…just…wanting you and not sure how to reach you." He touched her face. "Because I do want you Callie…very much."

She wanted him, too. She wanted more of his touch, more of his mouth, his breath. He gave her what her eyes asked for, kissing her passionately, cradling her against his body.

"Hey, Callie! I'm here for—"

Fiona. Noah released her instantly and she stepped back

on unsteady feet. Busted—and by the biggest blabbermouth she knew.

"Oh," Fiona said so chirpily it had to be a cover for her surprise. "Hey, Noah. So…I'll just go and make myself invisible."

Fiona Walsh invisible? Not likely. But to her credit she left the room without another word. Callie looked at Noah. He didn't look the least bit embarrassed that they'd been caught making out. "I should probably go inside," she said quietly. "Fiona is here for…"

"Don't run now."

She twisted her hands together. Her skin, her lips, the blood in her veins felt more alive than she'd believed possible. "Noah…I'm not ready for someone like you."

He stood rigid. "Like me?"

Callie exhaled heavily. "You're like this whole package— like Mr. Perfect." Suddenly the heat was back in the small room, charging the invisible atoms in the air with a heady pulse.

He laughed humorlessly. "I'm far from perfect."

Callie crossed her arms. "I mean that I don't think you're the kind of man a woman kisses and then forgets. I don't think you're the kind of man a woman simply has sex with. I think you're the kind of man a woman makes love with— and I'm not…I can't…"

His eyes glittered. "So this isn't a sex thing?"

Callie blushed wildly. "Well, of course it's a sex thing. I mean, I'm not denying that I'm attracted to you. It's obvious I am. It's not *just* a sex thing."

He didn't move. He stared at her with such burning intensity she had to look away. To the floor. To the side. Anywhere but into his eyes.

Finally, he spoke. "Within minutes of meeting you, Callie, I knew something was happening. I couldn't figure out what, but I knew it was big. I knew, on some level, that it would change my life. But I can't afford to be casual about this. I have a responsibility to my kids to keep myself in a good place and to do the right thing by them."

She took a deep breath as the sting of tears threatened. "That's just it. I know that about you…I feel that. You *have* to think about your children, Noah," she breathed. "And I…I'm not prepared to…I'm not prepared for that."

His gaze narrowed. "For what, Callie? My kids? Is that what you're saying?"

Her heart ached. *I'm saying I'm not ready to let go yet… I'm not ready to forget my baby son and move on. I'm not ready to fall for you and love another woman's children.*

Her heart contracted. "Yes." She whispered the word, knowing it would hurt him, knowing she was pushing him away because she was so afraid of all he offered her. "I don't want a ready-made family."

Silence screeched between them, like fingernails on a chalkboard.

When he spoke, his voice was quiet. "Well, I guess that's it, then. I'll see you next weekend."

Callie stepped forward. "Noah, I really—"

"There's no need to explain, Callie," he said, cutting her off. "I understand what you're saying. You don't want my kids. You don't want me. That's plain enough. I'll see you 'round."

She waited until he'd left the small room before taking a breath. And as she heard his truck pull away, she burst into tears.

Callie remained in the office for a while, but once her tears were wiped up she returned to the house. Fiona was waiting for her on the porch. Her friend sat on the love seat and held two glasses of wine.

"You look like you could use this."

She sank on the seat and took the glass. "Thanks."

Fiona's big eyes looked her over. "You've been crying. What happened? You two looked cozy when I walked in."

"I don't want to talk about it."

"You know," Fiona said, sharper than usual, "sometimes it doesn't hurt to open up a bit. That's what friends do for each other—in case you forgot."

"I'm a terrible friend," Callie said through a tiny hiccup.

"Yeah, I know."

Callie couldn't help the hint of a smile that curled her mouth. "I don't know how to feel," she admitted. "He wants… he wants…"

"Everything?" Fiona asked. "That doesn't seem like such a bad deal to me."

It didn't, no. But taking everything meant giving everything. "I can't."

Fiona took a sip of wine. "You can't live in the past forever, Callie. Believe me, I know that from experience." She leaned back in the love seat. "I know you lost a baby."

Callie gasped. "How do you—"

"I found some pictures," Fiona explained. "Remember when you first moved in and I helped you unpack? You were out with the horses and I was inside going through boxes…" Her voice trailed off.

Her memory box—given to her by the caring nursing staff at the hospital after Ryan had passed away. "Why didn't you say something sooner?"

Fiona shrugged. "I figured if you wanted to tell me, you would. The only reason I'm bringing it up now is that I like Noah. And so do you. I don't get why you'd send him away."

"It's complicated."

"Because he has kids?"

Callie wondered where her friend had gotten all this sudden intuition from. "I'm just not sure if I can do it."

Fiona watched her over the rim of her glass. "You won't know unless you try."

"And if I mess up, the children will be caught in the middle."

"I think you should cut yourself some slack. You're smart and from what I've seen you're pretty good with kids."

"This is different," she said quietly.

"Why? Because you're falling in love with him? With them?" Fiona asked.

Callie gasped. Was it true? Was she falling in love with him? She liked him…really liked him. But love? Could she? Overwhelmed, Callie couldn't find the voice to deny her friend's suspicions.

"Have you told Noah about your son?"

"No."

"Maybe you should," Fiona suggested. "You know he'd understand. Or is that what you're afraid of?"

She stared at her friend. Was that the truth? Was she so afraid of him really knowing her?

"I had a baby," Fiona admitted. "When I was fifteen."

Callie's eyes almost sprang out of their sockets. "What?"

Fiona nodded. "I gave her up for adoption. There's not a day goes by when I don't think about her, when I don't wonder where she is, when I don't pray that the family she's with are looking after her, loving her. I hope they don't love her less because she's adopted."

Thunderstruck, Callie stared at her friend, saw the tears shimmering in Fiona's eyes and pushed back the thick swell of emotion contracting her own throat. She had no idea her bubbly, eternally happy friend was holding on to such a secret. "I'm so sorry, Fee."

Fiona managed a brittle smile. "I guess what I'm saying

is that we all have things in our past that can stop us from looking for happiness or make us blind to it when it comes along. The trick is having the courage to take the chance."

Three days after the afternoon in the tack room, Callie went for a long ride. She rode into Crystal Point and headed for the beach. It was barely ten o'clock and only a few people were about, a couple chasing sticks with their dogs and a lone jogger pounding the sand. She maneuvered Indiana past the restrooms and onto the soft sand. She spotted a couple of small children building a sand castle and urged Indiana to a halt when she heard her name being called.

It was Evie. And the two small children were Hayley and Matthew.

"Hello," Evie said as Callie dismounted.

Hayley came running up to her and hugged her so fiercely Callie was amazed by the little girl's obvious display of affection. Evie stood back and watched the interaction keenly as Hayley showed off her thumbnail painted with transparent glitter polish compliments of her Aunt Mary-Jayne.

Both kids hovered around Indiana, and he stood like an angel while the little girl patted his soft muzzle. Matthew was a little more reluctant, but after a small amount of coaxing from his aunt he stroked Indy's shoulder.

"He's such a beautiful animal," Evie said with a whistle.

Callie smiled proudly. "Yes, he is." The kids lost interest in the horse and headed back to their sand castle. "They look like they're having fun."

Evie smiled. "They love the beach. I try to bring them as much as I can."

"Do you look after them often?"

"Every Wednesday," she replied. "My mother has them on Fridays and the rest of the week they're in daycare." Evie looked at the twins affectionately. "They're off to school next year and I'm already missing them just thinking about it."

Callie stopped herself from watching the twins. "They're lucky to have you in their life."

Evie shrugged. "They're easy to love."

Yes, Callie knew that. And she could feel herself getting drawn toward them. Evie patted Indiana for a moment and then slanted Callie a look she knew instantly would be followed by a question. "So, are you and Noah seeing each other?"

"Where did that come from?"

Evie smiled. "Jamie said you make a mean salad."

Callie tipped her Akubra down on her forehead.

"I knew you were going on a date. But I was surprised when the kids told me you'd been to the house," Evie said when she didn't reply. "You're the only woman he's invited home to be with his kids since his divorce. I figured that meant something."

Callie remembered Hayley's innocent remark about *grown-up girls* and her insides contracted. She'd known it, felt it...but to hear the words, to know he'd never had another woman in the house with his children...it made her heart ache.

"He's a good guy," Evie said quietly. "He had a tough time with his ex and deserves to be treated right."

Callie managed a brittle smile. "Are you warning me off?"

Evie chuckled. "Lord, no. And Noah would strangle me if he knew I was talking with you about this. Sometimes I get into my protective-sister mode and put my foot in it. But I like you, Callie. And I love my brother. So you can tell me to back off and stop meddling if you want—but I probably won't listen."

Callie was surprised by the other woman's frankness. "I hear you."

"She didn't want her kids, you know," Evie said as she looked over toward the twins. "Imagine that. I mean, she had a lot of emotional problems, no doubt about it…but to just walk away from two new babies…it's unfathomable to me." She sighed. "And Jamie was barely more than a toddler himself. As for Lily…sometimes she acts so impulsively and I'm concerned she has abandonment issues. And you'd never really know what Noah is thinking. But I guess when your wife packs her bags and tells you she doesn't want you or your children—it must make it hard to trust someone again."

Callie's breath caught in her throat and emotion burned behind her eyes.

Abandoned, motherless children…and a good man trying to hold it all together. She suddenly felt the shame of what she'd said to him right down to the soles of her boots.

She'd said the words to hurt…said them knowing they would hit him hard.

She'd wounded him instead of doing what she should have done…which was to tell him the truth. About why she was so afraid. Fiona was right—she needed to tell him about Ryan.

"I have to go," she said as she grabbed the reins and sprung into the saddle. "Thanks, Evie," she said as she turned Indiana back toward the boat ramp and began the quick canter home.

Twenty minutes later she was back at Sandhills Farm. She untacked Indiana, turned him into one of the small paddocks behind the house and then headed inside. One telephone call and a change of clothes later and she was on the road.

She'd called Preston Marine and was told Noah was working from home that day. Within eight minutes she'd pulled her truck into his driveway. Callie turned off the ignition and got out. She heard a loud noise, like a motor running, and followed the sound around the side of the house. She saw him immediately, behind the pool fence holding a chainsaw.

In jeans and a white tank shirt, he looked hot, sweaty and gorgeous. She observed for a moment as he cut branches from an overgrown fig tree and tossed them onto a growing pile. There was something incredibly attractive about watching a man work—a kind of primitive instinct, purely female and wholly erotic. As if aware he was being watched, he stopped the task, lay the chainsaw aside and turned. He walked around the pool and came to a halt about ten feet from her.

"Hello."

She took a breath. "Hi."

He looked at his hands. "I need to wash up."

Callie followed him through one pool gate and then another until they reached the patio. She waited while he slipped through the back door and then returned a few minutes later, cleaned up and in a fresh T-shirt and carrying two cans of soda.

He pulled the ring tab and passed her one. She took it, desperate to touch his fingertips, but she didn't. "Are you playing truant today?"

"Just working off steam."

Callie suspected she was the steam he needed to work off.

He put the can down on a nearby table. "Why are you here, Callie?"

She held her breath. "I saw your sister today."

His brows came up. "Did she embarrass me?"

"No." Callie stepped back on her heels. "But she said something. She said…she said you'd never invited a woman here…to be with the kids. Before me."

"She's right."

Another breath, longer, to steady nerves stretched like elastic. "Why not?"

He pulled out a chair for her to sit on and then one for himself. Once Callie was seated he did the same. Finally, he spoke. "When you're treated badly, when the person you've committed yourself to walks out the door and says she doesn't want you, she doesn't want your children, she just wants to be free, it breaks something inside you. It broke something inside *me*," he admitted. "I have no illusions about the kind of marriage I had. Most of the time it was a disaster. She'd left once before—the second time I told her that was it, no more. She had to make a choice. And she chose freedom." He leaned forward and rested his elbows on his knees.

Callie stood and walked across the patio. She looked at the pool and the immaculate garden and the timber cubby house she knew he would have built himself. When she'd gathered the courage to say what she come to say, she turned. He was still seated.

"I'm so sorry, Noah." Callie inhaled heavily. "About what I said the other day. I know I…I hurt you."

He didn't move.

Callie took a deep breath. "The way it came out, the way it sounded… That's not what I wanted to say. And certainly not what I meant."

He stood up and walked toward her. "So what did you want to say?"

She placed her hand on his arm and immediately felt the heat of their touch. "That your kids are amazing." She swallowed hard and kept her hand on him. "What I'm feeling, it's not about them. It's about me."

Noah covered her hand with his. "What *are* you feeling, Callie?"

Callie looked at him and her eyes glistened with moisture. She inhaled deeply, taking as much into her lungs as she could. "The reason I feel as I do…the reason I push people away…" She paused, felt the sting of tears. "The reason I push *you* away…it's because I lost someone."

Noah's grip on her hand tightened. "Your fiancé?"

She met his gaze levelly. And the tears she'd been fighting tipped down over her lashes. "No, not Craig."

"Then who? What do you—"

"My son," she whispered. "My baby."

Chapter Eight

"You had a son?" The shock in his voice was obvious.

Callie shuddered. "His name was Ryan," she said and felt the hurt right through to her bones. "He died when he was two days old."

She watched Noah think, absorb. "How long ago?"

"Three years," she said quietly and inhaled. "Ten months... one week...three days."

He swallowed hard. "How? Was he sick?"

She shrugged and turned, wrapping her arms around herself. "I was in an accident." She hesitated, took a long breath and then looked at him. "A car wreck."

Noah clearly knew what that meant. "The same one that killed your fiancé?"

"Yes."

She watched as the pieces of the puzzle came together in his head. "You lost them both?" He turned her back around and rubbed his thumb along her jawline. "Why didn't you tell me this before now?"

She looked down, taking a breath. "Because I don't talk about it. And we haven't known one another very long and I didn't…couldn't… Well, being responsible for someone's death, it isn't exactly the kind of thing I want to talk about."

Noah didn't try to hide his shock. "How were you responsible?"

"The accident," she replied. "It was my fault."

"Were you driving the car?"

She shook her head. "No, Craig was driving."

"Then how could—"

"I distracted him," she admitted. "I made him lose concentration. And I shouldn't have. I was angry because we argued." She didn't say anything for a moment. She looked up and around and then back to him. "Craig didn't want the baby."

"He didn't?"

"No. He didn't want anything other than to use me. I fell for him when I was seventeen," she explained quietly. "I moved in with him, wanted to be with him. Craig trained me, taught me everything I know. He was a gifted rider. I thought he loved me. But I found out too late that he only cared about his career. *Our career,* as he called it." Another breath. "We'd worked hard, trained hard, put in hours and used all our money. The Grand Prix Championships were at our fingertips—and after that, the big one, the Olympics, every rider's dream. But I got pregnant and everything changed. I couldn't ride, I wouldn't risk riding. Craig was furious. I'd never seen him like that. We argued about it for three days. In the end, he told me I had to make a choice."

She paused, took a long breath, gathered herself and blinked away the fresh tears in her eyes. "He wanted me to end it. The pregnancy."

Noah's mouth thinned. "What did you do?"

"Moved back in with my mom."

"And then?"

"I decided to get on with my life. When I was about five months along, Craig came back. He said he wanted to try and work things out. He said he'd changed his mind about the baby, about me. And I believed him."

She knew he heard the "but" in her voice. "What happened then?" he asked.

Callie shrugged. "For a few weeks it seemed like it would be okay. And as much as I felt betrayed by Craig, I knew my baby deserved a father. Craig even talked about setting a date for the wedding." She paused, thinking, remembering. "On the day of the accident he came around early. We talked about me moving back in with him, about turning one of the guest rooms into a nursery. He asked me to go for a drive. I was happy to do it, happy thinking everything would work out. We got in the car and drove for a while. But he seemed edgy to me, like he had something on his mind. And then... and then he said it. He said it and I knew I could never trust him again."

Noah held her tighter. "What did he say?"

"My horse," she replied. "He wanted my horse, Indiana. That was what he wanted. That was *all* he wanted. Not me, not our baby. You see, Craig was a gifted rider with a good horse, where as I was a good rider with a gifted horse. He wanted to ride Indy in the Grand Prix qualifiers. He said if I loved him, if I wanted him to be a part of my life, and the baby's life I had to do what he asked."

"And the crash?" Noah asked quietly.

"He was furious with me, called me a few names. He tried to touch me and I pushed him off." Her voice cracked, sounding hollow. "He lost control of the car. We ended up crashing into a guardrail and down an embankment."

Noah winced. He felt pain and rage rip through him. Anger toward a man he'd never met. A dead man. A man who'd hurt this woman so much, who'd broken her to a point Noah feared she'd never be whole again.

"Was he killed instantly?" he managed to ask, though he didn't know how. His heart thundered in his chest.

She nodded. "Yes."

"And you?"

"I was rushed to the hospital," she said. "I had a lot of internal injuries and the baby was in distress. I was pretty out of it. My mom was there and they told her there were no guarantees for either of us. So the doctors delivered him." Tears came again, brimming over. "He fought for two days. He was so tiny. I was so sick and only got to spend a moment holding him."

Noah swallowed, fighting the emotion in his throat. It was every parent's worst nightmare. And she'd endured it alone. He wished he could turn back the clock and be there with her, hold her through every awful moment. He took a deep breath. "I can't even imagine how you must feel."

Callie looked at him. "Ashamed that I didn't see through Craig's lack of integrity. If I had, maybe Ryan would still be alive, maybe my beautiful boy would be with me. He'd be nearly four years old now."

Four years old...

Noah drew a sharp breath. And the truth hit him with the force of a sledgehammer.

"The twins..." His words trailed and then picked up. "That's why you... Ah, of course."

Her throat convulsed. "Sometimes...it's hard to be around them."

Because they reminded her of all she lost.

"I'm so..." He stopped, searching for the words. Everything he considered seemed grossly inadequate. "Thank you for telling me," he said, and even that wasn't nearly enough.

"I needed to," she said, and Noah felt her pull against his

embrace. He let her go and she walked back to the seat and dropped into it. "I wanted you to understand that what I'm feeling is about *me*. Not them. Not you."

That didn't sound right. Her resistance, her pain was about him. And the kids. She'd lost her baby—and that loss stopped her from wanting to *feel* again. Noah could see her struggle. He could feel it. But he wasn't about to let her walk away from him.

He returned to his seat and grasped her hand. "Callie," he said gently. "What do you want to happen between us?"

She looked uncertain and he felt panic rise in his blood. He wanted her to say she wanted everything—him, the kids, the life he knew was within their reach. But her silence was suddenly deafening.

Finally, she spoke. "I've done a good job of putting my emotions on hold for the past few years. And as much as I'm drawn to you, Noah, I just don't know if I'm ready to feel again."

His fingers tenderly rubbed her knuckles as he kissed her. "I'm no expert, Callie," he said against her mouth. "But if you feel anything like I'm feeling right now, we're off to a good start."

She moaned slightly and the sound undid him. He wanted her so much. Needed her so much. He felt like saying something to her, maybe tell her exactly what she meant to him. Something uncurled in his chest, thudding loudly. *Liking* Callie, *desiring* Callie had swiftly turned into something else. And this Callie—this beautiful, fragile woman who now trembled in his arms, was suddenly the one woman he wanted for the rest of this life.

"Callie?"

She looked up. And one look did it. One look from blue eyes shimmering with tears.

I'm gone...

The feeling reached right through to every pore in his skin, every blood cell, every scrap of air that filled his lungs when he took a breath.

"Spend Saturday with me," he said quietly. He kissed her again, slanting his mouth over hers in a sweet, possessive caress and he felt her tremble. "Can you rearrange your lesson schedule?"

"Yes." She sighed. "And thank you for understanding."

He nodded. He did understand. She wasn't a woman to be rushed. And because he'd waited his entire life to feel this way, he'd do his best to give her whatever time she needed.

Wear a swimsuit.

Callie hadn't asked him why he'd insisted she make sure she had a bikini underneath her clothes for their date Saturday. However, when she spotted two long objects secured to the racks on the roof of his truck she knew why.

She frowned. "Boats?"

"Kayaks," he corrected and opened the passenger door.

"I don't really do boats."

He laughed deliciously. "It'll be fun," he said. "Trust me."

"I do," she replied. "I just don't trust boats."

He told her M.J. had arrived early that morning and was happily in charge of the kids for the day. Jamie had insisted on making Callie a matching pendant to go with the bracelet he'd gifted her and Callie was incredibly touched.

The trip to the boat ramp took about ten minutes and Callie relaxed. The nervous energy she seemed to have around him had disappeared. She felt calm and happy. And Callie sensed she was ready for the next step. Telling him about Ryan had been exactly what she needed to do. It gave her strength and, from somewhere, the courage to dare to imagine a future with the incredible man beside her.

When they reached the boat ramp he passed her something. "You'll need to wear this. There's a ladies bathroom over there."

He pointed to a concrete block building about fifty meters away. *This* turned out to be a black, stretchy, sleeveless wet suit that came to her knees and a pair of matching shoes with rubber grips on the soles. Once out of her jeans and shirt and into the wet suit, Callie ran her hands over her hips. With only a bikini beneath, she felt a little deliciously decadent. When she returned to the truck she saw he'd also changed into a similar suit.

It should be illegal for a man to look that good in black rubber.

She watched, feeling rather useless, as Noah unclipped the kayaks from the utility, prepped them for their outing and launched them into the water.

"Ready?" he asked and handed her a sun visor. It looked new, as if he'd bought it especially for her. "Can you swim?"

"Yes."

"Good," he said and passed her a life jacket. "Humor me anyway and wear this."

Callie didn't argue and slipped the jacket over her wet suit.

"We'll go up river," he said. "It's low tide at the moment. Just stick close by me."

She didn't intend to let him out of her sight.

Noah gave her quick but detailed instructions on how to use the single oar and maneuver the craft through the water. Half an hour later they were on their way.

Noah stayed at her pace and they paddled up river, splicing through the water in unison. On either side of the river the mangrove branches twisted and rose up onto the sandbank. Schools of fish crisscrossed below them and some flipped out of the water, delivering a salty spray across her face and arms.

"How are your arms holding up?" Noah asked after about an hour.

"Good. Although I think I'll be sore tomorrow."

"We'll stop for a bit," he said. "I owe you breakfast for making you get up this early."

Callie laughed. "Breakfast? Is there a café tucked along here somewhere?"

"You're sitting on it," he said, grinning. "There's a storage compartment beneath your seat. There's a cooler with food and a thermos of coffee."

Callie looked between her legs and chuckled. "So, what are you sitting on?"

He laughed. It was a rich, lovely sound. "The first-aid kit. Sunscreen. A spare life jacket. And my phone."

"You've thought of everything."

"Habit," he said, and indicated her to turn the kayak toward a smaller secluded inlet. "With kids you have to be prepared for any emergency."

Noah pointed to a tiny alcove ahead and they oared to shore. He got out first and dragged his kayak onto the sand and quickly helped Callie do the same. Once her feet hit the ground she felt the wobble in her calves and thighs. Noah grabbed her by the shoulders.

"Sea legs," he said with a smile. "It'll pass."

Callie let the warmth radiate through her. His fingers were strong and gentle against her skin. She placed her hands at his waist. That felt good, too. She wished she'd tossed off the life jacket so she could get closer to him. Then he kissed her with all the pent-up passion fuelling the long three days since they'd seen one another.

"Callie," he whispered against her mouth, before he kissed her cheek and the delicate and sensitive skin below her earlobe. "I'm starved."

She smiled. "Me, too," she admitted, not wanting to leave

his embrace but liking the idea of some food. She pushed past the nagging disappointment she felt when he released her. "What did you bring?" she asked as she slipped off the life jacket.

"Let's see."

They unpacked the kayak together. Callie grabbed the small rug he'd provided and spread it down farther up the bank in a spot shaded by a wiry native tree. She sat with her knees up, while Noah stretched out his long limbs beside her. There was fruit, soft bread rolls, cheese and smoked ham. They sat on the rug, eating and not saying much of anything for a while. Noah passed her a resin mug filled with coffee and she took it gratefully.

The weather was warm with a gentle hint of breeze and there were birds calling out from the trees above. Water lapped at the edge of the small sandy inlet and the sound was faintly hypnotic.

She put down her mug and uncurled her legs. "It's a lovely spot. Do you come here often?"

"Not much."

He wasn't looking at her, she noticed. He was looking at the sand, his feet and the drink in his hand. She said his name again and he looked up. His green eyes were vibrant and wholly aroused. Heat rode up her spine at a galloping speed.

"I didn't," he said quietly, interpreting her response, "bring you here with any motive other than to spend time with you."

"I know." Callie rested back on her elbows, felt the wet suit stretch with her movements and saw his gaze narrow. "I also know you won't rush me."

He sucked in a breath. "I'm glad you know that."

She relaxed fractionally. Dare she admit he was first man outside of her family who made her feel safe? "It's not that I'm afraid of…of…" She waved her hand between them.

"Of making love?"

"With you?" She pushed herself up and let out a long breath. "No. It's just that I've only ever been with one man in my whole life and it seems like such a long time ago."

"There's no hurry."

Noah looked so calm and controlled. But Callie wasn't fooled. He wanted her. Yet she knew he wouldn't take what she wasn't ready to give willingly. "There isn't?" she queried with a husky breath. "You're right."

His eyes glittered brilliantly. "You know, you're looking at me like that isn't helping my good intentions."

"Sorry," she said on a breath. "I guess I'm out of practice at all this."

"Don't be sorry."

The steady sincerity of his gaze raced directly to her heart. "Noah, I wish I was—"

"Come here," he directed softly. "Stop thinking. Stop talking. Just come here."

Callie resisted for a nanosecond and then she was in his arms. Noah captured her mouth in a deep, soul-wrenching kiss. She gripped his shoulders as he rolled her half on top of him. Their legs tangled and he grasped her hips, bringing her closer to the length of his body. "You're so beautiful," he whispered against her mouth.

Callie flung her head back and allowed him to trail hot kisses across her collarbone. She could feel him hard against her and her thighs parted, arching into his body. He touched her arms, her shoulders, her hands. He touched her over the wet suit, cradling her hips. Callie's hands curled over his biceps and she sighed against his mouth. Touching him became as intrinsic as breathing. They kissed and kissed, absorbing one another. Noah rolled over in one swift move, lodging a leg between hers. Callie could feel the force of his erection and it fueled her desire, driving her to kiss him more, touch him more. She sighed, a deep shuddering sound that echoed through them both. She heard him groan, felt the rising urgency in his touch, knew that he was as driven by need as she was. He kissed her as he tugged the wet suit off her shoulders. He cupped her breast through the thin fabric of her bikini top and Callie felt a flood of moisture between her thighs, a longing deep down, driving her to want more, need more. Her hips rose in anticipation, waiting, wanting and screaming with need. She reached down to touch him, felt him hard against her palm, felt the power in her hands as he grew harder still against her stroking fingers. It was as if they had been doing this forever—as if they had known one another in another time, another life.

"Callie," he muttered, like the word was ripped from his throat. "We have to stop."

She put her hands into his hair. "No, please."

"We have to stop," he said again, raggedly. "I don't have a condom. I can't protect you."

She clung to him. Some faraway voice told her he was right. But she wanted him so much. "It's okay," she breathed.

"No," he said, more groan than anything else. "It's not. I won't...I won't make you pregnant. At least, not like this. Not here. And not yet."

Callie's heart stilled, and pain filled every part of her chest. She felt herself move, retreat, pull away. She had to tell him of her pain. Her shame. "You're right, Noah," she whispered, suddenly cold. "You won't make me pregnant." A shuddering sigh came out. "I can't have children."

Noah pulled back immediately. He felt her hurt through to the blood in his bones.

She can't have children.

The pieces of the puzzle of who she was fell spectacularly into place. Of course. It made so much sense. Her son had died and she'd never have another.

Then share mine burned on the edge of his tongue. He wanted to tell her, make her see that she could have children if she wanted them. His kids, who would welcome her into their life. He knew it as surely as he breathed. Even Lily. They *needed* her. *He* needed her.

She scrambled up and took a few moments to readjust her clothing. Once she'd pushed her wetsuit back up she began collecting the leftover foodstuffs and blanket.

Noah adjusted his own wet suit and moved behind her. "Callie?"

She shook her head as she picked up the blanket and began folding. "I'd really rather not talk about it."

"I think we should," he replied, not touching her but so close he felt her nearness like a magnetic field.

"I can't have kids," she said, folding and refolding. "That's really all there is to it."

"Because of the accident?"

She turned around and faced him. "Yes." A simple response to a complicated situation. And not nearly enough. He looked at her and she continued. "I had a lot of internal injuries. The doctors told me I have about a ten-percent chance of ever carrying a baby to full term."

He stared at her. "So you can *get* pregnant?"

Obviously not the question she was expecting. "Well— yes, I suppose. I just can't stay pregnant."

"Then we did the right thing by stopping."

"I guess we did," she said stiffly.

Noah took the blanket from her. "We did, Callie. Come on," he said quietly. "The tide is coming in, we should get going."

They barely spoke on the trip back. When he dropped her home he stayed for a coffee he didn't really want. On the porch, with Tessa at his feet, Noah felt the tension of unfulfilled desire beat between them like a drum.

"You were right," she said unsteadily before she sipped her coffee. "We were sensible to stop. I don't think I could bear to get pregnant only to lose...to...well, you know what I mean. I guess that's why I tell myself I can't have children. It's easier to cope with."

"Ten percent is still ten percent," he said soothingly. "It's a chance."

She shook her head. "No. It's too big a risk. I didn't really think a lot about children before I found out I was expecting Ryan. I guess I just took it for granted." His gaze narrowed and she explained. "The feeling that a little piece of you keeps going on because of your children... It wasn't until I was told I wouldn't be a mother again that I realized just how much I really wanted it." She sighed heavily. "One of life's base instincts, I suppose."

Noah set down his mug and grasped her hand. "There are many ways to become a parent, Callie," he said and suddenly felt like spilling his guts and telling her everything about his disastrous marriage and Margaret's infidelity.

She shrugged. "I suppose."

It wasn't the response he hoped for. "You don't believe that?"

"I think...I think someone with four children wouldn't really know what I feel."

He stood up and walked to the stairs, turning around to face her with his hands on his hips. "And you once accused *me* of being arrogant," he said pointedly.

"What does that mean?"

"It means that you didn't corner the market on lousy relationships."

"I didn't say I had."

"But you imply it," he said quietly, completely frustrated. "I'm not going to pretend to fully grasp what it must have been like for you to lose your baby...or how it feels knowing you might never have another child. But despite what you might think, I do know a bit about disappointment…and loss."

Her blue eyes shone. "Because of your wife?"

"Because I married a woman I didn't love and who didn't love me," he replied. "And she spent the next ten years punishing us both for it. But I stuck with it because I'd made a commitment and I felt I owed my children a chance at a normal life with parents who stayed together." Noah dropped his arms to his sides. "It was a train wreck from the very beginning."

"But you stayed?"

"I stayed for the kids," he said honestly. "They needed me."

She stood up and reached him in a couple of steps. "You were right to stay," she said. "For Lily's sake especially. She's afraid, you know. Afraid you might leave."

Noah's chest hurt. "She said that to you?"

"She implied it. I think Lily is frightened things are changing."

"Change is inevitable, though."

Callie nodded. "I suppose. I'm not an expert on teenage girls, Noah, but I was one once. And in a way I understand what Lily is feeling. My father was sick for a long time before he died. And even though I knew my mom wasn't sick and wouldn't die, too, part of me always feared that she might. So maybe you simply need to talk to Lily and tell her you're not going anywhere."

Strange how good it felt to talk to her about Lily. The years of going it alone had been lonely ones. He could easily imagine Callie at his side, every day, every night. "Thank you for caring about Lily."

"I do care," she said quietly and looked away.

Noah stepped closer and took hold of her chin, lifting her face up. "But you're not sure you want to, right?"

"Honestly…being around you makes me more confused than I've ever been in my life." Her hands found his chest. "Would you…would you like to stay for a while?"

"Yeah," he breathed. "But I have to pick the kids up before three."

"Oh." Disappointment etched on her face.

"Evie's got guests arriving at two," he explained. "And my folks are golfing all day."

She moved her fingertips. "Another time, then?"

He grasped her shoulders and looked at her. "I *want* to stay with you." He pulled her close and her hands were imprisoned between them. "Believe me." One hand moved over her shoulder and he gently touched the back of her neck and tilted her head fractionally. "I want to make love to you so much I can barely think about anything else." Especially after what had happened between them down by the river. "I'll call you later," he said, kissing her. "And of course I'll see you tomorrow, for Lily's lesson."

"Of course," she whispered.

He kissed her again and the feel and taste of her was imprinted all over his skin. And Noah knew, without a doubt, that he wanted to love her for the rest of his life.

Only, he had no idea if Callie wanted the same thing.

Chapter Nine

Callie hitched the trailer to her truck and got Fiona to check the lights. Her friend gave her the thumbs-up.

"Can I *please* come with you?" Lily asked for the third time.

"Like I said the first time, no."

Lily scowled. "But I could help. You might need me."

Rescuing the three neglected horses would be tricky, but it needed to be done. Because Animal Welfare hadn't been able to trace the horses, Callie and Fiona had found out their location through a mutual friend and horse trainer. They'd planned the rescue for late Wednesday afternoon and would inform the authorities when they had the animals loaded on the trailer. Only Callie hadn't expected Lily to turn up and insist on helping.

"Definitely not," she said. "Get your bike and head home."

"Dad will let me go if I ask him," Lily said.

Callie looked at her. "No, he won't."

She knew how Noah would react. He was a stickler for doing the right thing. And what they were doing was not exactly protocol—even if their intentions were noble. She'd considered telling him about her plans because she didn't want there to be any secrets between them. But Fiona talked her out of it, insisting the fewer people who knew the better.

"But I *want* to help," Lily insisted and then said with a pout, "I thought we were friends."

"We are," Callie said, firmer this time. "But your father is—"

"More than a friend," Lily said bluntly and pouted again. "Yeah, I get that. I'm not a little kid. I know you guys are into each other."

Callie tried to ignore the heat climbing up her neck. She suspected Lily knew about their kayaking trip. Well, not everything. But Lily was smart, she'd work it out, even if Callie was reluctant to come clean and admit she and Noah were together. "I was about to say that your father wouldn't want you mixed up in this. And neither do I," she added.

"I can take care of myself," Lily said and crossed her thin arms. "And I wish everyone would stop treating me like I'm five years old. I'm thirteen…old enough to…well, old enough to do lots of stuff. And it's not like I'm about to go and do something stupid. And the way my dad's been acting lately you'd think I was some sort of glass doll."

Callie caught Lily's resentment. "He's concerned about you."

"No need," the teenager replied. "I get that he wants a girlfriend," she said and flashed her eyes at Callie. "But who says it would work out anyway? I mean, people get together and break up all the time, right? Even married people. *Especially* married people. In fact, I don't know why adults bother to get married at all. They should just have kids and break up straight away…that way the kids don't have to get used to the idea that having parents who are together is normal."

Once she'd finished her impassioned speech, Lily bit down on her lower lip. Callie's concerns about Lily's fragile emotions increased tenfold. For all the girl's bravado, she wasn't fooled. Lily was hurting. Lily felt things deeply. And Callie knew the young girl was concerned about her relationship with her father. Noah was all she had, Lily's rock, the one constant in her life. And Callie had no intention of threatening that foundation.

"Time for you to go home," Callie said gently. "I'll see you on Sunday."

Lily begrudgingly accepted her decision and took off on her bicycle.

"Let's get going," Fiona said after they'd filled up the hay nets. "We need to get the horses back here before it gets dark."

Callie agreed. She locked Tessa in the backyard and checked the house was secure. The windows all worked now, thanks to Noah.

She maneuvered the truck and trailer around the yard and headed for the road.

"So, big date this Friday, huh?"

Callie concentrated on the driving. The trip was close to thirty kilometers west of Bellandale and would take about half an hour. But she still managed to smile at her friend. "How did you find out?"

"Evie told me," Fiona said. "She's watching the kids and asked if I wanted to drop by for a game of rummy." Her friend rolled her eyes. "I get a game of rummy and you get a dreamy date."

Dreamy? She supposed Noah was a little dreamy. *A lot dreamy*. And she was looking forward to their date more than she could have ever imagined. She had only seen him during

Lily's lesson on Sunday because the twins had come down with a slight cold. But he'd asked her to dinner on Friday night. Although after what happened by the river, Callie wasn't sure she was ready for the next step in their relationship. Oh, she wanted Noah. What surprised her was the intensity of that desire. She'd never considered herself all that sexual in the past...her life with Craig had revolved around the horses and competition and hard work. Sex and romance had come last in the list of priorities they'd set for their life together.

But with Noah...well, she thought about sex a lot. And she felt certain he thought the same. Since they'd almost made love by the river she'd been distracted and unable to think about much else.

Except now she was thinking about Lily. The young girl's obvious confusion and pain lingered in the back of Callie's mind. She needed to talk with Noah before their relationship went any further. She needed to be sure she wasn't unsettling Lily too much.

"There's the turnoff," Fiona announced.

Callie slowed down and turned into a long gravel driveway. An old farmhouse came into view behind a row of wild bamboo. The settling dusk set up an eerie mood. "Are you sure this is the right place?"

"Absolutely. Put the headlights on, will you? It's getting dark."

Callie flicked on the lights and pulled the truck to a halt. "Looks like a gate over there," she said and pointed to a break in the fence line where an old timber gate was tethered between two posts. Fiona grabbed the flashlight on the seat between them and got out. Callie followed and retrieved three halters and ropes from the back of the truck before tracing her friend's footsteps.

"I can see them," Fiona announced when she reached the fence line. "Look."

Callie saw the three horses silhouetted against the diminishing sunlight. "You get the trailer ready," she said. "I'll grab them."

"Be careful," Fiona warned and headed back to the truck.

Callie looked at the chain and padlocks on the gate and tapped the pair of bolt cutters in her back pocket. She slipped through the barbed-wire fence and headed for the trio of horses who were now watching her suspiciously. The closer she got, the more appalled she became. They were clearly neglected. Two bays and one grey, all of them in need of decent feed and veterinary attention. She haltered one of the bays and the other two automatically followed. Once the three horses were secured, Callie grabbed the snips and cut through the barbed wire. Within minutes they began angle loading them on the trailer.

Fiona suddenly shrieked. "Callie, look. A car's coming."

Sure enough, a pair of headlights turned toward the long driveway. "It could be nothing," Callie assured her friend.

Fiona didn't believe her. She didn't believe herself. "They must have seen our lights. We have to get out of here."

Callie agreed. They quickly secured the horses, closed the tailgate, then jumped into the truck. Callie turned the truck and trailer in a sharp arc and headed down the driveway.

The car kept coming. Conscious of both their own and the horse's safety, Callie accelerated fractionally and stayed on the track. With just meters to spare, the car veered to the right with a loud blast of its horn. She kept going, giving the task her full concentration. Fiona told her the car had turned and was now on their tail as they headed out of the driveway. They hit the main road and Callie increased speed. Behind, the car closed in, tailgating them, striking the horn in an attempt to intimidate. The driver didn't give up, following them down the narrow country road. In the side mirrors Callie could see that the car was in fact a truck with a menacingly heavy-duty push bar out front. And it was getting closer to the back of the trailer with each passing second. At the first contact on the push bar against the rear of the trailer, Callie was thrown forward. Fiona screamed. Callie gripped the steering wheel and held on, managing the impact by pressing the gas and surging forward. She could feel the horses moving in the trailer and straightened the rig quickly. The truck collided again, harder this time, sending them into the gravel rut on the edge of the road. Callie held her nerve and pulled the wheel with all her strength.

"Should we pull over?" Fiona asked frantically.

"No," Callie said quickly. "Cameron's a police officer, right?"

Fiona nodded. "Yeah."

"So, call and tell him where we are and what's happening."

"But he'll—"

"Just call him," she insisted. "Hurry."

Thankfully Fiona had service on her cell and hastily made the call. Cameron instructed them to keep on their route at the designated speed limit if safe and said a police car would be dispatched immediately.

They endured a frightening ten minutes until the welcome sight of blue and red flashing lights came toward them. Callie slowed the truck down and pulled over. The truck took one last ram into the back, jerking them around the cab despite their seat belts. Another police vehicle appeared and cornered the truck behind them.

The offenders were out of their truck within seconds. Two men, hurling insults about how they had stolen their horses, didn't like having to answer questions about how Callie's trailer had dents on the tailgate.

Cameron arrived in plain clothes because he'd been off duty. He was quick to check they were unharmed and asked for a detailed account of what had happened. With the men now in the back of a police car and the horses jittery but in one piece, Callie began to tell her account of the events while Fiona called Animal Welfare to come and pick up the horses. But a sharp rapping sound interrupted them, followed by a shrill voice pleading, "Let me out."

Cameron followed the sound, Callie right behind him. He rattled the handle to the storage compartment on the side of the trailer. Callie quickly gave him the key and he opened the narrow door. None of them expected Lily Preston to unfold her gangly legs from the small space.

"Damn it, Lily," Cameron demanded as he helped her out. "What are you doing in there?"

The teenager straightened, rubbed her arms and looked at Callie. "I just wanted to help."

Callie's blood ran cold. "You stowed away when I told you not to. Lily, how can—"

"Because friends should help each other."

"Does your dad know you're here?" Cameron asked.

Lily shook her head, guilt written all over her face. "Maybe we shouldn't tell him."

Good idea—but not going to happen. Callie watched as Cameron stepped away and made a quick phone call.

By the time Noah received the call from Cameron, he was about to start calling Lily's friends to see if anyone knew where she was. He'd tried Callie several times thinking she'd be there, but she hadn't picked up. Nor could he get any service on her cell. Not surprising, considering Cameron's brief account of events that led to both Lily and Callie ending up at the police station.

He dropped the kids at Evie's and headed into Bellandale. He scored a parking space outside the police station and headed inside. Cameron greeted him swiftly, minus the regulation blue issue uniform.

"Where's Lily?" he demanded.

"In the break room. She's okay," Cameron said.

Relief pitched in his chest. "And Callie?"

"She's just finished making a statement. Room three. You can go in if you like."

Noah strode away without another word. She was sitting down when he entered the room. He said her name.

She looked up, swallowed hard and let out a long, almost agonized sigh. "Noah."

He stepped closer. "Are you all right?"

"Yes, fine."

"What happened?"

She took a deep breath and placed her hands on the small table in front of her. "Fiona and I heard that the three horses we've been trying to rescue had been moved again. We found out the location and went to get them."

"To steal them?"

She raised her hands and stood, scraping the chair back. "Well, yes."

"And what?" he asked, sharper than he wanted. "You thought you'd take my kid along for the ride?"

"No…I had no idea she'd stowed away in the storage locker."

Noah stilled. "She was in the *trailer?*" Cameron hadn't mentioned that.

"Dad?"

They both stopped speaking and turned their heads toward the door. Lily stood beneath the threshold. "Don't blame Callie," his daughter insisted.

"I'm not blaming anyone," he said and tried to stop thinking about the danger his daughter had been in. "I'm trying to understand what happened."

Lily shrugged. "I wanted to help. I wanted to do something. It's not Callie's fault."

"I'm not blaming Callie," he said and tried to push back the kernel of censure rising within his chest. He knew Lily. She was headstrong and impulsive. And Callie couldn't have known his daughter would be so determined to go along for the ride.

"Good," Lily said and raised her chin. "It was *my* fault. I'm the one who should be blamed. It's always my fault. That's what I do."

There was so much pain in Lily's voice that Noah's heart constricted. "Its okay, Lily. Why don't you go and wait by the front desk. We'll go home soon."

Lily looked at them both for a moment then let out a pained breath. "So you can do what? Talk about me and work out ways to get me out of your hair so you two can get it on?"

Noah stepped toward his daughter, but she moved back. "It's not like—"

"Maybe you should send me away somewhere," she said and cut him off. "Like boarding school—that way I won't be in anyone's way. Or maybe you should send me to Paris— you could always ask my mother if she wants me." Lily's eyes glistened with tears Noah knew she wouldn't let fall. "But we know what she'd say, right? She didn't want me four years ago, so she won't want me now."

The pain in his daughter's voice pierced directly into Noah's chest. Lily had kept her feelings about her mother locked away for years. And now they were leaching out. He was staggered and anxious and partly relieved. Realizing why, Noah swallowed a hard lump in his throat. In a matter of weeks Callie had somehow become the catalyst for Lily's stirred emotions.

"You're not going to be sent away, Lily," he assured her gently. "Not ever. Go and wait by the desk. I'll be with you soon."

Before she turned Lily looked toward Callie with eyes filled with apologetic resentment. Noah knew Lily liked and respected Callie, but his daughter was also afraid of the impact Callie was having on their lives.

Once she left Callie spoke. "She's in a lot of pain, Noah."

That much was obvious. "I know."

"She's confused and frightened."

He knew that, too. What he didn't know was why Callie looked at him with such blatant despair. "I'll talk with her."

Callie let out a long sigh. "I don't...I don't think we should do this."

Suddenly Noah knew exactly what she was talking about. And he knew what was coming. She wanted out. Before they'd even begun. It cut right through to the marrow in his bones. Perhaps because part of him knew she was right. Lily's needs had to come first. And whatever his daughter was going through, Noah knew his relationship with Callie would only amplify Lily's feelings of abandonment and anger toward her mother.

But...to lose her? Sensing that it was exactly what Callie wanted made him mad. Irrational and unlike him as it was, Noah experienced a deep burst of resentment for the fact she could give up on them so easily.

"So, I guess you get what you want after all," he said, not liking the way it sounded but too stubborn to stop the words from coming.

"What does that mean?"

"No ready-made family."

Callie looked at him, all eyes, all hurt. "That's unfair. I'm only thinking of Lily. She needs—"

"What about what you need, Callie? Or maybe you don't

need anything. Needing would mean feeling, right?" He pushed past the pain that had settled behind his ribs. "It would mean giving part of yourself to me...and I don't know if you have the heart for it."

She swallowed hard. "Do you think I'm that cold?"

"I don't know," he replied, frustrated and annoyed. "Only you know what's in your heart, Callie."

"I'm trying to do what's best for Lily."

You're what's best for Lily. You're what's best for me.

But he didn't say it. He didn't push. Didn't beg her to give them a chance like he wanted to. "I have to go. I'll see you... sometime."

She lifted her shoulders. "Sure."

Noah left the room. Walking down the corridor suddenly became close to the hardest thing he'd ever done.

Callie sat on the sofa, eating ice cream covered in crushed Oreo cookies and copious amounts of chocolate sauce.

She took a mouthful, anticipating the usual buzz from the sugary sweetness, and sighed heavily when the kick didn't come.

Hopeless.

She tried again and, when disappointed with the same result, plopped the dish on the coffee table and sank back in the sofa. It was Friday night and she was alone. The same Friday night that she should have been out on a romantic date with Noah.

I should be with him right now.

Except that everything was ruined.

Even though she knew there was nothing else she could have done when she realized the extent of Lily's fears, Noah's words had hurt her deeply. She did have a heart capable of feeling. A heart that was filled with thoughts of him.

She hadn't heard from Noah all week. Nor had she seen

Lily. She only had a message on her answering machine telling her he'd decided to take his daughter to Janelle Evans for lessons from now on. Callie had replayed the message countless times, listening for something, some indication he regretted what had happened between them. And because she'd heard nothing like that in the direct, clipped tones, each day dragged out longer than the one before.

She'd tried ignoring the pain suddenly and permanently lodged inside her.

She'd tried not to think about how much she missed him.

And how much she missed Lily. And the rest of his amazing family.

And as she'd thought her heart irreparably broken and imagined she'd never feel anything deep enough to really be hurt ever again, Callie came face-to-face with the truth. And it shocked her to the core.

I love him.

She was in love with Noah.

She wasn't sure how to deal with the feelings that were new, raw and strangely precious. Her head hurt thinking about it. She looked at the melting ice cream and was just about to trade it for some aspirin when Tessa barked and moments later the doorbell rang.

Fiona stood on her doorstep and walked across the threshold holding a bottle of wine in each hand. "We thought we'd come over and cheer you up," her friend announced.

"We?"

Evie Dunn stuck her head around the open door. "She means me." Evie's wildly curling black hair bobbed around her face. "Can I come in?"

"Of course."

Within seconds the door was shut and Fiona scooted to the kitchen for glasses.

"You don't mind?" Evie asked.

Callie shook her head. "I could use the company," she admitted and suggested they take a seat.

Evie sat on the oversize love seat and curled up one foot. "It was Fee's idea."

"I'm glad you're here," Callie said, and tried not to think about how much Evie looked like her brother. And *she* was glad for the company. She had the feeling Evie could become a good friend. She pointed to the bowl on the table and smiled. "I was just about to consume a gallon of ice cream."

"As a substitute for what?" Fiona chirped as she came back into the room.

Callie fought off the embarrassment clinging to her skin and ignored her friend's teasing. "You guys have saved me from a gazillion calories."

Fiona laughed then poured wine into three glasses and passed them around.

"If it's any consolation," Evie said quietly, "he doesn't look any better than you do."

Callie tried not to think about how hearing that made her feel. It wasn't as if either of them had made any kind of declaration to one another. Their relationship had fizzled out before it had really begun. What could she say that wouldn't make her look like a silly, lovesick fool?

"Noah told me some of what happened," Evie said and took a sip of wine. "Lily's pretty broken up that you're not teaching her anymore."

"It's probably for the best."

"I'm not so sure. Sometimes you have to push past the hard times."

"Noah has to focus on Lily," Callie said and took a drink.

Evie tutted. "My brother has focused solely on his kids for the past four years. And apart from Lily's gothic rebellion and typical teenage moodiness, she's never talked about how her mother's departure made her feel. And then wham, you walk into their lives and she starts letting things slip. There's a connection, Callie. Because of you she's opening up and that's a positive thing. Talking about her mother is good for Lily."

"I agree," Callie said. "But she needs to be able to do that without being afraid her world is going to be rocked upside down."

"By you?" Evie asked. "Lily worships you."

Callie's throat tightened. "As *her* friend. Not as…something else."

"You mean Noah's girlfriend? Or a potential stepmother?"

Stepmother? Heavens. How had this happened? How had she become so deeply involved with the Preston's that Evie was suggesting marriage? Loving Noah had changed everything. Not being with him hurt so much Callie wondered how she'd get through it.

"She needs stability," Callie said. "She needs to know her father isn't about to get sidetracked."

"She has stability," Evie said a little more forcibly. "What she needs is to know relationships can work and that not all women are like her mother and will leave her."

Callie agreed. Except she wasn't sure she was the kind of role model Lily needed.

And she suspected Noah thought that, too.

Noah thrummed his fingers on the steering wheel as he waited for Lily. The twins and Jamie, buckled up in the back of the utility vehicle, chatted quietly to one another. Harry was asleep on the front porch. The morning air was warm, typical of a November day. Summer would soon be here. And summer in Crystal Point meant the little township would be buzzing with tourists and convoys of camper trailers and weekend holidaymakers searching for some relief from the unforgiving heat in the clear waters of the surf beach and river mouth. He watched as Lily shut the front door and bolted toward the vehicle. She got into the truck and put on the seat belt.

"Ready to go?" he asked.

"Sure. I hope Maddy's okay."

Maddy Spears had been in a horse-riding accident and her mother Angela had called, asking if he could bring Lily to see her at the hospital.

"I'm sure she'll be fine," Noah assured her and started the engine. "How are the lessons going?" he asked, trying to take her mind off her worrying about her best friend.

Lily rolled her eyes. "I've only had one. And like you don't know that already? I'm sure *she's* told you everything."

She. Janelle Evans. Lily's new instructor. The enemy. Noah hung on to his patience. "I thought you liked Janelle."

She huffed. "You thought wrong. She's so *old.*"

He eased the vehicle into gear. "She's experienced."

Lily's eyes narrowed. "Old," she repeated.

"I think you should cut her some slack," Noah said quietly.

Another huff. "Well, you would. Seeing it was *your* idea that I go there in the first place."

"You said you wanted lessons," Noah reminded her.

"I do. But I don't want them with *her.*" Lily rolled her eyes. "I don't see why I can't go back to Callie. It's not like I broke up with her or anything. I knew I'd be the one who ended up getting screwed."

"Watch the language," he warned.

"At least you're not going to start dating *this* instructor," Lily snapped back. "I mean, she's like one hundred years old or something. So I'm pretty sure you won't marry her."

"Who are you marrying, Daddy?" came a determined voice from the backseat.

Noah spotted Jamie in the rear vision mirror and smiled. "No one, mate."

"You could marry Callie," Jamie said determinedly. "We like her. You like her, too, don't you, Dad?"

"Stupid question," Lily said.

"I'm not stupid," Jamie wailed.

"Yeah, you are."

Noah called a truce. "Stop the name calling." Lily made a face and he suspected Jamie stuck his tongue out in response.

"Are you going to *marry* Callie, Dad?" Jamie asked, almost jumping out of his seat.

Marry Callie? He'd thought about. Imagined it. Wanted it. "Lily and I are only talking."

But Jamie didn't give up. "If you marry Callie she'd be our mother, right?"

"Stepmother," Lily put in.

Jamie ignored his sister. "And would she come to school sometimes and work at the canteen, Dad?"

Noah didn't miss the longing in his son's voice. Such a small thing. But for a little boy who barely remembered a mother's love, it was huge. He'd tried his best, but juggling a business and four kids often made it impossible to do the small things. His sisters pitched in, especially Evie, and his mother did what she could. But it wasn't enough. Who was he kidding? His kids needed a full-time mother.

"Would Callie be our mother, Dad?"

Jamie again, still curious and not put off by Noah's silence. He tried to maintain casualness. "I guess she would."

Lily huffed again, louder this time. "Don't get too excited. We didn't have any luck getting our real mother to hang around. I can't see how Callie would be any different."

Chapter Ten

Callie had no idea that helping Angela Spears select a new pony for her daughter Maddy would end with the teenager taking a tumble from the first horse they looked at. She was relieved that Maddy's broken arm was the worst of her injuries. She had some superficial grazes on her face but none that would scar. The hot pink cast on her arm was finally wrapped and Callie offered to grab coffee for a fraught Angela while the doctor checked the results of a few cautionary tests, including a head scan.

She headed for the cafeteria and purchased coffee for Angela and a soda for Maddy.

When she returned to Maddy's room she saw Lily sitting on the edge of the bed, then saw Jamie and the twins perched together on a single chair and Noah talking closely with Angela.

The green-eyed monster reared its ugly head and she pushed the feeling down as swiftly as she could. A blended family—wasn't that the term used now? Angela was an attractive woman. Noah would be blind not to notice. She was a single mother, he was a single father. A good solution all round—yours, mine and possibly ours one day. Lily and Maddy were best friends. It would be the perfect scenario for Noah's troubled daughter.

And if Callie had any doubts that she'd fallen in love with Noah—they scattered the moment she realized the feeling coursing across her skin was blind, burning jealousy.

She swallowed the bitter taste in her mouth.

Callie placed the coffee on the table beside the bed. The twins rushed toward her and Callie had no hesitation in accepting their warm hug. Jamie quickly did the same. Only Lily hung back. But the teenager looked at her almost hopefully. And Noah's eyes grazed over her, from her feet to the roots of her hair. She felt the energy of his stare, felt her skin heat, felt the tiny hairs on the back of her neck come alive.

Angela's beaming smile didn't help. "Oh, you're back," she said breathlessly. "I was just telling Noah how lucky we were that you were with us today. And it was my fault," Angela wailed. "But it was so hot. I had no idea the pony would spook over a little umbrella."

"It happens sometimes," Callie assured her, fighting her awareness of Noah with all her strength. "Don't feel bad."

"Can we still buy the pony?" Maddy asked, still groggy from painkillers.

Angela looked at Callie. "What do you think?"

Callie smiled and turned to the girl in the bed. "How about we wait until your arm is better and try a few more horses out before making a decision?"

Maddy nodded. "Still…" Her voice trailed. "I'd really like my own horse."

"Me, too," Lily said and looked at her father. "You promised, remember?"

"I remember," he said, still looking at Callie. "We'll see."

Lily rolled her kohl-lined eyes. "Yeah, I know what that means." She looked at her friend. "Now you've busted your arm I haven't a chance."

Angela came across the room and hugged Callie. "Thank you for everything," she said, her eyes clogged with emotion. "If you hadn't been there, I don't know what I would have done. I wouldn't have known how to splint her arm like that. And the way you knew to keep her warm in case she went into shock." She shuddered. "I wouldn't have remembered any of that."

"I'm glad I could help."

"Help?" Angela hugged her again. "You were incredible. I'm hopeless in a crisis."

"Not hopeless," Callie said gently. "And I have to know basic first aid as part of my license to teach."

"It didn't look basic to me. Anyway, I'm so grateful you were there."

"Well, I'll get going." She looked quickly around the room, focusing on Angela. "Are you sure your sister will be coming to pick you up?"

"Oh, yes," the other woman replied. "You go, please. You've done more than enough. And thank you for coming here with us. I know it helped Maddy enormously knowing you were by her side."

She said goodbye to the kids and then turned without another word, pain slicing through her with every step she took. She made it about thirty feet down the corridor when she heard Noah saying her name. *I will not look back. I will not let him see how much I miss him.*

"Callie, wait up."

That stopped her. She inhaled deeply and turned to face him. "What?"

"Are you okay?"

Can't you see that I'm not? Can't you see that I'm crazy in love with you? But I can't come between your family. I won't.

"Why wouldn't I be?"

He looked into her eyes. "You had a fairly harrowing afternoon."

"I handled it."

"So Angela said."

Angela. Perfect single mother Angela. "Is there something else you want?" she asked and couldn't believe the sound of her own voice.

"Maddy's lucky you were there."

Callie felt prickles of annoyance weave up her spine. "I guess I have my uses."

He felt the sting of her response because he expelled an almost weary breath. "I just wanted to say…that it's…it's good to see you."

"I have to go," she said quickly and pulled her keys from her pocket. "I've got a student this afternoon," she lied.

He went to say something and then stopped. "Yeah, sure."

Her heart felt like it was going to burst. *I will not fall apart in front of him.* "Goodbye, Noah."

She turned before he could say anything and walked purposefully down the corridor.

By the time she'd returned to Sandhills Farm it was nearly two o'clock. Joe was there, wheeling a barrow of soiled manure from the stables when she pulled up. He asked about Maddy and she gave him a condensed version of what had happened.

"Saddle up Indy for me, will you?" she asked. "The Western saddle please. I'm going for a long ride."

Callie rode toward Crystal Point, through the cane fields, past sweet potato farmers cultivating their crops. She rode past the local primary school, took a trail toward the river and lingered by the boat ramp for a while, eating the sandwich and water she'd packed in her saddle bag while Indy happily grazed on Rhodes grass.

I'm such a fool. For years she'd frozen herself off from feeling anything. And then along came Noah and his incredible kids and suddenly she felt like she was *all* feelings. All want. All need. But she hurt, too. And she didn't know how to stop the hurt…or how to stop loving Noah.

It was past five when she returned home, and it was an hour later when she headed for the house after strapping Indy down, returning her tack to the stables and locking the gelding into his stall. By seven o'clock, once the animals were all fed and bedded down for the night, Callie had showered, put on a pair of sweats and sat on the sofa with her laptop to check her email. One from her brother, Scott, made her smile and she was just about to hit the reply button when she heard a car pull up outside.

He's here.

She knew it somehow. Felt it deep down. Tessa barked and Callie quickly made her way to the front door and flicked on the porch light. She opened the door.

It *was* Noah.

He stood beneath the light. "Hey." He looked so good in jeans and a white golf shirt. Her heart lurched in her chest. "I probably should have called first."

Callie crossed her arms, determined to be strong. "Why didn't you?"

"I thought you might hang up." He ran his hand through his hair. "Can we talk?"

She opened the screen door and waited until he'd crossed the threshold before closing both doors. "What did you want to talk about?" she asked once they'd moved into the living room.

He cleared his throat. "I wanted to…I wanted…"

Callie didn't move as she pushed her emotions down. "What?"

He let out an exasperated breath. "I don't really know. I let Lily stay with Maddy, and after I left the hospital I dropped the kids off at my parents. For the past two hours I've been driving around, thinking, trying to get things right in my head."

"What things?" she asked quietly.

He swallowed. "Us. The kids. Why I can't stop thinking about you."

Callie's knees gave up and she sat on the edge of the sofa. "It's the same for me," she admitted.

He came forward and stood a couple of feet from her. "So, what are we going to do about it?"

Callie shrugged. "Nothing's changed, Noah."

"You're right about that."

"You'd really be better off with someone else," she heard herself say. Stupid words. Words to cover the feelings coursing through her blood.

"Someone else?"

She shrugged. "Like Angela," she said, although her voice cracked and she knew he'd heard it. "She's a single parent, she obviously loves kids—she'd make you a good match."

"I'm not interested in Angela Spears," he said quietly.

"But Lily—"

"Tell me what *you* want, Callie."

"How can it matter, Noah? Last week you—"

"Last week I said something stupid and hurtful. And I'm sorry. I told you once that I'd never hurt you. But you were about to blow me off and I got mad and screwed up." He shrugged his shoulders tightly. "Can you forgive me?"

Callie nodded. "But it doesn't change anything. Someone like Angela would fit into your life. And with Lily and Maddy being friends it makes perfect sense."

"Not to me. I'm interested in you, Callie. I *want* you. Only you."

"But Lily—"

"Will be fine with this. With *us*. I know my daughter. And I know how she feels about you."

Callie wasn't so sure. She knew the teenager was confused and at a critical point in her young life. Callie didn't want to do anything to jeopardize the young girls well-being.

"If she doesn't…" Callie's word trailed.

"She will understand."

He stood in front of her, not moving, not speaking. Just looking at her from bright-green eyes. Finally, when neither could bear the silence any longer, he dropped to his knees in front of her and wrapped his arms around her.

He shuddered in her arms. "I can hardly breathe just thinking about you."

She wanted to deny him. She wanted to refuse the clamoring needs of her body and the deep longing in her heart. But refusing him, rejecting him, would break her into tiny pieces.

I love this man…

Callie ran her hands through his hair. "Me, too."

The air suddenly filled with heat. And need. She could feel the mounting tension in him beneath her hands. His muscles tightened and she instinctively gripped him harder. Warmth spread through her body, licking over every nerve, every cell. She knew he felt it, too. It rolled like waves, creating a turbulent energy in the quiet room.

Callie's hands slid down his arms, over strong biceps. She rubbed his skin with her thumbs and heard the unsteady sound of his breathing.

"Callie," he said, drawing the words deep from his throat. "I want…I want to make love to you." He stilled, taking in a profound breath. "But if you're not ready…we'll wait. And if you want me to go I—"

She smiled. "Shhhh." She traced her hands back to his shoulders. He felt so strong. *I can have this…I can have him.* "I'm glad you're here," she whispered. "I want you here. I think I've wanted you here my whole life."

Noah immediately moved closer, fisting a handful of her hair before he tilted her head back and took her mouth in a searing, hungry kiss. She met his tongue, felt the warm slide of it against the roof her mouth, and then tangled her own around his. His arms tightened around her and slid down her back, cradling her hips and then farther, curving possessively under her bottom. Callie arched forward and wrapped her legs around his hips. She pressed into him, all need, all want. She felt him hard against her and a rush of warmth pooled between her thighs.

"Where's your bedroom?" he muttered against her lips.

"Down the hall, first door on the left."

He kissed her again and stood up, lifting her with effortless strength, and strode down the hallway, shouldering the door open. The small lamp cast shadows around the room and created a welcoming intimacy. Noah placed her on the bed as though she were a fragile doll, flipped off his shoes, shucked off his shirt and lay down beside her.

He kissed her again, her lips, her throat, her neck, and dispensed with the four buttons holding her top together. His eyes glittered when he saw the white lace bra.

"You are lovely," he said, tracing a finger up and over the generous swell of cleavage.

She moved to her knees and slowly inched down the sweat bottoms, dispensing them to the floor. He looked at her with open desire and ran one finger from the top of her neck to the base of her spine, touching the edge of her briefs.

"A tattoo?"

The winged horse looked majestic in flight and Noah moaned his approval as he reached for her and coaxed her to lie beside him. He kissed her again, long and slow, branding her with his kisses, making her his own. He cupped her breasts and gently caressed them. His tongue trailed across her skin, brushing across the edge of the lace. Her nipples ached for his touch, the feel of his mouth, his tongue.

"Take it off," she begged. "Please."

He did so with remarkable efficiency, flicking the hooks at the back with his thumb.

"You've done that before," she breathed.

He chuckled. "Not for a *very* long time," he said as he chucked the bra to the floor and his mouth closed over one straining nipple.

Callie felt the pleasure of it through to her feet. She gripped his shoulders, wanting more, needing more. It was like nothing on earth. His breath was hot against the hardened peak as he suckled. He placed his leg between hers and Callie bucked against him. Pleasure ricocheted over every nerve ending as the abrasive denim he wore rubbed against her sex. She reached down to touch him, felt him shudder as her hand slid across the hardness of his erection straining against his jeans. Her hand moved up, over the zipper, to the belt and she pulled the leather strap free and flicked the top button. Her fingers played with the silky hair arrowing downward.

He groaned and kissed her again, taking her mouth with such hot, scorching possession Callie arched her back, straining off the bed. His hand moved over her skin, her shoulders, her hip and across her belly, then dipped below the tiny triangle of fabric covering her. She felt an intense pleasure as his fingers sought access between the sweet, wet folds and found the tiny nub waiting for his touch.

"Oh, Noah."

He touched her, softly at first, finding the rhythm she liked. She was so wet and welcoming he was surprised he was able to control himself. But he took a deep breath, and another, in between kissing her beautiful mouth. He wasn't going to rush loving her, no matter how badly his body wanted release. He had lips to kiss, breasts to worship, skin to touch and taste. Things he dreamed of doing since the first time he'd met her.

And he would. All night and into the morning.

She moved beneath the pressure of his hand, spreading her thighs trustingly, saying his name over and over. Noah thought he might explode. He felt her tense, heard the change in her breathing, felt her stiffen, waiting, climbing. His aching arousal pushed against his pants. She rocked against the pressure of his hand and he cupped her, then released, then cupped her again. He felt the pulse of her orgasm through his fingertips, saw her skin flush with pleasure and heard her earthy moans of satisfaction.

Desire for her washed over him; love for her filled every cell, every ounce of his blood, and every inch of his skin. He kissed her again—wild, needy kisses that she returned.

"I've never..." she whispered. "Amazing."

Noah dragged the briefs over her thighs, suddenly impatient to see her, marveling at how beautiful she was. He licked her breasts, her rib cage, her belly and lower. He kissed her gently, exploring the soft, moist flesh with his tongue, tasting the sweet musky scent that was uniquely hers. She was incredibly responsive, moaning her pleasure. Her hands gripped his shoulders as he continued his erotic kiss. When he trailed his lips back up across her stomach she writhed beneath him.

He was so hungry for her, so desperate to lose himself inside her, his entire body shook. She held on—his shoulders, his back, his waist.

When her hands hung from his belt, she whispered. "You're wearing too many clothes."

Noah got rid of his jeans and briefs in seconds and returned to her side.

She touched him, enclosing her fingers around his erection and he almost jumped out of his skin.

It's been too long since I've done this...

He took a deep breath and filled his lungs with air. Her touch was gentle, almost uncertain. Noah covered her hand with his and whispered encouragement. She didn't need much. She caressed him from the tip to the base, slowly, building a steady rhythm, driving him crazy with need. All he could think of was Callie—of this beautiful woman who held him, touched him, kissed him back with so much passion he felt truly humbled.

He took a moment and withdrew a foil packet from his wallet. She took the condom, her hands unsteady as she sheathed him. He let her do it and when the pressure became too much, when the need to be inside her drew the breath from his throat in a ragged groan, Noah moved over her. He kissed her and she parted her thighs. He entered her slowly, kissing her more, mimicking the movement of his body as she accepted him inside her

She moved, stretching to take him in, wriggling in a deliciously sexy way. Finally, he was home, filling her, more a part of her than he'd ever been of anyone.

There would never be a moment like this again...their first time...he'd remember the feeling for the rest of his life.

Noah rested his weight on his elbows and looked into her face. She smiled. He touched her hair, remembering how it was one of the first things he'd noticed about her. Such beautiful, luscious hair fanned around the pillow. He kissed her, glorious hot kisses she returned. When he moved against her she moaned, meeting his movements, matching the steady rhythm building between them. All he could feel was Callie, her heat, her wetness surrounding him, enslaving him. He heard her soft cries of pleasure, almost felt them through to his soul as her body arched and shuddered beneath him.

And finally, when the pressure built until he couldn't hold off any longer, it claimed him with white-hot fury, taking him over the edge, ripping through him with the sheer intensity and power of release.

"I love you, Callie." He breathed the words, feeling them with every fiber inside him.

Callie waited until Noah withdrew from her and fell back against the pillow before she took a breath.

I love you...

He'd said the words. It could have been an impulse, a sex-induced moment of euphoria where anything goes. A kind of mid-orgasmic madness. But Callie doubted it. Noah wasn't the kind of man who did anything by half-measures.

He loves me.

He took her hand and kissed her knuckles. "Are you okay?"

I'm out of my mind.

"Oh, yes."

He grinned and closed his eyes. "You're so beautiful."

She felt beautiful. She felt wholly desired and so completely pleasured all she could think of was experiencing it again and again. Callie touched his chest and felt him tense as she played with one flat nipple, then the other. She leaned forward and licked the spot and smiled as the small bud peaked beneath the gentle flick of her tongue. He lay perfectly still and for a moment she thought he'd fallen asleep. But, no—he was smiling, taking long breaths, letting her explore. She kissed his shoulder, nipping at his skin with her teeth before licking the spot. She ran her hand down his stomach and lingered at his belly button, playing with the soft hair trailing downward. When her finger inched lower he quickly covered her hand with his.

"Give me a couple of hours, okay?"

Callie maneuvered her hand from his and grazed her knuckles over him. "I'll give you an hour."

As it turned out he only needed forty minutes. Then Noah made love to her again. He teased her, taunted her with his mouth and tongue and finally, when she thought she could stand no more, he flipped over and dragged her on top. He held her hips, allowing her to ease her body onto his, taking him in, sheathing him inside her. Callie felt wild and wanton as she rode above him. He linked her fingers through his and he supported her weight as she moved, slowly at first, savoring each delicious slide. Then he pulled her forward and sucked her nipples every time her breasts bounced near his mouth. She flung her head back, driving harder, feeling the pressure build and calling his name as pleasure flooded every cell. He lifted off the bed as his climax ripped through him and Callie clenched her internal muscles, taking everything, giving everything, loving him more in that moment than she'd ever imagined she could love anyone.

Spent, they lay together, legs entwined. After a while she rolled onto her stomach and he fingered the tattoo at the base of her spine.

"Do you have any idea how sexy that is?" he said, kissing her shoulder.

"Uh, no. How?"

Callie felt his breath against her skin. "Shall I show you?"

She curled her fingers through the dark smatter of hair on his chest. "Absolutely."

They lingered in bed for another half hour then took a shower together. Afterward Callie made roast beef and mustard sandwiches and they sat in front of the television and watched a rerun of David Letterman.

By midnight they were back in bed, lying on their sides, facing one another.

"So," she said, touching his face. "You're staying?"

He frowned. "Of course."

Callie closed her eyes, feeling safe, feeling loved.

Waking up beside the man who loved you really was the most wonderful way to start a new day. Especially when that man roused you with a trail of kisses along your shoulder blade.

"Good morning," he said softly, slanting his mouth over hers.

Callie smiled against his lips. "Yes, it is."

"What are your plans for today?" he asked, moving from her mouth to her jaw and then to the sensitive spot below her earlobe.

"Oh, the usual," she said on a dreamy sigh. "Well, I used to have a student at eight o'clock."

"Used to?"

"She's with someone else now."

He smiled. "Actually, that's not working out so well."

"Oh. Why not?"

"Lily wants what she wants," he replied, still kissing her. "And she wants you."

"Janelle's a good teacher."

"Not as good as you," he countered. "Then again, I don't imagine anyone is."

Callie heard the lovely compliment and sighed contentedly. "Bring her back next week."

"She'd like that," he said.

"Good. What about you?" she asked. "What are your plans?"

"I've got to pick the kids up this morning. Do you feel like doing something later?"

Callie ran her hand down his chest and lower, lingering past his belly. "What did you have in mind?"

"The beach?"

Callie's hand stilled. "You mean...all together?" A family day out, that's what he meant. *I'm not ready for that yet.*

"That was the idea."

She shifted across the bed and grabbed her gown. "We'll see what happens." She stood up and slipped efficiently into the wrap. "How about breakfast?"

Fifteen minutes later Noah emerged from the shower, dressed and sporting an incredibly sexy shadow of beard on his face. When he entered the kitchen she passed him coffee and a plate topped with some kind of charred-looking bread.

"What's that?" he asked, looking at the contents on the plate.

"Toasted bagel."

He didn't look convinced. "Okay." He sat down, grabbed the toast and took a bite. "You were right," he said easily. "You can't cook."

Callie smiled. "Told ya."

He put down the toast and looked at her. "Are you okay?"

She shrugged and turned toward the countertop. "Of course."

"No regrets?"

Callie shook her head. She had no regrets about making love with him. "No."

"You look far away."

She swallowed, wondering when he'd gotten to know her so well. "I'm right here. Promise."

He drank his coffee and then stood. "I have to get going," he said when he reached her. He turned her in his arms. "But I'll call you later."

"I'd like that."

He kissed her softly and ran his hands over her hips. "I'll let myself out."

She nodded. "Okay."

Noah kissed her again and Callie didn't let out her breath until she heard the soft click of the front screen door closing behind him.

So, what now? She didn't have a clue. He'd said he loved her and she hadn't said it back.

And pretty soon, Callie was certain, he would want to know why not.

Chapter Eleven

Something was wrong. Noah felt it, sensed it. As he drove to his parents' house to pick up the kids he couldn't get the thought out of his mind. She'd retreated. She'd pulled back into a place he couldn't reach. The passionate woman he'd made love with had been absorbed by the woman he remembered from weeks earlier. The woman who didn't want to get involved.

Did she regret it? Was that it? She'd said no. But how could he be sure?

Noah certainly wasn't about to regret the most incredible sex he'd ever had. Because it was more than that. More than sex. Just…more. More everything. More in a way he'd never imagined possible. Touching Callie, loving her, waking up beside her had filled the empty place he'd had inside him for so long.

But the niggling thought stayed with him.

I said I love you. And she didn't say it back.

He'd felt it. In her touch, her sighs, the tears shining in her blue eyes. But, as much as he tried to convince himself it didn't matter, he knew he wanted the words.

He *needed* the words.

When he pulled into the driveway of his parents' home he saw Evie's car outside. His sister was in the kitchen, baking alongside their mother, while the twins and Jamie were in the backyard tormenting his father with a game of Twister.

His mother and sister smiled when he entered the room and then looked at each other.

"Hi. The kids are out the back," Evie said, elbow deep in a large bowl of dough. "Poor Dad," she said with a laugh.

When M.J. trounced into the room moments later, Noah felt the full scrutiny of three sets of curious female eyes.

"Is that a hickey on your neck?" M.J. asked with straight-faced innocence.

Noah's hand instinctively went to his throat.

"Gotcha," M.J. laughed.

"You should never have been taught how to speak," he said quietly, removing his hand and trying not to look self-conscious.

"So, are there wedding bells in the air?" M.J. asked with a big grin.

He scowled. "Watch yourself, kid."

"We have it on good authority."

Noah looked at M.J. and then his mother and Evie.

"Jamie said something this morning," Evie explained. "He's quite excited about the idea."

Noah remembered the conversation he'd had in the truck with the kids. He turned to his mother. "Thanks for watching them."

"How's Maddy?" Evie asked, still digging into dough.

"Broken arm."

"She's lucky Callie was there," Evie said. "Lily called and told us what happened."

He nodded. "Quite the hotline you girls have going."

"Well you never tell us anything," M.J. complained.

Nor did he intend to. "With good reason," he quipped. "Thanks again," he said to his mother, Barbara, who patted his shoulder affectionately.

It took ten minutes to finish saying goodbye and load the kids in the truck. Noah collected Lily on the way home, declining Angela's offer for coffee. When he got home he called Callie, amused by his own eagerness. She answered her cell on the seventh ring and he wondered if she'd considered not picking up. She sounded friendly enough and they talked for a while. She told him she had a new student that afternoon and would have to take a rain check on his idea for the beach.

Noah didn't push the idea. He ended the call with an invitation to his parents' home for the coming Saturday. But instinct told him something was wrong.

Callie knew Noah felt her pull back. And she knew she was acting like a first-rate coward. One mention of his kids and she'd panicked. It wasn't remotely rational. But since when was fear ever rational?

The kids were part of him. His blood. His life.

If she wanted Noah—and she did—then she had to learn how to deal with the reality of his children. She had to love them with her whole heart.

And without really understanding why, her heart simply didn't feel big enough for all that love. It was something she needed to talk to him about. He was smart. If he hadn't figured it out already, he would soon enough. He'd sensed something was wrong, and Callie knew if they had any chance of a future together they needed complete honesty between them.

But she put it off.

On Saturday night they were going to his parents' home for an anniversary party.

She waited on the porch for him to collect her while counting bugs brave enough to aim flight at the mosquito zapper hung from the ceiling. She was nervous about meeting his family. Foolish, she supposed. She already knew Evie, and M.J. and Cameron and she suspected his parents were good people—they would have to be to have raised such a son.

He arrived on time and her stomach did a silly roll when he got out of the truck. He looked great in dark cargo pants and a polo shirt. Her heart crunched up. The kids were in the backseat, she noticed, minus Lily, and she wondered if that was why he didn't kiss her.

"You look beautiful," he said as she got into his vehicle.

Callie smiled and looked in the back, and the three younger children greeted her with a chorus of hellos. They were clearly excited to see her. Shame licked along her spine. They were great kids. And they genuinely cared for her.

I just have to let myself love them without guilt. Without feeling like I'm letting go of Ryan.

Because *that* was what she was afraid of. Losing Ryan. Forgetting Ryan. Replacing Ryan.

"Where's Lily?" she asked, pushing the idea aside for the moment. She'd concentrate on the present and enjoy the moment. There was time for thoughts later.

"With Evie," he replied. "They're meeting us there."

He drove into Crystal Point and pulled up outside a large, two-story home one street back from The Parade in a quiet cul-de-sac. The gardens were immaculate; the home looked like it was made for a large family. A couple of cars were parked in the driveway and he pulled up off the curb.

The moment she walked into their home, Barbara and Bill Preston greeted her with smiles and a warm welcome. Barbara hugged her son closely and Callie didn't miss the gentle way she ruffled his hair and smiled at him, like they had a lovely secret between them. The twins and Jamie clearly adored their grandparents and were rustled away with their grandfather to play a game of Wii bowling before the guests began to arrive.

"The girls are in the kitchen," Barbara said. "Join us after you've shown Callie the house."

Callie followed when Noah led her upstairs.

"So," she said, standing in the middle of a room at the top of the stairway. "This was your bedroom when you were growing up?"

He smiled. "Yep."

It appeared to be as typical a teenage boy's room as you'd get. Blue quilt and accessories, shelves filled with trophies, faded posters of rock bands on the walls. She took a closer look at the trophies—some for sports, some for academics.

"So you were a jock?" she asked, picking up a medal awarded for a code of football she'd vaguely heard of. She fingered another one granted for rowing. "Looks like you were good at it." She placed the medal down. "How old were you when you moved out?"

"Eighteen," he said. "I moved to Brisbane to study engineering."

"Is that where you met your wife?"

He took a step toward her. "Ex-wife," he corrected. "And no. I always knew I'd take the business over from my father, but I wanted to experience life a bit before I came back to Crystal Point." He picked an old volleyball off the floor and tossed it onto the narrow bed. "I finished my degree in three years, then took off. I backpacked in Europe for about a year, until my money ran out. Then I worked at a pub in London trying to save enough for my fare back home, which is where I met Margaret. She was there on a dancing scholarship. We hooked up and I stayed for another year or so. But I always intended to come back." He shrugged. "A couple of months after I got home she called to say she was pregnant."

"And then you married her?" She hoped he didn't hear the tinge of jealousy in her tone.

He reached for her. "Let's not talk about that, okay?" His arms tightened around her. "I'd much rather kiss you."

And he did. So thoroughly Callie thought she might pass out.

When they returned downstairs the kitchen was a hive of activity. Mary-Jayne was there decorating a cheesecake, and Evie was wrapping potatoes in aluminum foil.

Both sisters' eyes popped wide when they saw them, but to their credit they didn't say anything. Lily was there, glaring at Callie with confused eyes. The teenager headed to the living room and mumbled something about how it was "typical" and no one cared what she wanted.

"Should I go and talk with her?" Callie asked.

Noah shook his head. "She'll be fine."

"He's right," Evie said. "She's just reacting. Lily doesn't know how she's feeling."

"All teenagers are obnoxious," Mary-Jayne announced. "Remember how I was?"

Noah smiled. "Was?"

Everyone laughed and Callie was struck by the deep affection they shared for one another. It made her miss her own family.

Within half an hour the celebration had taken itself outside. The outdoor entertainment area was huge and had been transformed with a long buffet table and chairs for those inclined to sit. Music filtered through strategically placed speakers. People started arriving, including Cameron Jakowski and Fiona, who were both well acquainted with the Prestons. He shook Noah's hand, kissed Barbara on the cheek while stealing a piece of cheese off a plate and teased M.J. about her Don't Blame Me…I Voted For The Other Guy apron.

Fiona gave Callie an unexpected hug. "I'm glad you're here," she whispered. She grabbed Callie's arm and pulled her aside. "So you're really dating now?" Fiona asked in a ludicrously excited voice.

Dating? They were lovers—did that count as dating? "We're…something."

She looked across the deck to where Noah stood with Cameron—and also the most beautiful woman Callie had ever seen, decked out in what was clearly a high-end designer dress of deep red and incredible four-inch heels. "Who's that?" she asked.

Fiona looked up and her pretty face turned into a grimace. "Princess Grace."

"Huh?"

"Noah's sister," she explained. "She's some hot-shot businesswoman in New York. A real cold fish. You can freeze ice on her—"

"I get the picture." Callie smiled. "She's stunning."

Fiona made a face. "Yeah, yeah. Beautiful and about as pleasant as global warming."

Callie's eyes widened. "Would your opinion have anything to do with the fact she's talking to Cameron right now?"

Fiona blushed. "No point," she admitted. "We're destined to be *just friends*."

Callie sensed the disappointment in her friend's voice. "There's someone out there for you."

Fiona raised both her brows. "Spoken like a woman who's fallen in love."

Callie froze when she felt a strong arm unexpectedly moved around her waist. She looked at Fiona and her friend's eyes popped wide open.

Had he heard Fiona's teasing?

She felt his breath in her ear. "Dance with me?"

She pulled back. "Dance where?"

"By the pool," he said.

Callie looked toward the pool area. Strategically placed candles created a soft, romantic mood and she couldn't resist joining the few couples already swaying to the music. "Okay."

Moments later she was in his arms. His parents were there, she noticed, dancing cheek to cheek and clearly still in love after many years of marriage.

"What are you thinking?" he asked.

"That your parents look happy together."

Noah smiled. "They make it look easy."

She looked at him, conscious of how close they were as he kissed her forehead gently. She could feel his thighs against her own every time they moved and a jolt of need arrowed low in her belly.

She knew what he read in her eyes, knew he could feel it in the vibration coming off her skin. "Ah, Callie," he said, so close to her ear his mouth was against the lobe. He kissed the sensitive spot. "I want to take you home and make love to you."

"I want that, too," she breathed.

"In my bed?" he queried.

His bed? Somewhere they hadn't ventured. "I'm not…"

"Not ready for that?"

Callie sighed. "I want us to be close, Noah. Really, I do."

"As what? Lovers?"

They were lovers. And she wanted to make love with him again. But she knew that for Noah that wouldn't be enough. "Yes…for now."

"We're going to have to talk about the future at some—"

"I know," she said quickly and pressed closer. *But later,* she thought cowardly.

For the moment she wanted to enjoy the dance, the moment, the knowledge that she was safe in his arms. She rested her head against his shoulder.

"Callie?"

"Mmm," she murmured, inhaling the scent of him, the mixtures of some citrusy shampoo and masculine soap.

"What Fiona said...is it true?"

So he had heard?

Callie's gaze dropped. "I...feel it."

"But you can't say it?" If he was frustrated by her response, he didn't show it. He rubbed her cheek with his thumb. "One day, maybe?"

She nodded, her head and heart pounding.

"One day," she said on a breath. "I promise."

Becoming lovers changed everything. With complete intimacy came vulnerability. Noah was an incredible lover—caring, unselfish and delightfully energetic. But despite all that, Callie felt the wedge growing between them, gaining momentum. *It's of my own making.* And she was positive Noah could feel it, too.

He didn't say a word. But he was on edge. Like he was waiting, anticipating.

He's waiting for me to say something. He's waiting for me to say "I love you..." or "I can't be with you..."

Four days later she still felt it, even as she rolled over, caught up in a tangle of limbs and sighed with a mix of pleasure and utter exhaustion.

It was light inside her bedroom, despite the thick curtains being drawn. The sun peeked through, teasing her, making her feel just that little bit wicked. Speaking of wicked, she thought, running lazy fingers through the hair on Noah's chest, which was still rising and falling as he took in deep breaths. He had such a wickedly good body...

"You know," he said between breaths. "I really can't keep taking time off during the day." He smiled. "Not that this isn't a great way to spend the afternoon."

She fingered one flat nipple. "Mmm…great."

"I've got a business to run."

The nipple pebbled. "Mmm…I know."

"My staff will start wondering why I'm leaving every afternoon."

She trailed her fingertips downward. "You could tell them it's a long lunch."

He smiled. "Speaking of lunch, we should probably eat something."

"Food for energy, hey?" Callie wriggled and rolled toward him. "Am I working you too hard?" she asked, smiling and kissing his rib cage.

Noah reached for her chin and tilted her face upward. "I'm not one of your horses you have to exercise to keep in shape."

Callie pulled herself up and lay on top of him. "No, you're not. I mean, I do love my horses…" She trailed kisses across his jaw. "But you're…I mean I'm…" The words got lost.

Noah cupped her cheek and made her look at him. "Don't backpedal now."

For the past three days they'd spent each afternoon in bed together. Callie couldn't get enough of him. She couldn't feel him enough, kiss him enough and love him enough. But she knew it was a fantasy. A fabulous fantasy—but still a fantasy. Being lovers, uninterrupted by the realities of life, wasn't sustainable.

They *had* to talk. About their future. About his children. About Lily.

About Ryan.

"Are you free Friday night?" he asked instead. "I thought you could come over and let me cook for you. What do you say?"

"I have a competition on Saturday," she replied. "And Fiona's staying over Friday night so we can get an early start."

"Right. What about Saturday night?"

She moved, shifting off him. "I'll probably be quite tired. Can I see how I feel after the comp?"

He sat up and draped the sheet over his legs. "Sure. And Sunday?"

"Lily's having a lesson Sunday."

Callie averted her eyes, trying not to get distracted by his chest as she slipped out of bed. She felt completely comfortable walking naked around the room and liked the way he admired her as she retrieved her clothes from the floor. She looked at the clock on the bedside table. It was three-thirty. "We should get moving. I have a student at four o'clock. And Lily—"

"Usually comes here Wednesdays," he said when she hesitated. "Yes, I know."

"Well I wouldn't want her to see you...see us..."

Noah frowned and pushed back the bedclothes. "She knows about us, Callie. I took you to meet my parents...she also knows I wouldn't do that unless we were serious."

"I just—"

"At least, *I'm* serious," he said, cutting her off. "You—I'm not so sure."

Callie inhaled a shaky breath. "Of course I'm serious. I just don't want to upset Lily."

Noah reached for his clothes, which were still on the floor. "Lily will have to get used to it." He pulled on his briefs and chinos and started adjusting his belt but then stopped. He looked at her. "You know, Callie, Lily is precious to me... but she doesn't get to decide who I fall in love with."

Callie's blood stilled. Her eyes never left his face. "Can't we just keep a low profile for a while?" she asked quietly and grabbed an elastic band off the dresser to tie up her hair.

He shrugged. "I won't hide our relationship from my kids."

Callie took a deep breath. "I'm only asking for a little time."

"It sounds like you're asking me to lie to my children."

She didn't like the accusation and quickly gave him a look that said so. "That's not what I want. But please just respect my wishes."

"As you respect mine?"

"That's not fair."

Noah pulled his shirt over his shoulders. "Neither is making me feel as though you're not in this for the long haul."

"Because I want to take things slowly?"

He grabbed his keys from the bedside table. "Slowly? Ripping one another's clothes off every time we're together isn't exactly slow, Callie." Noah grabbed his shoes and sat on the edge of the bed to put them on. When he was done he stood, turned and faced her. "It's pretty clear you don't want to spend time with the kids," he said quietly.

She shook her head, wanting to deny it because it sounded so incredibly callous.

"I can see in your eyes that you want to negotiate," he said. "And if I loved you less, Callie…maybe I could."

"Noah, I—"

"I've been hammered in the past," he said quietly and came around the bed. "And honestly, I didn't think I'd ever want to take a chance at feeling this way. I didn't think I'd ever want to share my life with someone again…or trust someone…or maybe get married again. But if I learned anything from those years with my ex-wife, it was that I intend on living the rest of my life true to myself. That's what I'm trying to do here." He took a deep breath. "And I can't be your lover if that's all it's ever going to be."

Callie couldn't move. "I don't know what to say to you."

He stood barely feet in front of her. "Well, when you figure it out, maybe you can let me know."

"Don't leave like this," she said shakily. "Not after we've..." She looked at the bed and the rumpled bedclothes.

"Sex isn't enough for me," he said. "Not even incredible sex." He rattled his keys impatiently. "I told you I couldn't and wouldn't enter into something casual. My kids deserve better...and frankly, so do I." He headed for the door and once there, turned back to face her. "And, Callie, so do you."

It took about thirty seconds for her feet to work. By then she'd already heard the front door close.

I'm losing him.

So do something.

Callie pushed determination into her legs and followed him. When she swung the front screen door wide she saw two things—Lily's bicycle left haphazardly at the bottom of the stairs and Lily standing by the bottom step, glaring up at her father who stood on the porch.

She looked like thunder. "Great," she said when she saw Callie. "This is just great."

"It's nothing to do with you, Lily," Noah said quietly.

"Ha." She rolled her green eyes. "It will be when it turns to crap. Adults can't get anything right." She crossed her arms. "It always turns to crap. Always. Look at Maddy's stepfather. And my mother." She made a pained, huffing sound. "She didn't hang around." She gave Callie a searing, accusing look. "And this will be the same."

Callie wanted to assure the teenager that it wouldn't. But the words got stranded on the end of her tongue.

"How about you move your bike to the truck and I'll take you home?" Noah said.

Lily's mouth pursed. "I came to see Samson," she said hotly. "See—it's starting already. You guys had a fight and now I have to do what you want."

"We haven't fought," Callie heard herself deny.

Lily's brows snapped up. "Yeah, right." She pointed to her father. "He comes out and slams the door and you come out after. That's a fight. I'm not a little kid, you know. So go ahead and fight—see if I care."

She turned around and raced toward the stables. Noah took the steps to go after her but Callie called him back.

"Let me go," Callie offered. "I'll talk with her. You know, girl to woman." She pulled on her boots near the door and headed toward the stables.

Callie found Lily by the fence in the yard behind the stables. Samson was with her, butting his whiskery chin against Lily's hand as he searched for morsels of carrot. As she watched them together she saw the bond forming between the teenager and the lovable gelding. It made her remember the early days of her relationship with Indiana and how sixteen years later they were still together.

"He's very attached to you," she said to Lily as she approached.

Lily shrugged. "He's a good horse." She stroked his neck. "Maybe I'll get to have a horse of my own one day."

Callie reached the fence and laid one boot on the bottom rung. "I'm sure you will. Lily, about your dad and me. I want to explain—"

"I think my dad loves you," Lily said unexpectedly.

Callie blinked away the heat in her eyes. "I know he does."

Lily took a deep breath. "So…do you love him?"

Callie felt the weight of admission grasp her shoulders with two hands. She wasn't about to deny it. She wouldn't dishonor what she had shared with Noah by doing that. "Yes… very much."

Lily's jaw clenched with emotion. "But what if it doesn't work out?"

Callie put her arms around Lily's thin shoulders and experienced a fierce burst of protectiveness inside her chest. "What if it does?"

Lily swallowed hard and flashed defiant eyes at her as she pulled away. "You don't know that. People leave all the time."

"Not all people," Callie assured her.

Lily shrugged but Callie wasn't fooled. She was in tremendous pain.

"Yeah, well, I know Dad said I could come back here for lessons, but I think I'll stick with Janelle." Lily lifted her chin, patted Samson one more time and pushed herself away from the fence. "She's a pretty good teacher after all. And she's got way better horses than you."

She took off and Callie gave her a lead of fifty feet before following. When she reached Noah, Lily was already tucked inside the truck with her bicycle in the back.

Another car had turned into the driveway. Her four o'clock appointment.

"I'll call you," he said quietly.

"Sure. Noah..." Her words trailed and she waited for him to respond.

He did. "I'm trying to give you space, Callie. I'm trying to understand everything you've been through and how hard it is for you to trust me, to trust *us*. But at some point you're going to have to meet me halfway. When you're ready for that, give me a call."

He walked off. There was no touch. No kiss. Only the sound of his truck disappearing over the gravel as he drove off.

Halfway. She was still thinking about his words the following afternoon. And trust. It didn't take a genius to figure the two things went hand in hand. Callie left Joe in charge of bedding the horses down for the night and headed into Bellandale. She stopped at a popular Mexican restaurant and ordered takeout, then drove back toward Crystal Point. By the time she pulled up outside Noah's house it was past five o'clock. An unfamiliar flashy-looking blue car was out front, parked next to Noah's truck.

Harry came off his usual spot on the porch and ambled toward her as she unloaded the plastic carry bags containing the food. She was a few steps from the porch when the front opened and Officer Cameron Jakowski stepped outside.

He flashed a too-brilliant smile when he saw her. "Hey, Callie."

"Hi. Is Noah—"

"On the phone," he supplied, rattling his keys. "Hey, I was going to call you."

He was? For what? "Really?"

"I have some news about your recent entanglement with the law." He was smiling and she relaxed.

Apparently the men who'd rammed her trailer had pleaded guilty and were due for a hearing in front of the local magistrate. Cameron suspected they'd get a suspended sentence, but Callie hoped it would at least be enough to stop them from doing anything that stupid again. She told him her insurance had covered the repairs to her trailer.

She said goodbye to Cameron and waited until he'd driven off before she headed inside the house. She could hear Noah's voice and followed the sound until she reached the kitchen. He stood by the counter and had his back to her, the telephone cradled against his ear. He still wore his work clothes and the perfectly tailored chinos did little to disguise the body beneath. Callie's heart hammered behind her ribs just thinking about it.

He turned immediately and looked surprised to find her in his kitchen. He quickly ended the call. "I didn't expect to see you tonight."

She held the bags in front of her. "I brought dinner," she said and placed the bags and her tote on the granite top.

"Don't you have a competition tomorrow?"

Callie nodded. "I do. But I thought dinner might be a good idea." She tried to sound cheerful. "Where are the kids?"

"With my mother."

Callie looked at the large quantity of food she'd bought. "Oh."

"They'll be home in an hour."

"And Lily?"

He didn't move. He didn't break eye contact. "At Maddy's, as usual."

Callie was concerned for his daughter. "Is she okay?"

"She's quiet," he replied. "But Lily gets like that."

Callie took a couple of steps toward him. "She was upset the other day. I tried to talk with her…but I don't know if I got through. She said she didn't want to come back to Sandhills."

"Lily doesn't know what she wants." He pushed himself away from the counter. "She likes you but doesn't want to admit it."

The irony in his words weren't missed. Hadn't he said the same thing about their relationship only yesterday? She'd come to his house to talk, to explain. It was time to open up.

She pulled out a chair and sat down at the table. "Halfway."

"What?"

"That's why I'm here. Yesterday you said I needed to meet you halfway. So, I'm here." She drew in a breath. "Halfway."

"Callie, I—"

"You know, all my life I've pretty much done what I wanted," she said quietly. "I left school at seventeen—I didn't even finish senior year. I wanted to ride. I wanted to be with Craig. And nothing could have stopped me from realizing my dream. Looking back, I was quite self-indulgent. But then I got pregnant and my life changed. Suddenly it wasn't just about me."

"Kids do change your priorities."

Callie nodded. "And I wanted the baby. Having Ryan was the most incredible gift. Even though he only lived for two days I will treasure those moments forever."

"You should, Callie," he said, with such gentleness. "You *should* celebrate his life."

"And get on with my own, is that what you mean?" She sighed heavily. "I want to. And I am trying. Despite how it might seem, I *have* accepted the fact I'll probably never have children. I know people can live full and meaningful lives without having kids."

"But?"

Moisture sprang into her eyes. "But I met you. And you have these incredible children who look at me with such... hope." Tears hovered on her lashes. "I know what they want. I know what they need. And I certainly know what they deserve. But because of Ryan...because I feel so much hurt...I don't know if I could ever give it to them. I don't know if I could ever feel what they would need me to feel."

He looked at her in that way no one else ever had. "Because you didn't carry them? Because you didn't give birth to them?"

She nodded, ashamed of her feelings but unable to deny the truth of them. "Partly, yes."

He stepped closer, bridging the gap. "Do you really think genetics make a parent, Callie?"

She shrugged, without words, without voice.

"What about all the adopted kids out there, the fostered kids, the babies born to a surrogate—do you think their parents love them less because they carry different blood?" His eyes never left hers. "Blood doesn't make you a parent."

"I know it sounds…selfish. It sounds self-absorbed and I'm ashamed to have these kinds of feelings. But, Noah, you have four children who—"

"One," he said quietly, silencing her immediately. "I have one child."

Chapter Twelve

Noah saw her shock and felt the heaviness of his admittance crush right down between his shoulder blades.

"What?"

"I have one *biological* child," he said with emphasis. "I have two who I know definitely aren't mine, another who might not be."

"But Lily—"

"Is mine," he said. "The twins, no…Jamie, I'm not sure."

She looked staggered by his admission and he couldn't blame her. "But you love them so much," she whispered incredulously.

He nodded and fought the lump of emotion that suddenly formed in his throat. "Of course I do. They are *mine*, Callie, despite how they were conceived. That's what I'm trying to say to you—it doesn't matter how they came into the world. What matters is how they are raised, nurtured, loved."

She nodded and he hoped she believed him. He loved her

so much and wanted to share his life with her and marry her as soon as she was ready. He wanted to ask her now. He wanted to drop to his knees and worship her and beg her to become his wife. But he knew they could only have that if she was prepared to accept his children as her own.

"And you're sure the twins aren't yours?"

"Yeah. Margaret took off to Paris to visit her mother and when she came back announced she was pregnant with twins. I knew straight away they weren't mine."

"You did?"

"I'd stopped sleeping with her a long time before. When I suspected she was cheating," he admitted, "I stuck it out for as long as I could for the kids. But I knew the day would come when we'd split. Margaret's moods were unpredictable. Looking back I'm certain she suffered from some kind of depression."

"What did you do?"

"I said I wanted a divorce. I was prepared to let her have the house, but I demanded joint custody." He moved to the table and pulled out a chair. "But instead she walked out after the twins were born. I think she knew, on some level, that leaving them was the best thing she could do for them. She just didn't want them."

"And Jamie?"

He sat down. "She told me the morning she left. That she wasn't sure if he was my son."

"You must have been devastated." Callie grabbed his hand and held on tight.

He nodded, remembering the shock and disbelief he'd experienced. "For about ten seconds I thought I'd been robbed of my son. But that feeling didn't last. He's my child in every way that counts. Just as the twins are."

"Does anyone know?"

"Cameron knows. My parents. Evie. And you."

"Do you think you'll ever tell them?"

He shrugged. "I'm not sure. Perhaps when they're older and can comprehend what it means."

He'd thought about it. Wondered how he would ever broach the subject with them.

"They'll understand," she said softly. "They love you."

"And that's really all it takes, Callie."

Callie knew he was right. And when the kids returned home a little while later and raced toward her with hugs full of unbridled excitement she couldn't control the urge to hug them back. Noah's parents stayed for dinner of reheated fajitas, enchiladas and refried beans, and it was such a delightfully animated and loving evening Callie was tempted to ask Noah to go and collect Lily so she could be part of it.

He was an amazing man. He cherished children that weren't his own. But Craig hadn't wanted his own child.

How could I have loved two men who were so very different?

Callie knew she had to let go of her hurt over Craig. And strangely, as though she'd willed it from sheer thought, her anger, the bitterness she'd clung onto, drifted off.

I don't hate Craig anymore.

It felt good to release all the bad feelings that had been weighing her down. And to know she could love again...to know she *did* love again...filled her with an extraordinary sense of peace. But Callie knew she had one more thing to do. One more hurdle to take. The hardest thing of all was ahead of her. It was something she had to do before she could completely let herself love and be loved.

I have to say goodbye to Ryan.

And the only place she could do that was in California.

The following day Callie called her mother, booked her flight for Wednesday evening, and arranged for Joe to stay at the farm for the time she would be away.

She hadn't stayed at Noah's the previous night. Instead, she'd gone home and stared at the ceiling. She hadn't told him of her plans. She was going to his home on Monday night and she would explain it to him. And she prayed he would understand.

On Monday afternoon Angela Spears arrived with Maddy. The young girl flew from the Lexus with lightning speed and showed Callie her cast. There was no lesson for Maddy, but she wanted to pet Sunshine and spend time with the horses.

Both women were surprised to see Noah's truck pull into the driveway and park beside Angela's Lexus.

The kids jumped out, headed straight for Callie and hugged her tightly. Hayley grabbed her hand and Angela didn't miss a thing.

"Goodness, you're popular," she said good-humoredly and looked toward Noah. "With everyone."

Callie blushed and turned her attention to the man who stood smiling. "I didn't expect you this afternoon. Are we still on for tonight?"

He nodded. "Of course. I'm here to pick up Lily," he said. "Is she with that horse?"

Callie shook her head. "Lily's not here."

He frowned. "What do you mean, she's not here?" His gaze snapped toward Angela. "She told me this morning that you'd bring her here this afternoon so I could pick her up."

Angela's face prickled with concern. "I haven't seen Lily since yesterday."

Callie looked at Noah. She saw the alarm in his eyes. "I'm sure she's somewhere close," Callie said quickly. "Perhaps she's with Evie."

"We just left Evie's."

"Well, your parents? Or Mary-Jayne?" she suggested, trying to sound hopeful. "Call them."

He did that while Callie questioned Jamie, but he said he

had no idea where she was. However, he did say he'd noticed her big backpack was missing and her iPod.

"No luck," he said after a few minutes. "I'll try her cell."

It was switched off. Angela called for Maddy and the teen-ager came toward them swiftly. She stood in front of her mother, wide-eyed, as if sensing the adults around her were on high alert.

"Madison," Angela said quietly. "Do you know where Lily is?"

"I—um…"

"Maddy?" Noah's voice, calm, deep. "Please…where is she?"

Maddy's eyes filled with tears. "I told her not to," she said. "I said she shouldn't do it. But she wouldn't listen to me."

"What do you mean, Madison?" Angela again, in formi-dable mother mode.

"When she didn't come to school today I knew she had really done it." Maddy took a huge gulp of air. "She's gone."

Gone. Callie's stomach sank. She clutched Noah's arm in-stinctively.

Noah took a heavy breath. "Where's she gone, Maddy?"

Maddy swallowed, looked to the ground, then back at her mother and clearly knew she had little choice but to tell the truth. "Paris."

Callie was certain their hearts stopped beating. Angela looked like she would hyperventilate. Noah paled when the reality of it hit him.

"How's she getting there?" he asked evenly, but Callie wasn't fooled. He was out of his mind with worry.

Tears flowed down Maddy's check. "She caught the train to Brisbane this morning. She said she was going to buy a ticket at the airport."

"Surely she wouldn't be able to do that," Angela said, all wide-eyed. "Oh, this is bad, this is—"

"Does she have a passport?" Callie asked, cutting off Angela.

Noah nodded. "Yeah. I took the kids to Hawaii last year."

"Why Paris?" Angela asked.

Callie looked at Noah. She knew why, as he did. But it was Maddy Spears who spoke.

"She wants to see her mother."

Callie got Noah into the house so they could make the appropriate telephone calls. She settled the kids in the kitchen with a snack and returned to the living room. Angela left with Maddy, but insisted she'd do whatever was needed to help.

Noah was on the phone, obviously to Cameron by the cryptic conversation. When he hung up he called Evie and instructed her to fill their parents in on the details. "Cameron's going to get her picture to the airport security," he said when he'd hung up.

"That should help," she said. "Is there anything I can do?"

He nodded. "Watch the kids. I have to get to the city as fast as I can," he said. He unclipped his keys and left one by the telephone. "House key," he said. "They'd probably prefer to sleep in their own beds."

Callie didn't hesitate to agree. "I'll take them home soon. You just…go…and call me when you know anything."

"Thanks." He ran a hand across his face. "This is my fault," he said. "I should have paid more attention. She's been quiet since…"

"Since she saw you here last week?"

He nodded and Callie saw the concern in his eyes. She knew what he was thinking, fearing. There were dangers in the big city, people who did bad things, predators waiting to pounce on a naïve young girl from a small town. She rallied instead. "She'll be fine. And she'll be found before you know it." She took a few steps toward him and placed her hands on his chest. "You have to believe that, Noah. For your own peace of mind."

She hugged him close and then watched as he drove off, waiting until she saw the taillights fade before she closed the door. The kids were relaxed enough in her company that they barely questioned their father's quick departure. Jamie talked to her about Lily, though, and because he was such a sensitive child she tried to put his fears at ease the best she could.

She left Joe to bed the horses down for the night, packed a small overnight bag, collected the children and Tessa and took them home.

Noah drove faster than he should have. A flight would have been sensible, but none would have gotten him to Brisbane airport in better time. Thankful that he had a full tank of gas, he drove straight through the four-and-a-half-hour trip without stopping. It was nine-thirty when he raced into the international terminal. He headed directly for airport security and, despite his impatience, was appreciative of their assistance.

"We have her picture here," a female officer told him. "But so far no one matching this description has shown up."

"Her train got in hours ago," Noah told them. "She has to be here somewhere."

"She can't pass this point unless she has a ticket," she assured him.

"Is there any chance she might get one?" he asked, his heart pumping.

"No," the officer said confidently. "The airlines are not in the habit of allowing minors to purchase tickets. You could try the domestic terminal," she said. "If she's resourceful enough, she could think it easier to try for a ticket to Sydney and then perhaps catch a connecting flight."

Noah's head felt like it was about to burst. "I'll go and check." He handed her a business card. "If she turns up here, please call me."

He jumped into a taxi to get to the domestic terminal and once there was scanned by a handheld metal detection device before a uniformed officer led him through. There were plenty of travelers about, browsing the shops; some were sitting in the departure lounges. Noah couldn't see Lily. Panic rose like bile in his throat. What if she wasn't here? What if something had already happened to her? Perhaps she never made it off the train.

He continued his search, checking cafés and a few of the stores that might appeal to a thirteen-year-old girl. He checked every one, showed her picture to as many sales assistants as he could and found some relief when one told him she looked a little familiar.

Fifteen minutes later he was almost out of his mind. He stopped by the escalators and looked up and down the long terminal while the security officer left to check the washrooms. Then just when his hope faded, he noticed a girl, standing alone, looking out of the observation window at the farthest end of the terminal. She had her back to him, and her hair was brown... *Not Lily.*

Noah turned to walk back to the main departure lounge but stopped. He had another look, longer this time. And suddenly his feet were moving toward her. Something about the way she held her shoulders, the angle of her head as she gazed out toward the runway and watched the departing aircraft niggled at him. The departure gates at this end of the terminal were all shut down for the night and she seemed oddly out of place in her solitude.

He kept walking, faster until he was almost at a jog. He halted about thirty feet from her. He noticed details within seconds. She wore a denim skirt and white top. Lily only wore black. And the hair—wrong color completely. And the shoes—not her trademark Doc Martens, but bright pink flip-flops with sequins sewn on them.

But there was a backpack at her feet. Lily's backpack. "Lily?"

She turned and Noah's jaw nearly dropped to his feet. No dark makeup, no piercings, just his daughter's beautiful face staring at him.

"Dad!"

Noah wasn't sure what to expect from her. He didn't have to wait long. She ran toward him and threw herself against him with a sturdy thump. *I have my kid. She's safe.*

"I'm sorry, Dad," she choked the words into his shoulder.

"It's okay." Noah touched her hair. "You scared me to death, Lily."

"I know...I'm so sorry."

"Come and sit down," he said to Lily.

She sat in one of the chairs and Noah retrieved her backpack.

"You travel light," he said, dropping it at her feet. He sat down beside her. "What are you doing here?"

She shrugged and inhaled a shaky breath. "I'm not sure."

"Maddy said you were going to find your mother," he said, gently because he sensed that was all she could cope with. "Is that true?"

Another shrug, this time accompanied by tears. "No. Yes."

Noah felt her pain right through to his bones. "Why now?"

"I wanted to ask her something."

Noah held his breath for a moment. "Do you know where she lives?"

Lily shook her head.

"How did you plan to find her once you got to Paris?" he asked.

She dropped her gaze. "I've got Grandma's address."

Noah could only imagine what seventy-four-year-old Leila would think about having Lily turn up at her door. "So what did you want to ask your mother?"

She shrugged again. "What we did. What *I* did."

"What you did?"

"To make her not want us."

Noah sighed and chose his words carefully. "You didn't do anything, Lily. Your mother was unhappy. And she didn't want to be married to me. But *you*," he took her hand and squeezed. "You didn't do anything. I promise."

"It feels like she left because of me. I mean, it couldn't have been the others—they were little. And everyone loves little kids."

"It wasn't you," he said again, firmer this time. "Lily, is this really about your mother, or is it Callie?"

Lily looked at him. Her bottom lip quivered and her gaze fell to the floor.

"Are you afraid she'll try to replace your mother?" he asked gently.

Lily turned her face into his shoulder and sobbed against him. "That's just it, Dad," she said brokenly. "I really want her to be replaced. Sometimes I forget what she'd looked like. Jamie doesn't even remember her—it's like she never existed."

"She did exist," Noah said, holding her. "You're proof of that."

Lily hiccupped. "But she left. We weren't enough for her. None of us. If she didn't love us enough to stay...why would someone else? She had to love us, and even that wasn't enough. And Callie, well, she wouldn't *have* to love us, would she? So I thought if I just asked her what made her leave, I could make sure it didn't happen again so that Callie...so that Callie wouldn't leave us, too."

Noah felt pain rip through his chest. Pain for the child

he held in his arms. And he understood, finally. Lily's fears weren't that another woman would come into their life and try to replace the mother she knew. She was afraid another woman might leave them in the same painful fashion.

He pulled back and made her look at him. "You know, Lily, there are no guarantees in any relationship. But if you trust me—you'll trust that I'll always do what's right by you and your sister and brothers."

"I do trust you, Dad," she said, hugging him. "I love you."

"I love you too, kid."

"I'm sorry I ran off," she said, smiling now, even though tears remained in her eyes. "I know you were worried. But I don't think I would have gotten on the plane. I was standing here before, thinking about you and Jamie and the twins and Aunt Evie and everyone else, and thought I'd miss everyone so much if I left. And I'd miss Maddy and Callie and Samson."

Emotion closed his throat. "And I'd miss you, Lily."

"Besides," she said with a sniff, "it's my birthday next week."

Enough said. "Okay. How about we get out of here?"

She reached for her backpack. "So, Dad, you haven't said what a dork I look like."

He ruffled her hair. "I think you look pretty."

She laughed. "Well, the hair's pretty cool…but these shoes have gotta go."

Callie spent the night in Noah's bed, wrapped up in the sheets, secure and safe. It was a lovely room. The huge bed was covered in a quilt in neutral beige and moss green, and the timber walls and silky oak furnishings were rich and warm.

He called her just before ten o'clock and told her that he'd found Lily and they were on their way home. He told her not to wait up and she hung up the telephone, missing him, craving him and feeling relieved he'd found his daughter.

Her heart went out to Lily. To all the kids. And to Noah. Being in his house, sleeping in his bed…it made their relationship seem very *real*. Perhaps for the first time since they'd met. And the responsibility of what that meant weighed heavily. Accepting the children into her heart was only a part of it. First her heart, then her life. Saying goodbye to Ryan was the first step.

But then what?

She'd return to Sandhills and everything would still be there, waiting for her.

Including Noah.

Only, a niggling thought lingered in the back of her mind. What if she couldn't say goodbye to her son? What if it was too much, too hard, too…everything. What then? Could she come back and face Noah and the kids, knowing she'd break their hearts into tiny pieces? Bathing the kids, dressing them in their pajamas, laughing over a botched dinner of grilled cheese and cookies had been wonderful. And she enjoyed their company so much. But there was doubt, too. And fear that she wouldn't measure up. They would expect all of her. An expectation they deserved. Did she have enough left inside herself for all that love?

Later that night, with the kids all tucked into their beds, Tessa locked in the laundry room and Harry guarding the front porch, Callie drifted into sleep.

She was quickly dreaming. Dreaming about Noah, about strong arms and warm lips and gentle hands. She could feel his touch; feel the love in his fingertips as he caressed her back and hips. Callie stretched her limbs, feeling him, wanting him.

And then the dream suddenly wasn't a dream. It was

real. She was in his arms, pressed against his chest. "You're here," she murmured into his throat. "You're home. I'm glad. Lily—"

"Shhhh," he said against her hair. "Lily's fine. Go back to sleep."

When Callie awoke a couple of hours later she could hear the rhythmic sound of the bedside clock and Noah's steady breathing. He lay on his stomach, his face turned away from her. She touched his back, rested her hand on him for a few moments and then slipped out of bed as quietly as she could.

When she padded downstairs a few minutes later she heard young voices whispering. The twins were awake, still in their beds but chatting to each other. Jamie emerged as though he had some kind of adult radar and quickly said he was hungry. Lily's door was still closed and Callie knew she'd still be sleeping. Breakfast was as hit-and-miss as dinner the night before, but the kids didn't complain. She gave them cereal and put on a pot of coffee and when they were done Callie herded them back to their rooms with instructions to stay quiet for at least another hour.

When she returned to the upstairs bedroom Noah was lying on his side with his eyes open. She closed the door softly and sat on the bed. "Sorry, did I wake you?"

He sighed wearily. "It was a long night."

"You should have stayed over and driven back this morning."

"I needed to get back."

"The kids were fine. Another few hours wouldn't have made any difference."

He looked at her. "Okay, I *wanted* to get back. As for them being fine," he said quietly and reached for her hand, "I knew they would be." He kissed her wrist and turned her hand over and kissed her knuckles. "In fact, I can't remember the last time the house was so quiet in the morning."

She smiled. "They're under strict instructions to be as quiet as mice for the next hour."

"What about you—don't you have to get back to your horses?"

"Joe will see to them this morning." She touched his face with her free hand. "How's Lily?"

"She's okay. She slept most of the drive home. We had a good talk about things. I think she'll be fine."

Callie had to ask what she feared. "Did she do this because of me? Because of us?"

"Not in the way you might think." He held her hand firm and told her how Lily was feeling. "You know, she's more like you than you realize."

Callie's breath caught in her throat. "In what way?"

Noah smiled lightly. "Impulsive. Sometimes hardheaded. But…extraordinary." He kissed her hand again. "I thought that the first time I met you. Those beautiful eyes of yours were glaring at me from under that big hat." He sighed. "It blew me away."

He shifted and raised himself up. Callie looked at his bare chest and then lower to where the sheet slipped past his hips and flat stomach. Her fingers suddenly itched with the need to touch, to feel, to taste.

"Keep looking at me like that and I'll forget how tired I am."

She colored hotly. What was she thinking? He'd just driven practically ten hours straight and she was leering at him. "You're right," she said and hopped off the bed. "You should hit the shower and have some breakfast when you've had enough sleep. I'll make sure the twins get to daycare and Jamie gets to school."

Callie sucked in a breath. She had to tell him now. Before she lost her nerve. Before they were any more involved. His name escaped from her lips.

He smiled again and kept his eyes closed. "Hmm."

She took a steadying breath, pushed out some courage and told him of her plans.

"You're going where?" he asked and pulled himself up.

"Los Angeles."

His eyes glittered, narrowing as he took in her words. "Why?" he asked. "Why now?"

Callie saw the confusion on his face. She knew he'd feel this way, knew he'd think her leaving was her way of running, of putting space between them.

Isn't it?

The truth pierced through her. Wasn't she running away? She took another breath.

"Please, Noah, try to understand…" She took his hands. "Please," she said again. "I know it might look like I'm—"

"What?" he said, cutting her off. "Running away? Running out? You forget I know what it feels like to be left, Callie."

She turned her hands in his and held them against his chest. "It's not like that."

He looked at her, deep, way down, like he was trying to absorb her with his eyes. Callie felt his frustration, his confusion, the sense he wanted to believe her but didn't quite know how. "Are you coming back?"

She hesitated and knew Noah felt it deep inside. "I'm… I'm…"

He grabbed her left hand and gently rubbed the ring finger with his thumb. "You know what I want, Callie. You know that I love you and want to be with you—as your friend and lover and husband."

Tears filled her eyes. "I know," she whispered and wrapped her arms around his waist.

"But that's not enough?"

She wanted to rest her head against his chest. "I just… don't know."

Noah pulled back. "Then I guess there's nothing left to say."

Chapter Thirteen

"You don't look so great."

Noah faked a smile. "Thanks."

Evie was never one to hold back her thoughts. "When's Callie due back?"

"I'm not sure." He felt like he had glass in his mouth. Because he had no idea when she was coming back. Or if.

His sister spun around in his kitchen and continued to chop watermelon with a big knife. "The kids are missing her."

So am I...

Noah tensed. He was in no mood for his sister's counsel. He wasn't in a mood for socializing, either. But it was Lily's birthday and the whole family had arrived to celebrate her day. "She'll be back when she's back." *If she comes back...*

"Have you spoken with her?"

"Is there a point to these questions?"

"Just trying to get you to talk," Evie said, raising both brows. "That's not an easy feat these days."

Noah didn't want to talk. He didn't want fake conversation with well-meaning relatives about how he was feeling. His mother had tried, now Evie. He just wanted to lick his wounds in private. He didn't want to talk about Callie. He didn't want to *think* about Callie.

But he remembered her look the night before she'd left. She'd made love with him, so deeply and with such an acute response to his touch it had felt like...it felt like...*goodbye*.

"So have you?"

Evie's voice shuttled Noah quickly back to the present. "Have I what?"

"Talked with her?"

He nodded. "Of course." Not exactly the truth. She'd called him when she'd landed in Los Angeles and he'd heard nothing since.

"Can I ask you something?"

Noah frowned. "Would it make any difference if I said no?"

Evie shrugged. "Probably not."

Noah grabbed the barbecue tongs and fork. "Go ahead."

"Why didn't you go with her?"

He stilled. Evie always knew the wrong question to ask. "Impossible."

"I could have watched the kids," she said. "So, what's your excuse?"

Because she didn't ask me to.

Part of him had longed to go with her, to meet her family, to see where she'd been raised, to be with her. He'd hated the idea of Callie traveling alone. Some base male instinct had kicked in and he wanted to protect her, to keep her safe. He should have insisted. He should have proposed marriage to her like he'd planned to do and taken the trip as an opportunity to meet her mother and brother.

"What's his excuse for what?"

Lily came into the kitchen. Without the gothic makeup and sporting only earrings—no other piercings—and jeans and a T-shirt, she looked so pretty, like a young version of his sister Grace. He smiled as she stole a piece of melon and took a bite.

"Were you guys talking about me?" she asked, suspicious but grinning.

"Of course," Evie said. "What else. How's the head cold?"

"Better," Lily replied. "I'm still sneezing."

Evie passed Lily the plate of fruit. "Well, if you're better, go and take this outside. Your Poppy loves watermelon." She looked at Noah. "You might want to light up the barbecue."

Lily was just about out of the room when Jamie raced into the kitchen. "Callie's here! Callie's here!" he said excitedly. "It's her truck coming."

Noah's stomach did a wild leap. He looked at his sister. "It's not possible."

"Go on," Evie said, shooing him out of the kitchen.

Noah headed for the front door, with Jamie and Lily barely feet behind him. Sure enough, Callie's truck was barreling down the long driveway. And it was hitching a horse trailer.

He opened the screen door. Lily was beside him instantly. So was Evie.

But it wasn't Callie behind the wheel. It was Joe. The skinny youth got out of the truck as Noah took the steps. He could feel Lily in his wake.

"Hi, there," Joe said. "Got a delivery."

Lily gripped Noah's arm. "Dad?"

He shrugged. "I don't know."

By now Evie and Mary-Jayne and his parents were standing by the front steps, with the twins squeezing between them, while Jamie jumped up and down excitedly.

Joe disappeared to the rear of the trailer and lowered the

tailgate. Lily's grip tightened when they saw the solid chestnut gelding step down from the trailer.

"Samson," she whispered. "Dad…look."

"I see him."

Joe led the horse around the truck and held the rope out to an astonished Lily. His daughter took the lead and buried her face in the animal's neck.

Joe pulled an envelope from his pocket and handed it to Lily. "Callie said to give this to you." He shook Noah's hand. "Well, I'll be seeing ya."

They waited until the truck pulled out from the driveway before Lily looked at the card inside. She read it out loud. *Dear Lily, I wish I was there with you. Happy birthday! Love, Callie.*

Tears welled in his daughter's eyes and tipped over her cheeks. "Oh, Dad." She hugged the horse. "I can't believe Callie did this."

Noah couldn't believe it, either. The woman he loved had given his daughter the one thing she longed for. It was an incredible gesture toward Lily. He ached inside thinking about it.

Lily didn't stop crying. "He's mine, he's really mine?"

"It looks that way."

Evie looked at Noah and raised her brows. "Some gift," she said.

Within minutes Lily had led the horse into the small pasture behind the house.

"That's one happy kid," his father said.

His parents had returned to the pool area with the kids and Evie pushed Noah to start up the barbecue. He was just flicking up the heat when Lily rushed through the back door and let it bang with a resounding thud.

"Dad!"

Her stricken look alarmed him and he set the utensils aside. "What is it?"

Lily shook her head frantically. "I want to call Callie."

Noah checked his watch. "Later tonight."

"I want to call her now," Lily insisted. "I want to call her and say thank you. And I want to tell her we miss her and want her to come home."

"You can't do that."

Lily tugged on his arm. "Why not?"

"Because you just can't."

Lily rolled her eyes. "No offense, Dad, but that sounds really dumb."

He shrugged, although he wasn't sure how he moved.

"So, you're not going to do anything?"

His back stiffened. "What exactly do you want me to do?"

Lily's eyes grew huge. "If you don't want me to call her—then you do it. You call her up and tell her we miss her. Tell her *you* miss her. She said in the card that she wished she was here—so call her up and tell her to come back."

Everyone stared at him. Evie raised her eyes questioningly.

He took a deep breath. "I can't tell Callie how to live her life." Another breath. "She's gone to see her family."

Tears filled Lily's eyes again. "I thought...I thought *we* were her family. So if she wants to be with her family she should be here, because *we* live here, *you* live here."

Noah wished he could stop his daughter's relentless logic. "She'll be back when she's ready."

Lily scowled. "Are you sure? What if she changes her mind? What if she stays there?"

Noah had spent the past week thinking of little else. He'd thought about it every night when he laid in his bed, twisting in sheets that still held the scent of her perfume in them. He missed her so much, wanted her so much he hurt all over.

"It's not up to me," he said quietly.

Lily hopped on her feet. "That doesn't make much sense. You love her, right?"

Eight sets of eyes zoomed in on him and he felt their scrutiny. "Well...I—"

"And she loves you," Lily said quickly. "She told me."

Noah rocked back on his heels. "She told you that?"

Lily looked at him like he needed a brain transplant. "I just don't get adults. You give all these lectures about being honest and then you can't even be honest with yourself." She puffed out a breath. "Why don't you just call her up and ask her to marry you?"

Noah's jaw almost fell to his feet. "What happened to your fifty percent of second marriages end in divorce speech?"

Lily swung her arm around. "Who listens to me? What do I know?" Lily blurted. "You guys are the grown-ups—work it out."

He saw Evie nodding. "Don't start," he warned his sister.

"She's got a point."

"Of course I've got a point," Lily said through her tears. "Callie loves you. You love Callie. We all love Callie."

"Yeah, Daddy, we love Callie," Jamie piped in, suddenly next to his sister. The twins weren't far away, either. And his parents hovered nearby.

She really does love me... She told my kid she loves me.

But she left.

And then, with a jolt, he realized he'd been so angry, so hurt, he hadn't really listened when she'd tried to explain. He'd cut her off, his ego dented, his heart smashed.

If he'd really listened he might have heard something other than his own lingering bitterness chanting inside his head. He might have heard that she needed to go home to lay her ghosts to rest.

Suddenly Noah understood. The past—Callie needed to

face her past, come full circle and deal with the grief of losing her fiancé and her son.

He felt the kick of truth knock against his ribs.

She loves me. He looked at his kids, all watching him, their little faces filled with hope. *She loves them.*

"Then I guess we'd better come up with a plan," he said and smiled when he saw everyone around him nodding.

Callie had been back in her old room for a week. It seemed so small now. And it didn't give her the comfort it once used to. But it was good to be home with her mother, especially since Scott had arrived two days after she had.

Her mother's stucco house was small compared to most in this part of Santa Barbara, but it was neat and her gardens were the envy of the neighborhood. She walked into the kitchen for a late breakfast and discovered her brother burning sourdough toast.

"Don't say anything," he cautioned. "I can still cook better than you."

Callie tapped him on the arm. "Ha, so you say."

She took the strawberry cream cheese from the refrigerator and waited while he scraped the burnt offering with a knife. Once he was done he passed it to her. Callie smeared it with spread and sat down.

"So, Mom said you're thinking of taking some time off?"

He shrugged. "Maybe."

"Because of what happened?"

Scott didn't like to discuss the tragic death of a friend and colleague a few months earlier. But she suspected the event had taken its toll on her brother.

"I don't know what I'm doing just yet."

"But you're not thinking of leaving the fire department, right?"

He shrugged. "Like I said, I haven't decided."

"You've wanted to be a fireman since you were four years old."

Scott grinned. "And you wanted to be a vet."

Callie shrugged and bit her bagel. "Nah—not smart enough."

"You could go back to school," he suggested. "Mom said you always got good grades. Not that I remember, being so much younger than you."

Callie held up three fingers. "That's how many years. Hardly worth mentioning."

He grinned again. "So would you?"

"I like my job. And I'm happy."

"Are you? You don't seem so happy to me."

Callie rolled her eyes. "Look who's talking."

"Well I never said I was happy," he replied. "So, what gives?" He smiled and ruffled her hair. "Why this sudden trip home?"

"I wanted to see you and Mom."

"And?"

And I'm in love…and I miss him so much I can hardly breathe. All I want is to go home and run into Noah's arms and stay there for the rest of my life.

"Stop badgering your sister."

Their mother came into the kitchen, a striking, willowy figure in a multicolored silk caftan, who looked much younger than her fifty-five years.

"Just asking," Scott said and grabbed another piece of bread. "You have to admit she showed up out of the blue. It makes me wonder what she's up to."

Callie placed her hands on her hips. "I am in the room, you know."

Scott chuckled. "So, spill."

She held her shoulders stiff. "I have nothing to say."

He bit into a bagel. "She's definitely hiding something."

Eleanor scolded her son and told him to take the dog for a walk. Still grinning, he grabbed his toast and left.

"Is he right?" her mother asked once the back door banged shut.

Callie nodded.

"A man?" Eleanor guessed correctly.

She nodded again.

Her mother sat down and swooshed the swirl of fabric around her legs. "I thought you might have changed," Eleanor said gently.

"Changed how?"

"I thought your time away might have loosened the tight control you've always had on what's inside you."

Callie knew what her mother meant. "I'm not good at talking about this stuff."

But she was with Noah. Callie had shared more with him than she had with anyone. Her heart, her body…all of herself.

"That's why things hurt you so much, Calliope. Even when you were a little girl you never talked about how you were feeling. You were always so happy on the outside. But I worried about you, keeping your feelings in. Your dad was like that, too." Eleanor pushed her bangs from her face. "After his accident, when he was really sick and knew he was dying, he didn't let me know how bad it was until the end."

"I remember."

"That hurt me for a long time," Eleanor admitted. "I thought he didn't trust me."

"He loved you, though. And you loved him."

"Of course," her mother said. "But when someone loves you, you should give them your whole heart."

"Like I did with Craig? That didn't turn out so great."

Eleanor raised her brows questioningly. "Craig was self-absorbed. And you were very young when you met. Had you met him now, as a woman, you probably would have seen right through his lack of integrity. He never deserved you, Callie…but if you've met someone who does, what are you doing here in my kitchen?" Her mother didn't wait for a reply and didn't hold back. "Do you love this man?"

Callie nodded. "I…yes."

Eleanor smiled. "Good. Because he called me yesterday."

"Noah called *you?*" Callie couldn't hide the shock in her voice.

"Mmm. We had a nice long talk about you."

Callie almost spluttered the coffee she'd just sipped. "What?"

"I liked him very much."

Callie was aghast. Why on earth would Noah want to talk with her mother? "Why didn't he call *me?*"

Eleanor widened her bright blue eyes. "Did you give him reason to?"

Did she? "Well, I didn't say he *couldn't* call me." She put down her coffee. Curiosity burned through her. "What did he say?"

Eleanor lifted her shoulders dramatically. "Oh, this and that. He asked how you were doing."

Callie's skin heated. "And what did you tell him?"

"Oh, this and that."

"Mom…please?"

Her mother stood up. "Come for a walk with me in the garden."

Callie followed her mother out the back door and across the lawn toward the small wooden bench in the far corner. They sat in front of a tiny rose garden her mother tended to daily.

"This is my favorite spot," her mother said as she arranged her housecoat on the bench.

Callie sat beside her and looked at the beautiful deep burgundy rosebush just about to bloom. "Dad's flower."

Eleanor smiled. "Not just that." She pointed to a small miniature rose shrub with tiny yellow buds on it. "That one is for my grandson."

Ryan's rose. Of course her mother would do that. Callie grasped her mother's hand. "Thank you, Mom." Callie sighed. "You know, I never thought I'd feel whole again. After Ryan died I shut myself off from everything." She looked at her mother. "And everyone."

She took a long, shuddering breath. "And then one morning Lily Preston knocked on my door and my life changed."

"Kids do that," her mother said fondly. "So does love."

He mother was so right and Callie didn't know whether she should laugh or cry. "The children are incredible. And they...they need me."

"So why are you here?"

Callie looked at the rose planted in her son's memory and said a silent prayer and thank you to the precious baby she'd never forget. And slowly the pain began to ease. She thought about Craig, and there was no anger, no lingering resentment for a man she now realized was never who she'd believed him to be. She felt sad for him. Sad for the time lost. But that was all, and it made her feel incredibly free. She thought about Noah loving children who weren't biologically his and knew he was right—blood and genetics were merely words. And Fiona—forced to give up her baby and living with the belief and hope that her child was being loved and cherished. And she knew, as her heart filled with a heady joy at what the future promised, that loving Noah was the greatest gift she could give his children.

"Why am I here?" Callie echoed her mother's words. "I'm letting go of the past."

"Are you about done?"

Callie nodded. "I'm done. I need to go home now." She

squeezed her mother's hand. "Will you come with me, Mom? I'd like you to meet Noah…and the…and my…"

"Your kids?"

Callie's heart contracted. "Yes."

Eleanor reached across and hugged Callie close. "We're booked to leave tomorrow. That young man of yours can be very persuasive."

Callie laughed with delight. "Oh, Mom, don't I know it."

Bellandale airport only accepted small aircraft, so Callie and her mother caught a connecting flight with a small domestic airline and because of the time difference arrived late Tuesday afternoon.

The airplane hit the runway and took a few minutes to come to a complete stop. Stairs were placed near the door and Callie felt the warm morning air hit her the moment she stepped out into the sunshine.

It was good to be back. And she couldn't wait to see Noah and the children. Fiona was picking them up and Callie intended to go directly to his house to surprise him. She clutched her cabin bag and followed her mother down the steps behind a line of other passengers. The walk across the tarmac took no time at all and when they reached the terminal and walked through the automatic doors the strong rush of the air conditioner was a welcome relief.

People disbursed in front of them, some greeting waiting relatives, some linking up with rental cars or taxis. Callie looked around for the familiar face of her friend and then stopped dead in her tracks as the throng of people in front of her disappeared.

For a moment she couldn't move. Couldn't speak. Couldn't think. She dropped her bag to her feet. Then, through the blur of tears she knew it was true.

Callie saw Lily first, then Jamie, then the twins. Lily held up a sign, as did Jamie, and the little ones had a hand each on a wide piece of cardboard. It spelled three words.

Please... Marry... Us...

The kids all looked hopeful. And Lily—looking so naturally beautiful with her newly colored hair and clean face, stared at her with luminous green eyes that shone brightly with tears. Jamie was smiling the widest smile she'd ever seen and the twins chuckled with such enchanting mischief she just wanted to hug them close.

I love these kids. I want to love them for the rest of my life. I want to be their mother.

She smiled through her tears and Lily came forward and hugged her so tight Callie thought she might break something. "Thank you for my birthday present," Lily said breathlessly. "Please say yes to my dad."

Callie hugged her back as emotion welled inside her. "Where is he?"

"Callie?"

She heard his voice, felt his presence vibrating though her entire body. He was behind her. Callie turned. Her breath caught in her throat. He looked so good. Sounds disappeared, people faded, until there was just him. Only this man she loved so much.

"You're here?" she whispered.

He nodded. "I'm here."

Callie saw Evie and Fiona from the corner of her eye, and watched as they ushered the children toward them and took Eleanor into their inner circle and headed for the exit doors. Noah stepped forward and took her hand. She felt his touch through to every part of her body.

"I can't stand being away from you," he admitted, drawing her closer. "It's killing me."

And right there, in the middle of the airport, with people moving around them, Noah kissed her.

"I'm sorry I left you," she managed to say, when the kissing stopped and she could draw a breath. "I know my reasons didn't make a lot of sense to you. But I had something I had to do before I could give you...all of my heart."

Noah held her in the circle of his arms. "What did you have to do?"

"I had to say goodbye to Ryan."

He swallowed hard and Callie saw the emotion glittering in his green eyes. "I understand."

"I'll always cherish him," she said, holding on to Noah, vaguely aware that people around them were dwindling to just a few. "But I knew I had to let go of all my anger toward Craig and my grief over losing Ryan. I guess it came down to this fear I had of messing up...of not being able to feel what I knew your children deserved me to feel."

"And did you let it go?"

Callie nodded. "Yes—once I realized that I *wanted* to love the kids and that I wanted to be part of their life."

Noah held her hands in front of his chest. "You know what it means, Callie? The whole deal—forever."

"I know what it means," she said on a rush of breath. "I want forever. I want the kids. I want you." She looked into his eyes. *"I love you."*

"It's about time," he breathed into her hair. He kissed her, the sweetest kiss she'd ever known.

"Thank you for not giving up on me," she whispered between kisses.

He held her in his arms. "I never will. Marry me, Callie? I need you. We need you."

She nodded. "Yes," she said, her gaze filled with love. "Yes, I will. I love you," she whispered. "I love you."

"Marry me soon."

"Mmm," she agreed through kisses. "Soon. How about Christmas Eve?"

He smiled against her mouth. "That soon? Good." He reached into his pocket and pulled out a small box. "Because I've been carrying this around with me for days."

Callie stared at the box as he flipped the lid. Inside lay the most beautiful ring she'd ever seen—a gorgeous champagne diamond surrounded by a cluster of pure white stones. She looked at the ring, then Noah. "It's beautiful."

He slipped the ring on her finger and it fit perfectly.

"The kids helped me pick it out." He kissed her forehead gently. "I love you, Callie." He lifted her chin and tilted her head. "And if you ever want to explore that ten-percent chance and look at trying to have a baby—then that's what we'll do. Whatever you decide, I'll be beside you."

Callie felt fresh tears behind her eyes. "Thank you for that. We'll see what happens. For the moment…I just want to learn how to be the best mother I can be to your children."

"Our children now," he said softly. "Maybe we should head outside and break the news?" he suggested and pointed toward the long glass windows and the sea of eager and clearly happy faces watching them.

She nodded and he linked their hands and they walked outside together. As soon as they hit the pavement Lily raced forward and hugged her close and Jamie and the twins followed her lead. With her mother, Evie and Fiona smiling, the kids laughing and hugging and Noah holding her hand so tightly she felt the connection through to her soul, any doubts disappeared. This was what she was made for. This man. This family. Her family.

* * * * *

TO WED
A RANCHER

MYRNA MACKENZIE

CHAPTER ON

"I'M sorry. It's obvious that I made a mistake. I was wrong to trust you. So, please, just go." Rachel Everly's voice wasn't as steady as she wanted it to be, but she managed to turn away from the car and the man she'd thought she'd known up until a few days ago.

"Rachel, stop acting stupid and hysterical. You're totally overreacting, so just get back in the car and let's go. Besides, I'm still your boss until this trip is over, and we have a photo shoot in Oregon in two days."

Oh, no, had Dennis really used the S word? And called her hysterical? *And* implied that trying to make another woman jealous by lying and saying he and Rachel were sleeping together was okay when he had claimed to have hired Rachel for her skill with a camera?

This morning, listening to him talking to the woman and then having him admit that his lies about Rachel had his ex-girlfriend wild to have him back, reality had hit Rachel hard. Dennis had been lying to her all along. He wasn't her friend. He wasn't fascinated by her skill as a photographer. He was a jerk who was just using her. And she had been used before.

No more.

Rachel wanted to whirl back toward the car and tell

thought, but right now she was almost as ...erself as she was with him. Darn it, she *had* .. stupidly. She'd always prided herself on being nobody's fool, but the man had discovered her weakness. He'd used their shared interest in photography to make her feel unique, when she was clearly just a convenience who could serve both as an assistant and a lure to play another woman for a fool. Using photography, her greatest passion, against her was…not cool. But allowing herself to be used was even worse. She needed to get out of here with as much dignity as she could muster.

She pushed her shoulders back. "You'll have to find a new assistant for Oregon. You're not my boss anymore. I'm through with you." With that, she walked away.

Behind her, there was silence. Then Dennis let loose with a string of profanities, his tires squealing as he drove away. She closed her eyes.

"That's it, Everly! That's the last time I trust so blindly. Ever," she muttered out loud as the sound of the car died away. For long seconds she couldn't even think about what to do or where to go in this unfamiliar town. She simply stood in the middle of the street alone.

Or…not alone. The sound of something scuffling against the pavement made her breath catch in her throat. Immediately her senses went on high alert. She opened her eyes…and locked gazes with a tall, broadshouldered man who, by the way he was looking at her, had clearly witnessed the whole exchange. Some sort of cowboy type judging by his boots, his jeans and his bronzed skin. He was standing just outside a store and must have been on the verge of entering or leaving when she and Dennis had begun their little scene. Her most personal failings had been viewed by this stranger.

She glared at him.

He didn't look even remotely fazed. "Do you need help?" he asked in a deep, whiskey-rough voice that sounded as if it came straight from some rugged cowboy movie.

Did she need help?

Yes, she thought, as a sense of failure tugged at her heart. Her past hadn't been the type that led her to build relationships. And, while this hadn't been a longstanding relationship, she'd thought she and Dennis had had something in common. She'd been wrong. Even worse, she'd been weak, and consequently blind.

Now, because of that uncharacteristic blindness, here she was. Alone. She was…she didn't even know where she was. Somewhere with a lot of cows and boots and cowboy stuff. In Montana. And talking to a stranger who had witnessed her humiliation. Still, she should be grateful for his offer, and a part of her was, but mostly she just wanted to escape those too-perceptive silver-blue eyes.

"I…what town is this?"

"Moraine. Do you need a lift somewhere?"

Oh, yeah, like she was going to get in a car with a stranger. She might have made a rookie mistake where Dennis was concerned, but she'd grown up around some big, bad cities. She'd taken her share of self-defense classes and knew how to behave when approached by unfamiliar men.

"No, thank you," she said primly. "I'm perfectly fine. I know exactly where I'm going and how to get there. I have friends." Which was, of course, a total lie.

But, self-defense classes or not, the thought of letting a man so much taller and more muscular than she was know that she was totally on her own in the middle of all this emptiness…if he carted her off somewhere, no one would ever even know she was gone.

"I have plans," she said more firmly, willing him to walk away so that she could figure out her next step in private. She tried to smile more broadly, lifting her chin and practically daring him to repudiate her words.

He studied her for several seconds, frowning all the while. Then he nodded once, turning away. Somehow, despite what she'd told him, a totally unreasonable part of her resented just how quickly he'd moved on. Maybe because men were not on her *nice* list right now. Especially tall, good-looking men. And, unfortunately, *this* tall man was gorgeous. He probably had women sending him sexy messages every half-hour. Irrational as it might be, it was easy to transfer her anger to him.

And then things got worse. When the man moved closer to the door of the store and turned slightly, looking back at her, she was sure she saw pity in his eyes.

A groan nearly escaped her. Pity was the worst. Maybe because she'd been forced to choke it down too many times in the past. She narrowed her eyes and pulled herself up to her full five foot three inches. "Did you need something?" she asked, trying to make it look as if she was the one in charge of her life and he was the one who merited sympathy.

He stared at her. She stared right back, doing her best to look totally unaffected by the recent turn of events.

"Not a thing," he said as he gave her one last dismissive look and walked away.

Immediately Rachel's anger vanished. No question

she was acting ungrateful and being unfair. But then, this whole situation was unfair.

Still, self-pity got a person nowhere, and she was used to depending on herself. So she turned and marched away as if she had a true destination in mind, when in fact she hadn't a clue.

It was only after she'd turned the corner and realized that she was already almost on the edge of town, with nothing beyond but lots of big, yawning stretches of land, that she began to panic.

"Stop, Rachel. Slow down. Think," she ordered herself, echoing the words of a favorite teacher. *What are the facts? What's the situation? What's the logical next step?* Good questions for an impulsive person like herself.

Questions she hadn't asked herself when she'd gotten out of the car. The truth was that she had been so shocked when the message and accompanying photo of that scantily dressed woman had appeared on the screen of Dennis's phone that she had simply reacted. The realization that she had been manipulated and used to con and hurt another woman had made her sick.

But now here she was, with no job and nowhere to go. Having planned to work with Dennis on the west coast, she'd given up her apartment. Her mother was on her umpteenth honeymoon, and her father's new wife felt about Rachel the way most people felt about gum on their shoes. And…

"My phone and my wallet were in the glove compartment of Dennis's car," she realized with a horrified whisper. It was enough to make some women sit down in the middle of the road and cry.

Rachel tried not to be that kind of woman most of

the time. *There's an upside to most situations,* she reminded herself. Unfortunately she was having trouble finding the upside right now, and time was against her. A few hours from now it would be dark. She'd need a place to sleep…and some way to pay for it.

Battling panic, she veered back toward the town. She glanced down at her camera, her one constant companion, the one thing she had always been able to depend on. Still, it wouldn't help her today.

She headed toward a small building with the words "Angie's Diner" on the window. There was only one customer and a large, friendly-looking woman behind the counter. Rachel opened the door and the bell jangled. The woman looked up and smiled.

"Can I help you?"

Rachel wanted to close her eyes at the prospect of begging for work. Instead, she took a deep breath and managed to paste on a smile. "Hi, I'm Rachel Everly. Are you Angie?"

"None other."

"Nice to meet you. Is there any chance that you're hiring?"

Angie looked around the almost empty room. The clock seemed to tick too loudly, emphasizing the lack of customers. "Sorry, no. You're new in town." It wasn't even a question. This was obviously one of those places where everyone knew everyone.

"I'm…visiting." Rachel didn't try to explain why she would need work if she wasn't staying. "Is there any place to stay in town?"

"Just Ruby's boarding house. Good food and service with a smile." Angie fired off directions. "But if you want work…well, good luck. Not much around here."

Rachel tried to tamp down her anxiety. "Thank

you." She wandered back into the street. Maybe if she humbled herself and begged, or offered to help Ruby with dishes or something, she could at least get through the night. Tomorrow she would figure out the next step, but she knew one thing. She was going to be extremely wary of men and their motives from now on. Because of idiotically trusting Dennis, she was home-less, stranded in the middle of nowhere.

"That's temporary," she told herself, battling her fears. Someday she'd finally have the home she'd never had. In Maine, the one place she'd been happy and the place she'd been trying to get back to for a long time. She'd be there now if...

Stop thinking about your mistakes. That isn't help-ing. Right now she had to concentrate on finding a bed. Maybe she could barter a free advertising photo of the boarding house for a place to stay, reach some sort of deal.

Just thinking the words made her feel a bit better. At least she wouldn't have to deal with any more men today. Her experience with the cowboy in town had been...well, she wasn't going to think about that. She'd never see the man again, anyway.

Shane Merritt wasn't in the best of moods. Being back in Montana, even temporarily, had him edgy, and that encounter with the woman in town hadn't done a thing for his bad mood. He hated feeling responsible for other people. He had a past that proved he was the worst kind of guy to turn to for help, but it had been clear from the little he'd seen that she was stranded in Moraine. It had also been clear that she didn't want his assistance.

"Which you ought to be grateful for, Merritt. The

woman did you a massive favor when she turned you down." The truth was that he was itching to get back on the road, back to his wandering life and his business that allowed him to keep moving. But he couldn't do that yet. He was as stuck here as she was, so for now he was going to have to settle for getting these supplies back to the ranch.

Unfortunately, his cell phone rang at that moment. "What's up, Jim?" Shane asked his business manager.

"Trouble. Your next job needs a reschedule. There's a conflict and you need to be in Germany in two weeks."

Shane blew out a breath. "Jim, you know I'm held up here until I sell the ranch. When I got here…well, let's just say that Oak Valley is in worse condition than I thought. Try to buy me at least three weeks." Even though in some ways the shorter time frame would be less draining. He'd inherited the family ranch a year ago, and for months he'd been eager to sell his less than happy childhood home, but this was the first time he'd had time to fly in and get the job done properly. And he needed to do it himself. There were things here…things that had belonged to his mother and his brother…

The overwhelming pain that followed that thought served as a reminder that he had failed them, and that, difficult as it was, he needed to be the one to supervise the disposal of their personal effects.

That conviction increased his resolve. "See what you can do, but three weeks is the absolute minimum for me to put things to rights. Things here look pretty messed up." Which was his own fault for staying away and letting things deteriorate.

"You okay?" his friend and employee asked.

No. Being here brought back memories he had to keep batting away, but at least once this was done it would be over, or as over as it would ever get. He never had to come back here again. He could spend the rest of his life circling the globe a free man. No ties.

"Shane?" Jim's voice was concerned.

"I'm doing just fine," Shane lied. "It's just a bit of an adjustment being back on a ranch after years of living in offices and hotels." That was one way of putting it. The trip to town had been a mistake. Moraine was filled with too many memories, regrets and ghosts. He wouldn't be going back.

"I can hardly picture you on a ranch," Jim was saying. "Or riding a horse or dating a cowgirl. *Are* there any cute cowgirls in the area?"

Immediately the image of the woman in town came to mind. She'd been tiny, pretty, spitting mad and full of grit. And not a cowgirl.

"I wouldn't know. I didn't come here looking for women."

"Yes, but they tend to find you." Jim didn't sound even vaguely concerned that he had wandered into personal territory. They'd known each other a long time. "Sometimes they even follow you here."

"That only happened a couple of times. It's not happening again."

"Too bad. I get some of my best dates that way."

Which was a lie. Jim had women lined up around the block, but Shane appreciated his friend's attempt at levity. It reminded him that there was more to life than selling the ranch. Oak Valley might have colored his world with bitterness at one time, but today it was only a temporary detour in his life. "Make the call to

Germany, Jim. I'll be back in three even if I have to give the place away."

"Will do, but if you meet any cute cowgirls give them my number. I've never been on a ranch." It was a direct bid for an invitation, but Shane didn't fall in line. Oak Valley had never been a place where fun lived. He ended the conversation and headed down the road.

But Jim's comments about women stuck in his mind. Or at least the image of the woman in town did. The scene with her and the man had been tense, the proverbial car wreck a person couldn't look away from. Her chocolate-brown eyes had been vulnerable, but she'd also been defiant and proud. When Shane had dared to suggest that she might need help she'd given him a withering look, as if she was offended...or suspected that he might grow fangs and fur every full moon.

So he'd backed off, which was a good thing. Despite those eyes that made a man think of dark nights and pleasure, the last thing he needed was to get even remotely involved with a woman he associated with Moraine, especially one with trust issues.

Besides, right now his life was centered on work and on expanding his business into more distant markets. It was a good life. It was enough.

"So, back to business, Merritt." The clock was ticking away, even faster now that he knew he had only three weeks. But this darn task...like it or not, he needed at least a little help. Some extra muscle, a short-term housekeeper and cook, someone who could take photos to help with the sales package.

"Hell." The word slipped out as he glanced up ahead and saw a small figure trudging down the gravel road, a red duffle bag banging against one leg, a very expensive Hasselblad he hadn't noticed before hugged tight against her other side. Her legs were covered in dust. She already looked beat up. And it was miles to anywhere.

He swore again beneath his breath, then pulled up beside her, prepared for another round of *Get away from me. I don't need any help.* He wanted to keep moving like fire wanted fuel, but several things stopped him. She was alone on a lonely road with night drawing near, and he couldn't just leave her alone in the dark. The woman didn't even have a flashlight to guide her; she wasn't wearing anything reflective. Besides, he couldn't forget those pretty, distressed eyes…or help wondering whether she could cook and just how skilled she was with that camera.…

Rachel heard a car coming up behind her and instinctively stepped farther off the road, hugging her camera closer to her body. Out here in the middle of what had to be Big Sky country, if the ceiling of pure blue was to be trusted, she felt naked, vulnerable. There was absolutely nowhere to go if she needed to run.

Not that she would need it, but self-protection was simply an instinct for someone like her. She took one more step to the right.

The car slowed.

Her heartbeat picked up. She didn't speed up—what was the point?—but she tried to take another step farther away.

"Don't," that deep, already familiar voice ordered as the car stopped. "Barbed wire is very unforgiving."

She stopped dead in her tracks and looked to the right. Okay, there it was. Barbed wire.

"What do you want?" She tried to make her voice

brave as he got out of the car. What would she do if he moved closer?

To her relief, he didn't take another step. He stayed on the driver's side, two tons of metal between them.

"What do I want? Not what you apparently think."

"What do you think I think?" She forced herself to stare him dead in the eyes. Those silver-blue eyes that made her want to look away…or keep staring at him. She frowned.

He scowled down at her thin-soled shoes that hadn't been made for walking long distances. "You're miles from anywhere, you know."

"Is that a threat?" She hoped she sounded brave.

"Not a threat. A fact." He held out his hands, open-palmed, as if to show her that he was weaponless or helpless or…something harmless…which she was sure wasn't true. He was a big man and, even if he wasn't a threat physically, he had that solid heartbreaker look about him. The kind of look that made a woman's chest grow tight and her breathing uneven. She hated that, and, given her recent circumstances and decisions, she looked at him more critically and came to the conclusion that a man like that was not to be trusted. Maybe if she'd done more critical thinking the day Dennis had given a workshop at the camera shop where she'd been working she wouldn't be in this fix now.

"Mind if I ask where you're headed?" he asked.

She did mind. She didn't want to talk to him. But the truth was that she'd been wondering for the past twenty minutes if she was walking in the right direction.

"The woman who runs the diner told me that some-one named Ruby would rent me a room."

"She's still doing that, is she?"

Rachel blinked. "Don't you know?"

"I don't live here anymore. But if you're looking for Ruby, then you missed the turn out of town maybe a mile and a half back."

The shot of energy that had run through her earlier had worn off after she'd realized that for now she was lost and stuck, tired and hungry, and in a really bad place. Now, with this bit of bad news, Rachel felt her spirits fall even lower than they already were. "And how far past the turn is her place?"

"Two miles or so."

She forced herself not to sit down in the dirt right then. Instead, she held herself as erect as she could and started to turn around.

"Do you have a phone?" he asked.

"Yes."

"Where is it?"

She didn't want to say. "Why?"

"I'm going to have you call Ruby."

"Does she have a shuttle service?"

The briefest of smiles transformed his handsome face into something truly, outrageously gorgeous before it disappeared as if it had never existed. Rachel wished that she hadn't noticed his looks. They were completely irrelevant and acknowledging them was… not helpful. Not helpful at all.

"A shuttle service? Not that I know of. But if you call her you can ask her about me, so that I can give you a ride."

"Why would you do that?"

"Let's just say that I don't need you on my conscience."

Ordinarily, Rachel would have bristled at that, but right now she was too tired. "How do I know that you and Ruby aren't in cahoots?"

"You don't, but if that's the case then Angie would have to be in with us, too, right?"

He had a point. Rachel wished that her mind wasn't so fried. Getting in a car with a stranger? A handsome, dangerous stranger who was probably used to getting his way simply by offering up a few dimpled smiles? "I'm sorry. I'm from the city. I don't take rides from people I don't know well."

The man blew out a breath. He gave her a look, and what she read in it was probably not what he was really thinking. She had been riding around the country with Dennis, and she clearly didn't know as much about him as she'd thought she had. Still…

"My phone was in the glove compartment of Dennis's car," she admitted.

"I see." He pulled an expensive phone from his pocket and moved just close enough to hand it to her. "I'd give you the number, but I haven't been here for a while."

She nodded, then dialed directory assistance. "What's your name?" she whispered loudly as she dialed Ruby's Rooftop Restaurant and Rooming House.

"Shane Merritt."

"So…Ruby will tell me you're a good guy?"

"No. She'll probably tell you some personal stuff I don't want to think about and that I'm a jackass, but I'm not the kind of jackass who kidnaps women."

Rachel stopped dialing. She stared up at him. "So… even though you've just admitted that you're not a good guy, you just want to give me a ride? That's all this is about?"

"Not exactly. I told you. I'm not stellar material. I do have ulterior motives, but nothing that should make you worry or run in the opposite direction. I have a few simple questions and I need simple answers."

What was this about? A sense of unease settled into her stomach. But this man apparently knew the woman who might, if she was lucky, let her stay the night for free. It wouldn't do to tick him off. "Ask."

He stared directly into her eyes. "How much do you know about cooking and cleaning?"

That was an easy one. Almost nothing. But clearly that would be the wrong answer. That kind of a question sounded as if there was a job attached. Right now, given her dire circumstances, she was entertaining all possibilities. She could always run if she didn't like the questions that followed.

"I know enough," she said carefully, desperately telling herself that it wasn't a lie. *Enough* was a relative answer.

He nodded, but she could tell that wasn't exactly the answer he was seeking. "How well do you know how to use that camera and...is it possible that you have a few weeks to kill?"

As if he'd said something about her child, she wrapped one palm protectively around the Hasselblad. "Okay, now you're creeping me out." She started punching in the numbers for Ruby's place again, as if just hearing a woman's voice would save her from this crazy man. "I don't know what this is about, but I don't take kinky pictures and I can't imagine what you would want with my camera or me or—"

He scowled and held up his hand, those dangerous blue eyes looking even more dangerous. "You're mistaken if you think I'm interested in anything kinky or even close to personal."

He looked so ticked off that Rachel knew she'd

taken a wrong turn. Her brain searched for answers and lit on one that seemed remotely plausible. If she was right, maybe there was a chance she *could* earn enough money to get her across the country. "I know. You have a wife. Maybe children. You need a housekeeper and maybe…you want a family portrait? Because yes, I can absolutely do that for you. I can take photos of your family." And she would charge extra this time, enough to earn her way to Maine. Where she would figure out the next logical step. Hopefully.

Unfortunately, Shane was looking at her as if she'd just said something obscene. "No family of any kind. No people. Things. I'm selling a ranch and all its furnishings and machinery. Everything has to go, down to the nails in the floor. There'll be an auction, maybe some bits and pieces offered on the internet. I just need someone to help get the house in saleable condition. And someone to take a few photos to help market the place. If you can do both, that's a bonus, because I have an extremely short time to hire people, pull this all together and get this deal done."

"I see."

"You don't, but it doesn't matter. Do you have time? Would you consider taking on a job? I can make it worth your while. Unless…"

She waited.

"Maybe you have to get back home?"

Well, she had to get away from here, and now that she'd set her sights on Maine she needed to look for work there, but it didn't have to be this minute. In fact, a little advance planning and money wouldn't be a bad idea, and this job Shane Merritt was offering looked to be her best bet to gain some breathing room and perspective and get her where she wanted to go. Still, Rachel knew better than to simply accept a man's word.

She dialed Ruby's number, completing it this time. Carefully, she explained that she had gotten a recommendation for Ruby from Angie at the diner, but she had gotten lost. She had a chance for a ride with someone named Shane Merritt.

"Shane Merritt?" The woman yelled Shane's name so loud that Rachel's eardrums cried out in pain. She held the phone away from her ear and punched on the speakerphone. "Shane Merritt is back in town? That wicked, heartless devil."

Rachel blinked. Shane, amazingly enough, didn't look even remotely surprised or upset. "You think I'd be crazy to get a ride from him, then?"

"He's trouble, all right."

That didn't sound promising. "So I should say no?"

There was a pause. "Tell me, does he still look as sinfully gorgeous as ever? Like you'd just like to lick him from top to bottom?"

Rachel's eyes locked with Shane's. She felt her face turning warm as blood rushed in. She punched off the speakerphone.

"He looks…he looks pretty good. Healthy, I'd say." She knew she was blushing even more as she struggled to get out of this mess.

"Hmm," Ruby said. "I guess that's one way of putting it."

"I—do you even have a room you can rent me?" Rachel asked, stumbling on.

"I do. I surely do. So, Shane's going to drive you here. Man, I haven't seen him in years. That jerk." Ruby's voice seemed to vacillate between excitement and anger. "He was always trouble and always *in* trouble, too. Plus, he was hardheaded, obstinate, slippery. Bad, unreliable, especially where women were concerned. Heartless. With you and making you feel loved one day and gone the next. Bad."

"I see," Rachel said quietly. "So I shouldn't ride with him?"

"What? Oh. No, hon, go ahead and ride with him. I've got no way to get you here. Just don't trust him to stick. He'll hurt you bad."

Rachel nodded, then remembered that Ruby couldn't see her. "All right. Thank you." She hung up the phone and looked at Shane.

"She says you're bad."

He shrugged.

"She says you're slippery and obstinate."

"Is that a problem? This is a short-term job. I'll be your boss. Obstinate comes with the territory." He stared at Rachel unflinchingly, and that direct gaze of his made her feel too exposed. As if he knew her thoughts and that much of her bravado was a bluff. Still, he had a point. They were talking about working together, not dating.

"Not a problem," she agreed.

"Good." The word was clipped. He looked impatient. For some reason impatient looked very sexy on him. Rachel reminded herself that Ruby had told her not to trust him.

Good advice. Especially because this man, this Shane person, looked...kind of angry. She could tell that he wasn't totally enthused about hiring her. Maybe he'd had no choice. Finding temporary employees in a town this small might be a challenge. Strangely, his lack of enthusiasm made her feel slightly safer. At least she would have no false expectations, unlike her experience with Dennis.

"So...you're going to give me a ride to Ruby's?"

"Yes." Obviously, he was a man of few words. That might be a good thing. Less interaction. If only he didn't look so...so...*virile*. Rachel frowned at the word, her tension and discomfort rising again.

"What if I decide not to work for you?" she asked suddenly, and immediately wanted to smack herself. After all, had any other jobs dropped out of the sky? No, but this man...this overwhelming man who stared at her as if could read the secrets and fears she kept locked away inside her...

Rachel swallowed hard. *Try to look nonchalant,* she ordered herself. *Try to look as if you don't even see him as a man.*

"You'll get a ride no matter what," he said.

"Because you don't want me on your conscience." Why was she pushing this, trying to peg the man's motives? No doubt because she was tired and frustrated and just plain mad as heck. Mostly at herself for being naive and impulsive and ending up stranded and broke. She hated feeling that all of her choices and power had been taken from her. And she needed to see things clearly and not miss things this time.

"I don't." And there was something in his eyes, some pained look, that told her that those words had meaning, too. He frowned. "So, does that mean that you're not taking the job? You didn't exactly say no, but you also haven't said yes."

She looked him directly in the eye. "Yes." A frisson of awareness slid through her. Saying yes to this man— this bad man, she corrected, remembering Ruby's warnings—might not be the smartest thing she'd ever done, and she needed to be smart.

"Despite Ruby's warnings?"

She lifted her chin defiantly. "I don't care how bad you are, because this is just going to be about work."

"Not a chance of anything more," he agreed.

Another woman might have been offended, but not Rachel. When a man said no, he was most likely being honest.

"And just so we're clear," he said, "I mentioned that I had a limited time frame. The truth is that this job won't last more than three weeks. I can't stay longer than that."

"I don't need more time than that. I just need enough money to get me out of here."

"All right." He held out his hand. "We have a deal then?"

Rachel stared for just a second. His hand was large, very male, with long, strong fingers. She slipped her palm against his and he—very briefly—closed his hand over hers. Warmth moved from his skin to hers in a most disturbing way that made her too aware that she was a woman and this was an overwhelming male she had just committed her time to. "A deal."

And then he released her just as quickly as he'd touched her.

Don't trust ricocheted through her mind, but she didn't have to be reminded. Not after today.

Hours later, on a narrow bed, staring at the moon, Rachel shivered, remembering all that had happened today. Her relationship with Dennis had been a horrible mistake, and she hadn't seen it coming. She knew it was because he'd made her feel that her skill with a camera made her stand out from the crowd in a good way, something she wasn't used to. She'd been naive. Now her eyes were clearer. She duly noted that there was a good chance that agreeing to work for someone like Shane would prove to be a mistake.

If she let it. "But I won't. I'll be on my guard," Rachel promised herself. Besides, it wasn't as if doing a little cleaning and taking a few pictures for some rancher was going to change her life.

CHAPTER TWO

"I PROMISE that I'll pay you for letting me stay here as soon as I can," Rachel said, drying a cup and putting it in the cabinet Ruby directed her to. She tried not to listen for the sound of Shane's car coming down the road. For some reason the prospect of riding in a car again with a man that potent had her spooked. Still, it was probably just a delayed reaction to her situation and the stress of yesterday. Nothing at all to do with the man.

Unfortunately, Ruby had noticed her nervousness. And misinterpreted it.

"Don't worry," she told Rachel. "He'll probably be here on time. When he was young, he was bull-headed and full of 'I dare you to make me try to do that.' If you put your foot down and demanded that he do something, he was almost sure to do the exact opposite. And he was a fighter. That landed him in jail a time or two. But I'm sure he's different now. He's a successful businessman, and since he was always a mathematical genius I'm sure he must spend some time on work and not so much on raising hell or loving up women."

The image of a half-naked Shane on a bed immediately sprang into Rachel's mind. She frowned. What was wrong with her?

Stop that right now, she ordered herself. She didn't even like the man. She didn't *want* to like the man. Hadn't she just yesterday shed one bad example of the male species?

Rachel shuddered. For two years, ever since Jason had broken her heart by leaving her for "a womanly woman," the woman he'd been waiting for all his life, as he put it, she'd sworn off associations with men entirely. Now she seemed to be making up for lost time, hooking up with one untrustworthy male after another. The thought that she might be turning into her mother, going gooey and giddy over any man who wandered near her, made Rachel feel suddenly sick.

She grabbed another cup and forced herself not to attack it. She needed to keep her mind on the work she'd been lucky enough to find, even if it was work she wasn't really qualified to do. She'd already nearly burned Ruby's boarding house down by trying to help her cook. That couldn't happen with Shane. Nothing bad could happen with Shane or he would fire her rear end.

Don't let that happen, she ordered herself. *Be professional. Just professional.*

"So, he's good with numbers?" Rachel said. "Kind of an accountant type?" That sounded safe. Good.

Ruby laughed. "If you're thinking you can take the edge off of a man like Shane by slapping a label on him, good luck with that. He'll still be just as much of a heartbreaker. Besides, he's got those smoldering eyes."

He did. "I hadn't noticed."

Her comment was followed immediately by the sound of a car door slamming, and Rachel nearly dropped a cup. In less than a minute those smoldering eyes were staring at her and Ruby. He hadn't knocked, but then, this *was* an inn.

"Ready?" Shane asked in that deep voice of his.

No. But that was the wrong answer. "Yes, just as soon as I finish up here. I owe Ruby big-time."

"That's okay. You run along," Ruby said.

At the same time Shane said, "All right. I'll wait."

"Thank you," Rachel said in her best prim employee voice.

"Well, then, did you eat already, Shane?" Ruby asked.

"I did."

"Could you eat again? If you had to make your own breakfast, you probably ate something disgusting."

A brief but wide smile flitted across Shane's face, revealing those devastating dimples before it disappeared. Rachel tried not to stare, sure that Ruby was watching her to see her reaction. No man should be allowed to look that good.

"I wouldn't want to trouble you."

"If your memory hasn't failed you, you'll know that there's always something on the stove here. Sit down and eat."

Shane moved toward the table. "Thank you."

Uh-oh, Rachel thought. Shane was a big eater and Ruby was a really good cook. What would he think when he had to eat Rachel's cooking? How soon would he fire her? She hoped she could at least make a few dollars before that happened. Maybe enough to get her a few miles closer to her destination.

Behind her, she could hear the clatter of dishes and the sound of a chair scraping against the floor as Shane sat down behind her. Rachel rubbed the dishes dry. When she was finished, she turned around to find

Shane already waiting for her. This time when he asked if she was ready she couldn't put off the inevitable.

Rachel Everly wasn't thrilled about this job. That much was clear to Shane as they got in his truck and drove toward the ranch. He'd never seen anyone take so much time drying a dish.

Not that he blamed her. If he'd been caught flat broke and forced to earn his way home he wouldn't be thrilled, either. Plus, Ruby was a colorful storyteller. There was no telling what she had told Rachel. There were plenty of stories circulating about him, and he didn't exactly shine in any of them. Some of them dealt with things he didn't want to think about. Most, if not all of them, were true.

Not that Rachel's enthusiasm for the task mattered. It was just a job that needed to be done, and the sooner they waded in, the sooner both of them could be free of the ranch, Moraine and each other. They might as well hit the ground running.

"You might want to pay attention to which direction we're headed," he said after a few minutes. "Some of these country roads aren't marked all that well, and it's easy to get turned around. You'll need to know how to get back to Ruby's."

He felt rather than saw her turn to him. "Is it close enough to get there on foot?"

"Only if you're a horse and you have a lot of time." Shane might not want to get to know this woman, but the fact that she had a habit of saying things that forced him to hold back his smile wasn't a good thing. He'd meant it when he'd said he didn't want there to be anything personal about this situation. He was here to cut the final cords that bound him to this place, and when he left he never wanted to look back again. So, there was no way he'd allow himself to do anything he might regret. Not this time.

"I don't understand," she said.

"You need to know the area, because there may be times when I'll be out on the far reaches of the ranch and won't be able to drive you back to Ruby's when it's time for you to go home. Or you might need to pick up supplies. At any rate, there are a lot of vehicles at the ranch. Hopefully, we'll find one that'll run and you can borrow it. Do you drive stick?"

There was a slight hesitation. "I do now."

"That'll do. I'll show you the basics."

He felt rather than saw her nod. "And you'll be very specific about what my job entails, won't you?"

"It pretty much just entails basic cleanup work and a few photos."

"And cooking, Mr. Merritt." She was clutching the handle of the door.

He frowned. "Shane. Just Shane. I'm not sure what Ruby told you, but I know she's a good storyteller and a romantic. Just so you know, you've got nothing to fear from me. I really meant it when I said that there would be nothing personal involved in this job."

Now he had her attention. She sat up straighter. "I never thought otherwise."

"You're practically ripping the handle off the door."

Immediately she released it as if it were on fire. "Sorry. I guess it's just being in unfamiliar territory. I'm a city girl and I've never been on a ranch."

"I see." But, remembering her rather magnificent tirade in the street yesterday and her long walk down the empty road, she didn't strike him as the type who was afraid of grass, fences and trees. Still, given the fact that she was stuck in Moraine and broke, she had other reasons to want to hold on tight to something, he supposed. Not that it was any of his concern.

"And in case it wasn't clear yesterday," she said, interrupting his thoughts, "you don't have to worry about me, either. I'll be totally professional. I'm not the type who has romantic notions. I'm not pining for a cowboy. I don't date people I work with. For the foreseeable future, I'm not dating anyone. If I'm slightly tense, it has nothing to do with anything Ruby may have said. I'm just getting my bearings."

"Point taken. I apologize for thinking that Ruby might have told you something that made you apprehensive."

She turned toward him then, her dark hair brushing across her cheek. He had a feeling she wanted to tell him that she wasn't afraid of anything.

"Excuse me, but Ruby said… Have you really been in jail?" she asked, surprising him.

As if a door had been opened, old bad memories rushed in. "Yes." No point in denying it, but he knew his tone said *back off.*

"Sorry. That was pretty rude of me, but I needed to know," she said. "I have a bad habit of being slightly impulsive and too direct. *Probing* is the way one person put it."

Great. He'd wanted an uncomplicated quick fix and he'd ended up with a woman who was going to pry into parts of his life that were open to no one, including himself.

"I'll work on curbing that. Just tell me if I get out of line," she said.

"Don't worry. I will." That was a promise.

For some reason, despite his grating tone, she seemed

to relax a bit, studying the landscape. They passed the timbered entrance gates to the Bella Bryce Ranch. A few miles down the road were the modest iron gates of the Regal R. Shane could sense Rachel's curiosity, though she kept silent. But when he turned in at Oak Valley, with its huge timbers with carved oak leaves climbing up and curling around the letters, she turned to him. "This looks big. It's all yours?"

Somehow that made it sound too personal. "Yes, I'm the sole owner of Oak Valley Ranch." Which was all wrong. He'd never wanted it, it should never have been his, and there were plenty of people who would agree with him on that.

"And yet you're selling it?"

Her voice was incredulous. He tried not to frown, but it was difficult. He didn't want to have to explain the whys and wherefores, what his life had been like growing up here, what had happened later and why he could never stay.

"I guess," she said, "if you lived in a place all your life, this would seem like no big deal?" Clearly she was trying to deal with his frown. "And even though this is your home—"

"It's not my home." His voice came out a bit too harsh.

His comment was met by silence. *Idiot*. Why had he cut her off and said something that made this seem even more personal? She was just here to do a job. He wasn't going to expose her to his history.

"I lived here most of my life, ever since I was three, but I've been gone for ten years and these days I run a business that keeps me on the move. I live in a lot of different places." He hoped that explanation was enough to satisfy her.

"That works for you? Living in so many different places?"

Yes. Hell, yes. "It suits me perfectly. I was made to be on the move."

"Not me," she said, shaking her head, her long dark curls sliding against her shoulders. "Not at all. The one thing I want is my very own home in my favorite place. Maine. Same place all the time."

He chanced a closer look at her and found that she had turned toward him. Those pretty brown eyes were intense, more than he would have expected given her casual lead-in questions. What must have happened to her to cause that kind of raw longing for a roots-buried-deep home of her own?

His curiosity must have been written on his face, because an enticing trace of pink painted her cheeks and dipped deep into the collar of her white shirt. Immediately a smoky trail of heat slipped through his body.

That wasn't good. He was her boss. She was his employee. He needed to start acting more like an employer and help her get her bearings.

"You said you were a city girl. So, if you have any questions, feel free to ask."

"About ranching?"

"About whatever you need to know."

"You might be sorry you said that."

He had no doubt she was right. He'd seen Rachel in action, stranding herself in Moraine when a man had wronged her. She'd been magnificent, but perhaps a bit impulsive. He'd already been treated to one or two of her more impulsive questions. And he had fences. High fences with padlocks.

"There's a good chance I might not answer every question in the way you'd like," he warned.

She nodded. "That's okay. You're my boss. You're allowed to tell me to slow down, to stop. You can tell me no."

There was that dreaded heat again. Shane wanted to groan. *No* wasn't the word he thought of when he looked at her. Certainly not *slow down*.

It occurred to him that he probably hadn't been dating enough of late if he was having these kinds of erotic thoughts about a woman who made him cringe with half of what came out of her mouth. It also occurred to him that he was going to have to watch himself. She was in his care now. That made him responsible for her well-being, and having the wrong kinds of thoughts about her wasn't allowed. The good thing was that their relationship wouldn't last long.

He only hoped she was going to get the house in order quickly, had some skills with that camera, and knew her way around a stove.

Rachel wished she could relax a bit. Discovering that she and her boss had different goals had been freeing, but she was still far too aware of him. Maybe it had something to do with the emptiness of the land they were traversing. She and Shane appeared to be the only two people within miles.

The thing was, she'd meant it when she'd told him that she wasn't a romantic. She'd been very young when she'd first learned that relationships weren't made to last forever and that a promise given wasn't necessarily a promise kept. Her grown up relationships had only served as more proof.

But, darn it, there was just something about Shane

that made a woman want to…to look at him. Closely. It was disconcerting. She had never been a very physical kind of woman. Lust had not been a part of her life. The fact that she was even having these kinds of thoughts was totally alarming.

So don't look. Get to work, she ordered herself. *Do something to create some distance.*

"So, Mr. Merritt, you have three weeks. What needs to be done during that time?" she asked casually, just as if she hadn't been thinking about what Shane looked like underneath his shirt.

He raised a brow. "Shane," he said, correcting her once again."

She nodded. "Got it. Shane." So much for distance.

"The ranch has been vacant for a while," he said. "Things have deteriorated. The hay didn't get cut, so that has to be done and then reseeded. At a minimum, fences have to be mended, buildings have to be repaired, irrigation systems checked out, weeds controlled. As I mentioned earlier, the house needs cleaning. The place has to look inviting if I'm going to be able to sell it quickly, and it has to be sold. Once it's in marketable condition, I'll ask you to take a few photos. We'll list it anywhere we can and end with an open house, followed by an auction if we haven't had any offers before then. Basically, we're getting the ranch show ready, not necessarily ranch-ready."

"The hay is for show?"

"Hay in the field will be more attractive. It's one less thing the new owners will have to worry about when winter comes and they need to feed their animals."

Rachel nodded. Once the two of them stopped talking, that sense of being alone with Shane in a world separated from everything else hit her again. "It's so quiet here other than the birds," she said. "You don't seem to have any animals. No cows or sheep or…whatever else a ranch has. I don't know. Llamas? Bison? Doesn't a ranch have to have animals? Aren't they what make a ranch…a ranch?"

He almost smiled that devastating smile, but—thank goodness—he put it away before she'd even gotten a good look. "Yes, most ranches have animals, but this one is for sale, and no one's been here since…it's been a while." She didn't miss that slight stumble, or the momentary pain that had flared in his eyes.

"When I inherited the ranch, I wasn't prepared to deal with the situation, so I just let things sit for the most part. Except you can't just let cattle sit unattended. I hired someone to sell them off."

"All of them?"

"All the cattle, yes. As for the horses…"

"Of course. You had horses, too."

"I still have them." He looked a bit sheepish at that. "I wanted to personally handle that bit, so I had them stabled in the next county."

"Is it nicer in the next county? Better grass or something? I mean…I know I don't know anything about ranching, but…why there when there were all those ranches we passed?"

He shrugged. "You were right. Better grass."

She could tell he was lying and that he didn't care if she knew it. He obviously had a reason and she, as his employee, wasn't entitled to it. Rachel zipped her lips. She had probably been talking too much, asking too many questions. It was a bad habit she'd developed early in life, the result of having to get to know large groups of people quickly.

Still, as they came over a rise and she saw a building in the distance, she couldn't help asking, "Is that it? The house…or…? I don't know much about ranches. Aren't there sometimes multiple buildings?"

"There are other buildings, but none of this size. Yes, that's the house." There didn't seem to be an ounce of pride in his voice.

Rachel understood why as they drew closer. She felt she should say something, but she wasn't quite sure what to say without sounding critical. "It's…it's an impressive building," she tried, which was no lie. In fact, it must have been very impressive at one time. A long, sprawling white building that looked as if it had been added onto multiple times, it dominated the land and looked out onto the mountains. But the paint was barely there, the chimneys were crumbling and there were porch boards that had worn through. A lone shutter clung to the side of one window, dangling at a crooked angle.

Shane stopped the truck, and he and Rachel got out. They walked up to the house and he opened the door, reaching around her. His arm brushed her sleeve, ever so slightly, and it was all she could do not to suck in a deep breath. Just that one little touch had called up such a giant reaction in her. How ridiculous. How unlike her. How unnerving.

Get your act together, Rachel, she ordered.

"My apologies." Had the darn man read her thoughts?

"No big deal," she said, as if his nearness didn't even affect her. "Could you…? If this is going to be my workspace, I'd like to see the rest of the house, please."

"Prepare yourself," was his response. And when she stepped over the threshold, Rachel understood why.

They took a quick tour, their steps ringing off the wood in the cavernous emptiness of most of the house. Dust and cobwebs lay over everything Shane hadn't already touched. There were no curtains at the windows, and one of the panes was broken. In the rooms that were furnished, Rachel noted that the furniture had probably been old when Shane was a boy. The kitchen appliances might have appeared in old horror movies, and all of the light fixtures looked questionable. Despite the condition of the house, or maybe because of it, Shane was moving quickly and they had soon covered all but one of the rooms. "I just want to fix it enough to sell it," he said.

"How about this room?" she asked, nodding toward the one room they hadn't gone in.

"Don't worry about that one," he said. "It was my younger brother Eric's."

Rachel smiled. "You think he's going to mind if I take a peek?"

Shane trapped her gaze with his own. "No. The ranch belonged to him. Now it's mine."

And he had apparently inherited it, which meant that his brother was dead.

Rachel wanted to drop her gaze. She didn't. "I'm sorry for your loss." She didn't say that she was sorry for her light comment. She hadn't known. He hadn't told her.

"I'm sorry, too," was all he said. "We'll leave that room alone for now."

But eventually, if he was going to sell the house—and he'd made it clear that he was—even that room would have to be fixed.

"Your call," she said. "You're the boss."

"Where that room is concerned...yes." And she was

only the employee. It would be good to remember that and not ask too many questions or get carried away. In any way. For once in her life she should learn to keep her mouth shut and not go poking at things with sticks. Because it was a good bet that if she poked Shane she might get a reaction she couldn't handle.

"Not going to happen," she muttered beneath her breath.

"Excuse me?" She looked up to find herself pinned by those awesome, fierce eyes.

"It looks as if there's a lot that needs to be done before you'll want to have an open house, even if you're only going for show ready," she said. And there was no hiding from the fact that she had zero experience of the types of things he needed doing. Her life had been a lot of moving. There'd never been a home she could call her own, let alone take care of. Her food had mostly been institutional, and when it hadn't been it had still been prepared by someone else.

"Rachel?"

She looked up into Shane's silver-blue eyes and saw…concern. Uh-oh. She'd shown her hand, hadn't she?

"Yes?" The word came out a bit too soft.

She almost thought he swore beneath his breath. He was standing so close she had to look up. She could feel his warmth. His gaze passed over her, and she could barely breathe.

"If you've decided you don't want the job, tell me now."

Oh, no. Here she'd trusted him and already he was firing her. "I need the job," she said, hoping she didn't sound too pathetic.

"Fair enough. I'll help with the heavy lifting."

The thought of having him in close proximity lifting things for her made her palms feel clammy. She felt awkward and fidgety. "I know I'm short, but I'm capable of doing this myself," she said, but she didn't know who she was trying to convince. Him or herself.

And, since she had punctuated her sentence by swiping a finger across a bit of woodwork in a dramatic swoop, she now had dust all over her fingers. She started to close her hand into a fist so that he wouldn't see what an idiot she'd been, but it was too late. Shane pulled a navy bandana from his pocket, cupped her hand in his own much larger one and gently wiped the dust away.

When he released her, her hand tingled, even though he had barely touched her.

It occurred to her that working with Shane would be a much bigger challenge than how to approach these chores she was so ill prepared for. Still, if she could bulldoze her way through and do the job quickly, if he could sell this place fast, she could get back to civilization and Maine, where there were no dangerous cowboy bosses. She hoped.

"Ever been to Maine?" she asked.

"Your favorite place," he remarked.

"Yes. And it's also my future, the place I intend to build my dreams."

He nodded at that. "I wish you luck. I really do, even though I'm not a big believer in dream-building. I'm strictly practical. As for Maine, I've been there, but not in years. No reason to show up there anymore."

Rachel felt a little pool of relief slip right through her. She would never cross paths with Shane once she left here. Oh, yes. Maine was looking better every minute.

CHAPTER THREE

"I'LL move everything out of the dining room so you can get started in there in a little bit, but for now let's take care of transportation for you," Shane said. It was time to move things along. Just dive in and get the preliminaries over so that he and Rachel could start the job in earnest. The sooner they started, the sooner they ended.

"That works for me," she said.

That seemed like a pretty enthusiastic response, considering how much had happened to her during the last day and given the terrible condition of the house. It had been going downhill ever since his mother had died many years ago, but he just hadn't cared. Now he had to, for several reasons. One of them was standing beside him, looking pale and scared but determined. He was lucky Rachel hadn't run out the door screaming. Many women—or men—would have walked rather than face this disaster.

He was grateful that she hadn't asked him more about Eric's room. He had taken everything that had belonged to his mother and Eric and locked the past away in that room. Sooner or later he'd have to face those memories, but not today. Or tomorrow. Or any day real soon.

"This way to the garage," he said as she followed him. "So driving stick will be a new experience for you? All right, let's see what we can find that you'll like."

"I'm not fussy. Dependable is more important than anything, I'd guess. You have some long, lonely stretches of road."

"Good point. Dependable it is." He led her out to a big gray building and pulled open the wide double doors.

For a second there was silence, just the birds and the insects chirping away. "Um…there are ten cars here," Rachel said.

"I know."

"That one in the back looks as if it's from another era."

"It is. It's a Duesenberg. Probably doesn't run very well."

She gave him a look. "Isn't that some sort of collector's item?"

"For those who collect, yes."

"And it's sitting there covered in cobwebs?"

"That's about the shape of it."

Rachel tilted her head, looking at him quizzically. "What?" he asked.

"Nothing. Just…I've known some people with money in my lifetime. Most of them like to flaunt it. If one of them had a Duesenberg they would be bringing it up in conversations, maybe have a print of it hanging somewhere in the house."

Shane shrugged. The Duesenberg had been his stepfather's pride and joy. Next to the ranch, of course. "I'm not much into collecting cars." Or ranches.

"Fair enough. What are you into?"

Kissing women with pretty brown eyes that snap when the woman is angry or nervous or that sparkle when the woman is amused. Stupid thought.

Keep it simple, Merritt, he reminded himself. *No complications. This woman is the serious type. That makes her off-limits.*

"Not a collector at all. I'm more into the working parts."

She looked suddenly self-conscious. Had he said something suggestive? Maybe he had, given how low his voice had dropped. "Of a car, that is. Engines. Systems. How things are engineered. The technical stuff." He flipped open the hood on the nearest car. "Not exactly looking good here." And neither were any of the others. "But I think I can get one of these two to run." He gestured toward the black sedan and the red sports car.

"Black is very practical and so is a sedan," she said. But somehow he could practically see her dancing on her toes when she looked at the sports car.

"I've always been partial to red myself," he found himself saying. *Why had he said that? What was that about? He was not a guy who gave a lot of weight to the color of his car, and given the choice of black or red he probably would have chosen black every time.*

"I don't know. Red seems flashy. I'm just the house-keeper. I should be practical."

"Are you always practical?"

As if he'd turned on a switch, she flushed straight down to the roots of those pretty brown tresses. "Not especially. Hardly ever."

Ah, now he saw. She'd been lectured about it, too, he was pretty sure. He wondered if that guy she'd been with had been the one who'd chided her about her impractical tendencies. "I'm fairly confident that the red one is in better shape." He wasn't. Not at all. And why was he doing this?

No clue. Certainly not because he was interested in the woman. That wasn't true. At all. Was it? Maybe it was just because if he thought about Rachel's situation he wouldn't have to think about his own and how being back here was like walking over eggshells filled with bad memories. If he didn't tread lightly, the shells would break and the memories would spill out. Concentrating on Rachel was easier, especially since there was no chance he'd ever get close enough to her to turn her into another bad memory. Yeah, that was probably it.

"Let's get the car running," he suggested.

In the end he had to make a phone call to Somesville in the next county for a rush delivery of a new battery, some spark plugs and fluids. In spite of the fact that he hadn't looked under the hood of a car since he'd left Moraine, all those years of keeping the engines here running had done the trick and he was sure that there was nothing major wrong with the cars. The biggest problem once he'd started appeared to be Rachel herself.

"Let me help, Shane. This is ridiculous. You're lending me a car, and here I am just standing around being useless. What can I do to help? Show me."

He looked at her pale blue slacks and white blouse and then at the greasy rag he was holding. "You'll get dirty."

She got a grim look on her face. "I'm not just some helpless female who fears dirt and spends all her time primping to make people think I look good." Then she put her hands on her hips and all he could think about for several seconds was how curvy her hips were and how good she really did look.

"I never said you were like that," he said, frowning at his own too-male reaction.

For one brief second she looked chagrined. "Sorry. You didn't. It's just that...I've known a few of those women. I...let's just say that it's a pet peeve of mine. And, really, I want to lend a hand. You're my boss. I should help."

"All right. Let's see what we can find to keep the grease off you." He began to open the drawers to the storage cabinets looking for some old shop aprons that might still be lying around. The cabinets were disorganized, not quite as bad as the house, but close.

"How about this?" Rachel asked, and he looked up to see that she was holding a pair of coveralls. Eric's old coveralls.

His heart felt as if someone had just punched him straight in the chest. He opened his mouth to tell her no, but Rachel was already shimmying into the royal blue coveralls, sliding them up over the curve of her hips.

All his objections died in his throat. Every cell in his body went on alert. Everything that was male in him stopped and paid attention as the coveralls that were meant for a stick-straight small male conformed to the perfect roundness of Rachel's rear end, the aged and worn soft material causing it to cling to her in places. The right places—no, the wrong places for a man trying to stay aloof...and sane. For several seconds Shane thought he might have stopped breathing.

And then it got worse. She reached back to find the sleeves, and there was no way he couldn't notice the soft curve of her breasts. It didn't matter that the legs of the coveralls were too long, that she had to roll up the sleeves or that the things barely touched her in places once she was inside them. As she raised the zipper, covering herself, he realized that he hadn't spoken through the whole ordeal…and that he was acting like a man who'd never seen a woman's body before.

Quickly, he ducked under the hood of the car, just barely missing banging his head. "Here," he said, holding out an oil wrench.

To his surprise, city girl Rachel jumped in with both feet. She slid under the dirty car and asked him to explain the basics of emptying the oil pan and removing the filter. She insisted on helping with the spark plugs and the new battery.

When they were done, he looked down to find her smiling. "You'd think we were doing something exciting," he mused.

"It was new for me, and I got one-on-one training. People pay big bucks to take classes in this very thing in my world."

It was the perfect opening to ask a question, find out more about her, discover what her world was like. But he wasn't going there. It was better that he not know too much about her. He needed to keep things impersonal.

"Besides, when I finally make it back to Maine and save enough money to get my own little dream house, maybe with a little clunker car of my own, I might need to know this stuff."

Another perfect opening. He firmed his mouth into a straight line and refused to ask about her dreams. Instead, he simply nodded.

She didn't seem to notice his silence. "But you," she said. "I'm amazed at people who can do what you've just done. You seem to be very good at this," she said, stepping over that line he had laid down and aiming straight for the personal information.

He frowned. "I've done it a lot." But not since he'd left the ranch.

"Is this kind of thing part of your business?"

"Changing the oil in cars?"

Perhaps he'd sounded too incredulous, since the result was a pretty blush that crept up Rachel's neck. This time he refused to look at where the blush disappeared into her coveralls. Not that it mattered. His imagination kicked in as he wondered just how far that blush traveled down her body before he managed to order himself to stop.

"I guess the answer is no," she said. "Ruby said you were very successful. I just thought…you know…do what you love, do what you know…"

"Makes sense," he agreed. "But I run a consulting firm that teaches companies how to use technology more efficiently."

"Oh, yes, the mathematical genius thing Ruby talked about."

"That was always an exaggeration." And it had often been a criticism. Apparently Rachel agreed with the criticism part. Her brow was furrowed.

"Not into math?" he asked, breaking his own rule about personal questions less than a minute after he'd resolved to steer clear of anything that drew them closer to each other in any way. What was it about Rachel that led a man to forget his own rules?

"It's not my best skill," she agreed, "but I admire those who know how to tame numbers and make them do what they want them to. I was just…" Her blush grew. "It's nothing."

"Obviously it's something."

"Nothing important. I'm just divesting myself of another stereotype—the nerdy numbers guy who's not good with women. According to Ruby you've got a reputation with the women here and…"

He pinned her with his gaze, raised a brow.

"Right," she said. "Let's just leave it at that. Not the kind of thing most employees discuss with their bosses, anyway."

But it was becoming obvious to Shane that Rachel didn't have much in common with most employees. Given his inability to just ignore her, or compartmentalize his reaction to her, he probably shouldn't have hired her, but now that he had…

We move on, he thought. *Quickly. Very quickly.* Already he was beginning to associate her with the ranch and Moraine, two places he never intended to think of again once he was gone. Already he could see that she had the kind of dreams a man like him would never fit. The sooner they were through with each other the better.

Rachel had barely arrived back at Ruby's in her borrowed car when Angie from the diner showed up. "Word in town is that you're working for Shane. I just thought I'd better pop in and give you a warning. There will be questions."

Rachel blinked. "About what?"

Ruby and Angie exchanged a glance. "Well, some women will want to know whether he's as devastating as he used to be. Whether he makes you get that fluttery feeling inside when he turns those blue eyes on you and says your name in that deep voice."

"What? No!" Rachel said.

Another glance exchanged by the two women. Clearly they didn't believe her.

"All right, he's good-looking. I'll give you that," Rachel admitted. "And he's kind of…I don't know…"

"Sexy as hell?" Angie suggested. "Yes, I saw him in town. Time hasn't done him any harm. He's definitely swoon-worthy."

"He's attractive," Rachel said, a bit primly. "But I'm just his employee."

Ruby opened her mouth to speak.

"*Just* his employee," Rachel repeated. "I'm not looking for a man."

"Hmm," Angie said. "I heard you just got rid of a bad one yesterday, but Celia Truro said she got a look at that guy and he couldn't hold a candle to Shane in the looks department."

"I wasn't dating Dennis. I was working for him."

"I know, but still…he was the man you were with, and if he was a jerk, tearing him down just a little by comparing him to Shane wouldn't hurt you. Just sayin'."

Rachel tried to look offended, but she ended up smiling. "Okay, Dennis was a jerk, and he didn't have Prince Charming looks. In the end he didn't have Prince Charming anything."

"I know. I can't believe he dumped you right in the street," Ruby said.

"He didn't dump me. I dumped him."

"Good. You were smart to do it. I read a lot of romances. I meet a lot of men in my business," Angie said. "And a truly good man—no matter the relationship—would have at least insisted on giving you a ride to the nearest train, or made sure you had money, or at the very least called someone who could help you.

Heroes don't drive away and leave a woman stuck with no way to get home, no matter what the situation. You don't want to get mixed up with any bad men."

Exactly, Rachel thought, and both Shane and Ruby had already pegged Shane as a man who had done some bad things.

"Now for the even bigger question. Is it true Shane's selling Oak Valley?" Angie asked.

"That's what I'm here for. To help him get it ready to be sold."

Ruby shook her head. "That's a shame. That ranch was the best in the area in its day. He's selling the whole ranch?"

"Every cup and saucer, every blade of grass."

"Everything? I'd really love to see some of that stuff," Angie said. "I've met a few people who worked there for a short time. They said that Shane's mother had some fancy things."

"You've never been there?" Rachel asked.

Another look was exchanged by Ruby and Angie. "Shane's stepfather was a bit of a hermit. Not into having folks over."

"Well, Shane's having an open house when he puts the ranch on the market," Rachel offered.

The women's eyes lit up. "When?" they asked, almost in unison.

"Three weeks. Maybe a little less." After all, one day was already done, and she was pretty sure that if Shane managed to finish up all the work he wouldn't wait to put Oak Valley on the market.

"That's going straight on my calendar," Angie said.

"We'll be there," Ruby declared.

"Lots of people will be there," Angie said. "Oak Valley opening its doors? That will pull people in."

"Hopefully to buy the ranch," Rachel offered.

"Maybe." Ruby looked doubtful. "Not too many people around here who could afford a ranch that size. Most people will just want to see the place."

"And the women will want to drool over Shane," Angie added.

Uh-oh, Rachel thought. Maybe she should have asked Shane before she shared this information. Maybe he'd planned to keep his open house "by invitation only." She doubted he was going to be pleased to know that his new housekeeper had just invited the world to his doorstep to drool and paw.

She hadn't even done one ounce of work for him and already she had given the man a reason to fire her. Other than her utter lack of skills...which he would find out about tomorrow.

Focus, Rachel, focus, she ordered herself the next morning. *Keep your plan in mind. Shane Merritt has nothing to do with your plan, nothing to do with your future.* But she'd spent a good part of yesterday working beside him, and later sitting beside him as he'd coached her through the paces of learning to drive a stick shift.

"Like this?" she'd asked, wrestling with the shift.

"Like this," he'd said, covering her hand with his own as he'd moved the stick through the gears, showing her, guiding her.

Driving her crazy just because he was touching her, even though it was a completely impersonal touch.

"You are an idiot," she whispered between clenched teeth as she put Shane's lessons to use and drove all the way from Ruby's to the ranch, only lurching a little and only stalling the car twice. "Don't start getting any ideas about Shane. Don't you remember what Ruby told you? And don't you remember that you have golden plans for your future?"

Yes, she was finally going to be free to put down roots and have her own life exactly the way she had always wanted it. Where she wouldn't have to move all the time, where she might finally get the chance to settle down and have a real life on her own terms. Doing something as crazy as losing her mind over a man like Shane, who would mess with her dreams and who was so very wrong for a woman like her... Well, she knew better than most people what the consequences of that kind of idiocy would be.

Stop feeling things, she ordered herself.

Simple. Easy. Should be a breeze to pull off as long as she put her mind to it. But the minute she climbed out of the car and Shane walked toward her, all broad shoulders, long denim-clad muscular legs and smoldering eyes, easy flew right out the door.

"Something wrong?" she asked. "Did I...? I didn't get a scratch on your car or anything, did I? I was really careful to park it far away from all the others at the inn."

He shook his head. "The car's fine. You were driving real smooth, too."

An inordinate sense of pride welled up in Rachel and she started to smile. Until she remembered that those were the types of comments Dennis had made about her photos, and he had merely been trying to butter her up so he could use her. Not that there was any question about her being used this time. She was, after all, a hired employee, and as such, Shane was openly using her services...and paying her well for them. And then, too, a compliment was a compliment.

She'd been trained by the best in how to handle compliments.

"Thank you. I appreciate your role in my smooth driving," she said politely. And then, because she had sounded like some of the prim, prissy girls she had known in school, the ones she hadn't liked and who hadn't liked her, she rushed on, "So, there's no problem?"

"Just a holdup. One of the men I'd hired to help out broke his leg yesterday. For a while I thought I was going to have to ride out and look for someone new, but he managed to talk a friend into subbing for him. He'll be here later today. We're all set to get started. A full complement of ranch hands."

Rachel blinked. "Is that what I get to call myself? A ranch hand?" That was a title she'd never thought to own. A bit exotic, at least in the world she'd grown up in. She liked it. "Could be awesome."

He almost cracked a smile, almost showed her those amazing dimples, and he held out his hands in a submissive gesture. "Go for it. Knock yourself out."

"I intend to. Chance of a lifetime. So…I guess I should start tackling the ranch house?"

"I'll just be over at the barn repairing the roof. Shouting distance away and in plain sight if you need me. I'll see you at lunch." Then he was gone. And she was alone with the house.

"And I'm expected to make lunch," she reminded herself. Gulp. *Okay, okay, this is nothing.* Cleaning. Cooking. People did this all the time. Ordinary people did it, and she had always wanted to be just an ordinary person. The kind who lived in the same place all the time and took care of that place, because that was what ordinary people with homes of their own did. This was her chance to have that for a few weeks. She could do it. Shane was counting on her to do it.

So…first things first. Find a computer, look some stuff up. She had wanted to do that last night, but Ruby had been working on her books and Rachel owed her too much to ask her to stop her own work in order to let Rachel access the internet.

Now Rachel headed toward the office she remembered Shane showing her. On her way there she glanced out the window.

And saw Shane climbing off a ladder onto the roof of the barn. He stood there, all male, surveying his territory, a tool belt slung low on his hips. As she watched, he leaned into the tilt of the roof. Casually. Easily. As if he'd done this sort of thing before.

And then he took off his shirt and she saw bronzed muscles. She saw those broad shoulders. Naked.

Her mouth went dry.

At that moment Shane started to turn. In a second he would see her staring at him if he looked this way.

She let out a muffled squeak and jumped back away from the window. Without turning around again, she scurried toward the computer and plopped down in front of it. She stared at the screen.

And remembered what Shane had looked like standing there like the king of the ranch. All male all the time. Ranch guy. A man who could run a company, fix a car or mend a roof without even blinking. The kind of men women lusted over. The girls in the countless boarding schools she'd attended all her life would have gotten into shrieking, calculated battles over a man like that. Her mother would have set out to charm a man like that. And win him…until the newest husband material came along.

"And both of those are just two of the many reasons why you're not interested." She didn't ooze charm. She didn't want to. And anyway, Shane was clearly out of her league. He could have all those charming women, and apparently had already had many.

I'm the housekeeper, she reminded herself. *I'm on the road to my future, to my dream.* And she had better start giving some thought to that future real soon.

"Yeah, just as soon as I figure out the most efficient way to clean a house quickly and how to make something palatable for lunch." A man who had spent the morning pounding nails in a roof would probably have a big appetite when he came in all hot and sweaty.

Rachel tried not to imagine that moment. She hoped Shane had put his shirt back on by then. She hoped he'd be so tired he wouldn't notice any problems with the food.

But first she had to find some food to make and directions on how to make it. Her fingers flew over the keys, their clacking sounding a lot like…desperation.

When Shane walked back into the house, nothing looked that different from the way it had looked that morning…except there seemed to be a few computer printouts lying about. He looked at the one lying beneath the hallway mirror. The Best Way to Clean Mirrors and Windows it read. There was another one on the oak sideboard called How to Make Woodwork Glow along with One Hundred Uses for Vinegar and The Easiest Way to Get Grease Off a Stove. There were more, but just then he heard a loud clatter, followed by, "Juno and Jupiter and…and…oh, darn it!"

"Rachel?" He rushed into the kitchen.

She was standing at the stove, and she whirled

around when he appeared. Red sauce had splattered her white blouse, there were smudges of dust on her cheeks and the light that had been in her eyes this morning had dimmed. She looked…pained.

"Did you hurt yourself?" The words sounded like an accusation. He didn't mean them that way, but his mother's death had begun as an injury. And—no, he wasn't going there.

To stop his thoughts, he slid closer to her and took her hand. He looked her over, searching for burns from the sauce. He reached out and placed two fingers beneath her chin, turning her face from one side to the other. Searching since she still hadn't spoken.

"Rachel, could you please say something? I'm sorry I shouted."

"I can't even make spaghetti. Anyone can make spaghetti. Look, it says so right here," she said, holding up a sauce-splattered computer printout.

She gazed up at him with those big brown eyes that looked so sad and he wanted to waltz her back across the kitchen, lean her against the counter and kiss the sadness from her lips until they tilted up into her sunny smile again.

But that would be mad. It would be bad.

"Who says you can't make spaghetti?" he asked, sounding grumpier than he had intended.

She bit her lip. "I lied about knowing how to do this stuff," she said. "I hate people who lie. Dennis lied. And…lots of people have lied. But I don't. I hate that, but I did this time. I wanted the job."

"Well…wanting things makes everyone do things they regret later. I don't quite recall any lies from you, though." He had to say that, because even though he knew what she was talking about, he hated that forlorn look in her eyes, and he felt partially responsible. He'd suspected her secret and had hired her, anyway. He'd treated her to his frowns, he'd worried about his all-too-male reaction to her, and in an attempt to escape that reaction he'd left her to tackle something she had no experience with. Guilt assailed him, and he already knew way too much about guilt.

Plus, there was no excuse for him having left her feeling so stressed about her duties. As a man who'd trained many people, worked with many employees, he knew the drill. He understood how to make sure people were comfortable in their work before he left them alone to do their jobs.

But with Rachel…he'd walked away because she messed with his senses, wreaked havoc with his resolve. She distracted him, and he seriously couldn't afford to be distracted. Nonetheless—

"I implied that I could cook," she said, cutting into his thoughts. "And that I understood the secrets of housekeeping. I told you that I knew enough, and I tried to convince myself that it wasn't really a lie because *enough* is a relative word."

He couldn't help himself then. She sounded as if she'd just done something truly heinous. And, much as he wanted to build a rock-solid wall between them, to keep all smiles and interaction to a minimum, he couldn't stop himself from smiling. "It *is* a relative word."

"Don't you dare let me off the hook. I have standards, and if I expect others to adhere to them, I have to adhere to them, too."

"All right," he said quietly. "You're entitled to your standards. That's a nice motto to live by, I suppose."

"It's not my own. Ms. Drimmons, Sidson School,

Grade Five. I didn't even realize that I'd absorbed or... stolen her motto."

He smiled more. "Rachel, you don't have to confess *all* your supposed sins to me. Or any of them, for that matter. Plus, as far as sins go, using someone else's motto isn't a very big one. All right?"

"I know that, but put together with my lying—"

"Which I'm not concerned about and we're going to move past, providing you don't tell me any more lies. Anything else I should know?"

She shook her head.

"Okay, then, why don't we look at the spaghetti?"

"It's easy enough to see," she said, wearing that delicious blush he was beginning to look forward to. "There was something in the instructions about flinging a bit against the wall. I think I may have flung too much."

Shane looked to the wall opposite the stove. At least a dozen strands of spaghetti were either making their way down the wall or lying on the floor.

He couldn't keep the amused look off his face.

"It's not funny."

He raised an eyebrow.

"Okay," she conceded. "It is funny, but I'm not laughing."

And then she was chuckling. And so was he. Shane realized that this was the first time he'd laughed since his return to Oak Valley. It felt like a release valve, helping him breathe. And while he knew it was a temporary release, because nothing had changed, for the moment it was welcome.

"Come on, I'll bet the spaghetti is entirely edible." He started toward the stove and she followed him. "The sauce is a little burned on the bottom, because the heat was a little high, but what's on top will be fine."

"I could probably make a meal out of what's on my shirt."

Okay, he could not let that pass, even though everything that was smart and good told him not to look at her shirt.

He looked…and was rewarded with that glorious, enticing blush again. He also realized that she was right. A lot of the sauce had bubbled out of the pan and plopped onto her shirt.

"I'll lend you one of mine," he said. And this time he did the right thing. He locked his senses down and didn't try to imagine Rachel wearing the same shirt that lay against his skin every week.

Instead he handed her a colander to drain the pasta. "Let's eat."

She hesitated. "You're being very generous. I hardly made any headway on the house, and this isn't the meal you had every right to expect. Why aren't you firing me?"

He hesitated. He didn't want to examine his motives too closely. But an answer that was just as true as any other reason slipped out. "You're trying, you're working. That's the truth, and…there's one more truth."

She looked up at him, waiting.

"For reasons I don't want to discuss, I never wanted to come back to Oak Valley and Moraine. Being here is barely tolerable. But…you're an incredibly interesting person. You distract me from things I don't want to think about."

And now those brown eyes widened. "I…distract you?"

"Yes." He wasn't saying more. He'd said too much. He hoped he hadn't been wrong to tell her that.

"Shane?"

"Let's eat," he said, changing the subject. "And then let's get back to work. This afternoon I might need you to take some photos. I assume you do know how to use that Hasselblad?"

Good. She'd raised her chin. He preferred a defiant Rachel to a sad one. Sparring with her, he had to keep his wits about him. That kept him from thinking too much about touching her.

Rachel felt much calmer now that she was back on familiar territory. For half a second she wondered if Shane knew that and had thrown out the topic of photography to help her get her bearings. But, no, she had never shared just how passionate she was about photography with anyone, not even Dennis, who had been a photographer himself. She'd learned as a child that being overly passionate about something sometimes invited criticism, even laughter or derision. Still, she was grateful for the chance to do something she understood even if she still had a lot to learn before she would feel that she had even come close to mastering her craft.

"You're safe," she said. "I know how to take photos. I'm not a pro by a long shot, but you won't have to go looking for someone else as long as you don't need anything too involved."

"Just basic shots," he agreed.

"And these basic shots...they're of the barn you're working on? Of the house?"

"A few of those, and some of the other landmarks on the ranch. Also I'd like some of the horses." Had his voice warmed just a little? Maybe. Maybe not. His expression gave nothing away.

Rachel wasn't nearly as successful at concealing her feelings. "You're bringing the horses back?" She couldn't help smiling.

"You like horses?"

"I—I don't know. That is, of course I've seen them, and they're beautiful, but I've never actually spent time with any. Still, they'll add some life to the ranch, won't they? I mean…it's beautiful, but so quiet. Lonely."

"You don't like solitude?"

"I do. Sometimes." But not too much. She'd spent too much of her life alone, or essentially alone. When she finally settled in Maine she wanted neighbors and friends she could keep for the long haul. But she hadn't started this topic to discuss her own past or preferences. She'd been trying to be practical, for once.

"It just seems that a ranch would sell better and faster if it had horses," she said. She remembered what Ruby and Angie had said about there not being many potential buyers around here.

"You're probably right. And horses are more than just beautiful creatures who'll help sell the ranch. They're useful, loyal and more. I'll teach you to ride," he said with a sudden devastating smile.

Oh, boy, there it was, that guy Ruby had referred to, the one who could talk a girl out of her clothes and her common sense, even though she knew he didn't have a thing to offer her.

"For practical purposes," he clarified. "Eventually I'll want you to take a few photos of some of the more remote areas of the ranch where there are no roads."

A vision of herself and Shane riding side by side through a meadow, stopping to water their animals while he reached up and helped her from her horse, sliding her down the length of his body, came to her. Darn it, why did she suddenly feel so hot? Was she blushing? And why did she always have to have such a vivid imagination? It made her feel things she shouldn't feel and long for things that just weren't smart. Sometimes she craved impossible things. Like now.

Trying to shut down her imagination, she fell back on her years of boarding school training. She knew how to make polite responses in her sleep. "I'll look forward to it."

The part of her that had conjured up that ridiculously foolish vision agreed completely with her statement. But the part of her that insisted on reality and truth knew that, as enchanted as she was with the idea of horses and riding horses, Shane was never in this lifetime going to get her up on one of those mammoth creatures.

She sure hoped he had an ATV stashed in the back of the garage somewhere. If she had to get somewhere remote she could probably manage one of those.

But horses were definitely out. In a minute, or maybe in a day, she'd have to tell him that. That and the fact that all of Moraine was probably going to show up on his doorstep for the open house…if they didn't storm the ranch and arrive sooner. A sudden vision of scantily clad women trying to look inside Shane's house or get a glimpse of his muscles and blue eyes slammed its way into Rachel's consciousness.

"Are you okay, Rachel?" Shane asked.

No, I'm clearly going insane if I'm worrying about other women coveting my employer, she thought. *My employer. My employer. Nothing more, Everly. You*

*don't want a man. Any man. Especially not a man with
as much potential heartbreak written into his DNA as
Shane Merritt. Remember that.*

"Rachel?"

"I'm sorry. I'm fine," she said. "Just planning out
my afternoon." Which wasn't a lie, because this afternoon her plan was to completely stop thinking of
Shane as a man and think of him only as her boss. Or,
better yet, not at all.

CHAPTER FOUR

RACHEL was down on her knees with a bucket of soapy water and a sponge trying to put her "don't think about Shane" plan into action. She was trying not to think about how her entire body had gone hot and steamy when Shane had tucked his fingers beneath her chin yesterday. She was trying to pretend that an almost painful glow of gratitude hadn't warmed her heart when he'd been so understanding about her lack of domestic skills. The thing was…she wanted to trust him.

The other thing was…she didn't trust her own judgment. She'd been known to trust the wrong people, Dennis being the latest example, so wanting to trust Shane would be super-dumb. Shane had a bad reputation.

She scrubbed harder at a worn bit of linoleum. She put her back into it.

"That must be some stain," a feminine voice said.

Rachel turned to see a curly-haired woman standing in the doorway, holding two young children by the hands.

Rachel got to her feet and stepped forward. "Can I help you with something?"

The woman smiled and laughed. "I think it's supposed to be the other way around. If you're Rachel,

Shane sent me to help you. I'm Marcia. My husband, Hank, is going to be working for Shane the next few weeks. We've been living with Hank's parents in the next county, and they're wonderful, but the space is tight. The fact that Shane's lending us a cabin on the edge of his property will be a vacation for all of us."

"I'm glad to meet you, Marcia," Rachel said, returning the smile. It was, after all, impossible not to smile at the woman. She looked happy to be here. And when Marcia looked down at the little boy by her side and told him that he needed to not interrupt when people were speaking she said it gently and with obvious love in her voice.

Still, Rachel retraced her thoughts to the other woman's earlier comment. "Shane sent you to help me?"

Because he clearly didn't think she could handle things by herself.

"Just for today," Marcia said. "While you and I both get settled and he makes sure the cabin is ready. He'd planned for a single man, and he wants to add some safety features now that children will be staying there. These, by the way, are my children, Ella and Henry. They're both four."

And both adorable, she might as well have said. Ella had huge blue eyes that seemed to take everything in all at once, and Henry had the cutest little cowlick, which was just about all of him Rachel could see right now. Now that Rachel had moved forward, he was hiding behind his mother's leg.

"It's so nice to meet you, Ella and Henry. If your mom is going to be nice enough to lend me a hand, we'd better find something interesting for you to do. I'm pretty sure I saw some blocks around here somewhere."

Marcia blinked. "I'm new to the area, but when Hank got the call this morning I asked him about Oak Valley and…you have toys? I didn't know there were any children here."

"There aren't," Rachel said, just as if she knew a lot about this ranch. "And they're not exactly regular building blocks. More like sanded down pieces of wood. Maybe from when Shane was growing up. I've been told he was good at mathematical things, making things, engineering things. But no one's using them now. Would it be all right if Ella and Henry played with them? After you've checked them over, of course. I don't have much experience with children, so I'd want to make sure they passed the Mom safety test."

"I would love that," Marcia said. "We had to throw things together in a hurry and already I've lost track of which box I threw the toys in. Not to mention that other people's toys are always more interesting than what you have at home."

Rachel pulled out the box she'd found in a cabinet, revealing its contents. The pieces inside really did look like building blocks, but very unusual ones. They were carved in intricate shapes that locked together, the wood polished smooth.

"They're beautiful," Marcia said. "Maybe Shane won't want the kids to touch them."

Rachel considered that. "No. Shane has told me that he's selling everything here, lock, stock and barrel. He hasn't forbidden me to use anything." Except she wasn't to enter Eric's room. But that bit of information wasn't for sharing, not even with someone as nice as Marcia.

Within minutes, the two little cherubs were playing with the blocks of wood. Ella looked up at Rachel with excited eyes, and Henry's little body was wiggling with excitement. "We got goats," he said.

Rachel must have looked confused, because Marcia smiled. "Henry must really like you. We have a Nigerian dwarf goat, only one, and she's his pride and joy, a present for them being so good when we dragged them across the country. He's very possessive, so the fact that he would even share this bit of information with you is surprising."

"That's so exciting, Henry. I've seen some pictures of goats like that. They're awesome," Rachel said.

"Tunia," Ella explained.

"Ah, your goat's name is Petunia. I see."

Ella's smile lit up her whole little face.

"You got it," Marcia said with a laugh. "Most people don't understand little-people talk and want to know what kind of name Tunia is."

"It's a great name. I really like it," Rachel insisted, and Henry, who was trying to connect two pieces of wood, paused to show her his approval with a tiny smile that made her heart flip. Given the fact that she had decided she wasn't ever going to repeat her parents' horrific mistakes and marry, she would never have an Ella or Henry of her own, so moments like this were rare gifts.

"So, let me help you with this house," Marcia offered, and Rachel gratefully accepted.

The two women dove into work, Rachel peppering Marcia with questions and mentally recording the answers. By the time Shane showed up to announce that the cabin was now child-safe and Marcia could put the children down for a nap without worrying that they could get into anything dangerous when they got out of bed, the kitchen and dining rooms were both gleaming.

Even if there was still a lot that needed repairing and dressing up in both of those areas.

Rachel thanked Marcia and knelt down to whisper in both Ella and Henry's ears. "All right?" she finished.

Both of them nodded.

"Because, you know, this is Shane's ranch, and Petunia is going to love it here, so I think we should tell him that he's very lucky to be the landlord of someone as special as Petunia."

"Ella, Henry? You have another sister?" Shane asked, widening his eyes and dropping down to one knee, making himself less big and man-scary. Rachel remembered being very afraid of tall men when she was as young as these two.

Ella giggled. Henry shook his head emphatically. "Goat," he said.

"Goat," Ella echoed. "Tunia."

"Ah, I see," Shane said. "Well, then, I'm honored that you would bring Petunia to my ranch. I hope she—and you—like it here."

"Box," Henry said, making all of the adults frown with concentration.

But Rachel's mind was flipping through all the possibilities. "Did you like playing with Shane's blocks?"

Henry nodded emphatically, but Rachel saw that Shane was looking at the box of blocks as if he'd seen a ghost. "I thought those were long gone," he said.

Marcia and Rachel exchanged a look. Had she been wrong to let the children play with them? Had they—?

"I...thought I'd misplaced those. I'm glad you had fun with them," Shane said to Henry.

Not long after that, everyone said their goodbyes. Soon Rachel was alone with Shane.

"That was a good save," she told Shane. "Were the

blocks supposed to be off-limits? Were they...your brother's? I'm sorry. I should have asked if it was all right for the children to use them."

"No. You were right. It's scary for kids that young to come to a new place. I'm glad you pulled out the blocks."

"They look handmade."

He stared directly into her eyes. "A guy has to have something do to with his hands when he's closed up inside in the winter."

Which led Rachel to look down at Shane's big strong hands. She swallowed hard. She tried not to imagine those hands on her body.

"How old were you when you made them?"

"Twelve."

"Twelve? Only twelve?"

He shrugged. "It began because I'd broken the law. I took the principal's car for a joyride."

"At twelve," she said, more shocked than she wanted to let on.

"I was an unpleasant boy," he admitted. "Anyway, despite everyone in town thinking he was crazy, he agreed not to press charges and instead put me to work helping do odd jobs at the school. He saw my fascination with the woodworking tools for the shop class, and when my punishment was over, he showed me how to use them even though they were usually reserved for older students. The blocks you saw were more a learning process than anything."

She nodded. "I know some people might think that that was a light sentence, but your principal sounds like a wise man."

"He was. He's long gone, but he was the best man I ever knew."

Which must say something about Shane's relationship with his stepfather. But that was none of her business, was it? Because she and Shane weren't friends. He was her boss. And only her boss.

"I hope you'll be happy to hear that Marcia helped me make some food that won't kill you. At least not too quickly. I'll be home before you start to feel the effects," she said, trying for a lighter tone to slam herself back into the role of employee.

He chuckled, the serious look in his eyes fading away. "You're pretty saucy for a cook."

"Oh, I'm more than a cook," she said, heading for the stove. "With Marcia's and the internet's help, I now know how to clean a floor that you can lie down on wearing a white suit. This morning I was nothing. Tonight I am a woman with housecleaning superpowers. Or…at least I know enough about housecleaning to make sure you won't die of dirt poisoning."

She stopped and whirled around to face him and found that he had been walking behind her. He had been right on her heels, and now they were almost toe to toe. When she tipped her head up, his mouth was only inches above hers. His blue eyes were doing that wonderful smoldering thing that made her tingle.

He reached down as if to place his palms on her biceps, then dropped his arms to his sides. "Don't make me like you too much, Rachel. I don't want to do something we'll both regret."

Her heart was beating like some wild, out-of-control drum. She could barely breathe. "I don't want to do anything I'll regret, either," she whispered.

He groaned. He reached out and touched her hair, smoothing back a strand that had crept out of the ponytail she'd been wearing while she worked. Just that one barely-there caress sent shock waves through her entire body and nearly sent her over the edge. She bit back a moan, closed her eyes. She placed one hand on his chest, and she had no clue whether she was trying to push herself away from him or whether she simply had to feel his heart pounding beneath her palm.

But he must have assumed the first. "Open your eyes, Rachel," he whispered, taking a big step away. Cool air slipped over her now empty palm. "I'm not going to touch you. I know you have serious trust issues. You know I have issues, too. One of them being the fact that I'm going to be gone in less than three weeks, and nothing is going to stop me from going. This project has to be done—this house will be sold even if I have to drop the price to nothing. And once I leave Moraine I'm never coming back."

"Me, either," she whispered. Even though she suspected that he was running away from an old life and she was trying to run to a new one. Either way, they were just together now on a very temporary pass.

She took a step back herself. "We should eat," she said.

So they sat. They ate.

"It's good," Shane told her.

It wasn't, but it wasn't horrible. And anyway, she mused, after she had returned to Ruby's, after the initial taste she hadn't registered a single bite she'd taken. Because she'd realized how close she'd come today to crossing a line that couldn't be crossed.

Despite years of avoiding the kind of relationship that had made her life a misery, she had wanted Shane to touch her. She had craved the taste of his lips so intensely that it was a miracle she hadn't shoved him down and had her kissing way with him.

Only Shane's resolve had saved her. Because if he hadn't backed off…well, she had the worst feeling that he could have told her anything, asked for anything, and despite the fact that she didn't actually trust him— and she knew for sure that he could and would hurt her—she might have given him much more than she could recover from.

Instead, he'd backed away. He hadn't kissed her. She should be drowning in buckets of relief right now. She should be thanking the stars that she had been saved from her own stupid desires.

If only she could stop wondering what it would have been like if they had a redo and this time their lips actually touched.

In the middle of the night, two days later, Rachel had an epiphany. "Decorating," she told Shane when she got out of the car and approached him the next morning. "You need decorating. Clean up, fix up, renovate up, decorate up. The ranchers will come for the ranch, I assume, but they have to live in the house. There's no life in the house. We have to change that."

Shane had been drinking coffee, leaning against the porch support, his ankles crossed as he slouched in that casual cowboy pose and surveyed the horizons of the ranch. The sun had risen but it was still a pink and gold ball reaching fingers of rose up to the sky. He turned to Rachel now as if she'd just suggested that he buy an elephant and put it on the porch.

"Slow down, Rachel. Back up. Why do we need to blow up the house?"

She gave him the evil eye. "You know what I mean. You said that you'd sell the house at any price, because you couldn't stay, but that seems such a shame. While

Marcia and I were cleaning, I scrubbed down to golden woodwork. There are some nice light fixtures underneath the grease that's built up. The place could look a lot better and it would sell faster if it just…looked a little nicer."

He was staring at her intently. "You're not getting too wrapped into this, are you?"

She started to say no. It was what he wanted to hear and what she wanted to say. "Maybe a little. I have a bad habit of jumping in with both feet. It goes…way back. It's gotten me in trouble on more than one occasion. I won't bore you with the details, but you're right. I'll try to slow down. But will you mind if I at least do a little with the place?"

"I don't mind. If you enjoy doing it, I have no objection at all. I just don't want things to get too complicated. I'm trying to keep my repairs to the minimum. This is more of a 'think of the possibilities' sale. I don't want to c— I don't want to spend too much time on it."

For a second there she'd thought he had been going to say that he didn't want to care. Maybe he had. That implied that he had feelings about this place, that there was a history here he wasn't ready to give up. There was, Rachel admitted, a lot she didn't know about Shane. He was a man with shadows in his life, a man with a patchy history. It was better not to know too much about him, she was sure. As he had started to say, it was better not to care.

"I'll be very blasé as I improve the ranch," she promised him, tilting up her chin and tossing her hair back.

"Somehow I don't think the word blasé has ever been used where you're concerned," he said. "I bow to your decorating expertise, Rachel. I'm sure there'll be a few people who will be just as interested in the house as the ranch itself."

"Maybe more than a few," she said, looking off to the side.

He stepped to the side so that he was looking into her eyes. "Care to clarify?"

"I might have mentioned the open house to Ruby and Angie. They might have told a few people. I think there may be a large contingent of Moraine women showing up on that day. You know. Just to look."

He swore beneath his breath.

"I know. I know. You don't like Moraine."

"It's more complicated than that." But he didn't elaborate.

"I'm sorry," she said. "But if the women come… they have friends and family and associates elsewhere. Even if they don't buy, they may know someone who might. And they'll have cameras and phones. Word will spread."

His face looked stony and…something else. There was that look in his eyes she could never quite decipher. As if ghosts lived in his eyes. And because she was standing so close, watching so carefully, she noted the moment when he closed off those ghost thoughts and gave in to the inevitable.

"I suppose you're right. And it's just one day. I can manage one day if in the end I achieve my goal."

Yes! she wanted to say. She had told her secret and he hadn't fired her. She had given him news she knew he would hate and he apparently didn't hate her yet. But she said nothing, because even though he had conceded her point, it was still obvious that he didn't like it. Gloating was not allowed.

"I'll give you a free hand with the house," he said,

"but for today can you spare me an hour or two? I need you to come with me, to document a few things with your camera."

"Not a problem," she said casually, although excitement was already bubbling up inside her. She hadn't taken a single photo in days. That was the only reason she was so eager. Wasn't it? It had nothing to do with the fact that she would be spending time with Shane.

Behave yourself, she warned herself. *Try not to act like some teenage nerd who just snagged a date with the prom king.* She hated, hated, hated that kind of thing. Still, her feet tripped along faster as she picked up her camera and returned to where Shane was standing.

"Today we ride," he told her.

Okay, so maybe there *was* a problem.

CHAPTER FIVE

"You need boots for riding," Shane mused as he walked with Rachel over to the corral, where Hank was seeing to the horses that had arrived a bit later than expected. "Those shoes are too slippery."

"No, I'm okay. I'm not…I'm not riding," Rachel said, her voice sounding slightly strained. Shane couldn't help glancing down at her. Was she looking a little pale?

"Rachel? Everything all right?"

"Everything's fine. Just great. Shane, your horses are so amazing. They're beautiful," she said, just as if everything was, indeed, all right. But something was slightly off here. Shane blinked at that. He'd only known the woman a few days. Why was he having thoughts like that? How would he know when something was right or wrong with Rachel? Why would he care?

In some ways, everything seemed perfectly normal. She had opened the case on her camera and was lining up a shot already, but when she'd finished taking the picture she didn't move closer to the horses.

He approached the fence, whickered softly, and a pretty chestnut mare tossed her head lightly and moved

up to him. "Rachel, this is Lizzie. She's very gentle."
He held his hand out and Lizzie nudged up against him.

"She knows you," Rachel said.

"Well, I don't know if she still does. We haven't
seen each other in a long while. But Lizzie was always
a friendly horse. You can touch her if you like. She'll
stand still for you."

When he looked at Rachel, her brown eyes were
glowing. "I've never touched a horse before." But she
looked eager enough. And even though she approached
Lizzie tentatively, she did manage to make contact.

Lizzie pressed up against Rachel's palm.

"Oh, you arc a sweetheart," Rachel said.

By now Hank and Tom, another new hand, had
brought a couple of the other horses over. "This one's
a stranger to me," Shane said. "And this is Rambler."
Rambler was a big, spirited bay.

"If you've been gone ten years, your horses must
have been very young when you left," Rachel said, her
voice soft and tentative.

"Some of them like Lizzie, yes. Some died during
that time and others were born. The horses are my one
regret about leaving the ranch, but my lifestyle doesn't
allow for pets. I should have sold them already."

"Leaving…things behind is difficult."

He glanced at her. Her voice had dropped. She
looked pensive, a little sad, but then she shook her head
and looked up at him.

"Are you going to sell them with Oak Valley?"

"I'm not sure. They're more window dressing right
now. Setting the stage."

"Actors?" she suggested. "Lizzie looks like she'd
like to be a star."

He chuckled. "She's a show off and yes, she's a star. Now—" he hesitated "—are you ready to ride?"

Rachel took a full step back. As if he'd just suggested that she wear a python for a necklace. "I—no. I'm sorry, but I'm not going to do that."

She was fidgeting in a way he'd never seen before, her fingers twisting up against each other.

As if she'd just realized what she'd said, her eyes opened wide. She looked horrified. "Maybe I should rephrase that," she began.

He shook his head. "Shh, it's okay. Just take your photos and then I'll drive you to the other sites."

"I'm sorry," she said.

"No need to be."

"You said that it was difficult to get to those other places with a car."

"I'll dig out the ATVs. Ever ride one?"

"No."

"Are you okay with trying it?"

"Totally fine with it."

Which sounded much more Rachel-like. She had already volunteered to learn how to drive a stick shift and change the oil and spark plugs in a car without a second glance. She'd been uncomfortable with cooking and cleaning, but in spite of that she'd tackled those tasks without flinching. And clearly she was enchanted with Lizzie and the horses, just not with riding one. Shane couldn't help wondering what had happened to her.

He scowled. From the beginning he'd known it wasn't wise to get too close to Rachel. That hadn't changed. In fact it had been more than obvious when he had been on the verge of giving her a full-on kiss the other day. He should just drop the horse issue.

Yeah, he really should do that. What difference did it make that Rachel would go through life without experiencing the joy of riding a horse? Not everyone in the world had to know that kind of pleasure.

"Why are you frowning at me?" she asked.

Shane blinked. "I wasn't frowning at you. Just thinking ahead to something I need to do, a problem I need to work out. Let's go find that ATV. I've got one with a rack for your equipment."

A short time later they were racing across the fields on ATVs, Rachel's dark mane flowing out behind her.

Shane stopped to show her the field where they were making hay. As the mower cut through the field, Rachel breathed in deeply of the cut grasses.

"It smells wonderful," she said. "What happens to it next? You just scoop it up into one of those hay baler things?"

"Eventually we bundle it up with the baler. But first we have to make sure that the moisture content is right, so once it's cut we leave it in windrows to dry. Then it's raked to help with the drying, and finally it's baled and stored until it's needed for the animals in winter."

"That's...nice."

He looked at her.

"No. I mean it. There must be something very satisfying about growing the feed for your animals all by yourself."

He tilted his head. "I grew up like this. Hadn't given it much thought. I never was much of a rancher."

"But you know how to do that?" She pointed toward the mower.

Shane shrugged. "I started this morning at first light and then turned things over to Tom when I went up to the house."

"Because you had to meet me?"

"Because you and I had things to do." But he couldn't deny that he'd felt a sense of anticipation waiting for Rachel to arrive. "Come on. Do you have some shots we might use?"

"I think so. Where to next?"

She was like a kid at a five-star amusement park. He led her around the ranch to a cabin meant as a winter shelter, and she entered the place as if it was some sort of treasure cave.

"I can imagine some pioneer woman cooking soup over a fire here, making candles, fighting the elements."

He couldn't help smiling. "I don't think it's quite that old, but, yes, the basic original idea was to protect a rider from the elements if he should get caught on the far side of the ranch. Not sure this one was ever used for anything more than a getaway."

She stopped to marvel at a field of yellow balsamroot and blue lupines. "I've never seen so many flowers in one place. There must be thousands of them." There were, but although he'd appreciated their beauty in the past, he'd never thought of them as anything special. They bloomed every year. On the ranch, they became just some pretty flowers he passed as he went about his chores.

"Let's move on," he said, not wanting to analyze his reaction too closely. It didn't matter, anyway. Soon the ranch would belong to someone else.

They made their way past grazing land, over hills and into valleys, until he stopped beside a clear, cold creek tumbling over rocks.

Rachel knelt and picked up a flat stone. "What a pretty pink! May I? Ranch souvenir?" she asked.

He laughed. "Be my guest. But it won't look nearly as nice once it dries."

"You sound so…adult," she said with a laugh. "But I'll bet you and…I'll bet you collected your share in your day." A guilty look came over Rachel's face at her stumble.

She was right. He and his brother had filled their pockets with stones, Eric always sure that the next stone would still be bright once it dried.

The familiar and still fresh pain flowed through Shane, but he wasn't going to have Rachel feeling guilty just for making a casual comment. Guilt was a cruel master, as he well knew.

"I ripped the pockets of plenty of jeans with the weight of those rocks. I used to camp by this stream in summer," he said. No need to mention that on one or two of those occasions it was because he'd run away from home.

"That sounds very romantic. The cowboy, his horse and a campfire beside a stream. The stuff that entices people to read Westerns and dream of coming to places like this."

It had never been that way for him. He'd been on the run…until duty had called him home. "Hey, I thought you were a Maine girl."

She smiled. "I am. I will be. But even a Maine girl isn't immune to the lure of a campfire under the western stars."

"I could see you here," he said suddenly. Because it was true. In a world gone dark, under a sky full of stars stretching from horizon to horizon, he could imagine Rachel looking up with those brown eyes that filled with wonder whenever she witnessed something new or exciting.

"Am I wearing a cowgirl hat and boots in your imagination?" she teased. "You told me today that I needed boots."

"I hadn't gotten that far," he admitted. "I wasn't imagining clothing." Although now that she'd brought it up and now that he'd said it in that ill-conceived way, he was definitely imagining her without clothes, wrapped up in a blanket with him. He wanted to groan.

"What were you imagining?" she asked, stepping closer.

"It's probably better not to say," he told her.

And there it was. The blush.

"I've never met a woman who blushes the way you do," he said. And then, as if he didn't have an ounce of sense in his head, he slid one hand beneath her hair and kissed her cheek, where the rose-pink blush had taken up residence. He tracked it down, kissing the delicate line of her jaw, her neck, where he could feel her pulse fluttering.

She was clutching his shoulders, trembling beneath his hands, and for a moment he forgot all reason. He touched his lips to hers, and his senses exploded. She was honey and cinnamon, woman and sunlight. He wanted more of her. Much more. Now. This second.

Rachel leaned into him when the kiss ended. She returned the kiss and the heat climbed. But soon he felt her hands against his chest. "I shouldn't be doing this," she said. "I shouldn't, because…because…"

She didn't have to explain. And she was right. So very right. He released her immediately. "Because you're a girl from Maine and I'm a man on his way out of Montana."

"And you're my boss and I'm your housekeeper.

And because I promised myself that this wouldn't happen," she said.

And so had he. He was a man who never made promises. This was just another reason why. "I apologize for stepping over the line."

Rachel shook her head. "I knew what I was doing. I'd been warned. Numerous times. I'd told myself not to do something like this. More than once. You might have kissed first, but I kissed last."

What could he say to that? She'd been warned about him, and with good reason. And now he had broken her trust. He wanted to tell her that it wouldn't happen again, but he no longer trusted himself. "I'd better get you back to the house" was the best that he could do.

She sighed. "I'm sorry this messed up the workday. I don't think you meant to finish this soon."

Finally he found a reason to smile. "Rachel, if you think this messed up the workday...there are millions of men who wish their workdays could end like this." But he *was* sorry. She'd been enjoying the day and now she wasn't. There was no way to fix that. The only good thing was that now he knew just how risky being close to Rachel was. He needed to be more careful. He needed to work faster. It was more important than ever that he finish with Oak Valley quickly. Maybe he should try to speed up the process.

Rachel felt as if twin storms were having a battle inside her chest the next morning. Shane had kissed her...and she had kissed him back.

What was I thinking? The question ran through her mind in a continuous loop. But why even ask that question, anyway? Because she hadn't been thinking. She'd just been feeling, reacting in that whole mindless man-woman way that had never worked out in her family. She'd sworn she would never let go that way. And she never had.

But, darn it, the man could kiss.

"Grr," she said beneath her breath.

"Rachel? Everything okay? You need help?" Shane's voice came from outside and Rachel jumped, banging her knee into the corner of a cabinet and biting back the pain to keep from yelling.

"No, I'm fine," she said quickly. "What are you doing out there?"

She got her answer when he came inside carrying a ladder. "I was just on my way to repair the molding around the window in the dining room and…why is your knee bleeding?"

Rachel looked down, and sure enough there was a thin trickle of blood seeping from a small cut, tracing a path down toward her sandal. The edge of the cabinet had been sharp, but she hadn't noticed the cut. She'd been so intent on avoiding contact with Shane. Now that they'd been intimate—or as close to intimate as they were ever going to get—she felt awkward in his presence.

"It's nothing," she said as casually as possible. "Go fix your molding. I'll just wash it off."

He frowned. "It's not nothing. It could get infected. Infection is dangerous. Sit down. We're taking care of this right now."

He was going to touch her? Touch her knee? With those big hands that had been touching her in her dreams last night? When both of them had been naked? She cursed her decision to wear shorts today. If she'd been wearing jeans, none of this would be happening.

"No, really, I can do it," she began.

"Rachel, stop it. I'm not going to do anything intimate." There was that word again. "I'm just going to make sure you're okay. You're on my watch right now. I can't have you getting injured. I've seen...I know what can happen if a person doesn't take care of something small and it becomes major. All right?"

She nodded slowly. Because while his words were asking permission, those stormy eyes of his told her that she didn't have a choice.

Rachel sat. Shane disappeared for a few minutes and returned with a first aid kit. He washed his hands, then pulled up a stool in front of Rachel. He took a cloth he had dampened, leaned forward and gently dabbed away the blood.

She tried to keep breathing normally. So far there was cloth between his skin and hers. "Um, how is your work going?" she asked, trying to appear nonchalant.

A trace of a smile appeared on his lips as he continued to work. Had he noticed the tremor in her voice?

"Got a lot done. The barn is finished, I have a small crew on fences. There's still a lot to do. Repair work on at least one of the tractors, some major windmill issues, other outbuildings that need work and some dead trees that need to be removed. But we might finish up sooner than later."

"Sooner?" So she had less time than she had thought. For some reason a sense of sadness pulsed through her. Probably just because she wasn't nearly as far along as he was, she told herself. It had nothing to do with the fact that she and Shane would be finishing their time together sooner. After all, her whole life had been about leaving places. She was good at it.

"I'd better pick up the pace, too. I've done at least the surface cleaning of all of the rooms. That is, I mean, most of the rooms." She faltered and took a breath. Why had she said that? It was just…Shane was touching her and she wasn't thinking clearly. And, okay, yes, she couldn't help worrying about the fact that Shane was clearly still in pain if he couldn't face his brother's belongings yet, and she—darn it, she'd always been a fixer type of person. Or at least she'd tried to fix the unfixable.

"I can work faster." She ended in a whoosh.

Shane paused. "Rachel."

"I'm sorry. I shouldn't have even mentioned it. Not the working faster. The other."

"I know what you meant," he said, his blue eyes dark, masking his thoughts. "I don't want you to worry about it. When the time comes I'll handle it, but…not yet."

She nodded tightly.

"I don't want you to be uncomfortable."

"I won't be. I'm not." Which was such a total lie. With Shane's hands still on her they were kissing close, even if no kissing was going on. And she was worried about him.

"Don't worry about the room."

"No. I won't."

He looked unconvinced. She didn't want to give him anything else to worry about. "I've got plenty to keep me busy. All that decorating to do," she said. "And if we're finishing sooner than expected, I'd better start thinking about where I go from here." She did her best to inject some cheer into her voice. "Maine's a big place."

Shane was looking down. He had resumed cleaning her cut, but now his hand stalled in his task. He had moved from the cloth to a much smaller disinfectant pad. His fourth and fifth fingers rested on her knee. He pinned her with his gaze. Rachel tried to keep breathing.

"You're telling me that when you leave here you have no specific place to go?"

"Well, I have a general area. But not one place, no. I should start looking."

"And how are you going to do that?" he asked, a bit too carefully, as he took a bandage out of a box and began to ready it.

Breathe. Breathe. Breathe, Rachel ordered herself. "I'll just do a general internet search. There are places where people list their apartments and you just contact them."

"Might not be safe." He gently smoothed the bandage into place, turning every nerve in her body to the *on* position. "You should only contact people you know you can trust."

What should she say to that? Not that there was no one she trusted that much, or that there was no one she would allow to help her with this important a decision. "Well, it's been a while since I was there last."

His hands were both resting on her leg now. He was staring into her eyes. "I know people in the business. They're very good at what they do. Let me put you in touch with them."

And now, with his hands against her, his voice rumbled through her body. She slugged in a deep breath, nodded fiercely. "All right. Yes. Thank you." Anything to end this before she leaned forward, grabbed his lapels, yanked him to her and repeated yesterday's kiss.

As if he knew what she was thinking, he released her. He stood. "Tonight," he promised. "If you don't mind staying a little later than usual?"

Oh, no. Ruby was going to have a field day with this, she thought, followed immediately by her own admonitions.

Stop worrying about Ruby. You just behave yourself. No more thinking about kissing Shane. Not unless you actually want your heart broken so badly that you'll never recover.

Not a chance. Ever.

"Tonight will be fine," she agreed.

No problem at all. She could handle anything.

Rachel tiptoed into the inn. Ruby always left the kitchen light on in case a guest needed a glass of water in the middle of the night. Pale light filtered out of the kitchen into the neighboring rooms, so Rachel had no trouble seeing her way through the house.

She breathed a sigh of relief that Ruby had already gone to bed. There would be no questions about what she'd been doing hanging around with Shane after dark.

And if Ruby was asleep she wouldn't be up until the next morning. Rachel's landlady slept the sleep of the contented. Nothing disturbed her once she was down for the night.

Slipping her shoes off and padding toward the staircase, Rachel was nearly to the first step when Ruby's voice stopped her. "Good, you're home. You were out pretty late tonight, weren't you, hon?"

Rachel turned. She was surprised to hear genuine worry in her landlady's voice. She wasn't used to anyone caring when she came home and guilt slipped through her. Dropping to the steps, she sat down. "I'm sorry I didn't let you know I wasn't coming back to the inn at my usual time. But it's only nine-thirty. I thought you were asleep."

"At nine-thirty?"

"Ruby, you just implied that it was late," Rachel pointed out with an exasperated smile.

"For young women cavorting with men who radiate testosterone. Not for old ladies waiting to hear what happened."

Uh-oh. There was too much interest in Ruby's voice. Rachel reminded herself that in Moraine nothing much happened. Little incidents made bigger splashes than they would in a larger town. Even when those little splashes didn't mean a thing.

"*Nothing* happened," she told her friend. "Shane was just helping me look for a place to stay when I get to Maine." And in truth, that was all that had happened. They had circled each other carefully at first, but eventually Shane had pulled up two chairs in front of the computer, brought out two glasses of wine, and they had discussed the pros and cons of different areas of Maine. He'd been there often in the past, even though his business hadn't taken him to that part of the country in recent years.

"So you like the tang of the salt air, the rocky coasts and picturesque little Cape Cod houses? Lobster traps and lighthouses?" he'd asked.

She'd laughed. "You say that as if it's a bad thing."

"Not at all. It's a beautiful part of the country. Any reason why Maine is your choice?"

Rachel had run her thumb over the stem of the wine glass. "I spent several years there growing up. It was the best time of my life."

He'd tilted his head in acquiescence. "Then Maine it is."

After that, they'd moved on to specific areas and he'd pulled out some ideas a former colleague had emailed him earlier in the day. By the time she'd gone home, Rachel had had a much better idea of where she might like to move and put down roots. That should have been one of the brightest moments in the past few weeks, but for now…

Something very close to sadness rippled through her. She felt as if she'd crossed something off on a list of things to do, but there was no satisfaction in the accomplishment. It was probably just because she was tired. Tomorrow the anticipation would finally kick in.

"Hello? Rachel?" Ruby snapped her fingers and Rachel opened her eyes wide.

"Sorry. I was just thinking about a house."

"*Yeah.*"

"What?"

"You spent the night sitting knee to knee with Shane and all you can think about is a house? Rachel, I'm twenty years too old for the man, but if I'd been closed up with him after dark my mind wouldn't have been on houses."

"It's not like that with us," Rachel protested. Except when it was.

"Okay, I'll stop pestering you. When are we going to get to see him again?"

"You want me to bring him here?"

Ruby grinned. "Hon, I'd like nothing better, but I was talking about convincing him to come back to town. The man has been here for a week but he's barely touched foot in Moraine and he'll be leaving soon. People would like to see him. He grew up here. He's Moraine family to us."

Uh-oh. If there was one thing Rachel knew, it was

that Shane didn't want to go to Moraine. She didn't know why, but she knew it was so.

"He's really busy and…I'm not a miracle worker, Ruby."

"You're a woman. Use your wiles."

Rachel should have laughed at that, but the truth was that it occurred to her at that moment that the only reason Shane was kissing her was because there were no other single women around. But there had to be single women in Moraine…which he was avoiding.

"Ruby, why do you think a man like Shane wouldn't want to go back to his hometown? What happened here? What did people do to him?"

Ruby shook her head. "I don't know. I know that Shane lost his mother at a young age, that he and Frank didn't get along and that Eric died in a ranch accident. But there's nothing anyone in town did or said to him that I can think of. Not a thing. But, believe it or not, I don't know everything. Maybe you should ask Shane. And if you can't get him there by using your wiles, maybe remind him that those are his potential customers."

That was a hoot. Wiles again? Rachel had none. Never had, never would. And she didn't want them. Wiles never got you anything good…or lasting.

But she did think that Ruby had a point about Shane going to town to meet his customers. If he really wanted to sell Oak Valley quickly—and he had made it clear that he did—and if he was a good businessman— and he apparently was—then why wasn't he using his networking skills with the people who might help him spread the word and sell the ranch?

Rachel didn't have a clue. Maybe Shane wasn't thinking clearly because he was still mourning Eric.

Maybe she should just mind her own business, stay out of things, keep quiet.

But she'd never been especially good at any of those things. Besides, Shane had stepped over a personal line when he'd opted to help her find a place in Maine. He was helping her. What kind of a person would she be if she didn't try her best to help him, too?

CHAPTER SIX

SHANE woke up the next morning the way he always did. Early. He headed for the bathroom to take a shower and shave the way he always did. He ignored the closed door of Eric's room, trying to pretend he wasn't going to have to open it soon and let the past beat him up for a failure he should have foreseen and a loss he could never get over. The truth was that he'd been running all his life, but now he had to run faster to stay ahead of his demons. The other truth was that he couldn't put off opening that room forever. Rachel was starting to worry.

He told himself he didn't care. His problems were his and only his, as they had always been.

That seemed to help. For about two seconds. Before he remembered just how difficult it was to look into her brown eyes and feel as if he was failing her.

He hated failing people. For some reason it was worse with her. Maybe because she was sunny most of the time.

Too bad, he told himself. It couldn't matter. It *didn't* matter. Because he knew what would happen once he started sifting through Eric's possessions.

Shane closed his eyes. He took a few deep breaths. Finally he convinced himself that it was all right to put the inevitable off for one more day, and he stepped into the shower and let the hot water melt the kinks he'd accumulated from the hard physical labor of the day before.

All right, he was in control of himself now. The day would be just fine. He had it all planned out. He was ready to get dressed, have coffee and hit the ground running, maybe do some repairs on the calving shed, pound some boards to take the edge off.

Then, when he was good and worn out, he would have lunch with Rachel, eat some of that stuff she was trying so hard to make edible.

He smiled at the thought. They'd talk, he'd sneak a few questions in about her plans for the future—why had he thought she had it all planned out? How had he not known she didn't even have a place to go?

But now he knew and he intended to help. Then he'd maybe sneak in a little time with her and the horses, get Lizzie to love her up a little more. Stupid idea. What difference did it make if she was afraid of getting on a horse? And why was it bothering him so much?

It's not, he told himself. Still…they'd have a go at Lizzie again. Yeah, that was the plan. Easy. Nothing too stressful. No tension.

He climbed from the shower, wrapped a towel around himself and stepped out into the hallway.

Right into Rachel's path.

She froze in her tracks. Her gaze took in the rivulets of water tracking down his chest.

"I-it's early, I know," she said hastily. "But I—the house. I wanted to talk to you about something. I wanted to catch you before you got busy."

He wasn't busy now. He was…fascinated by the way her eyes slid away from him, then returned, never rising to meet his gaze. But he was also aware that he was making her uncomfortable.

"Just let me get dressed and I'll be right with you."

Rachel gave a quick nod. "Okay, I'll…make some coffee, start some breakfast."

He wanted to smile at that. She hadn't cooked breakfast for him before. He either had her really discombobulated or she wanted to ask him something she thought he might not like. Maybe some froufrou thing for the house. Heck, he didn't care what she put in the house. He had the money to pay for it and he wouldn't be looking at it much longer, anyway.

"That'd be nice, but you know, I don't require you to make my breakfast."

She lifted one delicious dark eyebrow. "Are you afraid of my breakfast, Shane?"

He crossed his arms over his chest. "Do I look like I'm afraid?" He raised an eyebrow, too. Two could play at that game.

And now she surprised him. She stared directly at him, her eyes resting on his muscles, playing chicken. Where had she learned that kind of fortitude when he knew that intimacy made her nervous?

"Well, I can at least make toast," she said. "And coffee."

But in the end it turned out that she couldn't. When he came into the kitchen she shoved a bowl, a box of cereal and some milk and orange juice in front of him. The scent of burnt toast hung in the air.

"I would have eaten it," he said. "It tastes better that way."

She wrinkled her nose at him. "No fair going easy on me just because you know I don't know what I'm doing."

"I'm not. Really. You're learning and you haven't complained about the challenges, even though ranching and housekeeping are outside your familiar comfort zone."

Shane meant every word; he'd meant them to be encouraging, but Rachel was looking as if he'd just shown her a video of a sad puppy.

He tried again. "Everyone should be given a chance to learn. No one should be criticized for not being an expert at everything. We all have our strong suits." He couldn't begin to explain how strongly he felt about that. It was his mantra.

"Thank you," she said. "But I'm still not feeding you burnt toast."

He smiled and she returned the smile. Thank goodness. "Now, what can I do for you?" he asked.

She ran one hand down the leg of her jeans, looking as if she was about to ask for the moon. "I want you to come to Moraine with me."

Not happening, he thought. "Why would you want me to do that?" he asked, his voice careful and emotionless.

"I told you that I want to do some redecorating. I think—as the owner—you should have some say in what colors I put on your walls and what kinds of curtains I hang."

He shook his head slowly. "I'm not really that involved in that kind of thing. Whatever you do will be fine."

To his surprise, Rachel took a step closer. She held out a hand as if she was going to touch him. "What if I painted the walls purple and put curtains with big red butterflies in your bedroom?"

He tilted his head. "Have a thing for red butterflies, do you?"

She frowned, and he could practically see the wheels turning in her head. "You can see that I don't have much practice with domestic affairs. My taste might not match yours."

But he glanced down at her blue jeans, her pale blue blouse and the delicate gold chain on her wrist. He reached out, took her hand and rubbed his thumb gently over the delicate skin near the bracelet. "I like this," he said. "It's not gaudy and you haven't shown any signs of extremism in anything you've worn. So… what's this about, Rachel?"

"I—" She gazed up into his eyes, her lips parted slightly, and he realized what a mistake he had made. He'd been trying to overpower her, to get her to open up and confess what her motivations were, because they clearly had nothing to do with purple paint. But now, with his thumb resting on the soft skin of her wrist and with that pretty mouth urging him to kiss it closed, he was the one who was discombobulated. "I— Ruby and some of the other people in Moraine want to have some time to spend with you before you leave. They're all hoping that you'll come to town soon."

Just like that, he dropped her hand, stood up and took a big step back. "That's not happening."

"I don't understand."

"I don't expect you to, Rachel. You weren't here with me when I lived here."

"Did people mistreat you?"

He blinked at that. "Rachel, you've met Ruby."

"Well, Ruby, yes. But she's special."

"She is. She's very special. And she never mistreated me. Neither did anyone else. Rachel, I can't explain it, but going to town brings back memories I have to forget. I don't like to talk about my past. The most I can say is that no one goes through life without leaving tracks wherever they go. I'm not retracing mine."

Rachel frowned. "If you're talking about what Ruby told me that first day, or the episode when you stole the car…I haven't heard anyone saying anything negative about you. Well, other than Ruby's comments about you being…you know. But Ruby didn't say that out of malice."

"I know. She said it because she was concerned for you. But…I don't intend to hurt you, Rachel. Neither do I intend to set foot in town."

Rachel opened her mouth to speak. Shane stepped forward and gently laid two fingers over her lips.

"No," he said. "Just no. Go to town, Rachel. Buy whatever you like for the house and charge it to me. But I won't be going. That's final."

Or so he thought. He started to step away and she placed her hand—very lightly—on his bare arm. Sensation sizzled through him. What was that about? They were having a discussion, a painful discussion, and even then the woman's touch affected him. He did his best to ignore it, because if there was one thing these past few moments had brought home to him it was how close he was coming to leaving yet another person damaged. It could happen so easily if he didn't watch himself. Rachel acted tough at times, but she was held together with visibly fragile threads and she was here alone. There was no one to watch out for her.

Except for him. Someone needed to watch her back. He intended to make sure she was protected, even if it was from himself. So he looked down at where her fingers lay against his skin, trying to reestablish the employer/employee relationship. She was usually so conscientious about that stuff. He was sure she would back off, and then he could erect some walls around himself...which would be the best thing for her.

To his surprise, she didn't let go, although she did look very self-conscious about touching him. "Shane, I think this is a mistake. Whatever you said or did... you should never leave a place without settling your debts and doing whatever you can to make sure that everyone is happy."

"Is that another of your teacher's 'one size fits all' lessons?"

Her color rose high, but she didn't back down. "No, it's all Rachel Everly. Just something I learned at a very early age."

He had no clue what she was saying, but he knew for certain that somehow someone had hurt Rachel. And it wasn't just that jerk Dennis. The look in her eyes told him that this was a very personal lesson.

So, despite his best intentions, he slid one hand beneath her hair and gently rubbed his thumb across her lips. "Rachel, that's what I'm trying to do. I'm trying to make sure that I leave everyone here as happy as is possible."

"But they want to see you. They want your company. That's...such a gift. It's so special. I would—"

The intensity in her voice and the fact that she couldn't continue...what was *that* about? Shane realized once again that Rachel hadn't shared any real information about her past, and—amazingly—he realized that he wanted to know, even though knowing more of Rachel probably wasn't wise.

Still, he wouldn't pry. He more than most understood the need for emotional walls. "What would you do?" he coaxed, releasing her.

She shook her head. "What I would do doesn't really matter, does it? I'm the impulsive one, the one who ended up stranded here with no money."

"Don't," he warned with a scowl. "Don't demean yourself. You have a 'forge ahead' attitude and a gift for finding joy in the small moments in life that most people lack. If we could bottle that…people would pay buckets of money for it. We could all use a little Rachel in our lives."

And there it was, that beautiful blush that revealed the innocence beneath her "I can be anything" exterior.

But as the blush faded she crossed her arms. "I see what you're doing. You're trying to turn all business-man, all salesman on me, so that I'll leap for the compliment and forget that we were talking about you."

He raised one eyebrow. "Was that what I was doing?"

"You know it was."

She was wrong. He hadn't been trying to trick her. He'd meant every word. But he knew why she would think that. Trust was a fragile element and her trust had been broken. Maybe more than once, judging from the things she was leaving unsaid.

"You're wrong. Believe me." But he knew that she wouldn't. And why should she? Everything she'd been told about him urged her not to trust. And everything she'd been told was absolutely true.

"It doesn't matter," she said. "What matters is that… Shane, you have neighbors who want to see you. They like you. Do you really want to turn away from that?"

And they were back to him, back to doors he had

locked and didn't want to open. "I'm doing what I need to do, Rachel."

This time he managed to walk away. And this time she didn't try to get him to stay.

"What's going on out there at the ranch? Looks like you and Shane are setting up house," the woman at the register said to Rachel. Her name tag said that she was Cynthia Corvellis. To Rachel she was *the enemy,* if she was going to start spreading rumors about Shane.

Rachel forced a stiff smile. The part of her that was smart and sensible knew that she should just leave the store now, but the other part of her that had never been able to back down from ugly situations was out in full force today. She knew why, too. It was because Shane had complimented her during their argument and—Jupiter and Juno—warmth had slipped through her. She'd wanted to believe him. Worse, she'd wanted to touch him.

All of that was wrong. Believing compliments had gotten her in trouble before. Forgetting that Shane was her boss and only her boss was going to end up in big, big, heart-killing trouble. And here was this woman implying that she and Shane were…were *doing it* when that was just never going to happen in this lifetime. Nothing was going to happen between her and Shane, ever, unless you counted her nearly killing him with her meals twice a day. Having this Cynthia person fishing for spicy gossip today…it just crossed a line.

Rachel leaned over the counter slightly. She lowered her voice. "What would you think if I told you yes? Shane and I are getting married."

Cynthia blinked. "For real? He's settling down? Here? With you?" Her tone made it clear that she would be less surprised to see aliens from some distant planet walking around town.

And yet, when a smile of pure pleasure slipped over the woman's face, all the spunk and nasty slipped right out of Rachel. What was wrong with her? Why would she say something like that to this total stranger? "No. I'm very sorry. I was just…I lied. I'm only Shane's housekeeper, and I'm just here to buy curtains for his house because the ones there look as if someone put them through a cheese-shredder."

To her surprise, Cynthia reached out and patted her on the shoulder. "I know why you lied. He's a real hard man to love, isn't he, hon?"

Rachel blinked. "I—I don't love Shane."

But it was obvious that Cynthia didn't believe her by the pitying look in her eyes. "I've done more than my share of comforting the girls Shane has left behind in my time. He never stays."

Wasn't that almost exactly what Ruby had told her? What was wrong with the women of Moraine? Rachel wondered. The ones who fell for Shane and those who comforted them when things fell through? If *she* was in love with Shane and he left her, she certainly wouldn't go crying to every other woman in town.

No, you would just quietly cry into your pillow every night. You'd deal with your broken heart by yourself. And right there, in Cynthia Corvellis's Handy House store, Rachel realized just how much danger she was sliding into. Already she was beginning to care about the man, barging into his business, looking forward to when he came in for lunch. She could almost feel the pain of losing Shane this very minute. Which was wrong. It couldn't be happening. She was not going to allow herself to care. No.

"Shane's not a bad man," Cynthia was telling her. "He's just not the marrying kind. The world needs all kinds, including men who don't settle down and who raise a little hell now and then. And…what can I say? He's ours. It's been years since I've really seen him. I'd like to say hello. Any chance you could talk him into coming into the store?"

Rachel opened her mouth to say no. "I'm not sure," she said instead. *Idiot!*

"He used to come here with his mother when she shopped for dry goods," Cynthia went on, a smile lighting her face. "I always had licorice whips on the counter and I always gave him one when they left the store. He was the cutest little boy and he loved those things. His eyes would positively light up. But…I guess he's too old for licorice whips now."

She sounded so wistful that Rachel found herself saying, "I'll bet he still loves them." And then she asked Cynthia to help her pick out some curtains. It was the least she could do, since she had made up that awful lie and since her attempts to bring Shane to Moraine had failed.

When she was through, Cynthia turned to her and said, "I'm sorry I implied that something was going on between you and Shane. That was wrong of me. I just…Shane was always in trouble, but I don't know…I just liked him. And he made things exciting, you know?"

"I know," Rachel agreed. There was an energy about Shane that turned a beige world flame-red. Oh, no, there were those dangerous thoughts again. "When I get back to the ranch," she said, "I'm going to tell Shane that Cynthia Corvellis helped me pick out his curtains. They really are lovely, Cynthia. Just what the room needs."

The older woman positively glowed at the compliment. "You enjoy them, sweetie," Cynthia said. But of course that wasn't going to happen. At least not for more than a few days. Then the curtains would be someone else's to enjoy.

Rachel said goodbye and exited the store, heading toward the car. Across the street she noticed two men watching her, one elderly and the other one not so elderly. There was no malevolence in their perusal of her, and she had a hunch they knew who she was.

Her first instinct was to ignore them and just hurry to her car. Nice as Cynthia had eventually turned out to be, Rachel didn't need any more people asking her if she was Shane's newest conquest. How many women had the man had when he was living here?

She turned to go. But then it occurred to her that maybe all of this whispering and gossiping was part of the reason Shane didn't want to come to town. And years of girls' school training kicked in. If there was going to be talk, she preferred to have the chance to be a part of the dialogue instead of the powerless recipient.

Crossing the street, she held out her hand. "Excuse me, I'm Rachel Everly. I'm working for Shane Merritt at Oak Valley Ranch."

"We know. We weren't trying to be rude by staring. We were just wondering how to approach you without seeming too forward," one of the men said, looking a bit sheepish. "I'm Len Hoskins. I own the drugstore. And this is Jarrod Ollis."

Rachel said hello to both of them. "What…is there something I can do for you?"

"We just wanted to ask how Shane is doing." Len took the lead again. "I hear he stopped in town one day when we'd already rolled up most of the streets, that he bought some supplies and hasn't been seen here since. I missed seeing him that time and I wonder, if he plans to make another trip to town, could you ask him to let us know? Or could you let us know? It's been ten years since he left Moraine."

"I'd hate to miss having the chance to trade stories with him," Jarrod agreed. "I mean, he *was* in town for his brother Eric's funeral a year ago, but the arrangements were made in advance and he barely made an appearance. Not that I blame him. Some people need to be private in their grief. Still, Shane and Eric made this town rock, and it's been pretty boring without them."

"They were something," Len said with a laugh. "Eric was captain of the football team and Shane was always tinkering with machines and breaking hearts. But then, you know all that."

No, she knew almost nothing. Still, Rachel made a small sound of assent.

"And fighting," Jarrod said with a smile, grabbing his jaw in a gesture that indicated Shane must have punched him there once. "Shane had a mean right hook, and he wasn't averse to getting down in the dirt to wrestle you if it came to that." Obviously it had come to that more than once. "Wouldn't mind sharing old stories with him."

"Why don't you?" Rachel asked, and immediately wondered if she should have said that. Darn her impulsive mouth. But it was said. She wasn't backing down now. "Why don't you talk to him?"

"We just told you, Rachel. He hasn't come to town."

"But you could go see him. You could drop by the ranch."

Wasn't that what people did in small towns? They dropped by when they wanted to say hello? Ruby seemed to imply that people were always welcome at her place even if they weren't staying or paying.

Jarrod rubbed his jaw again, looking vaguely worried. "I don't know about coming to the ranch. Might make him mad."

"If it does, I'll protect you from him," Rachel said, drawing a big laugh from Len.

"I think I like you, Rachel," he said. "But I'm not so sure about stopping by the ranch, either. If Shane wanted to see us, he'd come here. That's just the truth. If he's staying on the ranch, then he doesn't want to have anything to do with his neighbors. But tell him hey from Len."

"And from Jarrod," Jarrod said. "Tell him if he comes to town there'll be payback."

Rachel blinked.

"I'm lyin', of course," Jarrod said with a wink.

"Of course," she agreed. But she had a feeling that Jarrod rather enjoyed fighting.

She also had a feeling that she had dodged a bullet. Maybe. Clearly she had been wrong about ranch and small town etiquette. At least in this small town and in terms of this ranch.

Len and Jarrod were probably right that it was a bad idea. Shane didn't want to come to town. And the people *were* the town. No matter her feelings about leaving places and people on good terms, those were her beliefs, not his.

"Good thing no one's coming," she muttered on her way back. "Saved from my own impulsiveness by the good people of Moraine." She smiled. It occurred to her that she liked Shane's hometown better than he did.

It might not be a good idea to tell him that she'd messed up again and invited people to the ranch.

But, good idea or not, she would have to do it.

CHAPTER SEVEN

THE next day Shane came back to the house at lunch-time to find that Rachel had transformed his dining room into something...

"Livable," he said as he stared down at the table dressed in his mother's cream-colored tablecloth and topped with an old bottle green vase he hadn't seen in years. The vase was full of golden blossoms and there were cream and merlot candles scattered about.

"Livable?" she asked. "Is that good or bad? Is it praise? Maybe?"

"Sorry. Yes, it's praise," he said with a trace of a smile. "And don't pretend you don't know what I mean by livable. This place has only been inhabited by men since I was eight years old. Lately it's mostly been the home of mice. It had gone beyond functional to funky. And I don't mean that in a good way. So, yes, the fact that someone might actually eat or entertain in here by choice rather than necessity is a good thing."

She held out her hand. "Note the curtains."

They were nice—plain cream-colored curtains with bottle-green scalloped edging and tiebacks—but nothing to write ballads about.

"Cynthia Corvellis helped me pick them out," she said.

The name opened up a wound in his soul. Cynthia

had been Eric's piano teacher. She had adored Shane's brother. No question why. Eric had been the most lovable person on earth. According to everyone. According to me, Shane thought. *Don't think about it,* he thought.

"Cynthia always had good taste," he said.

"She's a nice woman," Rachel agreed. "She told me that you used to love licorice whips and she kept a container of them on the counter for you."

A tiny smile flickered over his lips, then died. "I know what you're doing, Rachel. Cynthia is a very nice woman. I'm happy that she helped you find what you needed. But I'm still not going to town."

"I know. What if town came to you, though?"

He froze. "Rachel, what do you mean?"

There was a pause. A long pause. "I might have done something you won't like."

He stared at her. He could tell that she was waiting for the whip to come down on her back. "What is it that you might have done?"

"I—I'm not sure. Maybe nothing." She told him about her conversations yesterday.

He studied the ceiling, fought for composure. The thought of trading stories with people who had known him when...

"Rachel, why would you do that after I'd specifically stated that I didn't want to go to town to meet my neighbors?"

She bit her lip and glanced to the side. "You didn't exactly say that you didn't want to meet them. You just said you didn't want to go to town."

Before he could say anything she rushed on. "No, that's not right or fair. I knew you weren't just avoiding the location. It's just that...friendship is such a valuable thing. I-it's not good to waste it, even if it lasts for only a very short time."

"More words of wisdom?" He blew out a breath.

"Yes," she said quietly. "I—I'm really sorry. I had no right to try to foist my ideas on you. And while I don't think that any of those people will actually show up—they seemed reluctant to invade your privacy— just in case, I'll get in touch with each one of them and explain that I was wrong to issue the invitation."

It was an eloquent little speech, a perfectly pretty speech. And Shane had no doubt that Rachel would follow through. She was naive and almost innocent in some ways, but tough when toughness was required. Tougher than he was, he thought. And what was the source of all that moral toughness? Of all her pretty and, yes, naive, little rules? He didn't know, but he knew that there was a sadness in her. He remembered that she had chosen to move to a state where she apparently knew no one.

"No. Leave it. Don't make the calls," he said. Because somehow he didn't like the idea of making Rachel humble herself to retract her invitation. "But Rachel?"

She waited.

"I'm sure the rules you live by are very nice and all, but don't try to turn me into something I'm not. Don't expect me to live by *your* rules."

"I won't," she said, her voice coming out soft and strained. "I promise."

That word. That word. The one word that meant so many awful things to him.

"Don't." He practically bit off the word. "Please, don't promise me anything."

He might as well have slapped her, he thought later.

Her eyes went puppy dog wounded, but to her credit she pulled herself together almost instantaneously.

"It was only an expression," she said. "I said it out of habit. It meant nothing."

But he knew that she was lying. Those little rules she used…he had no idea where they had come from, or when she had picked up the habit, but he knew that they meant something important to her. And he knew he'd been a total jerk.

His words had stolen Rachel's smile, her sunshine. And when it disappeared… When had he started looking forward to her smile? How long had he been waking up and anticipating her arrival at the house just because he coveted that smile?

He didn't know. He couldn't allow himself to think about that. Because in the end it couldn't matter. He and Rachel would be parting ways soon.

But he knew one thing. He needed to fix things and bring back Rachel's smile. If he could. He planned to concentrate on that this afternoon.

But then Rachel went missing.

Rachel needed advice, and she didn't want to go to Ruby. Ruby had known Shane for too long. She was a little biased. Plus there was the fact that she was a bit of a romantic. She would read something into Rachel's questions that wasn't there.

The perfect person would be someone who didn't know Shane very well. That was how Rachel ended up on Marcia's doorstep and how she ended up spilling her guts about what she had done.

"I just had to confess my sins to someone, and any woman who can decipher the ins and outs of Shane's antique appliances ranks as a practical sort of person who might give me practical advice," she said.

Marcia laughed at that. "Hank would probably disagree about the practical part. He thinks I'm a dreamer. But I see what you mean. It's always easier to be objective about other people's relationships than about your own."

Rachel froze in the act of lifting the cup of tea Marcia had just given her. "Shane and I don't have a relationship."

"Hmm, not sure I buy into that. That day at his house, the wattage on your smile turned up twice as high when he walked in. And I saw you looking at his biceps."

"I didn't."

Marcia drummed her fingers on the table. "I thought you wanted truth, objectivity."

"Okay. I do feel a little breathless when he's around. But it's probably just due to all the exercise I'm getting lately. And, anyway, I don't like it."

"Don't have to."

"This isn't solving my problem. I was hoping you could tell me what to do."

"About your infatuation with Shane?"

"About the possibility that I may have opened the door to unwanted visitors," she said, explaining what had happened. But when Marcia opened her mouth to speak, Rachel shook her head. "No, don't say anything. I was wrong. I thought I wanted advice, but then I've never been good at taking advice. I think what I really wanted was just someone to listen. I've been feeling a little tense lately."

"Because you're afraid you might fall in love with a man who can't offer you a future?"

"Not really."

Yes, Rachel thought. She'd had her heart scraped raw by people and she'd spent the past few years trying to learn to be smarter, less susceptible. Shane threatened that plan; he made her feel weak and wanton and afraid of what getting too close to him could do to her. But she was also afraid of more.

"I'm afraid of failing him. Somehow."

"Cooking? Cleaning?"

Rachel smiled a little. "Well, I fail on those counts every day, but that's not it. He seems like such a hard man, especially the way he's so set on dismantling and selling his childhood home, but he's not. And me with my blundering, acting without thinking ways... Just look at how I invited the world into his life when he's been trying to close it out. What damage I might have done. Maybe even now someone is driving toward Oak Valley and something terrible will happen. What kind of a woman would do something like that?"

"A loving one, Rachel. You had good intentions."

But good intentions didn't always count for much, she knew. "I'd better get back," she said. "I only meant to stay a few minutes."

"Okay, but can you at least stop and say hello to Ella and Henry? They've been dying to show you their goat."

Rachel's heart lifted immensely. "Lead me to the cherubs and Tunia. I wouldn't miss it. Mind if I snap some pictures of them?"

"They love smiling for the camera. And don't you dare forget to send me copies."

That was how Rachel ended up on her back, trying to get an upward shot of Ella and Henry, when another subject moved into her viewfinder.

"Hello, darlin'," Shane said. "Have I mentioned how much trouble you are?"

No, but lots of people had over the years. Rachel stared up at Shane and noted that his eyes seemed to be fiercer than usual. His frown was out in full force. Her immediate instinct was to scramble to her feet, because she was most definitely at a disadvantage lying on the ground. But that wasn't her way.

"Hello, Shane," she said. "I was just here collecting recipes in the hopes of saving your life." Which wasn't a lie. She had asked Marcia for some new "recipes for the hopeless" and she had them stashed in her camera bag.

"Were you, now?" He reached out and held a hand out. And even though Rachel knew how dangerous it was, touching Shane in any way, she placed her hand in his.

The kick was immediate. The tension traveled through her body quickly, clicking on every nerve ending, turning on that lust thing that she could never quite seem to control whenever Shane was around. But that was for her to know and no one to find out. "Thank you," she said as she regained her footing and Shane released her. Was that disappointment she was feeling when he let go of her?

"Sorry, munchkins," she told Ella and Henry. "Gotta get back to work."

Ella looked as if she was going to cry. She blinked hard and her lower lip trembled.

"Tunia?" Henry asked. "No Tunia?"

Shane dropped down beside them. "Was Rachel going to take a picture of Petunia?"

Henry nodded slowly. Shane picked him and Ella up and held one of them in each arm. "Well then, I apologize for interrupting. Rachel's yours for a few more minutes. Some things are way more important than lunch. Right?"

He got his answer when little Ella wrapped her arms around Shane's neck and hugged him while Henry patted him gently on the arm.

For no reason Rachel could think of, her chest suddenly felt tight. She tried to say "thank you" and had to clear her throat.

"Work your magic, Rachel," Shane said quietly. "I'll be waiting at the house when you get done."

Within minutes Rachel was struggling to capture the essence of the little lively goat and get Ella and Henry in the picture at the same time as all three of them jumped around with excitement.

"Did you get what you wanted?" Shane asked when she finally walked in the door.

"Yes," she said, thinking of the photos and the recipes and the companionship with Marcia. And, *no,* she thought, staring up into Shane's eyes and thinking of how messed up her heart was becoming and how there were no easy answers on how to protect herself or how to fix what she had messed up with him.

"Good," he said as he crossed the room. "I'm glad. But...please don't leave without at least telling someone where you've gone, Rachel. This is a ranch. There's water and rock, barbed wire and rough terrain. And heavy machinery that can hurt you. I didn't know where you were. I didn't know where to look."

His always deep voice was deeper, thicker. She looked up at him and her heart lurched at that dark, smoky and anguished expression. "I'm sorry," she said. "I didn't think."

"I know," he said. "But Rachel?"

She looked up.

"Next time…think. Tell someone. Tell me. Don't make me worry about you again. I've lost people on this ranch before." And then he placed one hand on the door frame she was standing next to. He kissed her. Hard. Fast. Done. The kiss was over almost as soon as it had begun.

"I'm not apologizing for that. I had to touch you."

Which made her heart hurt. He had lost people and she had gone missing on a ranch the size of Texas. The kiss had been a reassurance kiss. Nothing more.

"I won't wander off without notifying you again."

He nodded, and turned as if he was going to leave to go back to work. Instead, he stopped mid-stride and looked at her. "I'm glad that Marcia is close. You get lonely out here, don't you? That's what my mother used to say, that the ranch was a lonely place."

Rachel shook her head. "No, actually, I don't. That is, I love that Marcia is nearby, too, but…I like the ranch. I haven't felt lonely once." And she knew what loneliness was. She was on intimate terms with it.

"Still, you haven't seen much of the fun side of ranching. Come on." He took her by the hand and led her outside. It didn't take a cartographer to realize that he was leading her toward the corral. "Let's go see the horses. Lizzie misses you."

Rachel laughed at that. "I've gone to see the horses more than once since I've been here. I didn't notice that any of them had any special interest in me."

"That's because you haven't gotten close enough to talk to them."

"That's because they're big."

"But you can charm her. You have carrots."

"I do?"

Shane laughed. "Yes." He produced a carrot and showed her how to hold it on the flat of her palm so that her fingers couldn't get nipped by Lizzie's teeth. The horse lapped the carrot up and then snuffled around for more.

"Oh, she's hungry. Do you have another one?" Rachel asked.

"Yes, and she's not hungry. She knows you're a sucker. And you like to feed people."

"Lizzie, I promise you that these carrots are much healthier than my cooking and not nearly so lethal." The horse's gentle whinny seemed to say that she understood. Within no time Rachel and Lizzie seemed to be talking back and forth as Rachel rubbed Lizzie's coat. "I haven't really been out here much. I've been so busy."

"I know. I should have taken the time to make sure you had fun and not all work."

She shrugged. "I don't think bosses have to do that. Besides, there's that deadline."

"Even so, you've never been on a ranch, and you might not get near one again. I—Rachel, I won't push you, but...are you really afraid of Lizzie? I mean of riding Lizzie? Because I think you'd love it."

"I think I'd *want* to love it, but...I'm really, really terrified of heights. One of my stepmothers made me climb up on the roof when I was twelve because I'd thrown a Frisbee up there. I slipped and nearly fell off."

A low curse escaped Shane's lips. "That's criminal."

She shrugged, trying not to think about that day, an echo of her fear resounding in her memory even today. "I guess it wasn't a totally high roof. I practically dared her to make me do it. But still...I can't forget that swooping, out-of-control sensation as I gathered speed sliding toward the edge or the feeling that I might not be able to stop, trying to clutch at shingles and not being able to. Only my shoe jamming against the gutter saved me."

Shane's brows drew together. His hands were curled into fists. "Were you afraid of heights before?" The words shot from his mouth. Cold. Hard. Angry.

"No. I loved climbing."

He took deep, visible breaths, glancing down at the ground. Then he pinned her with his gaze. "I wouldn't presume to say I could help you forget that day. But... maybe I can help you take a baby step. I can hold Lizzie while you're up there. Rachel, horses and I...we go way back. They tell me their secrets. Lizzie likes you. She told me so."

He said the last in a whisper, conspiratorially, and Rachel knew he was trying to make her laugh, to distract her from her fears.

She looked up at the pretty horse with the gentle eyes. As if Lizzie understood, she gave a soft whicker.

"I don't know," Rachel said. "She looks really huge."

"Shh, you'll hurt her feelings. Lizzie worries that her rear end looks fat in a saddle."

Rachel couldn't hold back her smile then. "You have a lovely...um...rear end, Lizzie, but you're a bit taller than I am." Which wasn't saying much. Most people were a bit taller than she was.

Again as if she understood, Lizzie tossed her head. She gave Rachel another one of those sad looks. If she didn't know better, Rachel would have thought that Shane was coaching the pretty creature.

"Will you promise not to let me fall?" she asked Shane.

"No."

She blinked wide, startled.

"Sometimes you fall when you're on a horse," he said. "And I hate it when people promise what they can't deliver. Let's just say that I'll do my best to make sure you don't end up facedown in the dirt. And, if you do, I'll pick you up and dust the grass off of you."

"Ah, Ruby was right that first day. You're a real sweet-talker, Shane," she said.

He smiled. "You're stalling. And you know you want to try. I'm betting that a belief that trying new things is healthy is one of those handy little sayings you fling about."

"It's not," she said. "But it probably should be. Okay, I'm willing to try…once. Show me how to do this," she told him.

Within a very short time Shane had wandered off and located a pair of boots that were a size too big, but which served the purpose. He had her up on Lizzie's back. "Lizzie's no youngster, so she'll be slow. She won't run off with you."

In fact Lizzie was standing quietly, seemingly unperturbed to have Rachel on her back. Rachel felt the big animal's muscles shift beneath her and her breath caught in her throat. She reached out to touch Lizzie's back. "I'm counting on you, Lizzie," she whispered. "No bad surprises." She'd certainly had enough of those in her life.

"Let's try a leisurely walk down to the corral and back," Shane said, and he showed her what to do. To Rachel's surprise, Lizzie did just as she was asked.

"Are you giving her some secret commands?" she asked Shane.

He laughed. "She's just responding to *your* commands. You're letting her know what you want and she knows the drill."

Rachel knew that there wasn't anything magical about riding a horse. People had been doing it for years. But there was something so heady about asking her horse partner to take her somewhere and having Lizzie do exactly as she asked. She held the power, she had control in ways she'd rarely ever been in control during her life. Riding this slowly was simple stuff, feeling powerful because of it was silly, and yet…

"I like this," she said. "I can feel her moving and it's as if we're a team."

"You *are* a team."

But they were a slow team, probably a very slow team. Rachel was pretty sure that an experienced person like Shane wouldn't have been moving at anything near this crawl if not for her. "I should be working," she said suddenly. "I'm keeping you from what you need to do."

"Not true. The horses are an integral part of the ranch and they need to be exercised. You're helping."

"If this is as much exercise as Lizzie gets, she's going to start putting on some pounds real soon. Maybe we should go faster." She couldn't help the hopeful sound in her voice.

Shane laughed. "Not now. Those boots don't even fit you. You might fall if we speed things up." But they did speed up…just a bit. And she didn't fall.

She fell in love with Lizzie and with horseback riding and with Oak Valley. Beyond that, Rachel refused to think, but when Shane lifted her from the saddle and slid her down to the ground, her body touching his, it was all she could do to keep from wrapping her arms around his neck and begging him to kiss her. Thank goodness there wasn't too much time left with Shane or there was no question that she was going to be in serious, heart-shattering trouble.

CHAPTER EIGHT

WHEN Rachel arrived at Oak Valley the next day, Shane noticed two things. She was wearing his favorite smile and...

"I like the boots," Shane said. "Did you pick those out all by yourself?"

To his delight, she blushed, just as he'd known she would. Rachel always looked pretty, but when she blushed she was darn near irresistible. Which was a good sign that he shouldn't be trying to make her blush, but...those boots...

"As a matter of fact, I did pick them out," she said, lifting her chin in a defiant gesture. "I liked the blue flowers curling around the instep. They look pretty against the golden leather, and, yes, I *was* told that they were impractical and that they would get dirty, that they were really more for rodeos and things like that, but I bought them anyway."

He smiled. "Impulsive. Stubborn."

She sighed. "Yes, but I bought them because...it's just that I'll probably never have another pair of cowboy boots. If I'm only going to have one...well, you know."

"You don't seem like the type of woman who allows

anyone to dictate her style. You could wear boots for the rest of your life."

"I know. But it would be different then. I would just be posturing. These boots are going to be real. I'm going to actually use them. If Lizzie lets me back in the saddle."

Shane shook his head, confused. "Why wouldn't she?"

Rachel laughed then, that spontaneous, pretty, bell-like sound that turned his body hot. "I think I might have bored her to death yesterday. Next time you show me how to keep her entertained."

"Entertained?" Shane couldn't hold back his grin. "Rachel, I don't think I've ever met anyone who worried about whether the ranch animals were having fun. Lizzie is a working horse."

"Who hasn't been working for a while."

"Can't argue that."

"Do you think she'll mind getting moved around again when the ranch sells? I mean, she lived here with you, then she got moved to the other stable. Now she's here again. But for how long? Someone might buy her and take her elsewhere. Do you think that horses feel stressed about moving around the way people do?"

Shane hesitated. She had injected the subject of the ranch selling, the only reason they were here and something that was quickly coming up on the calendar. And she was right, too. "Yes, I think they do feel stress. Are you trying to guilt me into making sure that Lizzie stays here, Rachel?" Not that he blamed her. The truth was that he *had* felt guilty about moving the horses away from their home.

Rachel looked up, her eyes wide. "I don't know.

I was just wondering. I—seriously, I'm sorry about that."

"Don't be. You're right. I'll do what I can to make sure this experience is as stress free as possible for them. Now, I have a few things I want to discuss with you this morning. Have a seat."

She sat, and he noticed the sunlight glinting off her hair. She was as lovely as one of her photos, he thought. He wished he could capture this image and hold it, but…

"Let's discuss the schedule, first of all," he said, and he told her what he had done and what he had left to do. "The house is looking very inviting. Warm," he added. "You've made a big difference here."

"Thank you. I wanted it to feel like a home," she said softly.

The very words made his heart hurt. This house had never been a home, and he knew from things she'd said in the past how much she wanted one. Louise, his Realtor friend, had called him last night.

"Louise told me that she thinks she's found you an apartment and that you concur."

"Louise is a genius."

"She is. So, tell me, what are your plans when you move to Maine?" The days were flying past, and it had occurred to him—several times—that Rachel was rootless. She had her dream of a home, but she'd left her job with Dennis. "Do you have another job as a photographer lined up?"

Those brown eyes flickered. "Shane, I think I may have mentioned that I'm not really a pro. You've seen my work. It's adequate, but not more."

It *was* more.

"In fact," she said, "I've been meaning to ask—"

Now she looked nervous, her tongue sliding over her lip in a way that was driving him crazy. He took a deep breath. "Ask."

"Those shots I took of the ranch…I know they're not great and I was wondering if you wanted me to redo any of them. I don't want to fail you."

That was it. Shane sat down and took her hands in his. "Rachel, I don't need art to sell this ranch. The shots of the ranch are good. If I was going to buy a ranch, your photos would sell me on this one." He glanced at one she had hung on the wall, the one with the field of flowers. "Who wouldn't want to stare at that every day?" he asked. "But…" He could feel her fingers tense beneath his own. "Who made you so unsure of your talent? Was it that stepmother who nearly killed you?"

"That sounds *über*-dramatic, like Hansel and Gretel." She was trying to make a joke, to keep it light, and Shane wanted to give her what she wanted, but ever since yesterday he'd known that bad things had happened to her. Her stepmother had sent her onto a roof and he didn't care how "not very high" it had been. It had certainly been high enough to have made her fearful.

"Rachel, you're a trouper. You're a tough one. But…I need to know that you'll be safe and settled when we part. I need to know how you ended up on a roof. And that something like that won't happen to you again. Because I won't be there to try and save you, and that's going to make me insane."

"Don't," she said, pulling her hand away. "Don't pity me or feel responsible for me. I don't like even mentioning this stuff. I never tell anyone. But if it will keep you from worrying, I'll tell you this much.

I had…*have* self-absorbed parents who didn't want a child. So, as soon as I was old enough, they sent me to boarding schools. Lots of them. They moved me around on whims. And they married and divorced over and over, always trying to one up each other in the spouse department. I was called home when I might serve a useful purpose, such as sealing a deal with a potential new husband or wife. So, *yes,* there have been some bad moments and one or two bad stepparents. And, yes, my life has been rootless and unpredictable, and I've never stayed in one place long enough to have lasting friendships. But I don't need or want pity or concern. I learned how to make friends fast and how to jump in and figure out how to make each place my own quickly. Above all, I know how to take care of myself."

"I think that's clear. I'm amazed at how much you've accomplished here."

"One gets to be self-sufficient."

"I don't think many people would have such an optimistic outlook as you do. You're an amazing woman, Rachel."

She looked to the side. "What?" he asked, seeing that she was upset.

"I think you might have really meant that," she said.

Now he was angry. "Hell, yes, I did. You can't tell me that no one's ever said something similar to you."

"Dennis did. He said my photos were almost as good as his."

Little angry fires started in Shane's soul. "Dennis is a snake. And he's wrong about your photos."

Her head whipped around. "You don't like them?"

He smiled, just a little. "You know I do. What I meant was that I looked Dennis up online. Your photos put his to shame. Especially the ones with Ella and Henry. Hank showed me what you sent to Marcia last night and…you're amazing with children. You must have taken a hundred shots to catch the perfect expression. They were stunning, far beyond anything Dennis has ever produced. I suspect he knew that you are better than he is."

She gave a tiny nod, but she didn't look happy despite his compliment.

"So what do you plan to do in Maine?" he asked, getting back to what was worrying him even more now that he knew about her parents.

"I'll land on my feet. I always make sure that I do."

"That's not good enough."

"It's all I've got."

"Then you're selling yourself short."

"I don't think so. I know what I can and can't do."

"I don't want to know what you can do. I want to know what you're really *going* to do. Whether you like it or not, I'm going to worry if you're not set up with a way to feed yourself."

She shrugged. "I'm sorry. I really am. I wish I could tell you, but I'd just be making stuff up. I won't know until I'm there, facing reality."

"So it's just do or die when you get there? That works for you?"

"Well, it keeps me in food. I'm not dead yet."

Shane frowned.

"I'm sorry. I shouldn't have said that. It was insensitive."

"Don't. You don't have to muzzle yourself for me. But, yeah, I hate that when you leave here you'll be standing on a ledge waiting to see which side of the drop-off the wind will blow you to. So…how about this? It's not unusual for writers or artists to have another career to keep them solvent. With your natural way with children you could be a teacher. Maybe an art teacher. You'd be a sure success at something like that, and I just thought…why don't you go to college and explore your options?"

She didn't look convinced. "I did begin college right after I got out of school. My mother stopped paying the bills, and without a loan or a grant I was left hanging. Then she insisted that she was desperately ill and I needed to come home and help her."

"*Was* she ill?"

"Sort of. She'd had a face-lift and then she'd fallen while she was ignoring the doctor's orders to slow down. So I went home." The way she said it led Shane to believe that it wasn't the first time something like that had happened.

"She doesn't have servants?"

"When Mother is between husbands she tends to fire her servants. Me, she can't fire. It's why I'm such a hot commodity with the parents when they're between spouses and need someone to listen to them. Anyway, from there we went overseas for a year, and by the time we returned and Mother had met a man, I was two years behind. I got a job at a camera shop and never went back to college. Now it feels too late."

"You're twenty-five. I've met people who went back in their fifties. People have gone to college in their seventies."

"It takes money."

"You'll get a loan."

"I have to work so that I can eat."

"So, take classes when you can. In fact…start now." Rachel frowned, confused.

"You can get some of your gen eds via web-based classes. Rachel, why not try? You can still keep working at your craft—it would be a total shame for the world to lose your art—but security can also be a very good thing."

"Says the man who changes addresses every six weeks."

"True. But I *am* always gainfully employed when I move."

"Touché. I'm seldom gainfully employed, even though I'd like to be."

"The world needs more people like you at the helm, Rachel. More spit in the eye people, more enthusiastic people. Some lucky employer is going to be fortunate to get you."

"I don't know. I've gone to so many schools. I—"

"Is that it? Because you're not coming in as a freshman you'll feel like the new girl again?"

"I—yes."

"That's the beauty of college. People transfer all the time. Go to a big school. Lots of other people are guaranteed to be new, too. You won't be the only one. Just…think about it."

She didn't answer.

"Rachel?"

"I'm thinking about it," she said. "Seriously. I'm thinking about it."

Apparently that was as good an answer as he was going to get, Shane realized. He wanted to be happy with that answer. For her sake he would have to accept it.

But happy?

No. He couldn't be happy knowing that Rachel could simply disappear off the face of the earth and there wasn't a thing he could do about it. That had happened to him before.

This situation with Rachel might not be life or death, but having her vanish and be swallowed up where he might never even be able to locate her still promised to be incredibly painful.

Rachel was trying not to think about the fact that she had spilled her guts to Shane. She'd never done that before and now she felt naked. Uncertain. So she was throwing herself into work, trying to avoid the big questions about his suggestion, but mostly...him.

The calendar days were dropping off. Goodbye was right around the corner and she didn't want to think about it. So today she'd tackle one of her last cleaning tasks. She had almost worked her way to the back of the massive hallway closet, which housed decades of coats, mittens and hats. Boxes of greasy tools shared shelf space with old jelly jars with no lids. Torn and yellowed journals on ranching contained articles on such subjects as the pros and cons of different types of fencing.

"Pitch it all," Shane had said whenever she'd asked him about anything she found in the various storage spaces in the house.

And she was in the process of doing just that when she came upon a large black lacquered box with an ivory scrimshaw cameo of a woman set into the lid. When she opened it up it smelled faintly of tea, as if that was what had once been housed there. But there was no tea in the box, just lots and lots of packets of seeds. The box was so full that when Rachel opened it some of them fell out. Phlox and pinks, zinnias and sunflowers, columbine and daisies, delphiniums and marigolds. The once brightly colored packets were slightly faded now, and a few of them were opened. She took them out and spread them out on the table. At the bottom of the box were charts outlining where each plant would find a home.

Pitch it all, she heard Shane saying. But...

Gathering up her find, she went in search of Shane and found him repairing an overhead light in the tool-shed. He was standing on a ladder, his arms over his head, the muscles in his back beneath his white shirt tensing with his movements.

For a moment she just watched him...until she realized that she was looking like some ridiculous plain-Jane schoolgirl salivating over a boy who would inevitably never notice that she was even in the room.

She cleared her throat, loudly.

And Shane hit his head on the light fixture. A string of low curses dropped from his mouth and he turned around.

Heat traveled up from her toes, making all of her feel...hot. Very hot. She knew she was blushing. Horrid habit. Why couldn't she just control her body's reactions to the man?

"I'm so sorry," she said. "I startled you."

"Don't apologize. You were just trying to let me know you were there. I'm the one who swore the air blue. I'm the one who's sorry."

Then he smiled, and her inner schoolgirl emerged again. She held out the box mutely.

His smile disappeared. He came down from the ladder slowly.

"Where did you find this?" he asked.

"Buried in the hallway closet. It must have been in there a very long time. The colors on the packages are faded. I know you told me to throw everything in there away, but this seemed…special. The box is very pretty, unique, probably expensive. And the seeds…" The seeds interested her more than the box. "There are so many of them, and there are these wonderful planting charts with comments like 'Phlox reminds me of home,' or quotations by Wordsworth like 'Daisies: The Poet's Darling' scribbled in the margins of the charts."

She stared up at him, waiting for him to tell her about this treasure, because it was obvious that he knew what it was. But the look in his eyes…was it pain? Was it remembrance? "Were these yours?" she asked. "Or…?"

"My mother's. I remember her planting a garden every year. She could never have enough and always tried to cram too many into the space she had plotted out. If a frost came she would run out in the night and try to cover everything up. I remember my stepfather, Frank, chiding her for that. 'Flowers aren't that important,' he told her."

"But they are," Rachel said. "Even if you're sad, a flower can cheer you up. Not that I know anything of gardens. I never had one. My mother…well, you know about my mother. She would be horrified at the thought of kneeling down in the dirt. And I was never in one place long enough to plant one of my own. There would have been no place for a garden, anyway."

"Rachel…"

"No. That was bad of me. That sounded self-pitying and I'm not. I hate that kind of thing. It makes me feel small and icky. Besides, flowers are everywhere. I've had my share."

"From men?" Shane was wearing that smoky look again, the one that made it hard to breathe…or talk.

She gave him a haughty look. "I—I don't need a man to give me flowers," she managed to say. "They were mostly from me to me. Those count."

"They do. They count a lot."

She glanced down at the box. "This was your mother's. Not like the other stuff in the closet. What should I do with it?" She held it out to him. "You should keep it. Seriously. Just this one thing."

He placed his hands over her own, shook his head and slowly restored the box to her arms. "No, I want you to keep it. Please."

"But it's special. It's your mother's."

"It *is* special. And my mother would have liked it to be used by a gardener. When you get to Maine and find a bit of land, plant your own garden. The seeds won't grow. They're too old. But you'll fill the box with your own. That's a much more fitting end to it than sitting on a shelf in my apartment or hotel room. And someday you'll have flowers."

But the very next day she had flowers. Several vases of them arrived. When she approached Shane to thank him, he looked sheepish. "Have to have flowers for an open house," he said.

"You're a softie, Shane Merritt," she said. "You know these won't last that long. You just did this because I told you I hadn't had any flowers from a man."

"I did it because I can't believe what a low class of men you must have been hanging around with if none of them sent you flowers."

She smiled. "Well, I've obviously met a higher class of man now."

He scowled. "No. You haven't. This was bribery, pure and simple. Now, let's get back to work."

She did, but several times that day she stopped to

bury her nose in the flowers. She tried to remind herself that these weren't special. Shane had surely sent flowers to many women. And would again long after all she had left of him were memories.

Her heart hurt. She really needed to think about the future.

Soon.

Rachel wandered through the next few days in a fog of gratitude and pain and regret. She had finally taken Shane's suggestions to heart and had enrolled in an online class. It was a small start, but maybe it would be something to look forward to when she was tempted to look back to her days on the ranch. That was the gratitude part.

For the rest...

"He's not coming, is he?" Ruby asked one day. "Let's face it. He's going to leave here and never come back and we'll never see him again."

"Ruby..." Rachel said, her heart breaking for the woman.

"I know he has a good life and a good business, but...I don't know. You watch a child grow up and become a man, you have a part in his life, and... I don't have any children of my own. I never married. So the children in town are the closest I'll ever get to having my own. I know I'm not the only one, either. It was awful when Eric died. He was so young. He'd been engaged, but he'd barely become an adult. He didn't leave us by choice. Shane's refusal to interact with us... it feels a lot like rejection," Ruby said.

Rachel's throat was closing up. She'd been dealing with the reality of leaving Shane for days, maybe ever since she'd come here. And, no matter how much she wanted to deny it, she'd developed feelings for him. Feelings she was doing her best to shut out. She had no choice. She wasn't free to care. A man like Shane, who had told her from the first that he liked his life unfettered...falling for a man like that would be like ripping your own heart out voluntarily.

But Ruby...wonderful, warmhearted, fun and funny Ruby, who seldom was serious...to see her this way...

And Shane...whatever was keeping him from people like Ruby had to be something that hurt him badly. She knew he wasn't a man who would harm someone uncaringly.

Swiping her hand across her eyes hastily lest Ruby see the tears that threatened to fall, Rachel made a resolution. One way or another she was going to confront Shane about the way he was ignoring his neighbors and ignoring his own history. And punishing himself, she supposed, for youthful indiscretion.

And if he fired her...

She took a deep breath. *Well, I'm going anyway,* she reasoned. But she didn't want to think about that. Like everyone else, she wanted every last drop of time she could get with Shane.

Still, she would take the risk. He wasn't going to be happy about her intrusion into his life again.

Too bad.

Rachel sat at the kitchen table waiting for Shane to come in for dinner. Her stomach felt as if a million miniature gymnasts were staging a show, doing cartwheels and handstands and stealing all of her air. She had waited until this late hour so that there would be time, but she didn't relish making Shane angry; the fact that he was late only added to her nerves. Why was he late? Shane was not a man who showed up late with no explanation. She remembered his lecture about the dangers of ranching.

The phone rang loudly, startling her. "Rachel?" he yelled as she picked it up.

"Shane, what's wrong?" His voice was strained, and she could hear air whishing past, so he was moving fast as he talked. He was incredibly late for dinner. Fear lurched through her.

"I'm not coming in." He sounded as if he was running. "Rambler's hurt. I—does blood make you faint?"

"It never has before."

"Good. The vet's on another call, Tom's on the outskirts of the property, Hank's getting over a cold and I'd rather not risk any more infection here. Meet me at the barn."

She didn't hesitate. She just ran, her legs pumping fast as she entered the barn to find Shane already there examining the horse with gentle yet persistent movements. At the sound of her entrance, he rose.

"You need to wash up," Shane told her. He gestured to a sink and soap and began to scrub his hands. "I won't need you to do more than hand me things, but I don't want any extra germs."

Rachel did as he said. She glanced at Rambler, who was clearly in distress, and at Shane's tense expression. "Tell me what you need."

"Saline first. Some sterile gauze, bandages and disinfectant." He grabbed the saline and moved off toward the horse, clearly expecting her to follow. She scrambled to locate the other supplies and hurried over to where he was kneeling, next to the frightened and quivering animal.

"Shh, boy. How'd you do this, anyway? Were you

dreaming of some pretty little filly and not paying attention to where you were going? It's okay, Rambler. We all get hurt now and again." As he spoke, his words soft and low and soothing, he gently washed the wound with saline, pressing his body against the horse's, calming him. "But I'll make it right. You'll heal. You're going to be just fine, boy. I know it hurts, but we're going to do our best to make that better right away."

As he spoke, he gestured to Rachel, who handed him whatever he was pointing to. He kept up the low, gentle conversation as he worked. "Just a little bit longer, boy," he said, as he made the final wrap of the bandage. "I know this disinfectant doesn't smell pretty, like Lizzie, but it'll do the trick. Soon you'll be galloping off around the fields faster than ever. You'll play Romeo again. You'll be just fine."

He stood, straightening to his full height and patting the giant horse's side. As he did, Rambler tossed his head just a bit. "Oh, already feeling a bit better?" Shane asked. "Or are you just showing off for Rachel?"

Rambler whickered weakly, just as if he was answering, and Rachel finally realized that she was standing next to a creature much bigger and wilder than Lizzie. But…what could she do? The animal was hurt. That had been a nasty cut.

"Will he really be all right?" she asked.

"He'll be sore for a few more days, but he should be fine. The wound looked bad because of the blood, but it wasn't deep. Thank you,' he said. "I didn't want to ask for your help, but I wasn't sure what I was dealing with when I first got here."

"You're very good with horses, aren't you?" she asked. "You calmed him. He knew you'd take care of him. There was something rather beautiful about the whole experience. The man caring for his horse."

He shrugged. "Practice," he said. "This was nothing."

"Not to Rambler." And not to her, either. But as her words trailed off, Shane finished up in Ramber's stall, peeled off his bloody shirt and began to wash off. The muscles of his chest were slick as he reached for a towel.

Rachel closed her eyes. When she opened them again, he was staring at her with a fierce expression. He has clearly seen her looking at him.

"I should go back to the house," she said, her voice weak.

Shane nodded. And then he smiled that glorious dimpled smile. "I'll be right up. We can share a meal and celebrate your successful baptism as a veterinary assistant. Another notch on your résumé."

He looked happy. But Rachel knew that he wouldn't be happy for long. She still had to do what she had sworn she'd do today.

CHAPTER NINE

SHANE was just taking his last bite of Surprise Casserole, or, as Rachel called it, Super Surprise Casserole, when he looked up to find Rachel watching him with worried eyes.

She'd been quiet throughout the meal. He was pretty sure he knew what the problem was.

"Rachel, I apologize for asking you to help me with the horse. I know you're a city girl, that you're not very comfortable with large animals and that Rambler's much bigger than Lizzie. Believe me, if there had been anyone else around I wouldn't—"

She had placed her hand on his wrist, and now those big brown eyes were looking at him as if she was going to tell him something very bad.

He'd seen that look in someone's eyes twice before in his life. "Something's wrong."

"It's Ruby."

His heart dropped like a rock in water. "She's sick? She's hurt? No, you wouldn't have waited to tell me that—"

"Shane, no. It's nothing like that. It's just...she's depressed and hurt that you would come here and then leave without seeing her. And she's not alone. I know that whatever happened here, whatever made you hate this place so much is none of my business, but…I just can't leave this alone."

"Did she ask you to talk to me?"

"She didn't have to. She told me that she had no children and you and Eric had been like her children. And…it's not just that. I know part of why you hate this place has to be tied up with your brother and that room. I just… You've done so much for me. You've helped me so much and I… Shane, I'll be gone in four days. You'll be gone. And I know I'm just your house-keeper, I don't have a right to your personal business, but—"

He rose from the table, knocking his chair over in the process. Anger washed over him. At himself. At how Rachel was trying so hard to help him, to help Ruby and the others, and how he was mucking it all up. Again. As he had done before.

"You know you're not just a housekeeper. Damn it, Rachel. You just helped me bandage an animal that weighs ten times what you do. You've taken on tasks I know you had no interest in. You've befriended my neighbors."

"I just don't want to overstep—"

"You're not. It's not your fault you've been driven to this. Come on. It's time."

"Time for what?" Those big brown eyes looked un-certain.

"Time for several things. You're leaving in just a few days. So am I. But when you're gone I want you to take some memories. Some real ranch memories. And I want you to leave here knowing exactly what kind of man I am. Ruby plays me like some bad boy who's good at heart, but I'm not that guy."

"Who are you, then?"

"I'm a guy who made some serious mistakes and I can't ever forget them or forgive myself."

"Are we talking about Eric?" She looked toward the room.

Shane's heart hurt. His throat hurt. He knew the little-boy items that were in that room, pieces of his brother's past, baby pictures, so many things frozen in time. He just…couldn't do this here.

"Rachel, I need to be outside tonight, if you don't mind. Will you come with me? Will you…mind?"

To his consternation, she didn't hesitate. "I'll come."

He frowned. "You should hesitate. Not follow blindly. I need to know that you'll be safe when I'm gone, not just walking into danger without thinking."

"I was thinking. I was thinking that I trust you."

He scowled. "See, that's a mistake right there. You call Ruby and you tell her that I'm taking you out to Settler's Creek, to the camp zone. And that I'll have you back bright and early tomorrow morning. That's called insurance, Rachel. You always let someone know where you're going. When you'll return. Will you do that?"

"Only because Ruby will worry if I don't."

He wanted to swear, but he knew Rachel needed her independence. It was one of the things he loved about her.

That acknowledgment made him flinch. It wasn't her fault that he had done what he'd said he'd never do: fall in love. She would never know. He wasn't mixing another person up in his life, especially not Rachel, who was finally, finally, for once in her life, catching a break and on the road to realizing her dreams.

"Will you mind if we ride? I'll ask Tom to check in

on Rambler, but Cobalt needs exercise and Lizzie is always available for you."

"I'll get ready," she said, and soon they were on their way across the fields to the spot she'd once told him would be perfect for a cowboy fantasy.

But fantasies weren't on the menu tonight. Truth was. Rachel deserved truth. All of it. She'd been bleeding for his sin, trying to make things right with his neighbors, and he wasn't going to make her do that anymore.

When they got to the camp area he lifted her down from Lizzie and while he savored the chance to hold her in his arms, he didn't allow himself the kinds of thoughts he always had with Rachel. Instead, he spread a blanket and made a place for her to sit. Then he began to gather firewood.

"I can help," she said, starting to rise.

"No. Not tonight. Tonight you're my cowgirl guest. You stare at the mountains and watch as the stars begin to come out." He knelt by the cleared space and began to stack the wood.

"Shane?"

He looked up from his task. The last drops of sunlight were squeezing from the sky, and the fire-pink reflected back in Rachel's eyes. She looked more beautiful than ever, this tough-sweet woman. But she wasn't staring at the glorious sunset. She was looking at him. Was she trembling? Was he making her nervous?

"I'll keep the tale short," he said. "And then for the rest of the night you can just enjoy the beauty of the sky. That is, unless you want to go home after you've heard my story."

"In the dark?"

"I've got provisions and a lantern. I'd keep you safe."

"I know you would."

He breathed in deeply, wondering what he had done to deserve the appearance of Rachel in his life. But he already knew the answer to that. He didn't deserve her. He'd simply been lucky that day; he'd been blessed.

Now that was over. He'd had his turn. He reached for the last piece of wood, set fire to the kindling and waited for the flames to build. Then he took a place on the blanket, facing her. Not near enough to touch.

And he ripped off the bandage he had placed over his heart long ago. He began to speak.

Rachel realized right away that Shane had placed his back to the fire so that his face was in the shadows and hers was in full light. He'd made it clear that this was not a conversation that he relished. He was doing this because she'd asked. No, she'd needled, practically demanded. And as he began speaking, even though she couldn't see his expression, she could hear the change in his voice.

He was in pain. Real pain.

"My birth father was friends with my stepfather, and when my mother got pregnant and my father disappeared, Frank stepped in. He'd loved my mother from the first and eventually, when I was three, she married him even though she didn't love him. She did it for me, so that I would have security."

"Because she loved you."

"Yes. I don't think she would have agreed to the marriage otherwise. I was four when Eric was born, and eight when my mother died from an infected wound. One day she was there, the next day she was dying. By then, it was obvious that Frank didn't like me at all. I was a symbol of the man my mother really loved. And I was also the healthy brother. Eric was frail when he was young and he followed me around everywhere. Everywhere."

Shane's voice cracked a bit. He turned away slightly and waited until he had himself under control. "As she lay dying, feverish and weak and scared, my mother begged me to promise that I would watch over Eric. I think she had grown to loathe Frank, and she was afraid that a man who revered ranching and physical strength as much as he did would grow to hate his fragile son even more than he hated me. And by then she knew that I was the strong one. I was terrified and sobbing but I gave her my promise."

Rachel couldn't hold back her murmur of distress. "You were just a child."

He shook his head. "I was never a child. I had an attitude and a serious disregard for authority figures and rules. I learned to swear and spit, kick and bite, and ignore authority. But I took my responsibility to Eric seriously. And my little brother was my polar opposite. He was the friendliest, most lovable guy, like a big puppy or a very generous friend. He'd give you everything he owned if you'd let him, he'd lend a hand wherever it was needed and he surprised everyone by eventually shedding his fragility. He became an athlete, an outdoorsman, a true rancher, not an angry, spiteful math nerd who felt stuck on the ranch like I did."

"In other words he became the son Frank wanted."

"Yes."

"And you were the troublemaker, the one who wouldn't fit the mold."

"I was arrogant and angry at everyone, including my mother for dying, and especially at Frank for insisting he would turn me into a rancher or die trying. He hated the fact that I liked math and science more than raising cattle. I did anything I could to keep from doing the right thing...except where Eric was concerned."

Rachel could understand Shane regretting his wild childhood, but...the other...the way he still flagellated himself and shut himself off long after his tormentor was gone...

"Did your stepfather beat you?" She heard the horror in her voice.

"No. That wasn't Frank's way. That might have brought strangers to our door, and Frank didn't like strangers. No, Frank was a man of words, slurs, derision. But in public, in the rare times we appeared together, he never said a word. No one ever knew what went on here, and if they did...it wasn't illegal. A man can tell his sons whatever he wants to tell them.

"The only thing was...as I got older my arguments with Frank became more heated, and more frightening to Eric, who hated conflict of any kind. The day I brought him to his knees, begging me to please just go to my room and let Frank bellow, I decided that it was time to go. I tried to tell myself that it was for Eric's sake, but the truth was that I felt trapped. By my life, by Frank and..."

He stopped, looked up, clenching his fists.

"You felt trapped by your promise to take care of your brother?"

"Yes. I told myself he was old enough, but he was only sixteen, and I know my leaving hurt him. Tore him up."

Shane stopped again, trying to regain his composure. Rachel waited, silent.

"After that," he continued, "I only saw Eric away from here, I'd ask him to come to my hotel. Once or twice I flew him out to where I was. But I had stopped watching over him. And then Frank died, and Eric truly was alone, but I still didn't come home."

"How old was Eric then?"

"Twenty-two."

"A man."

"You wouldn't say that if you'd known Eric. He was a late bloomer, young for his age."

"But a talented rancher and outdoorsman."

Shane ignored that comment. "He met a girl, fell in love, got engaged. They were having a party. I was supposed to come, but I got snowbound and missed it. I sent flowers, and when the snow melted I just went back to work. The next day Eric went out to the field with the tractor to feed the cattle alone. He wouldn't have gone alone if he hadn't been upset with me. I'm sure of that. Eric was very safety conscious. And while he was pitching the hay to the cattle in a snow-covered field something went wrong. The tractor tipped and he was pinned beneath it. Crushed."

"You blame yourself?"

"Of course I'm to blame. I left him alone at sixteen, living with an uncommunicative and sullen father. I ignored his life as if only mine mattered. I might as well have been driving that tractor that took him to his death, because *I* had always been the reckless one, not him. He learned that maneuver, that wildness, from me. Because I cared too much about myself to care about anyone else."

"Is that why you avoid the people of Moraine? Because they witnessed all of what you consider your sins?"

"Not because they witnessed them. Because they were my victims. I wronged them over and over, cared nothing for their feelings and then I took their brightest sun, the best that Moraine had to offer. Eric was the boy who took in stray animals, he served as a make-shift vet when the real vet was unavailable, he shoveled people out of the snow. He was the go-to guy when anyone needed a strong shoulder, the peacemaker. And I hurt him so much that he...he died. Rachel, he *died*."

Rachel couldn't help herself then. She crawled across the blanket and wrapped her arms around Shane. She just held him while he wrestled with his demons. Silently struggling.

Eventually, when he seemed calmer, she looked up and kissed him on the chin. "The people of Moraine don't blame you, Shane, or if they ever did, they've forgiven you."

He looked down into her face. "I know. I've known that all along."

Oh, this was bad. This was difficult. "That's why you won't let them in? Because they've forgiven you but you haven't forgiven yourself? You don't want them to forgive you."

"I don't deserve their forgiveness."

Rachel didn't know what to say. She had spent a lot of time in her life learning how to deal with adversity and unhappy situations, loneliness, friends who could only be friends for the short term, but this was beyond her experience. And yet she couldn't let it go. This was Shane. This was...the man she cared for far too much, and it was impossible to leave things as they were.

"I know you loved your brother, Shane, but Eric was an adult. He made a choice."

Shane didn't answer.

"If he loved you—and I'm sure he did—he wouldn't want you to be this way."

Still no answer.

"Shane?"

"Rachel, do me a favor."

"What?"

"Don't— please don't try to save me. Just lie here with me beneath the stars. No touching. Nothing like that. Just be here with me."

"Anything," she said, her heart breaking.

He pulled her into his arms and lay down with her. "This isn't the romantic evening under the stars you once mentioned."

No, it wasn't, but she was right where she wanted to be. Not that she could tell him that. Ever. "It's…peaceful," she whispered, although it wasn't really peaceful. It was quiet. It was sad.

"Shh. Sleep," he said.

And what could she do but give him what he asked. It was all she *could* do. She knew she wouldn't sleep, but she tried, and eventually she slept. Because Shane's arms were around her.

Some time after that the stars disappeared behind a threatening cloud and Shane gathered up their things and gave Rachel a helmet with a light on it. He led them home.

"Don't go now," he said. "The roads are dark and deserted. You can have my room. I'll sleep in the spare."

She wanted him to hold her again, but he didn't. He simply walked away.

So she lay there in the dark, thinking about how she'd only made things worse for him by pushing. She'd forced him to face things he had put in a box. And now the scab had been removed from the wound and he was distant and unhappy.

Shane woke and got dressed the next morning feeling as if some of the heaviness he'd been carrying in his chest had been lifted and yet…it wasn't a pleasant feeling. Probably because he'd done what he hadn't wanted to do. In his urgency to give Rachel the truth he'd felt she deserved, he'd saddled her with more worry.

That wasn't right. There were a whole lot of things that weren't right. And it was no longer just about *his* pain now. He'd seen her face when he'd lost it last night. He'd dragged Rachel in. Down.

"Fix it, Merritt," he ordered. Yeah, and the first thing he was going to do was what should have already been done. The open house was in four days. Rachel had offered to let him off the hook and find a place to store the contents of Eric's room. But that wasn't fair or right.

Tension rose within him, hard and hot, as he thought of opening that door. But he beat it back.

Silently, he walked toward the room and turned the knob.

CHAPTER TEN

RACHEL felt the difference in the house when she woke up. There was a silence, a sense of anxiety, as if the whole world was just waiting to implode. As soon as she walked into the main part of the house she sensed what had happened, and her footsteps carried her to the room where Shane had buried his past.

The door was open. She didn't even have to be nosy or rude. And in the middle of the room, surrounded by boxes, by photo albums, by bits of paper and old souvenirs, Shane sat on a small sofa, the upholstery sagging.

He looked up when she came in, and she saw that he was holding a bundle of yellowing letters tied with a bedraggled pale peach ribbon.

"Are you…all right?" she whispered.

His response was to call her to his side. He brushed aside a pile of clothing, making a place for her. "I'm sorry about last night," he said.

"Sorry?"

"For hitting you with all that brutal stuff. For not—"

"Holding it in?" she said, standing up. "Shane, how can you say that? I'm so…honored that you agreed to tell me. I just hope I didn't push too hard."

To her surprise, he smiled slightly. "You always push. It's cute."

She blinked, unsure of how to react, but he took her hand and drew her to his side again. "You've spent so much time dealing with the detritus of this ranch. You deserve to see some of its history. Will you sit?"

She wedged in beside him, his warmth, the length of his thigh near hers, making her want to move closer. She resisted.

"It's all here, the pieces of their lives," Shane said. "Here's my mother's home in Boston. Here's Eric when he lost his two front teeth."

Rachel looked down at a photo of a very young smiling boy, clinging to the hand of his older brother, a much younger Shane. And the Shane in the photo was smiling back at Eric as they shared a private moment.

"He looked up to you," she said.

Shane shrugged. "He was a kid." Just as if Shane hadn't been "a kid," too. "Here's my mother's garden in better times." And now Rachel could see just how awesome a gardener Vera Merritt had been. The flowers were full and fat, purple and pink, white and gold blossoms a perfect contrast to the mountains in the distance and the green of the fields.

"She could have won prizes. She was an artist," she said.

"She would have liked to hear you say that. But..." He picked up the discarded letters. "These detail the events that led to my birth and to my mother marrying Frank. To her credit, she didn't lie to him or promise him anything. She was upfront about her reasons for marrying him. But it's clear that she wasn't happy. Unfortunately, Eric would have seen these after Frank died."

"He didn't know?" she asked incredulously.

"He was only four when she died. Why expose him to the dark stuff?"

"I don't care what you say. You were a good brother," she said, "and your mother must have loved you and your brother very much to make the kind of sacrifices she did. Mothers like that aren't born every day," she said, unable to keep the wistfulness out of her voice.

"Rachel, I wish—"

"No. My parents are imperfect, but they're mine and I'm fine with that. I'm okay," she said as he brushed his knuckles across her cheek. She couldn't help herself then. She leaned into his touch, but in her leaning her gaze fell on something.

"Shane, look at this," she said. She was staring down into a box, its contents a mess of papers. "These must be your brother's school papers." She picked up a hand-ful and saw reports on "Calf Roping by the Numbers," "Alfalfa and Oats as Feed" and "The Road to Being a Quarterback."

"He wrote about what he loved," Shane said. "There's Eric right there in your hands." He took the papers, devouring the words as if now that he'd opened the doors and let the past in, he couldn't help himself.

"Shane." Rachel's heart nearly stopped.

He looked up. She held out a single sheet of paper. The title read, "Why My Brother is My Hero by Eric Merritt."

"I never knew he wrote that," Shane said.

"He wrote it after you left. Look at the date," she said.

When she turned to Shane he was staring at the ceiling. A single tear tracked down his cheek. Quietly, she got up and left him alone, closing the door behind her.

It felt as if this was already goodbye. Shane would be all right now, she hoped. He could be happy with his work, knowing that Eric had remembered the years when Shane had watched over him, cared for him and loved him.

Eric had just returned the favor. He'd given Shane a gift that was worth more than gold, silver and diamonds combined.

It was wonderful. They were a family again.

And she? She would soon be on her way elsewhere. Like always.

She was just about ready to go about her work when Shane came into the kitchen.

"I want to thank you," he said.

"For what?"

"For being in the road that day. I'm not sure I would have found that report if you hadn't been there. I might have burned everything."

"Shane…"

"Sorry. I can't seem to lie to you. That's why I'm not going to lie and tell you that some miracle has happened. It hasn't. I'm not eager to visit with the people of Moraine, but I'm going to."

"Because it's the right thing to do?"

"Because you want it so much."

Rachel felt a lump in her throat, and not a happy lump. To have Shane do something just because she wished it broke her heart. It touched her, but…

"You can't—"

He held up his hand to stop her. "And because even though I don't think I deserve forgiveness from my neighbors, I feel that they deserve the right to call the shots, not me. I'm not even sure how to approach them, though."

"Then you're lucky I've been thinking about this," she said, risking a smile.

His answering smile was the kind that was wide enough to reveal his dimples. "Why am I not surprised that you have a plan to get me to town?"

"Oh, not to town. Here. I was thinking…a gathering. Not the open house. That's four days away, anyway, and it's about business. This would be…I don't know… tomorrow. And just people."

"I wasn't thinking anything quite that formal. Or that soon."

"It doesn't have to be formal. Just all-inclusive. A party."

He looked a bit taken aback. "A party? Tomorrow? I don't see—"

"I'll make it happen."

"I don't want to put that kind of work on you."

"You won't be. I really do want this get-together, Shane. I'll be gone in four days. I'll never be a Moraine girl again, never a cowgirl again, never here with all of you again. They're nice people. You're nice people. Nice people should get together."

"And have parties?"

"Of course."

"Another rule to live by?"

"When you change schools every year or six months, you learn ways to get in quickly and connect with people, parties being one way. Because even if you never get to see them again, you still get to count them as friends."

"Damn it, Rachel."

Shane moved up beside her. He trailed his index

finger down her cheek. She felt the heat rise within her. She heard his breath quicken.

"I'm not going to kiss you this time. I promised that I wouldn't hurt you, but you…amaze me."

"I wish you would kiss me. And don't say 'Damn it, Rachel.' I know I'm being outrageous, but time is short."

"Kissing…accelerates things. Situations tend to get out of hand. At least that's how I know it's going to be with me if I kiss you."

She shook her head. "It won't. I won't let it."

He reached out and cupped her elbows, pulling her toward him. Their bodies weren't touching other than his fingertips feathering across her elbows. Then he leaned forward slowly and traced her lips with his tongue. Softly. Gently. He kissed her.

Her elbows tingled. Her lips tingled. Her…everything tingled. Heat rose within her. Higher. Higher still until she was swaying toward him. She was just going to wrap her arms around his neck, but she heard herself only seconds before, saying, "I won't let it." She remembered that Shane was the king of guilt. If something happened, he would not let her take the blame even if it was totally her fault.

And yet…she quickly looped one arm around his neck, kissed him quick, hard, drinking in as much of him as she could, tasting as much as she could manage. Then she squeezed her eyes tight and pushed away.

"You're safe," she said. And she didn't know whether she was talking to him or to herself.

"I don't feel safe," he said.

"Me, either," she admitted.

"How do you feel?"

Lost. So lost. She was losing him. Only four more days. Four short days and then a lifetime of no Shane.

Rachel took a deep breath. "I feel frustrated and as if I need to do a lot of stuff to take my mind off of kissing. Fortunately, I have a big party to plan." And, with that, she ran off to start planning.

Shane walked out onto the grassy area where Rachel and Marcia had hastily set up tables and chairs decorated with white tablecloths and Rachel's favorite flowers. He and Hank and Tom had constructed a makeshift wooden dance floor in record time. There would be musicians. There was food galore. "Some of which Marcia let me look at but not touch," Rachel had teased.

He had laughed. Hard to believe he had been able to laugh or look her in the face after all the things he had confessed the other night. He should be feeling self-conscious. He probably would be if the person on the receiving end had been anyone but Rachel.

Because Rachel wasn't like anyone else, he thought as he looked up to see her walking toward him. She was wearing her pretty blue-trimmed boots and a white fringed skirt with a blue blouse. A white hat hung down her back on a string, and she kept trying to look over her shoulder and see it, to no avail.

"Does any true cowgirl ever wear one of these?" she asked. "I'd hate for anyone to think I was making fun of real cowgirls."

He smiled at her because…he just couldn't help himself. "You can wear whatever you like. No one will mind."

And that theory was proven correct when the guests began arriving.

"Nice hat, Rachel," someone said.

"Beautiful, Rachel," a male voice said.

Shane swung around to see Jarrod Ollis staring him in the eyes.

"Want to fight over her?" Jarrod teased. "I'll wrestle you for her."

"Are you actually trying to manipulate me into a fight?" Shane asked with a smile. "If I recall—and I do—the last time we fought, you walked away with a broken arm."

"A scratch."

It had been much more than a scratch, and it hadn't been a good-natured fight that time, either. Shane took a deep breath. "I'm—Jarrod, I'm sorry."

"About the broken arm? Forget it. I was probably asking for it."

He hadn't been. Not really. "About the arm, but also…about everything." That covered a lot of territory. He wanted to be more specific, but when he opened his mouth to speak, Jarrod punched him in the arm. Gently.

"Hey, man, no. I didn't come here to humiliate you or for an apology. Lots of things happened. We were young and stupid, then not so young. Maybe still stupid at times. Whatever. Things change. Some bad things happened to both of us. Probably to all of us. But I'm still here. And so are you. I came to see you."

Shane's chest felt tight. He could see Rachel over Jarrod's shoulder. She was fanning her face as if trying not to cry. So, for her sake, he couldn't lose it right here. But he slapped Jarrod on the back. "I'm glad you're here," he said.

By then the guests had started arriving fast and furious. Ruby and Angie and Cynthia cornered him.

"We missed you, you big…Shane," Angie said.

"Come into the store anytime," Cynthia offered. "I'll pull out your favorite licorice whips."

"I'll be sure to come by the store and the diner before I go," he promised. And then… "I've missed you," he said, and meant it as he gave them each a big hug.

"Don't think you're going to get away with one hug from me," Ruby warned. "I want two hugs and a kiss on the cheek."

"I can do better than that," Shane said, meeting her demands and then swinging her around in a circle.

"Shane," she shrieked. "Put me down. I weigh a ton."

"You're a feather," he told her.

She laughed. "Oh, I've missed you more than you can ever imagine."

And that was when he lost it. He pulled Ruby close and hugged her again. "I'm sorry, so sorry for holding you at arm's length. You mothered me a lot when I was growing up. Even when I was bad."

"You don't ever have to apologize to me," she said. "But I'm so glad to see you again. I owe Rachel a lot."

"I owe her more."

"You're really going to let her get away?"

"Ruby…"

"All right, I won't pry."

"You'd better have a good time, though," he warned. "Rachel worked like the dickens to pull this off. I want it to be the best night ever."

Because after this…the open house didn't really count. There would be lots of people. The ads had gone out, complete with Rachel's photos, to five counties. He might not get to see her alone for more than a minute or two that day. They had reached the top of the mountain and now they were rushing to the bottom. Shane took a deep breath and dived into Rachel's party.

At some point he took the mike and thanked everyone for coming. Despite Jarrod's words, Shane told everyone he was sorry he had been rude and distant and in general a jerk, and was shushed by the crowd. But he saw a damp eye or two or three, and some sad faces when he finished thanking them for loving his baby brother and for being good neighbors to Eric in his absence, so he was glad he'd been allowed to apologize.

And then he found himself searching out Rachel. As if she knew he'd been looking for her, she came to him. The band was tuning up their fiddles and mandolins and banjos. And then they began to play.

She grinned and mimed dancing with him.

He took her hand, even though what he really wanted was just to walk with her, talk with her, be with her.

Rachel walked right into his arms. "I'm not the best dancer," she confessed.

It didn't matter. He would have her in his arms.

"I'll muffle my screams of pain if you step on my toes," he promised.

She hit him, lightly, and that was good. Because while he was teasing her, and she was reacting, he couldn't do what he really wanted to. Which was to kiss her crazy.

Dancing with Rachel was torture. Exquisite torture. And over too soon.

Everything with Rachel would be over too soon. And he would have to smile through his pain. Because she was following her dreams.

* * *

Rachel couldn't stop humming even after the last guest had gone home. The evening had been magical, and she didn't want it to end. Even though she knew it was already over. And tomorrow…tomorrow…

"One more," Shane whispered, coming up behind her and taking her in his arms as he swung her into a dance, just as if the party was still going on.

Except it wasn't. They were at the ranch, they were alone and she was so in love with him that she couldn't think straight. She was in deepest danger of doing something stupid, showing her hand. She had to lighten things up.

"So…what do you think? Ruby and Len? Maybe an item?" she asked.

Shane tilted back his head and laughed. "She was beating him over the head when he stepped on her foot. He was hopping around like a bunny that had lost its sense of direction. And the dog…the dog…"

They stopped dancing. They laughed, holding each other. "The dog…" Shane said. "I thought the dog was going to be trampled between them. I don't know if Otter was trying to save Len from Ruby's blows or if he just wanted to dance with them. Good thing you got in there and saved him. You're as good with animals as you are with children, Rachel."

"He looked as if he needed a friend," she said.

And that was when the laughter stopped.

"You've been just what I needed, what everyone in Moraine needed. You made this happen," Shane said. "This whole wonderful evening was your doing."

"No," she said quietly. "No, it wasn't. You made them happy, Shane."

"They made me happy. And this night…it was time. You were right. All along. Maine doesn't know just how lucky a state it is," he whispered fiercely. While he was talking, he was slowly walking her up against a wall. He took her hands in his.

"I'm not sure a state can be considered lucky," she said, a trifle breathlessly.

He lifted her hands and placed them against the wall on either side of her head, his palms holding her there gently as he nudged her head to one side with his nose and kissed right beneath her earlobe.

She melted.

"Lucky. Like me. I feel lucky to have you with me tonight," he said.

His lips slid down to the curve of her neck. To her shoulder.

She shivered and his eyes turned molten. He released her as his lips met hers. He gathered her to him and slid his hands over her shoulders, just beneath the curve of her breast...

The sound of Hank closing a gate somewhere in the distance registered. He wasn't close. He wouldn't come to the house. But Shane backed away. "I promised I wouldn't do this," he told her. "I shouldn't have started it."

"Not smart of either of us," she agreed. "But...you didn't want it?"

He looked at her with astonishment. "Do I look like I'm insane and unaware of how desirable you are?"

"No one's ever told me that before, that I'm desirable."

Shane growled. "Then the men you've known must have been wearing their heads on backward, because you are the most desirable woman I know," he said as his hand snaked around her waist. He slammed her up against him. He kissed her hard, his body molded to hers. Every inch of her body was curved against his. "Bodies don't lie, so don't lie to yourself. If it weren't for Hank reminding me that it would be a major mistake for us to sleep together, I would be begging you to come to my bed."

She looped an arm around his neck. "All right. You win. I'm what you wanted tonight." Then she smiled up at him sadly. She kissed him, just once. Somehow—she didn't know how—she managed to back away, because backing away was the only choice when so much was at risk.

In only a second she would be far enough away to break the spell of being near him. She hoped.

But then she made the mistake of looking directly into his eyes, and that always messed with her common sense. "You wouldn't have had to beg me to come to your bed. I was already there in my mind," she confessed. "Thank goodness one of us thought things through, or we would have been naked together and regretting it ever afterward."

And then she turned and ran for her car.

"Idiot. Fool. What's wrong with you?" she whispered as she began to drive home, just a bit too fast. But that answer was already obvious. She was in love with Shane.

And her heart was already preparing itself for the pain to come. Because, no matter what milestones he had passed tonight, he was still going. Mending fences didn't negate the fact that he loved his work. He loved moving around. He didn't want a relationship.

If she were very smart—and she had once thought that she was—she would start putting on the emotional brakes. She could pull away right now, just get on a bus and ride away. She had enough money now, and not going was going to land her in major hurt territory. There would be broken pieces of her that might not go back together again. There would be substantial scarring of her heart, the kind that never disappeared.

Still…not staying would leave Shane alone to face that open house and the auction, selling off the house where his mother and brother had lived and died.

"So suck it up, Everly. You know you're not leaving him until it's all done and he's back on his way to happy." Still, she had to be very careful. Who knew what foolish things she might do between now and then?

CHAPTER ELEVEN

RACHEL and Shane sat on the porch beneath a star-filled sky. *Last time to do this,* she thought. The house was finished. Tomorrow was the sale. But she didn't want to think about that.

"They're so beautiful. There are so many of them," she said.

"I meant for you to have a chance to enjoy them that night we camped out. I'm sorry you didn't get the chance."

"I'm seeing them now. I suppose some people would find this mundane, but I've never really spent much time looking at stars. Most of the places I've lived have too much light pollution to see more than a few of the brightest ones."

"My mother used to tell Eric and me that stars were a giant's dandruff. Mostly, I think, because Eric had this amazingly contagious laughter. We used to think up things to make him laugh just to hear it."

She smiled. "What a nice memory."

"I'd almost forgotten it."

"I'm glad you didn't. Remembering your brother's laughter is a good thing, isn't it?"

"It was one of the best things about him. Are you sure you're not cold? It's a bit chilly tonight."

She sighed and leaned back against the porch support. "I'm...just right. In fact, I could fall asleep right here in this very spot. Did you ever do that?"

"Sleep on the porch? Lots of times. Lots of mosquito bites in the morning." He flicked an imaginary one away from her nose.

She leaned toward him, following his touch. "Shane, do you think we've done enough? I want tomorrow to be perfect," she said. "Lots of people coming to look at your house. I want it to shine like silver. Nothing left undone."

He laughed. "You've checked and double checked everything."

"As if you didn't," she teased.

"Yeah, but that's what I do. I'm a numbers man, a checklist kind of guy."

"And I'm a 'try to make everything right' woman."

"Do you seriously want to look one more time?"

No. She seriously wanted him to lean closer and kiss her. She wanted them to slide to the porch wrapped in each other's arms. She wanted to plunge her fingers into Shane's thick, dark hair. And because she wanted those things so badly...

"I think one more look around wouldn't hurt." She got to her feet.

He groaned, but then he laughed. "The royal tour, then?"

"Nothing but the best for us."

So they opened the door and stared at the wonders they had created. The living room was perfect. "I still love that green vase, even in lamplight," she said. "Maybe especially in lamplight. I hope someone gives you bundles of money for it."

They moved to the kitchen, redone in sunshine

yellow and turquoise, with black and white tile on the floor. "If anyone makes one remark about tearing this place down, don't tell me. This room is perfect as it is."

The tour continued. The dining room, the enclosed porch. Finally they came to Eric's room. Rachel had come in early and she and Shane had worked as long as they could.

"You were right about the very subtle cowboy theme, the hat on the shelf, the boots in the corner," he said. "I thought it might be tacky, but done up in rust and brown and gold this place is Eric through and through. And I'm glad. It feels warm. It feels complete."

"Thank you," she said softly. "I tried not to change too much. And now…I guess there's nowhere else to go, no more rooms to inspect. Everything is in its place."

"Tomorrow we let the masses give it a yes vote or a no vote, I suppose."

"They wouldn't dare give it a no vote," she said, making him laugh. She laughed, too, but there were tears in her heart. Because when tomorrow was over Shane would turn over anything that hadn't sold to a company that would continue the sale online. And then she would leave him.

"And then we'll both leave," he said. "You'll go to Maine."

"You'll go to Germany."

"I'd like to know that you're all right," he said.

Her heart stalled. She'd experienced so many endings, but this one…she couldn't drag out her goodbyes. Her heart was ripping in half already. "I'll—I'll send you a postcard," she said.

He froze. "Damn you, Rachel. That's cold."

"Said the boy who was born to break hearts."

"Not yours. I don't want to break yours. Not that I could, but…I don't want…"

"*I* want," she said suddenly.

This whole situation, this polite farewell. Everything was so clean, so neat, so dry, so terrible. And she had always been a messy person.

"I want a souvenir," she said. "Just one thing." She wrapped her arms around his neck and kissed him.

He kissed her back. Fervently. And then…more fervently.

"I don't want to forget you," she whispered.

"I want you to forget me," he said. "I don't want to be a regret for you."

"You won't. You'll be a memory. A great memory. The kind I couldn't possibly forget."

"That's what I want, too," he said. "Wait here." And he took off as if the house was on fire.

In a few seconds she heard the sound of banging and clanging. She started toward the bedroom.

"Don't come in here," he warned. "In fact, go into the living room and close the door."

"I don't think—"

"Good. I don't want you to think right now. Just feel." And then he was gone again. Ten minutes later he came to get her. His hair was disheveled. His shirt was half untucked. "Come on, my little astronomer."

"Astronomer?"

"You wanted to sleep beneath the stars. Well, I can't promise you sleep, but I can promise you something better than the porch." He led her out of the house into the yard, and there beside the garden, with the fragrance of night roses wafting over them, was a bed fully assembled.

"We're having a sleepover?" she asked, and her heart started pounding.

"I hadn't gotten that far yet. I just wanted you to finally have your wish, your souvenir. A night beneath Montana skies."

He held a hand out toward the bed, and she saw that he had piled up pillows. A person could lie back and easily, comfortably look up at the heavens. If looking up was what they wanted to do.

"I can see now what all those women saw, why so many of them cried when you left. You're a master of the gallant gesture."

He chuckled as he sat on the side of the bed, took her hand and drew her down beside him. "Believe me, this is a first for me. Beds aren't made to be dragged out into the night."

"But you did it. Thank you. It was a heroic effort, and I—"

"Rachel?"

She looked up at him. He smiled down at her.

"Shh," he said, and he slipped his hands into her hair and kissed her.

He drew her down so that they were lying on the bed. And he kissed her some more. Deeply. His mouth driving her slowly crazy, his hands wandering over her body, slipping beneath her blouse, leaving trails of fire burning within her.

She clutched at him, unbuttoned his shirt with more speed than skill, popping a button as she revealed his chest. She slid her palms up over his naked skin and loved the sound of his breath catching in his throat.

"Rachel," he said on a groan.

"Yes."

"No. I shouldn't have started this. We're not doing

this." He reached out and began to rearrange her clothing where he had left her skin exposed.

Her heart went cold, like a rock in winter. "We're not?"

"No. And not because I'm not dying to. I'm burning up for you. My hands are shaking with the need to touch you. But tomorrow..."

"Tomorrow it ends."

"I want it to end right for you. With no regrets. I don't want you to hate me afterward."

She would never hate him. But the fact that he cared... She leaned forward and kissed him on the chest. He visibly swallowed. His breathing became more shallow.

"And I also don't want you to have to worry about falling asleep and having Hank find us this way," he said in a raspy voice.

She shrieked. "Hank? I hadn't even thought of Hank."

"Neither had I when I came up with the not so bright idea of dragging the bed out here. Still, Hank isn't the main reason we're just going to lie here and stare at the stars while I hold you. I want...I want you to be different. I don't want you to be the topic of gossip. You're so strong and beautiful and proud. I would hate to have anyone use that sympathetic, sorrowful tone when they talked about you."

"Shane, that's so...nice." But she didn't think she could bear it if he didn't at least kiss her some more. She placed her palm low on his stomach and leaned closer.

A shudder ripped through his body. He placed his hand over hers, stopping her. "Damn it, Rachel. For once I'm trying to do the right thing, and I'm not sure

I've ever done anything that tested me so much in my life. Now…the stars…please."

She gave a tight nod, kissed his arm and lay back in his arms. "Show me your stars, Shane." He was trying to make her different from all his other women. Despite the pain in her heart, the knowledge that she would never spend a night in his arms, Rachel intended to help him do—or not do—this thing.

So she lay beside him as they whispered about the constellations and he showed her the sky he'd grown up with. He showed her Sagittarius and Hercules and Corona Borealis. As he spoke, his deep voice echoed through her body. His left arm tightened around her as he pointed out the stars with his right. Gradually, she began to relax, to appreciate the beauty and the wonder of simply lying here with him, sharing this with him.

She felt…special…and as his voice died away she looked up at him to tell him so.

He smiled down at her, and then a curse word left his lips. Rachel blinked, then learned the reason why as fast-moving clouds started blotting out some of the stars and a few drops of rain fell on her face.

Without even talking, they leaped from the bed. Rachel grabbed the bedding, Shane muscled the mattress up on the porch, then came back for the frame. By the time they were done the clouds had obliterated all of the stars and both of them were wearing wet clothes.

"I can't believe I did that to you," he said, but he was laughing. "I can't believe I didn't know there was rain in the forecast."

"Well, you're a numbers man, not a weatherman," she told him, laughing up at him. "Shane?"

He looked at her.

"I'm really wet. I'm going inside to take my clothes off."

"Rachel?"

"Yes."

"I'm going to follow you, and I hope you'll understand when I tell you that I think I used up my last drop of willpower back in that bed. If you take your clothes off, I'm going to want to look."

"I'm so glad to hear that." She didn't even wait to get inside. She shucked her boots, pulled her blouse over her head and tossed it aside, then removed her pants until all that remained was her candy-apple-red bra and panties.

Shane came at her like a madman, wrapping her in his arms, crushing her to him and kissing her crazy. "Tell me to stop," he told her. "I'm not even close to being in control."

"Don't stop," she begged. "I love all your fancy constellation talk, but…don't stop." She rose on her toes. She kissed whatever parts of him she could reach.

Somewhere along the line his shirt and pants and… everything came off. He removed the remaining scraps of red silk from her body and dropped with her onto the bare mattress lying on the porch.

They kissed, they clutched and finally they created some new constellations of their own as the rain came down and the darkness enfolded them. He loved her long and well throughout the night. And as the sun came up he kissed her throat.

He stared down at her, a worried look in his beautiful blue eyes. "I don't want you to ever be sorry for this, to regret this summer," he told her.

She tried out a shaky smile. Because she knew that what he was asking her just wasn't completely possible.

She would love him forever. She would regret the pain that would follow her all her days. Still, this…

"This was wonderful," she told him. "Thank you for everything." And that was all she was going to say.

He didn't look happy.

She didn't feel happy. Because the night was over. The auction was today. The words "the end" loomed large in her mind.

When she came out of the shower, where she had retreated, she knew that something was wrong. Different. Shane was staring at the phone.

She moved to his side.

"I've already had an offer on the ranch. On everything in it. A group of local investors saw it on the internet, pooled their funds and want the whole thing. Now. No auction."

His voice sounded… She didn't know how it sounded. Her heart had fallen out of her body, or maybe it was simply being squeezed by a giant fist, because all she could think was, *It's over. Too soon. This is goodbye, the last conversation, the last anything.* She wasn't even sure she could speak without her voice catching. And if she didn't speak he would know just how much she was hurting. That would hurt *him*. Again. It just wasn't happening. She wasn't letting it.

Rachel cleared her throat. "Are you accepting the offer?"

He looked at her, but she couldn't read his expression. "It's what I came to do."

She nodded, even tried a smile. "All right. Good. That will save you a lot of trouble. Do you need me to…?"

She looked around, trying to seem cheerful. Here

was where he'd kissed her. There was the vase she loved, Cynthia's curtains, the rooms Shane had walked in and grown up in and where she'd learned to love him heart and soul. It was going, going, gone…and not even an auction in sight.

"I think…we should both leave today," he said. "Now. It's what we planned, anyway. Just earlier than expected. I'll make some calls, take you to the airport, get you on an early flight and…"

"No." She touched his hand. "Don't drive me." She couldn't bear a public goodbye at an airport. "I'll leave now. Hank can pick up the car. Ruby will make sure I have transportation. I think this is the way we should end. Here at the ranch. Maybe…this minute." Because if they didn't end right now, she was surely going to let her tears fall.

"If you like."

No. There was no *like* about it. She wanted the impossible. She wanted Shane. However she could have him. She had become one of those women Ruby comforted.

Without another second of hesitation, Rachel looped one arm around his neck and kissed him quickly. "This was the best summer ever," she said fiercely. "Kiss Lizzie goodbye for me and give her some extra oats. Make sure the new people aren't mean to her. And—"

"Rachel—" Shane's voice broke. He pulled her hard against his chest and his lips met hers. She leaned into him as tears threatened.

Just a few seconds more, she pleaded. *Don't cry now. Don't, Rachel.* She ran for the car, climbed in and hit the gas. Shane disappeared from her rearview mirror.

And the tears fell.

* * *

Shane kicked the wall. He kicked a few other things, too. She was gone. Gone forever. And the look in her eyes...

Something was wrong. And he was pretty sure that he knew what it was. Rachel wasn't a jump-into-bed kind of woman. She wouldn't do that lightly. But when that call had come this morning it had caught him by surprise. So much so that the sense of loss at ending things so quickly and finally had hit him sledgehammer hard, and he had just wanted to get past it. He'd been callous in his suggestion that they end it now. Hell, he hadn't said any of the things he'd wanted to say. Things like, *Thank you for being you, thank you for bringing light into my life, thank you for saving me from myself.*

And then there had been all the things he never *could* say. Things like, *I love you. I love you. I love you.*

He kicked the bedpost, the one he had still not put back together, and it fell over with a bang.

She was gone. *Get used to it, Merritt.*

But that was never going to happen. Slowly, he began to gather his things, getting ready to leave. Rachel would soon be living her dream life, and he owed it to her not to be a pathetic lovesick guy. He could never call her. If he did, she would know something was wrong and she would worry.

He just couldn't do that to her. And yet...something was flat out wrong ending things this way. She'd had so many aborted stays in her life, being dragged here and there with no fanfare at all. And here was another aborted ending.

Just once in her life she should have a joyful farewell, with people saying all the right things.

"She's already gone," he said. "It's too late."

Yes. Most people would think that way. But Rachel had never been like most people, and she had taught him a thing or two.

He picked up the telephone.

Rachel couldn't figure out what was wrong with Ruby. The woman wasn't herself at all.

"I'll see about getting you a ride, but I think there may be some problem at the airport. I heard something on the news earlier. This could take a while," Ruby said.

"What kind of problem?"

"Oh, I don't know. Some holdup. Planes stacked in. They're telling people not to show up yet."

Rachel raised an eyebrow. "Maybe I should call and get an update."

"Oh. No. There are lots of flights today. You need some breakfast. You didn't even eat breakfast."

She hadn't, but…

"How do you know that?"

"I just…I think I know you a little bit by now, Rachel Everly. I just know it. Are you calling me a liar?"

Rachel didn't have time to say no. The phone rang, and Ruby jumped up and ran into the next room to answer it. "Sorry, got to take this. A businesswoman has to always be available, you know."

Apparently there was a lot of business today. The phone kept ringing. Ruby kept talking in low, fervent whispers. Was she having problems with her business? Rachel would make sure that Ruby at least was okay before she left today.

The thought made Rachel sad. So many friends

she would never see again, never know what had happened to them. An image of Shane reared up in her consciousness. Rachel closed her eyes.

"Honey, are you sure you're all right?"

She opened her eyes to find Ruby frowning down at her.

Lie. Lie, she told herself. *What purpose would it serve to worry your friend?* "I'm just fine," she tried to say, but her voice came out garbled and thick. "I really need to leave," she finally managed. "I have to call the airport, and if there's a problem there call Shane and let him know." She couldn't get trapped in an airport with him. Not after she'd managed to make it this far without letting him see that she'd been stupid enough to love a man who had told her from day one that he couldn't love, couldn't promise.

"Sweetie, he knows," Ruby said, and she enfolded Rachel in her arms.

Panic erupted in Rachel like a volcano. "He knows what?" That she loved him? No, no, no. Don't let him know that.

Ruby looked panicked, as if she'd made a mistake herself. "He knows about the airport, I'm sure. He has people to do those things for him, and I'm—I think—"

The sound of sirens blaring interrupted her. Both women looked up. There was yelling, screaming, something that sounded like a drum and a fiddle and—

Rachel raced Ruby to the window.

"Thank goodness. I thought I was going to have to tie you down," Ruby said. "Come on, sweetie. Shane knows you need something better than a handshake and a peck on the cheek goodbye."

Fear gripped Rachel's heart. "I don't understand."

"You will. Come on."

A part of Rachel wanted to dig in her heels. She was pretty darn sure that if this had something to do with Shane she should back away. If she saw him again, or had to talk about him to anyone, she was definitely going to make a fool of herself. But the part of her that was desperately, pathetically in love with him didn't have the strength to run away again. She followed Ruby out onto the lawn of the boarding house.

A group of people had gathered there. Len and some men were in the back of a pickup truck with musical instruments.

"Have to have music at a going away party," he said, smiling and tipping his hat to her as they began to play some soft, lonely tune that pulled at Rachel's heart.

Other people held homemade signs that read, "We'll miss you, Rachel," and "Good luck in Maine," and "Don't forget us, Rachel." Some of the signs had been painted, and the paint was clearly still wet.

"Rachel, we wish we'd had more time, but we brought food. You can't say goodbye without cake," Angie said, and she and Cynthia and some of the other men and women began to set out folding tables and chairs and bring out food.

There was chatter, and people began to hug her. She hugged them back, thanked them and turned to Ruby. "You did this so fast!" A lump nearly choked her, but she got the words out and hugged her friend, kissing her cheek.

"Not me," Ruby said. "I told you. I'm thrilled this is happening, but this was all Shane."

But Shane wasn't here. Rachel knew then that he had wanted her to have a goodbye party, but they had already said their goodbyes. She tried to accept that and smile at her friends. They had gone to so much trouble for her.

There were even games of several types, and someone gave Rachel a horseshoe. When she turned to throw it in the wrong direction a cry rang out. "I'm just getting my bearings," she said, a bit sheepishly. "I wasn't going to throw it yet."

But apparently it wasn't her lack of skill with a horseshoe that was causing the uproar. People were pointing and calling out Shane's name, and Rachel looked up to see him flying down the road in his pickup truck, the dust curling in a low cloud behind him.

Her heart began to thump wildly, erratically. Her throat felt thick with tears. For the first time in her life she thought she might actually faint. Somehow she didn't.

Shane drove close to the crowd, jumped out of the truck and walked right up to her. "Hello again, sunshine. I'm sorry. I know you wanted it to be a short goodbye, but...I just couldn't do it. It had to be right. You need to know how important you are, how much you'll be missed, that this wasn't just an ordinary summer. It was different, better. It was special because of you."

Oh, no. The first teardrop slipped down her cheek. She just couldn't stop it.

"Don't," Shane whispered. "I didn't mean to hurt you." He stepped forward, took a handkerchief out of his pocket and wiped the tear away gently.

"They're tears of joy," she said, and that was partly true and partly very much a lie. "Thank you. For this." She gestured to the crowd. *This* was so wonderful. People had obviously stopped their busy lives to make this happen for her. She was not going to ruin it for them by crying. If only she could stop.

"She's crying." Jarrod stated the obvious. "I—Rachel, I think those are presents Shane has in his truck."

That Jarrod was trying so hard to cheer her up only made the tears flow faster. She swiped them away.

The crowd turned to look at the back of the truck, which appeared to be crammed full. There was a log cabin quilt covering whatever was inside. "I'm sorry I didn't have time to do this right," Shane said. "You should have had everything wrapped in gold ribbons and silver star paper. This isn't all I hoped it would be."

She looked at him, hoping her heart wasn't in her eyes. "I don't need silver paper. But I don't understand. What are you giving me?"

"A home. Or at least some of the things from the ranch you've grown to treasure." He handed her the green glass vase that had gotten her eyes glowing so many times, her favorite mug, a small and exquisite oak table. Slowly he revealed the secrets beneath the quilt.

"Not your mother's favorite china? Shane, I love it. You know that. But you can't give that to me."

"Why not? You're building a dream life. You'll need things, and you should have things you love."

"But they're yours."

"And I was going to sell them," he said. "You treasured them the way I should have."

Suddenly, something wasn't right. "You said the buyers wanted the house and all its contents. Shane, you can't do that. You can't let me have these things. That would be stealing."

His fierce, steady gaze suddenly flickered. "No, it wouldn't. I—I decided not to sell the ranch."

"Just like that?"

"Quicker than that."

"Why?"

"I'd rather not say."

She shook her head. "But Shane—"

"Because that house *is* a home now. It wasn't before you came. You loved it up and changed it. You changed *me*. And now…things are different."

"Will you rent it out?"

He took her hands. "It doesn't matter, does it? What matters is that you're going to have what you want and need. I'm glad of that. But I want you to know, if you ever pass this way again, we'll be here for you. You have family here. You have a permanent place to come to."

"You're staying?" The words came out on a whisper, on a breath.

"I don't think I can do anything other than stay. You made me see the ranch through your eyes. You taught me to let people in, not shut them out. This place feels like family now. It's where I belong."

She bit her lip. She nodded. "I'm glad."

As if no one else but the two of them were there, he cupped her face with his palms. "I want you to be happy. Supremely happy. To have all the things you've ever dreamed of."

But of course that was no longer possible. She gazed up at him with her heart in her eyes.

"What if my dream changes? What if I've realized that a home isn't one never-changing place?"

"Rachel." He said her name on a breath. Somewhere someone sighed. "What are you saying?"

She set down the vase she was still holding. "All those other times when I had to leave a place I didn't fight back. I went because there was no one on my side, no one I could trust. But…I trust you. You've opened up my world, inspired me to take risks and make better choices. I'd like to make one of those choices right now."

"Do it," he said. "If it's that you don't want my mother's dishes, I can find you something you'll like better."

She bopped him on the arm. "I love your mother's dishes. I don't want to talk about dishes. I want to talk about you. About me. About how I want to stay here and how I don't want to be another woman who ends up crying on Ruby's bosom. I want you to love me, but if you can't—"

Rachel never got the chance to say the words. Shane tugged her to him and she tumbled into his arms. "I've been in love with you for weeks." His voice was a fierce, dark whisper.

"And you didn't tell me?"

"You had things to do. In Maine. Without me. I wanted you to have your dream."

"You *are* my dream. Every night. Every day."

"Good," he said. "Because I'm never leaving you. Not now. Not ever."

"Can you afford to keep the ranch?"

"If I want to, I can afford never to work again in my life. I'm rich, Rachel, but I think I'd like to ranch even though I'm not a cattleman. I'll be a horse rancher."

"And I'll be a horse rancher's wife. If you'll have me."

Shane laughed out loud. He kissed her hard. "That's

my beautiful, exciting, exhilarating Rachel. Impatient. Mouthy."

"Shane, you didn't answer my question. Everyone is waiting. I'm—I confess that I'm a little nervous. I didn't mean to blurt that out."

And then her wonderful rancher went down on one knee. "I'll have you. I'd never have any other. And I'll love you until the stars turn their lights out."

"Shane, there's still something in that truck, isn't there?" Jarrod asked. "Something big. What is it?"

"It's a secret," he said. "It's just for Rachel."

She looked at him with a question in her eyes, but she was willing to wait for the answer. She had what she wanted, after all. Her rancher.

"I always knew he was a rancher," Ruby said, and everyone laughed. "More importantly, I knew he was Rachel's rancher. She flipped him over and found all the hidden parts none of us had ever looked for. She found his heart."

"And she owns it," Shane whispered against Rachel's hair. "I don't need to move around anymore. There's no longer anything to run from, and what I've spent my life searching for is right here."

Hours later, as they pulled up at the ranch and climbed out of the truck, Rachel started to go inside.

"I'll be right there," Shane said. "There's something in the truck that we need."

"Dishes?" she asked. "Shane, I don't think so. We've been eating all afternoon."

"I know, and I'm not hungry for food. But we might need a bed. It's in here somewhere."

Rachel shrieked. She ran to him and put her arms around his waist. "You were giving me your bed? The one we made love on?"

"It wasn't my bed, it was ours after that," he said stubbornly. "I kept the pillows that still carry the scent of your perfume and gave you the rest. I wanted to feel that you were with me when I slept. I wanted you to remember the man who loved you on that bed. It was selfish, I guess. A better man wouldn't have tried to remind you of our last night together."

She slid in front of him, rose on her toes and kissed him. "There isn't a better man than you, Shane."

"I hope you always feel that way," he said. And he lifted her into his arms and started toward the barn.

"Shane, where are you taking me? What about the bed?"

"I'll get to that in just a minute, my love," he said. "For now I'm taking you to tell the kids that their mother's home. And this time she's staying forever. She's ours."

Rachel laughed. "I do love Lizzie and Rambler and all the others," she said.

"And I love you, Rachel. No more endings. No more moving. Just you and me, beginning the rest of our life together. Every single morning."

EPILOGUE

Two weeks later, Rachel walked across the grass near the creek at Oak Valley. She was dressed all in white, her long veil flowing out behind her.

And waiting for her beside the creek was her cowboy.

She reached him and he pulled her straight into his arms, kissed her long and slow and sweet.

The minister cleared his throat.

"Sorry," Shane said, "but I waited a long time to come back to Oak Valley. Too long. I don't want to wait for the good stuff anymore."

"Well, you'll wait for this woman if you want to wed her," the minister ordered.

"In that case, I'll wait forever," he said, backing away as Rachel rushed forward and launched into his arms.

The minister rolled his eyes.

"You might as well give up for a while. Once they start kissing, it tends to go on and on," someone said.

But Shane and Rachel heard, and both of them stepped away. "We like to kiss," Rachel said, "but we want to get married."

"We're *going* to get married," Shane said. "Today."

"And then they're going to be so happy," Ruby said.

"Rachel is going to college here, and she's going to be a teacher and our local photographer. Shane is going to be a rancher."

"I thought that Shane hated ranching," someone called out.

"He only thought he did. Until he looked at it through Rachel's eyes."

The conversation was going on all around Shane and Rachel until someone said, "Shh."

Shane was very quietly saying his vows. For Rachel's ears alone. "I promise to love you," he ended, repeating the words he'd already said.

"I promise to adore you," Rachel added.

"I promise to…" He leaned over and whispered in her ear. She turned a delicious shade of pink.

"Now?"

"Tonight," Shane promised.

"I now pronounce you man and wife," the minister said, rushing in. "You may kiss the bride."

But he already was. And as he tipped his bride back and her skirts rode up, the toes of a pair of boots with blue trim peeped out.

"Am I a real cowgirl now?" she asked her husband.

"You're *my* cowgirl now."

"That's the very best kind. And you're my cowboy."

"Right from the start, sweetheart. And to the end of time."

THE MUMMY PROPOSAL

CATHY GILLEN THACKER

Chapter One

"I hear you work miracles," Nate Hutchinson drawled.

"Sometimes I do." Brooke Mitchell smiled and took the sexy financier's hand in hers, shaking it briefly as she stepped into his downtown Fort Worth office.

"Good." Nate looked her straight in the eye. "Because I'm in need of a home makeover—fast. The son of an old friend is coming to live with me."

Still tingling from the feel of his warm, hard palm clasped in hers, Brooke stepped back. "Temporarily or permanently?"

"If all goes according to plan, I'll adopt Landry by summer's end."

Brooke had heard the founder of Nate Hutchinson Financial Services was eligible, wealthy and generous to a fault. She hadn't known he was in the market for a family, but she supposed she shouldn't be surprised. Nate's four best buddies were all married, with kids. It made sense that as he approached his late thirties, the dark-haired, six-foot-five Texan would want to enrich his personal life, too. Brooke had just figured that a man as successful and handsome as Nate would want to do so the old-fashioned way. By finding a woman to settle down with and *then* have babies. Not that this was any of her business, she reminded herself sternly.

She turned her glance away from Nate's broad shoulders and powerful chest. "So how old is this child?" she asked in a crisp, formal tone, trying not to think how the marine-blue of Nate Hutchinson's dress shirt and striped tie deepened the hue of his eyes.

"Fourteen."

Brooke sank into a chair and pulled out a notepad and pen. She crossed her legs at the knee and continued. "What's he like?"

"I don't know." Nate circled around to sit behind his massive antique mahogany desk. He relaxed against the smooth leather of the chair. "I've never met him."

"You've invited this kid to live with you permanently and you've never laid eyes on him?" Brooke blurted before she could stop herself.

Nate flashed a charming half smile, the kind car salesmen gave when they were talking about gas mileage that was less than ideal. "It's complicated," he murmured. "But I'm sure it's going to work out fine."

Obviously, Brooke thought, calling on her own experience as a parent, Nate Hutchinson knew as little about teenage boys as he did about decorating. But that wasn't her problem. Finding a way to do the assignment and collect her commission without getting emotionally involved was. It seemed there hadn't been a child born yet in this world who did not possess the capability to steal her heart...and that went double for a kid in any kind of trouble.

The phone on his desk buzzed. Nate picked up. "Yes. Send him in. I want Ms. Mitchell to meet him." He rose and headed for the door.

Moments later, a tall, gangly teen sauntered through the portal of the executive suite. He wore jeans and a faded T-shirt he had clearly outgrown, and had peach fuzz on his face and shaggy dishwater-blond hair. His only nod toward propriety was the tender deference with which he treated the elderly white-haired woman beside him. She walked with a cane and looked so frail even a mild Texas breeze might blow her over.

Brooke could feel Nate's shock, even as he resumed the perennial smooth of someone who made his living charming people into investing with his firm. "Mrs. Walker. It's been a long time." He moved to help her into a chair. The youth assisted from the other side.

The elderly woman gratefully accepted their help. "Yes. It has."

"And this must be your great-grandson." Nate moved toward the fourteen-year-old boy, genially extending his palm. "Hello, Landry."

Hands shoved in the pockets of his jeans, Landry looked around the luxuriously appointed office, ignoring Nate entirely. Finally, with a disgruntled sigh, he cast a sideways glance at his great-grandmother. "Obviously, this isn't going to work, Gran. So...can we go now?"

"Landry, dear, I explained..." Mrs. Walker replied in a feeble tone.

Landry scowled at Nate. "I don't care how much money this dude has!" he blurted. "There's no way he's going to adopt me and be my dad!"

NATE COULDN'T BLAME the teen for being upset with the quick turn of events. He hadn't seen this coming, either.

Had it been anyone but Jessalyn Walker asking him to do this, he would have been on the phone to his lawyer, seeking another solution. But it *was* Jessalyn who was here, orphan in tow. And it had been her granddaughter Seraphina making the request, through a letter left for

Nate. A letter Jessalyn had held on to until yesterday, while she, too, tried to do what was best for all concerned.

Nate dropped his hand. "I'm very sorry about your loss," he said quietly.

"My mom died a year and a half ago." The teen glared at him, still hovering protectively next to his great-grandmother. "If you were really my mom's friend, where were you then? You should have been there."

What could Nate say to that? The kid was right. "Had I known your mother was ill, I would have been," he assured him.

Landry looked at him contemptuously.

"He's here now, Landry, ready and willing to help us— just the way your mom wanted, when the day came that I could no longer care for you." Jessalyn Walker reached out and put a comforting hand on her great-grandson's forearm. "That's all that counts."

Landry's chin quivered. "You don't have to take care of me," he declared. "I'll take care of you."

"That's not the way it's supposed to be," Jessalyn reminded him patiently, giving his arm another beseeching pat.

Landry broke away abruptly. "I don't mind. I want to do it!"

"Landry—" Jessalyn pleaded.

"If you don't want me around, fine! Go ahead and move into that retirement center!" Landry huffed. "But I'm not signing on for *this!* And none of you can make me!" He spun around and strode toward the door.

Nate took off after him, catching up with Landry before he reached the elevators. Nate had no experience with wayward teenagers, but he was pretty certain he knew what was called for here. "If you care about your great-grandmother as much as you say you do, you'll come back to that office and work things out like a man instead of running away."

Landry snorted. "Whatever." He did an about-face and marched back to the office, spine straight, attitude intact. Nate followed him.

Brooke, who had been consoling Jessalyn, gently squeezed the woman's frail hand and met Nate's gaze.

"I know you are furious at my failing health. So am I," Jessalyn Walker told her great-grandson wearily. "But my doctor is right. I need more care than I can get at home. And you can't live with me in the assisted-living home I'm moving into tomorrow. So it's either go with Nate today, and give that a try as I've asked, or enter the foster care system."

Landry's scowl deepened.

To Nate's surprise, Brooke stepped into the fray. She fixed Landry with a kind look. "I know this is none of my business, but I would advise you to go with Nate. I was in foster care as a kid. I got moved around a lot. It was…not fun."

This, Nate had not known.

Landry's eyes narrowed. "Is that the truth?"

Brooke nodded sadly. "I lost both my mom and dad when I was fourteen, but unlike you, had no relatives or old family friends to take me in." She paused, regarding the teenager with a gaze that was as matter-of-fact as it was softly maternal. "Not having any family at all to care about you is a tough way to grow up. I really wouldn't recommend it, honey."

Landry's shoulders sagged. "Can I live with you then?" he asked Brooke.

She seemed as taken aback by the request as everyone

else in the room, and exhaled ruefully. "I'm sorry, Landry, but that is not an option."

He crossed his arms in front of him. "Then I'll take foster care," he insisted.

Seeing a situation he had hoped would go smoothly rapidly deteriorate into emotional chaos was not part of Nate's plan. Determined to regain control of the moment, he caught Brooke's attention and gestured toward the door. "If you two will excuse us, I'd like to talk to Ms. Mitchell alone a moment."

Brooke didn't appear to want to go with him, but complied nevertheless. Her posture regal, she walked down the hall to the boardroom. Nate held the door, then followed her inside.

The room was elegantly appointed, with a long table and comfortable leather chairs backed by a floor-to-ceiling window overlooking the Trinity River and downtown Fort Worth. The spectacular view was nothing compared to the tall, slender woman standing in front of it.

Nate paused, taking in the glossy fall of walnut-brown hair brushing her shoulders. A sleeveless tunic showcased her shapely arms. Matching silk trousers fluidly draped her legs. But it was the inherent kindness and empathy in her golden-brown eyes he found the most captivating. It was no wonder Landry had gravitated to her. Brooke Mitchell was an intriguing mix of savvy business entrepreneur and empathetic woman. She seemed like someone who would know what to do in any situation. And right now, Nate and Landry both needed a woman like that in their lives.

She glanced out at the skyline, then turned back to him. "I understand you have a big problem," she told him with all sincerity. "I *feel* for Landry. But there my involvement ends."

Nate remained determined. "I understand you're a single mother with a thirteen-year-old boy."

A delicate blush silhouetted her high, sculpted cheeks. "How did you…?"

"Alexis McCabe mentioned it when she gave me your name and suggested you were the ideal person to help me make the mansion I just purchased a home." Nate walked over to stand next to her. He glanced out at the view, too, then back at her. "I need help getting Landry situated."

Brooke inclined her head slightly to one side. "As a single parent, you have to get used to handling these challenges by yourself."

Again Nate followed the spill of glossy hair brushing her shoulders, and couldn't help but notice her fair skin and toned body. She was one sexy lady, in the woman-in-the-office-across-the-hall kind of way. And due to the circumstances he and Landry were facing, totally off-limits. Nate needed to keep his thoughts trained on the issue at hand.

"I will handle these problems myself," he promised her, "as soon as Landry adjusts to the idea of becoming my son."

She remained silent, but gave him a look that said *Lotsa luck with that!*

Undeterred, he braced a shoulder against the glass. "In the meantime, you have a son close to Landry's age, and I have a two-bedroom cottage on the property. You and your son could stay there while the makeover of the main house takes place, under your direction. The boys could swim in the pool, play on the sport court, and you could help bring me up to speed on this whole parenting thing."

Brooke shot him a censuring glance. "You presume a lot."

Nate countered with what experience told him would be

the winning hand. "I'm also willing to pay a lot," he said bluntly. "Double your usual rate for the next two weeks, if you'll help me out here."

Silence stretched between them, as palpable as the sexual sparks he'd felt when he had first taken her hand. Brooke's services were expensive to begin with. They were talking a lot of money here. "You're serious," she said.

"As a heartbeat."

Brooke sighed and then muttered something under her breath he couldn't quite catch. "All right," she said finally, lifting a nicely manicured hand to her hair. "I'll do it on several conditions."

Nate stepped closer, inhaling the soft lilac fragrance of her perfume. "And those are?"

Her fine brow arched. "When my work at your place is done, I'm done with the whole situation."

Nate lifted his hands in surrender. "No problem."

Her pert chin angled higher. "Two, if the boys don't get along, they won't be forced to hang out together."

Nate agreed readily. "All right."

"Three. My son, Cole, is already enrolled for the summer in a prestigious academic day camp that focuses on computer skills, and he's going to go."

Nate had been involved in organized activities—mostly academic—every summer when he was a kid, too, and always enjoyed them. "That might be good for Landry, as well."

"If you can get him in, it probably would be great for him," Brooke agreed. "And four, I make no guarantee how this will all work out. Except to say that you will be pleased with how your home looks when the redecoration is complete."

Nate admired her confidence. Curious, and more than a little intrigued by the beautiful and accomplished woman in front of him, he asked, "How do you know that?" She hadn't even seen the property or heard what he had in mind.

Brooke's radiant smile lit up the room. "When it comes to my work, I never give up until the customer is completely satisfied."

Chapter Two

"Not exactly child-friendly, is it?" Brooke observed, walking through Nate Hutchinson's multimillion-dollar residence an hour later.

The ten-thousand-square-foot abode had a postmodern edge to it. Everything was black or white. Glass tables and lamps abounded, as did expensive statues and paintings. The overall impression she got was sleek, cold and sterile.

Nate shrugged. "It's an investment. I bought it as is. It can all be changed."

He glanced over at Landry and his great-grandmother. The teen was glumly inspecting the marble-floored foyer and sweeping staircase. Jessalyn was sitting wearily in the formal library, off to the left. Cane in hand, she kept a worried gaze on the boy. Probably wondering, Brooke thought, if Landry was going to be able to accept his new living arrangements.

"Obviously," Nate continued, oblivious to the concerned nature of Brooke's thoughts, "we'll set a budget that is appropriate for the scope and scale of this house." He paused, close enough now that she took in the fragrance of his soap, cologne and heady male essence. "I'm going to need it done as quickly as possible. Two weeks, at the outside."

Brooke shook off the tantalizing fragrance of leather and spice. "That's a tall order."

He eyed her with lazy assurance. "I'm not worried. You have a reputation for providing your clients with the home environments they always dreamed of having, in record time."

Brooke could not contest that. She was good at what she did. She worked hard to keep at a minimum the chaos and disarray that went along with redecorating. Usually, however, the homes were not nearly this large. A feeling of nervousness sifted through her. "It's going to require a lot of time on your part, as well," she warned.

He regarded her with maddening nonchalance. "I don't move furniture."

Famous last words, Brooke thought. No one got through a major upheaval of their personal belongings without eventually having to heft or slightly reposition *something.* It didn't matter how many professionals were hired. At the end of the day, there was always something that wasn't quite right. Something that begged the owner to reach out and touch and, in the process, claim it as his or her own. But figuring Nate wouldn't understand the need to put his own signature on the place if it were truly to become his home, she let it go for now.

Giving him the smile she reserved for her most difficult and demanding clients, she tried again. "I meant you're going to have to sit down with me—pronto—and talk about what kind of style you envision having here."

Brooke turned as she saw Landry heading up the staircase.

Nate lifted a staying hand. "It's okay. He's going to have to explore the place sometime."

Meanwhile, Brooke noted, the seventy-nine-year-old Jessalyn appeared to be drifting off to sleep.... "So when can we get together to do this?" she asked.

"How about tonight?"

If only that were possible, she mused, as anxious to get a head start on this task as he. "I have to pick up my son at summer camp."

"Bring him, too. Say around seven? We'll all have dinner. If you want, you could even move your things into the caretaker's house at that time."

Brooke had heard Nate moved fast. His indefatigable drive had turned his solo financial advising practice into a firm with six thousand top-notch certified financial planners, and a national reputation for excellence.

She gazed up at him. "I know you want to get this done," she began.

"It's important for Landry that this feel like a home instead of a museum," Nate said.

Brooke couldn't disagree with that. "But there's such a thing as moving too fast. Decorating decisions made in haste are often repented in leisure." And she had her own problems to triumph over, starting with her promise to reconfigure her priorities and bring balance back into her life.

Nate brushed off her concern with a shrug. "I'm counting on you to help me avoid that."

The doorbell rang before she could answer him.

Nate moved to get it.

A stunning ebony-haired woman in a Marc Jacobs suit strode in, cell phone and briefcase in hand. She was in her mid-thirties, of Asian-American descent.

"Brooke Mitchell, my attorney, Mai Tanous. Mai, this is Brooke Mitchell."

Mai nodded briefly in acknowledgment, then leaned toward Nate. "We need to talk."

NATE HAD AN IDEA of what Mai was going to say. He also knew she would be much more circumspect if they weren't alone. He motioned for Brooke to stay put, and regarded Mai steadily. "I presume you brought the papers?" he asked in a voice that tolerated no argument.

Mai cast an uncertain look at Brooke, as unwilling to talk business with an audience as Nate had presumed she would be. "Yes," she said politely. "I did. But—"

He held up a hand, cutting off her protest. "Then let's sign them so Jessalyn can go home. She's exhausted."

Exhaling in frustration, Mai frowned. "Are you sure you want to do this?"

He nodded. For a moment Mai seemed torn between doing her job and being his friend. Finally, she pivoted and headed for the library, where Jessalyn was seated. As Brooke and Nate entered the room, the elderly woman roused.

Mai extended a hand and introduced herself. "Mrs. Walker, are you sure you don't want to have your own attorney present?"

Jessalyn waved off the suggestion. "I trust this man every bit as much as my late granddaughter did. If Nate says he'll do right by Landry, then he will."

"I would still feel better if we slowed down a bit," Mai said. "Perhaps began the process with a simple visit."

Nate gave his attorney a quelling glance. "I told you it wasn't necessary," he stated firmly. "Now, if you have the Power of Appointment papers…"

Her posture stiff, her expression deferential, Mai opened up her briefcase, extracted the documents. "Basically, this agreement states that Landry will live with Nate now. It gives Nate the power to take him to the doctor, and to school or camp while he is in Nate's care. In the eyes of the law, however, Landry's great-grandmother, Jessalyn Walker, will remain his legal custodian until the court transfers custodianship to Nate."

"Why can't we just make Nate Landry's legal custodian now?" Jessalyn asked impatiently.

Mai regarded the elderly woman gently. "The court will need to be certain this arrangement is in the best interest of your great-grandson."

Nate noticed Brooke visibly react to that admission.

"I don't see why, since Nate has agreed to be the father that Landry needs." Jessalyn appeared upset.

Mai knelt in front of her and took her hand. Looking her in the eye, then explained, "The authorities are still going to want home studies to be done by social workers, and reports given to the court, recommending placement. But that won't happen until the petition for custodianship is filed with the court. And in fact—" the attorney gave her hand a final pat and stood, addressing all of them once again "—I would suggest that until Landry settles in a little bit and feels like this is something he wants, too, that we hold off on taking him before a judge. And instead just let him live here for a few weeks and get used to things, before we actually petition the court to begin the process to make it permanent."

Although Brooke had said nothing during this whole exchange, Nate noticed that she seemed to agree with Mai on that. Probably because she was a mother herself and understood how unhappy Landry was right now....

No one there seemed to have confidence that Nate could make the teen any happier. When it came right down to it, he wasn't certain, either. His own familial background left a lot to be desired, in that regard.

Jessalyn studied Mai with faded blue eyes. "You're worried what will happen if Landry decides he doesn't want to live here with Nate, aren't you?"

As direct as always, the lawyer nodded, her expression grim.

"Why don't I check on Landry?" Brooke interjected helpfully.

Appreciating her discretion and sensitivity, Nate shot her a grateful glance. "Good idea."

She slipped out. The mood in the room was somber as Jessalyn and Nate read and signed the legal documents Mai had drawn up. Finally, it was done. Everyone had a copy of the Power of Appointment to take with them.

"Obviously," Nate told Jessalyn, "you are welcome to call or come by at any time to see Landry. And I'll make certain he visits you at the retirement village, too."

"Thank you," Jessalyn said, her eyes moist. "And thank you for coming to our aid. Especially under the circumstances." Her words were rife with meaning only Nate understood.

Reminded of the situation that had prompted him to cut ties with Seraphina and her grandmother, Nate bent and clasped the elderly woman's frail shoulders in a brief hug. "I wish you'd come to me sooner," he murmured in her ear.

Jessalyn looked at him. "You know why I didn't," she retorted, just as quietly.

Nate did. He exhaled deeply. Before he could reply, Brooke appeared in the doorway.

"A small problem," she said with a rueful twist of her lips. "I can't find Landry anywhere."

MAI STAYED WITH a visibly upset Jessalyn Walker. Brooke and Nate split up. She covered the east half of the house, while he covered the west. Both were diligent in their search. Neither found a trace of the wayward teen.

Mute with worry, they headed out to the lagoon-style swimming pool, complete with elaborate greenery. He wasn't there. Ditto the sport court. The detached six-car garage. The only thing left was the caretaker's cottage.

"Naturally," Nate murmured, as they approached the

porch of the ranch-style domicile and spied Landry settled in front of the television inside. "He's in the last place we looked."

"And also," Brooke noted thoughtfully, "the most eclectic."

Unlike the house, Brooke observed, which had been decorated with style and cutting-edge decor in mind, the cottage was a ramshackle collection of mismatched furniture and odds and ends. It was, in short, a designer's nightmare—and a disgruntled teen's hideout.

Surprised and a little disappointed to suddenly find herself in the same situation she had endured in her youth, she pivoted toward Nate. He stepped nearer at the same time. Without warning, she was suddenly so close to him she couldn't avoid the brisk masculine fragrance of his cologne, or the effect it had on her senses. Turning to her cool professionalism, she stepped back slightly. "This is where you wanted me and my son to stay?"

Nate's brow furrowed. Obviously, he saw no problem with the arrangement, but was astute enough to realize she was momentarily disconcerted. Not just at the obvious discrepancy between this and the main house, but what the decision obviously said about his estimation of her. This was no cozy abode, or the sort of lodging suitable for a respected colleague. Rather, it was a place for a servant one didn't care much about. Worse, there was a thick layer of dust on every surface, which would play havoc with her son's asthma.

"It doesn't look like it's been cleaned in forever," Brooke stated grimly. And Nate had wanted her and her son to stay there that night!

"I apologize for that," Nate murmured, clapping a hand on the back of his neck. "I was unaware."

Typical man. Brooke sighed in displeasure. This job

hadn't even started yet and it was already a mess in practically every respect. She had half a mind to forgo the lucrative contract and walk out.

"I suggested it because it was separate from the house, and therefore private. I hadn't really thought about the condition of the place or the decor. I haven't used it in the two months I've lived here. Nor has anyone else, since I don't employ any live-in help." Nate took another look through the window. "But I see why you're less than tempted to accept. I guess for someone like you, who pays attention to the aesthetics, these accommodations could be..."

"Insulting?"

"It's not what I meant when I issued the invitation." He ran a hand through his thick black hair and looked seriously chagrined.

Brooke let him off the hook with a raised eyebrow.

Clearly not one to let a mistake of any kind go, Nate persisted with narrowed eyes, "Obviously, we'll get this place scrubbed from top to bottom, and fixed up, too. And we'll take care of that before we even start on the main house, if you do agree to move in here with your son."

Brooke had not come this far in her career to get the reputation of a diva. And if the story got out that Nate had been forced to redo her quarters before starting on his own, her competitors would have a field day. She stopped him with a glance. "It's not a problem. I've lived in worse. Foster care, remember?"

"Oh."

"I can make anyplace a home." In fact, she told herself sternly, she welcomed the challenge.

At the moment there were far more pressing problems to deal with.

Brooke cast another look at the fourteen-year-old slumped on the hideously out-of-date orange-green-and-brown-plaid sofa. "Let's go inside and talk to Landry," she murmured, touching Nate's arm.

The boy was the picture of defiance as the two adults entered the cottage.

"You can't run off like that," Nate chided, switching off the television.

Landry leaped up, hands balled at his sides. "Who are you to tell me what to do?" he demanded. "And don't go saying you're going to be my dad, because you're not!"

Nate explained about the legal papers that had been signed.

Landry fell silent. "So I'll live here," he grudgingly agreed at last. "It doesn't change the fact that you're just some guy doing a favor for my great-grandma." He stormed out of the cottage and back toward the house, leaving Brooke and Nate no choice but to follow.

In Landry's place, Brooke knew she would have been wary, too. Seeking a reason that would alleviate the orphaned child's distrust, she inquired matter-of-factly, "Why haven't you been part of Landry's life until now?"

For a moment, Nate didn't answer. Finally, he explained, "I didn't know he existed until twenty-four hours ago, when Jessalyn Walker called me. She told me Seraphina had died of cancer a year and a half ago, and that Landry had been living with her ever since. Jessalyn said at first it was all right. He was clearly grieving the loss, as was she, but they were a team. Then, in the last month or so, as her health began to fail and she had to sell her home and arrange to move into the assisted-living facility, he became really angry about the hand fate had dealt him."

Understandably so, Brooke mused.

"He did his best to care for her, apparently, and convince her she didn't need nurses looking after her, when she had him," Nate related. "But she knew Landry deserved a better life. So she took a letter that Seraphina had left behind, for a worst-case scenario, and had it messengered to me."

And the combination of phone call and letter had worked to get Nate involved.

"What did the letter say?" Brooke asked, telling herself that her curiosity had nothing to do with her interest in Nate the man and his previous relationship with Landry's mother, and everything to do with trying to create a home decor that worked for both Nate and his charge. There might be clues in that note about what his mother thought her son would one day want and need....

Nate reached into the pocket of his suit jacket. Wordlessly, he handed over a piece of cream-colored stationery. Brooke opened it and read:

Dear Nate,
Landry needs a man he can look up to in his life. I know I have no right to ask you this after the way our engagement ended, but please put the past aside and be the family to my son that my grandmother Jessalyn and I can no longer be. And if you can't do that, I trust you to find someone who can give Landry all the care and attention he is going to need in the years ahead.
   I never stopped loving you.
Seraphina.

Finished, Brooke handed the letter back. It was obvious Seraphina had really looked up to Nate, despite whatever had transpired to break them up. "Why didn't she ask you to do this before she died?"

Nate's tone grew turbulent. "Probably because she didn't

know how I'd feel or what I'd do. When she knew me, I was all-career, all the time."

"And yet she trusted you either to be the father Landry needed or to find one for him."

"What can I say?" The emotion in Nate's eyes dissipated and he flashed a charming grin. "I'm a trustworthy guy."

What wasn't he telling her? Brooke wondered. Did it have anything to do with the reason Nate and Seraphina had stopped communicating and made little or no effort to remain friends after their breakup?

Brooke studied Nate, the mother in her coming to the fore. "Are you sure you want to take this on?" Landry had already weathered a lot of loss. Nate had no experience with children, and gallantry, no matter how well intentioned, took a potential parent only so far.

He nodded, his blue eyes serious. "In the end Seraphina and I may not have been right for each other, but I loved her, too, and always will. And I know I can—and will—love her son."

"You've got to be kidding me!" Cole said, when Brooke picked him up at day camp several hours later. He regarded her with all the disdain a thirteen-year-old boy could muster. "What about the promise you made to me about not taking on any more ridiculously demanding clients and 'restoring balance' to our life?"

Brooke had meant it at the time. She still did. "I had to take this job," she explained.

She eased away from the carpool line and pulled out onto the street. Her minivan picked up speed as she drove. "Because the circumstances were extenuating—and Alexis McCabe asked me to do it, as a special favor. And I owe her…you know that." Brooke let out a beleaguered sigh.

"Not only was she one of my very first customers, after your dad died. She helped me get my business off the ground, with tons of referrals." To the point Brooke was now doing only big projects, with unlimited budgets.

"I liked it better when your clients weren't so rich they felt they could ask you to do anything and you'd have to say yes."

So had Brooke, in the sense that she hadn't felt so pressured. That the more prestigious jobs brought better pay... well, she was happy with that. "I know. And if my last client hadn't canceled the job abruptly—"

"When you refused to fly to Paris to look at fabric."

Brooke nodded. That client had been outrageously demanding—and unreasonable. "I guess it all worked out for the best. If I'd abided by his wishes, I wouldn't have unexpectedly had two weeks open...or been able to take this job with Nate Hutchinson." She couldn't help smiling. *Now I'm going to get paid double my usual rate for two weeks!*

"This Hutchinson guy...he's an important dude?"

Brooke glanced at her son. As usual, Cole looked relaxed and content after a day spent alternately learning cool stuff and playing in the summer sunshine. He was dressed in a yellow camp T-shirt with a computer emblazoned on the front, khaki cargo shorts and sneakers. That day's athletic activity had been swimming, so his blond hair was wet and smelled of chlorine.

"One of the most high-profile businessmen in Fort Worth," she confirmed.

"And he knows a lot about money."

"Apparently so, judging by the success of his financial services company."

Cole sighed. "Yeah, well...I still don't want to live in some guy's house!"

Nor did Brooke, to tell the truth. But every time she remembered the look on Landry's face, she thought about her own experiences in foster care—what it had felt like to get shunted around to places you didn't know, with people you'd never met—and her heart went out to him. She knew she could help him adjust. And if doing so eventually repaid the universe's kindness to her...

"It's actually a caretaker's cottage, and it's a rush job. The only way I'll get it done in the time allotted is if I'm at the Hutchinson estate day and night for the next two weeks. And if I'm there till all hours and you're at our place..."

Cole grabbed the half-finished sport drink from his backpack and unscrewed the top. His golden-brown eyes were wiser than his years. "We'll never see each other."

"Right." Brooke turned onto the entrance ramp that would take them to the freeway. "I know you're at camp all day. But I still like hanging around with you during the evenings, even when I have to spend part of that time working."

Cole ripped open the wrapper on an energy bar. "If I'm a good sport about this, you're going to owe me."

Brooke had no problem putting the carrot ahead of the stick. Incentives were a great way to motivate people into going the extra mile. She smiled at her boyishly handsome son. "What would you like?"

Cole beamed and bartered resolutely, "A whole day at the Six Flags amusement park in Arlington! We're there when the park opens and we stay until we see the fireworks. Deal?"

Brooke consented with a nod, glad to have come to some accord. "Deal. But it's going to have to wait until I finish the job," she cautioned.

He wiped the oatmeal crumbs off his mouth with the

back of his hand. "Or sooner, if you get a day off before then."

Brooke wouldn't count on that. She had just met the man, but... "Mr. Hutchinson can be quite the slave driver."

"You can sweet-talk him into letting you have a day off next weekend. You can sweet-talk anybody, Mom."

Brooke knew that was true. But only to a point. "And there is one more thing," she added, turning into the neighborhood of palatial estates Fort Worth's wealthiest citizens called home.

"Uh-oh," Cole said. "I know that look…."

Brooke tried to focus on the positive. "Mr. Hutchinson has a boy your age who is just now coming to live with him. Landry's mom died a year and a half ago, so he's having a hard time." Briefly, she explained what had transpired.

Cole fell silent, no doubt thinking about the death of his own father two years before, and the grief he had endured.

Finally, he asked, "Was Landry's great-grandmother nice when you met her?"

"Very nice. She's just too old and too ill to care for him." Brooke turned into the drive. She keyed in the pass code that Nate had given her before she left. The electric gates opened.

"Wow," Cole murmured, sitting up in his seat. "This is rich!"

At the end of the driveway, near the huge detached garage, Landry was kicking a landscaping stone across the pavement. Scowling, he barely looked up as she parked her minivan.

Cole's compassionate expression faded, and wariness kicked in. "Is that the kid?" he asked.

Brooke nodded.

Her son tensed. "He doesn't look friendly at all."

It didn't matter. The success of this particular job meant the kids had to develop a rapport. So for all their sakes, she would use every one of the skills she possessed to make sure they did.

Chapter Three

Landry grumbled the moment he laid eyes on the supper selections. "There are dead fish on this pizza."

Brooke knew it was a mistake to have Landry's first meal with Nate in the formal dining room. The black lacquer table seated fifty. But there was no other place to eat inside the house, since the equally enormous kitchen was set up like a fancy hotel cook space, with stainless-steel counters and massive state-of-the-art appliances. So she had ignored her own instincts—which were to dine at one of the wrought-iron tables outside on the terrace—and gone along with Nate's suggestion.

Nate looked momentarily taken aback by Landry's disdain. "I had them put anchovies on only one of the pies."

Landry stared at the dinner laid out for them, thanks to the local upscale pizza-delivery service. "That purple stuff looks gross, too."

Nate glanced down at the colorful assortment of veggies topping another crust. "That's grilled eggplant. And if you don't like it, you could remove it and just eat the rest of the vegetables."

That suggestion was met with mute resistance.

"Maybe you could try the Hawaiian pizza," Brooke suggested kindly.

Landry scowled. "Who puts pineapple and ham on top of cheese and tomato sauce?"

"Actually, you'd be surprised. It's pretty good." Cole held out his plate. "I'll have some," he said.

Nate cheerfully handed over a generous slice.

"You might like it," Brooke told Landry.

The boy stared glumly at the last option—a pale pizza with spinach and garlic—then looked back at Brooke. His great-grandmother had only been gone an hour, she thought. Already Landry was near meltdown. Her heart went out to him. Leaving Jessalyn would have been tough under any circumstances. Going to a place he didn't know, to be with an old family friend he had never met...

She touched his arm lightly and offered a comforting smile. Landry gazed into her eyes, then wordlessly held out his plate. "My mom used to look at me like that, when she wanted me to do something I didn't want to do," he muttered beneath his breath.

Which was as close as they were going to get to verbal capitulation, Brooke thought, as she served him a slice of Hawaiian pizza. "You have to eat," she said, using every ounce of motherly persuasion in her arsenal. "Otherwise, you're only going to feel worse."

Landry exhaled, bent his head over his plate, took a bite. Then another...and another.

Nate asked Cole how summer camp was going. Smiling, he launched into an account of everything he had done in the first two weeks. Brooke's pride in her son's outgoing nature and accomplished social skills was tempered by her concern for Landry. The orphaned child was so out of his depth here. Worse, she wasn't sure Nate had the tools to reach him.

"Perhaps your attorney had a point," she said half an hour later, when the two boys had gone outside to hit some tennis balls around the sport court behind the swimming pool. She cleared the table while Nate put the leftover pizza away. "Maybe you should slow this process down a bit, have Landry get to know you better first."

"And put him where? Jessalyn's heart is failing. She's moving into a retirement village with round-the-clock nursing care tomorrow."

"She can't put it off even a short while or move in here with him temporarily?"

"I've already suggested both. It is Jessalyn's opinion that Landry won't bond with me or anyone else unless there's no other option. She does think that he'll enjoy academic camp. Apparently, he's been extremely bored since school let out for the summer, and he's as interested in computers and technology as Cole is." Nate paused. "So I'll work on getting that set up first thing tomorrow. In the meantime, I have to figure out what to do about the sleeping arrangements tonight."

"What do you mean?" Brooke asked.

"Initially, I thought I would just put Landry in one of the guest rooms, and have you and Cole bunk in the caretaker's cottage. Now I'm thinking it might be better to have you all stay in the main house this evening."

"Or we could simply go home and come back tomorrow," she offered hopefully.

Nate's glance narrowed. "I don't think Landry would like that."

She sighed. "Probably not."

Nate stepped closer.

She noticed the evening beard darkening his jaw. It lent a rugged masculinity to his already handsome features. Irritated to find herself attracted to him—again—she stepped back. She had a job to do here. One that did not involve lusting after the boss...

Oblivious to the desirous nature of her thoughts, Nate looked into Brooke's eyes. "Landry's bonding with you."

She felt drawn to him, too. Landry needed a mom in his life again. So much so that he had immediately latched onto her.

But that was no solution, Brooke realized sadly.

She fought getting any more emotionally involved in a situation that was not hers to fix. She was trying to bring *balance* to her life, not more conflict. "He needs to bond with you, Nate."

"And he will…over time," Nate concurred calmly.

A little irked to see him treating this like just another life challenge, when it was so much more than that, Brooke murmured, "Never met a target you couldn't charm?"

His persuasive smile faded, and with an understanding that seemed to go soul-deep, he murmured, "I never wanted to be in a situation where I had no family."

But here he was, Brooke thought, unmarried and childless—until today, anyway.

"And I'm certain Landry doesn't want to be in that situation, either." Nate paused, before finishing resolutely, "When he realizes we can help each other, he'll come around."

Brooke hoped so. Otherwise, all four of them were in for a bumpy ride.

"Psssst, Mom! Are you still awake?"

Her heart jumping at the urgency of the whisper, Brooke sat up in bed. "Cole?"

The guest room door eased open. Seconds later, Cole and Landry tiptoed in. Both were barefoot, clad in cotton pajama pants and T-shirts. Cole's were stylish and vibrant: Landry's were faded and on the verge of being too small.

Promising herself she would get Nate to take care of the clothes issue for Landry as soon as possible, Brooke turned on the bedside lamp. "Why aren't you two asleep?"

Cole perched on the foot of her bed, then signaled for Landry to do the same. The boy came around to the other side.

It seemed being in the same boat had forged a bond between the two, Brooke noted. Realizing a first tentative step toward Landry's future had been made, she smiled. Maybe Nate was smarter about all this than she had realized....

"Because the place is too big and too quiet." Hands clenched nervously, Landry sat down, too.

"It feels like we're in a hotel—only we're the only ones here," Cole acknowledged with a comically exaggerated shiver. "Which is kind of spooky if you think about it too much."

Ten thousand square feet of space *was* overwhelming, Brooke agreed. Especially the way the residence was decorated now, with a postmodern edge and minimal furnishings. The only television was in the master bedroom, where Nate was sleeping, so she couldn't even offer that as a distraction.

"You boys have a big day tomorrow." Both would be at summer camp all day. "I've got a lot on my schedule, too."

"Can we hang out here for a while?" Cole asked.

Landry's stomach grumbled loudly.

Suddenly, the mom in her kicked in, and Brooke knew what was really keeping them awake. "You guys wait here," she told them. "I'll be right back."

NATE HAD JUST CLIMBED into bed when he heard the soft sound of footsteps in the hallway.

He sat up, listening. It wasn't his imagination. That last creak had been the back stairs! He clamped down on an oath. Certain Landry was running away again, Nate flung back the covers and padded soundlessly down the hall, in the direction of the escape route.

But it wasn't Landry he found standing in the bright light of the kitchen—it was Brooke.

Clad in a snug-fitting tank top and yoga pants, her brown hair tousled, she was standing at one of the two big stainless steel refrigerators, staring thoughtfully at the contents.

"I know," Nate said. "I've got a little bit of everything in there."

She shot him a look over her shoulder, as at ease in his home as he wanted her to be. "And here I didn't imagine you could cook," she drawled.

"I don't. But I found out most of the women I've dated do, so it makes everyone happy if the fridge is well-stocked."

Brooke's smile faded. "Right," she murmured.

The word had a wealth of undercurrents. "Meaning?" Nate prodded.

Her lips curved upward even as the light faded from her eyes. She said in a low, cordial tone, "You have a reputation for making the women in your life very happy, while they are in your orbit."

Nate certainly tried. What point was there in spending time with someone unless it was a pleasurable experience? That didn't mean, however, that he pretended something was going to work long term when it clearly wouldn't.

"I don't fall in love easily." Although not for lack of trying. He wanted to be married and have a family.

She studied him as if trying to decide whether or not he was the womanizer some made him out to be, then brought out a bowl of fresh fruit, a loaf of artisan bread and a block of sharp cheddar. "Have you ever been in love?"

Nate handed over the serving board and bread slicer. "Once, with Landry's mother."

Brooke set to work preparing a snack, with the skill of a mom who spent a lot of time in the kitchen. "What happened to break you up? Or shouldn't I ask?"

Normally, Nate followed the gentleman's rule and did not talk about his previous relationships with women. For some reason, this was different. He wanted Brooke to understand. "I was working really long hours, getting my company off the ground," he admitted, moving restlessly about the sleek, utilitarian kitchen. "Seraphina was pretty involved in planning our wedding, and she had an old friend living in her building. Miles Lawrence was trying to make it as a stand-up comedian, and she went to as many of his appearances as she could. I didn't worry about the amount of time they spent together. As it turns out, I should have," Nate reflected ruefully. "She broke off our engagement to run away with him."

"And had a child," Brooke interjected, perceptive as ever.

Reluctantly, Nate met her eyes. "Some eight months later."

Her hand froze in midmotion. She stared at him, already doing the math. "Is it possible that Landry is yours?"

Nate had been wondering the same thing. All he could go on was what he knew for sure. "The birth certificate lists Miles Lawrence as Landry's father."

She went back to slicing up fruit and arranging it on a serving platter. "What about this Miles? Where is he?"

Nate lounged against the counter and watched the competent motions of her dainty hands. "Jessalyn told me yesterday that he left Seraphina before the baby was born. Miles wanted to focus on building an act that revolved around being a single guy, one always in love with a woman he could never hope to get."

Brooke looked horrified. "Don't tell me the man insisted he had to be chasing skirts to get material…."

Nate folded his arms across his chest, sharing her disdain. "Apparently so. Anyway, Seraphina was still in love with him and hoped he would come around and change his mind about marrying her and building a family together, if she gave him a little time. That's what Jessalyn told me. But they never had a chance to find out. He died in a plane crash when Landry was just two months old."

Brooke offered a commiserating glance. "So Landry never knew him."

Nate shook his head. "According to Jessalyn, all he has are a few old photographs and stories from his mom."

Brooke's smooth brow furrowed. "So what are you going to do?"

What could he do? "Raise him as mine."

"Without finding out?" Once again, Brooke looked shocked.

She was beginning to sound like his attorney. "There's no point in it. I've already agreed to adopt Landry and bring him up as my son." What counted, Nate knew, was the commitment made, and kept. Love would follow, over time. At least he hoped that would be the case. Thus far, Landry didn't seem to have his heart open to anything except rebellion.

The tromp of youthful footsteps sounded on the back stairs. Seconds later, Landry and Cole came barreling into the kitchen. Cole nodded at Nate, then turned back to his mom. "Where have you been?" he demanded.

"We thought maybe you got lost," Landry added, ignoring Nate altogether and looking at Brooke with concern.

Abruptly, the teenager swung around toward Nate, suspicious as ever. "How come you're up?" he demanded.

Nate straightened. He had to find a way to get Landry to respect him. The first step was telling it like it was, in situations like this. "I heard something and thought you might be taking off again," he informed him matter-of-factly.

An inscrutable light came into Landry's eyes. It was followed swiftly by a smirk. "And so what? You were going to stop me?"

Nate nodded with the quiet authority he knew Landry needed. "That's my job now."

When Landry sullenly turned away, Nate knew he'd gotten his point across.

"It's going to take time for Landry to adjust," Brooke told Nate, after the boys had taken their snacks and headed upstairs.

How long? Nate wondered, aware that Landry was already giving Brooke a much easier time.

But then again, Nate realized, Brooke wasn't the adult legally aiding Landry's great-grandmother in keeping Landry here against his wishes....

Brooke patted his arm before heading back upstairs, too. "In the meantime you've got to be patient and follow the plan you've set out and give him plenty of positive things to do."

NATE KNEW BROOKE WAS right. So first thing the following morning, he took Landry to the academic camp where Cole was enrolled in the summer program. He and Landry talked to the director, took the tour. As they headed back to her office, the teen shrugged and muttered, "I guess it'll be okay. Can I be in the same group as Cole?"

The director nodded.

Nate filled out the paperwork, wrote a sizable check and said goodbye to Landry. Then he headed for downtown Fort Worth, and the weekly meeting with his four business partners at One Trinity River Place.

Knowing the four guys would have invaluable advice to offer, since they were all experienced parents, Nate filled the group in on everything that had happened the last few days, starting with Jessalyn's phone call and the letter from her late granddaughter, Seraphina.

"Time helps," Travis Carson said, with the expertise of a widower who had shepherded his own two daughters through the demise of their mother.

"In the meantime…I have to agree with your lawyer," Grady McCabe told Nate seriously. "You are jumping the gun a bit, deciding to adopt Landry before the two of you have had a chance to develop any real rapport. The promise may not ring true to him."

Nate respected Grady's inherent ability to look at the big picture. Not just in the skyscrapers and other mixed-use development projects they built, but in their personal lives, too.

Dan Kingsland added matter-of-factly, "I know you've already hired Brooke Mitchell…."

Nodding, Nate was glad he'd had the foresight to bring her on board. She was the one ray of sunshine in his chaotic life right now.

"But redecorating your house just highlights the fact you're going to have to make a lot of changes to take Landry in," Dan continued. "I can't say how he would respond to that, since I've never met him, but I know my three kids would interpret it to mean they're a burden."

Jack Gaines added, "The faster change occurs, the harder it is to accept."

Nate knew Jack and his daughter had just weathered

a lot of upheaval due to a hasty wedding in their family. But that had worked out okay in the end, too. "I have faith Brooke Mitchell will be able to pull this off," he told his friends.

"The home makeover, sure," Grady said. "Everyone knows Brooke can work miracles in that regard. That's why her services are in such high demand."

"But she's not going to be there two weeks from now when the task is finished," Dan cautioned.

"At that point," Travis interjected, "you have got to be prepared to parent solo. And the rest of us know from experience that is one of the hardest things to do."

But it could be done, Nate thought, as the meeting concluded and he headed home to confer with Brooke over the lunch hour. All he needed were a few more tips and parental insights from her to get Landry moving in the right direction. After that happened, Nate was confident that the tension in his household would fade.

When he drove in the front gates, he expected to see the cleaning van on its way out, not furniture dotting the lawn. Nor a Cadillac next to Brooke's van, with a faculty parking sticker for a local university prominently displayed. Curious, Nate walked across the lawn, hearing the voices as he rounded the house.

"You gave me no choice," the bearded, white-haired man said. "You've been ducking my calls."

"I had hoped," Brooke said archly, "that would be enough for you to *get the message*."

The elderly man countered, "You and Cole have to be at the publication party for Seamus's book."

Wary of intruding, but not about to leave Brooke to fend for herself if help was needed, Nate reluctantly stayed where he was and continued listening in.

"If you and Cole don't show up, people will start asking questions."

"And we wouldn't want that, would we?" Brooke's voice rang with contempt. "We wouldn't want anything to reflect poorly on the university!"

"We were protecting you and Cole."

"While turning a blind eye? If you had wanted to help, you should have let me know what was going on, long before that night."

"Brooke…" The gentleman held out a hand in entreaty.

She glared. "You have to leave."

He pushed a book and what looked to be some sort of engraved invitation into her hands. "Not before you agree to attend the party."

Her expression distraught, Brooke backed away.

Enough was enough. Nate walked briskly around the landscaped swimming pool toward the caretaker's cottage. He extended a hand toward the bearded man. "Nate Hutchinson. And you're…?"

"Professor Phineas Rylander, from the university where Brooke's husband taught. I was just inviting her to a prepublication party that the English department is giving for her late husband, Seamus. It's his last work and we are very happy to be able to promote his collection of poetry. Naturally, we want Brooke and her son to attend."

Brooke pressed her fingertips to her temple. "I don't think it's going to be possible."

Professor Rylander refused to give up. "I beg you to reconsider."

Nate clapped a hand on his shoulder. "Thanks for stopping by."

"I—" the man began.

"I'll walk you to your Cadillac."

Reluctantly, the professor assented. Nate escorted him out, waited until he drove away, then returned to Brooke. She was sitting on one of the half-dozen pieces of mismatched furniture that had been moved to the lawn outside the cottage. She had the book and the invitation in her hands, and was staring down at the photo on the jacket cover.

Nate followed the direction of her gaze.

Seamus Mitchell had been handsome and distinguished. Yet Brooke was regarding the photo with utter loathing and contempt. Not exactly the reaction Nate would have expected. "Are you okay?"

She rose with quiet dignity. "No, I'm not," she said frankly. "And you know why?" Bitterness underscored her every syllable. "Because I know what it feels like to be betrayed by a loved one, too!"

Chapter Four

Brooke hadn't meant to blurt that out. But now that she had, she found she needed to unburden herself to someone who knew what it was like to be on the receiving end of such betrayal. Carefully, she set the book and the invitation on the chair she had been sitting on. "My husband didn't just die of a heart attack." That scenario would have been so much simpler to deal with. "He was in another woman's bed at the time."

Nate responded with an oath that perfectly summed up Brooke's feelings on the matter. Appreciating his empathy, she swallowed around the tight knot of emotion in her throat. She threaded both hands through her hair and continued with as much grace as she could muster. "The university didn't want a scandal. And there would have been one had word about what really happened gotten out, since Iris Lomax was Seamus's graduate assistant." Brooke exhaled deeply. "So the head of the English department, Professor Rylander, told everyone—including me—that he and Seamus had been out jogging when Seamus had the coronary." Her son still thought that was what had happened….

Nate gave her a look that said, *Not cool*. He reached over to squeeze her hand. "How did you find out that wasn't the case?"

In the worst possible way. Brooke lifted her gaze to his. "The nurse in the E.R. had no idea there was a mistress involved. She thought what the paramedics on the scene had initially been led to believe—that Seamus had been having sex with *me* at the time of his coronary. She had questions about Seamus's medical history, including a very mild heart attack the previous year that I knew nothing about." Brooke added with self-effacing honesty, "I have to say the way I reacted was not one of my finer moments." She was still embarrassed about how she had completely lost it.

Nate kept listening, his eyes kind.

Needing him to understand, as well as needing to unburden herself, Brooke confessed, "I had come to terms with the fact that my husband flirted with women the way some people breathe. I just thought it ended there." Her former naivete still hurt and embarrassed her. "Finding out it hadn't, and that Seamus had been taking some performance-enhancing drugs to keep up with all his extramarital activity—despite the known risks to someone who had already suffered a mild heart attack—was pretty devastating." She had been angry at her husband for his recklessness and his infidelity, and furious with herself for being such a fool.

"Does Cole know any of this?" Nate asked softly.

Relief softened the set of Brooke's shoulders, worked its way down her spine. "Heavens, no," she muttered emotionally. "He still thinks his oh-so-charming father walked on water." Despite the fact that Seamus had barely known Cole existed, except on the few occasions when the Irish poet had trotted him out, to show him off and enhance Seamus's own ego. "Which is why I don't want to take Cole to the book party."

Nate's eyes narrowed. "You're afraid someone will say something," he guessed.

"Although many faculty members remain in the dark about the circumstances surrounding Seamus's death, I have since come to realize some knew about his philandering." She took a deep breath. "Some of them thought I knew and was turning a blind eye, to keep the marriage intact. Others actively covered for him when he was out carousing, and helped him keep his infidelity from me."

"So if any of them were to look at you sympathetically..." Nate guessed where this was going.

Brooke nodded. "Or just react in a way that would stir questions in Cole's mind, it could be a problem. I worked very hard during the years of our marriage to protect Cole from anything unpleasant. Right now, he's secure in his father's love and the memories he has of our times together as family. He doesn't realize that anything was amiss." She crossed her arms self-consciously. "And I don't want to do anything that would take away from that. Because there were parts of our lives together that were very good." *Times when Seamus had really poured on the Irish charm.* "And that's all I want to dwell on. So going back to the English department, where Seamus and I first met..."

Once again Nate looked shocked. "You were his student, too?" he asked in surprise.

"I took one of his classes when I was a senior," Brooke admitted, with no small amount of cynicism. Looking back, she could see how gullible, how ripe for the picking she had been. But at the time, their age difference and Seamus's history as a tortured artist, and a known womanizer with a penchant for getting involved with female students, hadn't mattered. With effort, Brooke found her voice. "He was twenty years older than me, and when the writing was going well—as it was at the time—he was very sweet and kind and funny and loving." That was all she had seen. All she had needed to see.

"He made you happy."

Not ashamed to admit it, Brooke nodded. "When he asked me to marry him and give him a child, I was thrilled. I'd finally have a family again, and so would he." Maybe she'd been blind, but her first years as a devoted wife and mother had been one of the happiest times of her life. "We had Cole right away. Seamus wrote a few new poems and continued teaching. And I became consumed with building a part-time business on the side, and being a mom."

"And later?"

"We still had good times. But Seamus was under a lot of pressure. In academia, what they say about publish or perish is very true. The powers that be were on him to produce another book of poetry the university could promote." She swallowed uncomfortably. "Seamus didn't think it was that simple. He wanted to wait to be inspired, but that wasn't an option if he wanted to keep his standing in the department. So eventually he did what was expected." Brooke tried not to dwell on the fact that Seamus's mistress had no doubt supplied the muse for the latest collection of love poetry, just as Brooke had allegedly inspired his earlier work.

She sighed and went on. "He had just submitted *Love Notes from the Soul* to his previous publisher, The Poet's Press, and was waiting to hear back about whether or not they were going to buy it, when he died. Eventually, they decided they wanted to publish it posthumously, since it was his last work." Even though it wasn't his best work. Far from it, actually.

Nate studied her, as if sensing there was more. "So what are you going to do?" he asked finally.

Brooke put away her lingering feelings of anger and

resentment. "I'm not sure. The university has notified all the newspapers in the state that the book is coming out, and they're trying to get it reviewed. Since Seamus isn't here, they'd like me to speak with the press and help promote it."

"But you don't want to," Nate noted, perceptively.

She picked up the invitation and advance copy of her late husband's book and held them at her side. "Every instinct I have tells me it would be a mistake, especially since my feelings on the matter are so complicated. So I'm going to sidestep that minefield and let the university handle it. In the meantime—" she put her personal angst aside and got back to the business at hand "—I'd like to show you what I've done with the guesthouse."

"THIS IS ABSOLUTELY AMAZING," Nate murmured several minutes later, after he had completed the tour of the caretaker's cottage. The mismatched furniture had been covered with soft blue denim slipcovers, and colorful braid rugs adorned the newly polished wide-plank pine floors. Art was on the walls. Blue-and-white paisley draperies dressed up the plantation shutters on the windows. The old appliances in the kitchen sparkled, and a round table for four had been brought in and set with dishes that were as pretty and useful as everything else in the home.

Nate cast another glance at the cotton quilts on the beds, the fresh towels, rugs and shower curtain in the lone bathroom. It was like a guesthouse out of a magazine, with all the comforts one could possibly desire. "How did you make it so livable so fast?"

"Well, as you can see, I had everything moved onto the lawn, then had the cleaning service do a thorough scrubbing of the space. I put half the furniture back, keeping the pieces that were in the best shape and leaving the others outside. Which brings me to my next question." She walked out to the yard and gestured at the odds and ends. "Do you want to put these things into storage or give them to an auction house for resale, along with everything you won't be using?"

"Auction everything." The money from the sale would go a long way toward funding the makeover.

Brooke made a note on her clipboard. "You said you wanted to get away from the black-and-white color scheme."

"Right." Nate sauntered back into the cottage and gestured toward the inviting decor. "I want the main house to look as comfortable as this." Like the cozy, welcoming homes all his married friends had. A place where he could come home and put his feet up.

Brooke tapped the pen against her chin. "That's a pretty big undertaking. We're talking about furnishings for ten thousand square feet of space. And we'll have to come up with a new color scheme."

Nate felt his eyes begin to glaze over. That always happened when the discussion turned to decorating. "Whatever you decide is fine with me."

She looked at him, clearly unconvinced.

He lifted both palms in surrender. "I'm not kidding—I like your taste. You understand a lot about boys and what they need. Speaking of which..." He took a deep breath and plunged on. "I'm planning to take Landry to get a haircut this evening after camp. And then to buy the clothes he needs. Any chance you and Cole might want to join us?"

Brooke hesitated.

Nate knew he was pushing it, dragging her further into this situation. But he had no choice. Edging closer still, he threw himself on her mercy. "I know nothing about any of this. And Landry can tell. You, on the other hand, are Supermom."

She raked her teeth across her lower lip. "I don't know about that."

"I do," he said. "I could use your help. Please don't make me beg…."

As their eyes locked, Nate sensed a wall going up between them. "I meant what I said yesterday. You're going to have to learn to do this on your own eventually," Brooke stated, sizing him up with golden-brown eyes.

"*Eventually* being the key word," he agreed.

After another moment, she finally relented, as he had hoped she would.

It was Landry Nate had trouble convincing.

"No way!" the teen said when he and Cole got home from camp, and they were told the plan. "I'm not getting a haircut, and I don't want or need any new clothes."

"Why do I have to go?" Cole chimed in.

"Because you need a haircut and a new pair of shoes," Brooke told him firmly.

Cole apparently knew that tone, Nate noted. Both boys sighed in resignation and tromped back out toward the driveway, muttering under their breaths the entire way.

"Nicely done," Nate said, falling into step beside Brooke.

Her expression as resigned as her son's, she murmured back, "Don't congratulate either of us until we complete our tasks."

Nate wasn't sure what she meant. He found out twenty minutes later, when they entered the unisex hair salon. Brooke went over with Cole to talk to the stylist taking walk-in appointments, and then sat down to read a magazine.

Landry glared at Nate, cutting off any attempt on his

part to do the same. "If I have to do this, I'm doing it my way," he growled as another available stylist walked toward them.

Figuring anything would be an improvement if it got the hair out of the boy's eyes, Nate nodded and gave him free rein. "I've got a call to make. I'll be right outside."

He stepped out into the mall. When he came back twenty minutes later, Cole was finished. His hair was cut in traditional adolescent-boy layers. He looked preppy and well-groomed. Brooke seemed pleased.

Landry was finished, too.

"You don't like it, do you?" he challenged, after Nate had paid the cashier.

But Brooke's son did. "You look like a punk rocker," Cole observed admiringly.

Which, Nate figured, Landry had done to tick him off.

Aware that Landry was waiting for him to lose his cool, Nate glanced at the new cut. The hair on top of Landry's head was short, spiky and stood straight up. The rest was thinned and layered, and fell almost to his shoulders. "Looks trendy," Nate said, and left it at that.

The teen scowled. "You can't like it," he insisted.

Which meant, Nate thought, *Landry* didn't like it.

Nate shrugged. "Your hair, your choice."

The boy's eyes narrowed. All rebellious teenager again, he pointed out, "You didn't say that when you were making me *get* my hair cut."

"My bad," Nate admitted, realizing too late he shouldn't have forced the issue.

Landry continued to glare at him. Finally, realizing Nate was sincere in his reversal, he scowled and said nothing more.

Brooke glanced at Nate as the boys walked on ahead.

The empathy in her eyes made him feel better. Although he still didn't know what he was doing in terms of being the dad Landry seemed to want and need.

The two teens paused in front of a popular clothing store known for its appeal to teenagers.

As they stood there, Nate noticed the longing on Landry's face. It had obviously been months since anyone had bought clothes for him, and Jessalyn would probably not have known to come here. "This okay with you?" Nate asked.

Landry's expression transformed. He looked at the cargo-shorts and T-shirt-clad model in the window with exaggerated disdain. "Sure," he drawled sarcastically, "why not? If you're going to torture me, why not torture me all the way?"

"Enthusiasm," Nate murmured, resisting the urge to clap an affectionate hand on the lad's shoulder. "Just what I want to see." Stuffing fingers in his pockets, he followed Landry inside. Brooke and Cole sauntered in after them. The boys headed straight for the racks of T-shirts.

An hour later, they walked out with enough clothing to see Landry through the rest of the summer.

Next stop was the shoe store, where Landry and Cole both got new athletic shoes and sandals.

Hamburgers, shakes and fries followed. It was nine o'clock before they returned to Nate's place.

"We're sleeping in the caretaker's cottage tonight," Brooke told Cole, when he got out of Nate's Jaguar.

"Then I want to sleep there, too," Landry said.

Brooke looked at a loss.

Nate figured it was one battle best not fought that evening. Tabling his own disappointment, he said, "If it's okay with you, it's okay with me." His primary concern was that Landry be safe.

Brooke hesitated. It was clear she felt like a traitor to what Nate was trying to do, but also knew the dynamics of the situation. She turned and put a hand on each teen's shoulder. "Then let's go, guys."

FOR THE NEXT HOUR, Nate roamed the mansion, trying to envision how it would appear when Brooke was finished with the makeover.

The more he looked around, the more it seemed he had given her an impossible task.

The rooms were all too large. There were too many of them. Even without the contemporary black and white furnishings, it was too big and cold and sterile.

No wonder Cole and Landry had eagerly gone off with Brooke to the now-cozy caretaker's cottage.

Given the choice, Nate would have preferred the smaller abode, too.

And no wonder Landry preferred being with Brooke over him. Spending time with her probably reminded him of home.

Ironically, Cole didn't seem to mind spending time with him, Nate thought as he changed clothes and went down to the pool for a swim. In fact, Brooke's son seemed eager to get acquainted with him. It was only his son-to-be, Nate thought as he swam lap after lap, who couldn't have cared less if they developed a rapport.

And that could spell trouble in the future, he realized, as he climbed from the pool, his workout ended.

Just then the cottage door opened and Brooke crossed the lawn. Nate ran a towel over his face and hair, then draped it around his waist.

Brooke had changed out of her business clothes into a figure-hugging T-shirt, running shorts and flip-flops. She'd swept her hair into a silky knot on the back of her head. She looked pretty and at ease in that mom-next-door way.

"Landry and Cole asleep?" he asked.

"Yes." Her expression went from genial to concerned.

"You don't have to say it." Nate grabbed the water bottle he'd brought out with him, and drank deeply. Aware they'd known each other only a few days, but were already talking with the candor of two people who had known each other for years, he sighed. "I know I blew it tonight."

Brooke's eyes softened. "That's not what I came over here to say."

Maybe not in those exact words… Disappointed in how he was handling the situation, Nate made no effort to hide his mounting frustration. He wasn't just a CEO, capable of starting a company from scratch and building it into a resounding success, he also had a background in sales. Years of experience honing the winning pitch had schooled him on how to gain the confidence of those who barely knew him. Yet despite all that he was failing mightily with the one person who needed to believe in him most. Failing Landry in the same way Nate himself had been let down in his youth. "Then…what did you want to say?" he asked impatiently.

Brooke perched on the edge of a round, wrought-iron patio table, gripping the edge. "You're pushing him too hard."

As Nate moved closer, the shimmering blue from the swimming pool illuminated the otherwise dark night with a soothing glow. There was enough light for him to see the self-conscious color creeping into her fair cheeks. "All that stuff had to get done today."

Brooke inhaled, the action lifting, then lowering the soft curves of her breasts. A pulse worked in her throat as she kept her eyes meshed with his. "I'm not arguing that."

Nate couldn't say why, he just knew it frustrated and embarrassed him to come up short in front of her. "Then what?" It wasn't as if they could have let Landry continue to go around with his hair in his eyes, wearing clothes he'd long outgrown, when Nate had the power and the means to remedy both.

"I disagree with your timing." Brooke rose gracefully to her feet. "If you want this to work, you have to start looking at the situation from Landry's point of view. Right now he has no say in anything. Grown-ups have decided where he's going to live, and with whom. Two days ago he was residing in his great-grandmother's neighborhood, where he spent all his free time fighting boredom and taking care of her." Brooke looked Nate squarely in the eye. "Now he's in an intellectually challenging summer camp and living here. That's a huge change."

And a good one, Nate thought fiercely, still sure taking Landry in was the right thing to do. "He could be in foster care."

Brooke moved closer. "To him, it's the same thing." She propped her hands on her hips. "I know you're used to just snapping your fingers and making things happen. All CEOs are. But Landry can't just put on a happy face and make this situation work. He's a kid. He needs time to process it, to understand what it is about you that made his mother decide you were the one to bring him up, once his great-grandmother could no longer do so."

"You want me to sing my own praises?" he asked disparagingly.

Brooke leaned toward him. "I want you to pull back, not be so results oriented when it comes to Landry's happiness and his attitude. Just give him space, Nate. Let him be…."

In normal circumstances, Nate would agree with her.

In this particular situation, it sounded like emotional desertion—an action Nate was well-acquainted with, too. "And just hope that he doesn't feel even more abandoned in the process?"

This time it was her turn to concede his point.

"It's a fine line," Brooke said eventually.

"You don't know the half of it," Nate agreed in a flat voice.

"Then tell me," she murmured, her warm tone wrapping him in tenderness.

"My parents are both executives for major corporations." Despite the fact that another wall had just come tumbling down, Nate tried not to make it sound any more important now than it had been then. "Career was everything to them when I was growing up, and it still is."

"You were alone a lot?"

That depended on the definition of alone. Nate finished the last of his water in a single draught. "I always had a nanny. And when I got older, a housekeeper." What he hadn't had were parents who cared as much as he needed them to, then or now.

God help him if he left Landry feeling the same way....

Brooke seemed to intuit all he wasn't saying. Her glance became even more empathetic. She edged close enough that he could inhale the faint citrus fragrance of her skin. "Are your parents still around?"

Nate nodded. "My mother is in China, my dad works in Brussels. Global economy and all that. We get together once a year, usually around Christmas."

"That sounds…"

Cold. It was. Nate turned and looked Brooke in the eye. "I want something different for Landry and me."

This time she smiled. "It'll come." She reached out and

squeezed his hand reassuringly. "You're only just starting to get to know each other right now."

Nate absorbed the heat of her skin pressed against his. Fighting the urge to ditch propriety and take her into his arms, he pointed out, "He's already bonding with you."

Brooke shrugged her slender shoulders. "I'm a mom. He lost a mom. He never really had a dad."

And maybe I don't know how to be one. Nate sighed. Her candor allowed him to say the unspeakable in return. "And maybe Landry doesn't want a dad."

"Maybe not," she said with the wisdom of a woman who had spent years parenting effectively. "But he needs one. He needs you, Nate."

BROOKE HADN'T MEANT THAT to come out that way. Hadn't meant for this conversation to get so personal, so fast. Yet that was what seemed to happen every time she was alone with Nate. They'd find themselves talking about things that were far too intimate for two people who had just met.

"Anyway—" she forced herself to regroup and step away from Nate "—like I said before, that isn't why I came over here."

"So what did you need?" Nate asked curiously.

Talk about a loaded question.

She pushed away the idea of kissing Nate. Just because she had noticed how sexy he looked standing there, with his dark hair rumpled, water still beading on his powerful shoulders, and a beach towel wrapped around his waist, was no reason to be thinking this way.

Brooke swallowed and made herself stay focused on the task, even as she failed to slow her racing pulse. "I came over to borrow a pillow and blanket—I'm low on bedcovers. I didn't anticipate Landry spending the night in the cottage with Cole and me. The boys are occupying both beds…so I'm going to have to sleep on the sofa."

His eyes gleamed in the shadows. "You couldn't have put one of them on the sofa?"

Not without showing favoritism of some kind and causing a problem that way. "It's fine, Nate," Brooke replied. "I can rough it for a night or two."

He shook his head in silent approval. "You're one of a kind, you know."

"Thank you…. I think."

He pivoted and started for the mansion. "Not many women would step up the way you have the past few days."

Brooke fell into step beside him. She had to struggle to keep pace as he swiftly led the way into the house. "You may be underestimating the female species."

Nate paused at the base of the back staircase. "I don't think so."

She tilted her head, not sure what he meant. Only knowing that the words sounded soft and seductive.

So alluring, in fact, that it wasn't as much of a surprise as she would have expected when Nate flattened a hand against her spine, guided her close.

Brooke had plenty of time to pull away.

The surprise was she didn't want to.

She yearned to experience the touch of Nate's lips on hers.

And when it happened, his kiss was everything she had expected—tender and evocative, possessive and masculine. She moaned softly as he threaded his hands through her hair, tangling his tongue with hers. With their mouths fused together, she reveled in the taste of him and the tantalizing fragrance of his aftershave. He was so warm, so solid, so strong. He wanted her so much. She could feel it in the way he pressed against her, urging her to curve her body all the way into his. Brooke hadn't ever felt seduced like this. Or had such a strong yearning to be touched, held, loved. Which was why she had to come up for air. Take a moment. Regain some common sense!

She splayed her hands across his chest. "Nate..."

He lifted his head slightly. He had a dazed, besotted look in his eyes that mirrored the unwanted emotions she harbored deep inside.

"That's been a long time coming," he told her gruffly. And then he kissed her again.

Chapter Five

Brooke had never been one to spend a lot of time kissing. But as Nate pulled her flush against him once again, and delved into the kiss with breathtaking dedication, she began to see what she had been missing. She was light-headed with pleasure as his lips touched one corner of her mouth, then the other, teasingly warm, temptingly reassuring. Her body went soft with pleasure. She wrapped her arms around his neck and tilted her hips into the hardness of his. He made a sound low in his throat and continued kissing her ardently, one hand in her hair, the other coming around to cup her breast.

Engulfed in his touch, in his smell, Brooke felt the possibilities of a liaison with Nate and longed for more. So what if the guy had a string of ex-girlfriends ten miles long? It had been years since she had been wanted like this, or felt like a woman with needs. Years since she had acknowledged the aching void deep inside her.

With his thorough, provocative kisses, Nate brought it all back. The feel of her heart slamming hard against her ribs. The blossoming heat that started in her breasts and spread outward in deep, pulsing waves. The throb of awareness between her thighs, the boneless feeling in her knees. She knew she should play it cool, but when he pursued her like this it was impossible to mask her response. One stroke of his tongue or brush of his fingertips, and she was trembling all over.

There was something primitive and satisfying about being held against him and savored this way. She could feel his hardness, his need, and knew that whatever normalcy she had been holding on to in his presence was completely gone. There was no point pretending they didn't desire each other, or that his kisses were anything but spectacular. She could only imagine how magnificent his lovemaking would be...if they took this to the next level.

As if hit by the same erogenous thoughts, Nate drew back. Still holding her tightly, he looked down at her. "I could do this all night," he murmured.

"So could I." *If you weren't a client. If I were childless.* Unfortunately, she reminded herself with what little self-discipline remained, she was neither.

With effort, she forced herself to be sensible. "But we both have responsibilities."

For which he apparently cared not a whit, as he continued to stare at her with lust in his eyes.

So she forced herself to say, "Sons to parent." *Emotional baggage still to be dealt with.* "And we can't afford to be distracted."

Finally, she got through to him.

Brought back to reality, Nate inhaled sharply and buried his face against her throat. "And I thought I was the one given to weighing risk," he murmured.

Brooke shifted so that he had to look at her, trying not to think about how good he made her feel. She wasn't sure she followed what he was saying. "In financial terms...in your work?"

"In every way." Their gazes locked and the corner of his

mouth curved upward. "And this," he said, kissing her ever so briefly again, before letting her go, "is a risk worth taking."

BROOKE WAS HALFWAY BACK across the lawn, the borrowed pillow and blanket in her arms, when she saw an ancient Volkswagen pull into Nate's driveway. Her first thought, when she saw a lithe female figure emerge, was that the man who had just kissed her had a visitor.

Her second realization occurred when the woman turned and looked straight at her.

Brooke's heart sank as she recognized the petite auburn-haired grad student with a body that would have given Eva Longoria a run for her money.

"Professor Rylander said I'd find you here," Iris Lomax told Brooke as she neared.

Deciding this conversation should not happen out in public near the caretaker's cottage, Brooke clasped the bedding close to her chest and turned to face her late husband's mistress. "You shouldn't be here," she told Iris. "Especially this late." It was nearly midnight.

"I just got off work. I wait tables to supplement my assistantship. And it couldn't wait." Iris reached into the canvas carryall she had slung over her shoulder. She withdrew an advance copy of Seamus's last book of poetry. "I know you're angry with me for being with your husband, but I can't believe you would stoop this low."

The deep anger in her voice took Brooke aback. "I have no idea what you're talking about."

Iris advanced. "Where do you get off passing off my poems as Seamus's?"

For a second, Brooke was sure she hadn't heard right. "What are you talking about?"

Iris waved the volume with a shaking hand. "Two-thirds of the love poems in Seamus's collection are mine!"

Furiously, she angled a thumb at her chest. "I wrote them! And I helped construct the rest of them, too!"

Brooke could barely breathe. "Surely there's been some mistake."

"You're darn right there has. I'm going to sue Seamus's estate for plagiarism!"

Nate stepped out of the shadows. "How do we know you're telling the truth?"

Brooke was startled by his presence. She'd thought she and Iris were alone.

The grad student sputtered, clearly taken aback. "I've got the originals on my computer!"

Nate stood next to Brooke, silencing Iris with a look. "That doesn't mean anything. You were sleeping with Seamus. You could have copied his work while he was alive. Now that he's gone, you're trying to pass it off as your own."

The woman's jaw dropped.

Brooke was a little surprised, too. She hadn't expected Nate to come to her defense, never mind so gallantly.

"That's not what happened," Iris said heatedly.

In CEO mode once again, Nate withdrew his wallet from his back pocket, took out a business card and handed it to her. "Why don't you gather your proof? Hire an intellectual-property lawyer to represent you. And then call me tomorrow. I'll facilitate a meeting with lawyers for you and Brooke and the publishers."

"The university should be involved, too," Brooke said with a sigh.

Iris glared at her. "Just so you know…I'm not going to let you get away with this. I'm not going to let you and your son benefit financially from my work."

"Believe me, that is the last thing I would ever want to do," Brooke retorted.

Nate draped a comforting arm around Iris's shoulders. "Let me escort you to your car," he murmured.

She relented.

Brooke walked as far as the patio next to the pool, then sat down on a chaise, dropping the bedding beside her.

In the driveway, Nate stood talking with Iris for several minutes. Brooke had no idea what he was saying, but the effect of his words was palpable. When Iris got in her car and finally drove away, it was in a calm, deliberate manner.

Nate returned to Brooke's side. He hunkered down in front of her, took both her hands in hers and searched her face. "Are you okay?"

She gestured impotently, not really sure if she was or not. As she worked to steady her nerves, she said, "I can't believe Seamus did that. And yet…"

"You do?" Nate guessed.

She inhaled deeply and held his gaze. She needed a sounding board. For many reasons, Nate was it. "Seamus had writer's block the last three or four years of his life. No matter how much he tried, he was unable to finish anything. He said he just didn't feel inspired. And then the last year or so, he told me the muse had returned, and he was doing all this great work. It was his excuse for staying away so much, working late."

"You think he was collaborating with Iris?"

"Maybe. She had just started at the university then, as a PhD candidate in poetry. So it's possible he was mentoring her and working with her to improve her writing, and there's just been some confusion about who came up with which lines." Brooke swallowed and forced herself to deal with the worst-case scenario, too. "Then again, maybe what Iris says is true—Seamus was just stealing her words and planning to pass them off as his own all along."

Brooke buried her face in her hands, doing her best to recall. "Whatever happened, the poems for the collection were turned in to Seamus's editor before he died. Nothing has been added or deleted since. The only thing that was done was some very minor editing."

Shifting the pillow and blanket, Nate moved to sit next to her. "It seems like an awfully foolish thing to do. Surely Seamus would have known he would be caught."

That was the logical conclusion for anyone who hadn't possessed illusions of grandeur. Brooke sighed. "Maybe he thought he could 'handle' Iris, if and when she ever found out." Seamus had been known for his ability to lay on the Irish charm. "Or...I don't know. Maybe it wasn't so much the medicine he was taking to help him out in the sack as the stress of the deception that really caused his fatal heart attack. Maybe he was already having an attack of conscience and second thoughts about what he'd done."

"I meant what I said earlier." Nate clasped her hands in his. "I'll help you find an intellectual-property lawyer. I'm sure something can be worked out."

The urge to throw herself in his arms and let him handle everything was almost overwhelming. Knowing she couldn't risk being a passive participant in her life again, even in difficult times like these, she pushed away, bounded to her feet and began to pace. Talking as much to herself as to him, she said, "I have to keep this quiet. I can't let Cole know his father was a fraud. It would destroy him."

Nate paused, his brow furrowed.

It didn't take a body language expert to know what he was thinking. "You don't agree," Brooke surmised.

He gave a small shake of his head. "Cole is a smart kid."

"It would destroy him," Brooke exclaimed, moving

closer. She took his hands once again, gripped them hard. "Promise me, Nate. You'll never breathe a word of this to him."

Nate eyed her reluctantly. Finally, he relented, even though she could see he thought it was the wrong move to make. "I promise."

"Mom!" Momentarily disoriented, Brooke opened her eyes and became aware she was stretched out on the living-room sofa of the caretaker's cottage. Early-morning sunshine filtered in through the closed blinds.

Cole waved the volume of poetry and the embossed invitation in front of her face, while Landry lounged in the background, taking in everything.

"Why didn't you tell me Dad had a new book coming out?" Cole demanded. "Even if it was mushy stuff, I would have wanted to see it."

Brooke blinked.

Realizing she must have fallen asleep while perusing the writing, to see if she could figure out if Seamus had actually written any of it or not, she brushed the hair from her eyes and struggled to sit up. Not easy, given how tangled she seemed to be in the blanket she had thrown over herself for warmth.

Landry edged closer, curiosity mixing with the concern on his face.

"I…" Brooke faltered.

"So how come you didn't tell me about this?" Cole repeated intently. As she rubbed the sleep from her eyes, her son plopped down beside her. Too late, Brooke realized she should have hidden the book and invitation away before she fell asleep. Either that or set her alarm, which she had also apparently neglected to do.

"Are we going to the party?" Cole asked eagerly as

Landry roamed the room, his hands stuffed in the pockets of his shorts, as usual. "The invitation is addressed to both of us."

"Yes, it is." Something else she hadn't really noticed when she'd received the invite from Phineas Rylander. But it was fitting, since Cole had attended all Seamus's other book signings.

Brooke cast another look at Landry. "But…"

"So we're going!" Cole beamed.

"No!" She stopped short at the crestfallen look on her son's face, and the perplexed expression on Landry's. Why did Cole choose this morning to look so much like Seamus, especially around the eyes? How was it that Landry knew she was hiding something?

She turned back to her son, shaking off her unease. "I meant…" She faltered again.

"We're not going?" Cole echoed in disbelief.

Brooke held up a hand. Never a morning person to begin with, she felt completely overwhelmed and out of her league today. Especially since she had lain awake half the night worrying about what to do. "Cole, I just…" Guilt and indecision warred within Brooke. Wary of blurting out the wrong thing again, or further alerting Landry to the turmoil roiling inside her, she rose and said beseechingly, "Can you give me a moment to get a cup of coffee?"

Hurt registered on her son's face. "I don't get why you do this."

"Do what?" she asked nervously.

His lower lip trembled. "Act so weird whenever Dad's name comes up, instead of just talking to me about whatever you are worried about!" Cole spun on his heel and bolted out the door. Then came back in to add furiously, "I hate it when you treat me like a little kid who doesn't know anything about anything! 'Cause I am mature enough to go to that book party and not get all bent out of shape just because Dad died and can't be there!"

Brooke latched onto the idea that it was residual grief keeping them from going, rather than the scandal Cole still knew nothing about. She approached her son and put a reassuring hand on his arm. It wouldn't be much longer before he was taller than she was. "Honey, I know it used to be fun when you went with your dad to his poetry readings and book signings. But this wouldn't be the same."

Scowling, Cole clamped his arms over his chest. "Why can't we do what we did at the wake? Have everybody make a toast and remember him fondly?"

Because, Brooke thought, that would only invite someone like Iris Lomax to make a scene. The kind that, thank heaven, had not been made at the funeral, since she had been persuaded by Phineas Rylander not to attend. Now, it was different. Iris had something Professor Rylander did not want revealed, not the other way around. And if it was a university event, there was no way to bar her without raising a lot of eyebrows—and some very fair questions—since she was still a teaching assistant in the English department.

"Why can't we tell stories about Dad and make it fun, Mom?"

Once again, Brooke had to think on the fly. "Because it would be inappropriate. This is a literary function, and I believe they're planning for it to be very stuffy and intellectual—not something either of us would want to sit through for hours on end."

Cole glared at her. "What you really mean is you don't want to go."

What could she say that her son wouldn't see right through, except the truth? "No, honey, I don't."

"Well, I do!" Cole stormed back out of the cottage.

Landry shoved his hands through his newly spiked hair, which actually looked kind of cute, in a disheveled-rock-star kind of way. "You sure blew that one," he commented, his brow arched in adolescent disapproval.

"No kidding," Brooke muttered. She folded the blanket and set it on the pillow, then looked around for her flip-flops. "Stay here," she told him.

Landry seemed to appreciate that directive as much as Cole liked being kept in the dark.

"I'll be back to fix breakfast for you boys in a moment," she added.

Clad in her sleepwear of athletic shorts and a T-shirt, she raced outside. To her dismay she saw that Cole was standing next to Nate, who appeared to have just come back from a run.

She had to admit that Nate's athletic pursuits kept him in really buff shape. Even his legs were amazingly powerful and sexy.

"...so completely unfair," Cole was saying.

Nate wiped the sweat from his face with the hem of his damp, clinging T-shirt. "I'm sure your mom meant to tell you," he soothed.

Brooke joined them. "I just found out about the party yesterday," she said.

"But you had to know this was coming," Cole waved the volume. "Books don't just appear overnight."

He was quoting his father now, Brooke realized.

"Especially poetry books." Cole flipped the hardcover over to look at his father's photo on the dust jacket. "They take years to write and get published."

Brooke turned her gaze away from the handsome face that had fooled her for so many years. "That's true. And I did know the publisher was bringing out a new volume of your dad's poetry." After all, she had signed the contract.

"Then why didn't you tell me?" Cole persisted.

"I wanted it to be a surprise," she said lamely. It wasn't the first time she had lied to Cole to shield him from his father's frailties, but it was the first time she had done so in front of Nate.

The look in Nate's eyes told her what she already knew in her heart—that it was a mistake. "The proceeds from the book are going to be added to your college fund."

Cole seemed mollified. "You still should have showed me the book the moment you got it."

Nate clapped a paternal hand on Cole's shoulder. "Point taken, buddy."

"Hey, I thought you were coming back to make breakfast?" Landry had ambled out to join them.

"Sounds good to me," Nate stated cheerfully. "That is if I'm invited."

Increasing the intimacy between her and her client was not wise—Brooke felt they had already crossed too many boundaries as it was—but right now she really needed the diversion. She flashed an enthusiastic smile. "Absolutely. I'll get those pancakes started right away."

NATE WENT UP TO THE HOUSE to quickly shower and change. By the time he returned, short minutes later, Brooke had breakfast going.

"Did you know my dad?" Landry asked him.

The question came out of left field, and had Nate feeling as off balance as Cole's third degree had left Brooke. Parenting was harder than it looked, Nate realized. Doing his best to be honest and forthright, he nodded. "Yes, I did. Miles Lawrence lived in the same apartment building as me when we were just out of college."

Landry helped himself to a strip of crispy bacon from a plate that had been set on the table. "Did you ever see his stand-up act?"

Nate poured a cup of coffee and lounged against the counter next to Brooke. "A couple of times."

Landry rocked back in his chair. "Was it any good?"

Brooke kept her attention riveted on the pancakes she was cooking.

Nate turned to face the boy. "He was a funny guy."

Hope shone in Landry's eyes. "My mom always said if he'd lived my dad would have been really famous."

Nate forced himself to be generous. "I think she was right."

The teen frowned. "He never married my mom."

It was no comfort, knowing the woman who had shattered Nate's illusion suffered heartbreak, too. "Your great-grandmother told me that." The knowledge had made him sad. If he had wished anything for Seraphina, it was for her to be happy.

Landry broke another strip of bacon in half. He was quiet for a moment. "Do you think that was right?"

This was definitely not getting easier. "I...don't know."

Brooke shot Nate an empathetic look from beneath her lashes, which neither of the boys could see, then swept by him with a plate of steaming hotcakes in hand.

"You're dodging the question," Landry complained.

Warmed by Brooke's steady presence and unspoken support, Nate took another sip of his coffee. "It's complicated."

The instant Brooke set the platter on the table, Landry stacked several golden-brown pancakes on his plate and doused them with maple syrup. He picked up his knife and fork. "If you were the baby daddy, would you marry the baby momma?"

Nate had no doubt whatsoever about that. "Yes."

"Why?" Landry asked with narrowed eyes.

Feeling the warmth of Brooke's approval, Nate answered, "Because I think whenever possible kids should have two parents, a mom and a dad."

Brooke tensed. Although what she could find wanting in that answer, Nate didn't know.

Cole looked over at Brooke, curious now, too. "Do you feel the same way?" He also helped himself to several pancakes.

She nodded and poured more batter on the griddle.

Cole considered that, while he took his first bite. "My dad didn't feel that way," he announced when he had finished chewing. "He said marriage was a trap, and unless I was really in love I should avoid it."

Nate choked in midsip. "You must feel that way, too," Cole said to him, when he'd stopped coughing. "Because you're not married."

Brooke's eyebrows rose. "Cole, for heaven's sake!"

Nate held out a hand, glad this had come up. He wanted to lay it on the line for both boys, set an example. "It's not because I don't want to be," he explained, then paused to look at Brooke, too, before turning his gaze back to them and continuing with heartfelt sincerity. "I want a wife and family more than anything."

Cole and Landry remained skeptical.

"Have you ever been married?" Cole asked.

"No," Nate admitted.

"Engaged?" Landry pressed.

This was more difficult. "Yes," Nate said.

"Who to?" the boy asked curiously.

There was a beat of silence. Aware he couldn't sidestep the question now, Nate confessed, "To your mother."

For a moment, both boys were frozen in shock. Then anger and resentment permeated the room.

"How come nobody ever told me that?" Landry fumed.

"LANDRY HAD A POINT," Brooke said to Nate later, after the boys had disappeared into their rooms to get ready for summer camp. She and Nate had seized the opportunity to step outside with their second cup of coffee and engage in some private conversation. "Someone should have told him about the relationship between you and his mother."

Nate didn't like receiving criticism that was ill-founded, but in this case it was worth enduring, since he needed a sounding board. "I assumed someone had."

Brooke paused, mug halfway to her lips. "You don't mind the questions it's going to create?"

He shrugged. "They would have come up anyway." Kids were curious. Heck, *he* was curious. About Brooke in general…and specifically, in whatever she'd put into those pancakes to make them taste so good. They were hands down the best he had ever eaten. And he'd dined in some mighty fine places over the years.

Brooke's delicately shaped brows knit together. She hadn't had a chance to get dressed in the clothes or put on the subtle make up that comprised her work armor. Her slightly tousled hair and bare lips made her seem more accessible. She twisted her mouth in disagreement. "You don't know that."

Nate knew avoiding problems never worked, in business or at home. He wouldn't pretend otherwise, even to score points with a woman he found more sexually attractive with every second that passed.

He walked a little farther from the house. "I know I'm not going to hide the truth from him."

Brooke sauntered after him, not stopping until they had reached the waterfall in the lagoon-style swimming pool. She looked up at him, bewilderment lighting her eyes. "You'd really tell him you're unsure about his paternity?"

Nate wouldn't enjoy doing so, but the way he saw it, he had no choice. Not if he wanted Landry to trust him. "If and when he asks, yes."

Her expression grew troubled. "You don't know how he would react."

Nate was beginning to see how Brooke would react. "Then I guess we'd find out."

She blew out a gusty breath. "It could hurt him, Nate."

He raised an eyebrow. "Being lied to or deliberately misled would hurt him more."

The door to the cottage opened. Both boys tramped out, backpacks over their shoulders. "Mom! Camp! We're going to be late!" Cole called.

"Why don't I take them today?" Nate offered.

Brooke looked at the kids, who both shrugged. She turned back to Nate, gratitude in her eyes. "I'd appreciate the help this morning," she said.

"Then let's get a move on," Nate told the guys.

He wanted to spend time with them, and then get back to Brooke.

BROOKE WATCHED THEM all amble off toward Nate's Jaguar sedan, then she hit the shower. When she finally headed over to the main house to await the arrival of the moving crew, Nate was just coming down the sweeping front stairs. Since returning from taking the kids to camp, he'd changed out of the casual slacks and shirt he'd put on after his run. In a dove-gray business suit, coordinating shirt and tie, he looked handsome enough to take her breath away. He smelled great, too, she couldn't help but note as he crossed to her side. As if he'd taken time to slap on some of that leather-and-spice cologne after he shaved. "So what's happening here today?" he asked.

Brooke put her hormones on ice and switched to businesswoman mode. "The auctioneer and I are going to do an inventory of everything you're sending over to be sold. And then the house is going to be emptied out."

"Except for my bedroom and the library," Nate said. His gaze drifted over her as he favored her with a rakish smile.

Insides humming, Brooke nodded. "Those will remain as is."

"For now," he added. "I'm going to want my bedroom changed out eventually, too."

"No problem." She consulted her clipboard as she pushed away a mental image of Nate lounging between the sheets. It was not something she would likely ever see. She lifted her head again and looked into his eyes. "We'll just have to sit down and go over what you want."

And we won't think about what I want.

Which is a man like you in my life.

Nate glanced at his watch. "How about today?" Pulling the BlackBerry from his suit jacket, he checked the calendar. "Can you meet with me at my office downtown? Say around one o'clock?"

Brooke tried not to think how good it felt to be standing here with him like this. "Sure." He was a client, and that was all.

He flashed a disarming smile and touched her gently on the arm. "Then I'll see you then."

Chapter Six

"What's going on here?" Dan Kingsland asked, four hours later.

Nate paused in the door of the conference room where a private lunch had been set up. Resting beside his place setting was the palette of paint colors Brooke had given him to peruse. Good. Everything was exactly as he'd wanted. Glad his business with his partners had been concluded, he turned back to the guys as he attempted to usher them out. "It's a lunch meeting."

Grady McCabe eyed the china and silver. "You never set out roses for us when you invite us here to dine with you," he ribbed.

"We usually get take-out containers and no tablecloth," Jack Gaines remarked.

"And you never mix business with courtship," Travis Carson observed. "So who is this lady who's prompting you to break your own rules? And where is she?"

Nate knew the fastest way to get rid of his friends was to tell them the truth and send them on their merry way. "It's Brooke Mitchell."

The guys chorused approval with big grins. "Ah, the home makeover expert," Travis said.

"Sure she's not making over you, too?" Dan drawled.

"Or just making do," Jack joked.

Nate winced. "Funny."

"Seriously, Nate," Grady said, "don't even think about adding Ms. Mitchell to your string of broken hearts. 'Cause if you do, Alexis will have your hide."

"Make that all our wives," Dan warned. "Emily, Holly and Caroline are friends with Brooke, too. They won't take kindly to you flirting with her, then deciding she's not The One, either."

Nate had been given a bad rap in that regard. "I don't do that," he argued.

More than one of the guys grunted skeptically. "You're pretty picky," Grady observed.

Nate frowned. "I don't want to invest in the wrong relationship again." This time he needed to approach love with the same caution and thoughtfulness he managed his business, and connect with the right woman first. Then and only then would he allow himself to get more involved.

The fact that Brooke seemed like the right woman put him one step closer to his goal of having the loving, supportive family he had always wanted—and never had.

"Maybe no one told you?" Dan chided. "Women don't come with any guarantees."

Travis held up a hand. "Relax, guys. From what I understand, Brooke is every bit as romance-shy as our pal here."

That was true, Nate silently acknowledged. And clearly it was going to make moving forward in his pursuit of her even harder.

A knock sounded on the door. Looking as gorgeous as ever in a lemon sheath and short-sleeved white cardigan, Brooke stuck her head in. "Am I interrupting?"

"Not at all." Grady gave his friends a look that told them to exit ASAP. He turned back to Brooke. "Our meeting is done."

But she was not done talking to his pals. She sauntered in and set her leather carryall on the floor next to the table. "I have to tell you guys, One Trinity River Place is amazing. You should be very proud of yourselves."

Nate's partners beamed. "Go on," Jack urged.

"Yeah," Grady teased with his typical "if you've done it it ain't bragging" attitude. "We can take it."

An appreciative light sparkled in Brooke's pretty eyes. "Okay, Grady, you get kudos for putting together the development deal that made the high-rise possible. Dan deserves 'em for designing the skyscraper, Travis for constructing it. And I'd be remiss if I didn't single out Jack for making sure all communications and electronics are state-of-the-art high tech. And last but not least, Nate—" Brooke paused, her eyes locking with his for an extra long second "—for having a business that is so successful you can afford to house it in a place as luxurious as this."

And here Nate had thought she wasn't impressed with all he had accomplished, building a multimillion dollar company from scratch!

"Ever thought of going into public relations?" Travis teased.

Dan winked. "We could use you on our team."

Brooke grinned, enjoying the banter and camaraderie with the guys as much as Nate was. Unfortunately, their time together was limited. And when he had the opportunity, he wanted her all to himself. "She has a job," Nate reminded them. "Which she is trying to do, if you guys would all clear out of here."

Hands raised in surrender all around. "We get the hint."

Nate shut the door behind his pals after they filed out. "Sorry."

For the first time, Brooke seemed to take in the details

of their surroundings. "I didn't realize we'd be doing lunch here."

Telling himself that was not disapproval in her golden-brown eyes, Nate ushered her toward the table and held out her chair. "It's an environment that is more conducive to work."

WAS IT? BROOKE WONDERED. Looking at the table set for two, in a private room with a spectacular view of downtown Fort Worth, all she could think about was what it would be like to have a date with the handsome CEO.

Not that he was asking for anything but help with Landry and in redecorating his home, but he had kissed her. And those kisses had stayed with her like nothing ever had before.

Which was exactly why she shouldn't allow herself to be distracted this way. Business was business, and this meeting today should be all about his home makeover, she reminded herself.

Brooke settled into the chair Nate offered. "Then let's get down to it."

He sat opposite her.

"Have you had a chance to look at the color palettes I gave you this morning?" she asked.

"I liked them all."

And I like you. But she was digressing again…. She forced herself to return to business. "That's not exactly the response I was looking for."

After they exchanged smiles, Nate gestured. "I can't make a decision about something like that."

He seemed genuinely lost at sea. Brooke leaned toward him and soothed, "You probably have stronger opinions than you realize."

The lift of his black brow said he doubted it.

She brought out a notepad and pen. "Describe a space you really like," she suggested.

Mischief turned up the corners of his lips. "The caretaker's cottage. Since you made it over, it's very…I don't know." He struggled visibly for the correct terms. "Serene…calming…yet cheerful and homey."

"I started with a neutral base—the sand-colored paint that was already on the walls. Added durability and texture with the washable denim slipcovers, and brought in splashes of color with the rugs, bedcovers and other accessories."

Nate thought a moment. "Let's do the same thing in the main house."

"Sounds good. Any colors you truly detest?" She struggled not to notice how sexy and self-assured he looked.

"Orange and purple. Lime green."

Same with me, she thought. Although she had done spaces in those colors for clients. "What about styles of furnishings?" she asked crisply.

"Nothing dainty," he specified. "Everything should be comfortable and kid friendly."

Got it. Brooke made another note. "What about your bedroom?"

Nate shrugged, not the least bit interested. "We'll do that last," he said. "But you should probably talk to Landry about what he wants and get started on his bedroom right away."

And now for the bad news… "I tried last night," Brooke said with a wince.

Nate tensed. "And…?"

As much as Brooke wanted to protect Nate, she couldn't. If he was going to help Landry adjust, he had to know where things stood. She put down her pen and reluctantly shared, "He told me not to worry about it. He didn't think he'd be staying with you for long. He said bunking in the guest cottage was fine."

Nate's face registered the same disappointment Brooke had felt at the time of the exchange.

"He'll come around." She reached across the table and briefly squeezed Nate's hand. Fingers tingling from contact, she took a deep breath and sat back, counseling gently, "You have to give him time. In the meantime, it might help if he went to see his great-grandmother."

The brooding look was back on Nate's handsome face. "I think so, too. I offered to take him this morning, when I was driving the boys to camp." His lips compressed. "He declined."

Brooke played with her fork. "Maybe it shouldn't be an option."

An unreadable emotion appeared in Nate's blue eyes. "That was my first instinct," he admitted slowly. "And then I got to thinking, we're already forcing him to do so much. Maybe Jessalyn is right. Maybe Landry shouldn't see her again until he accepts the reality of the situation and settles in a bit."

"And maybe," Brooke countered equably, "what he needs is to see her, so he'll finally understand this is all for the best."

Nate's BlackBerry buzzed. He glanced at the screen. "Percy Dearborn is waiting to see us."

Brooke lifted a brow, confused.

"He's an intellectual-property lawyer—the best in the area."

She did a double take. "Excuse me?"

The CEO was back full force. "I assumed you wouldn't have time to find someone, so I made a few phone calls this morning."

As if it was the most natural thing in the world to

do for a woman you'd just become acquainted with and kissed...

Nate leaned back in his chair and forged on. "I told him the situation and he offered to represent you and your late husband's estate in the plagiarism claim being made by Iris Lomax. It's important we go on the offense here."

Memories of similar situations surfaced. "This isn't your situation to manage!"

His eyes narrowed. "You need help."

Brooke had been trying not to think about that. Dealing with Iris's sudden reappearance in her life had been disturbing enough. "Then I'll find it on my own," she insisted.

"*Have* you hired anyone?" Nate pressed.

"No, but..."

Determination tautened his jaw. "Do you want Cole to see this played out in the newspapers?"

Brooke flushed. "Of course not."

Nate rose and moved around to pull out her chair. "Then I suggest you meet with Percy and get his advice on how to proceed." He touched her shoulder gently. "You can give me hell later."

Brooke glared at Nate. "We will talk about this," she promised.

"Of that," Nate said drily, "I have no doubt."

Brooke spent the next half hour answering Percy Dearborn's steady stream of questions. Finally, he put down his pen. "I do not think the court would find you personally liable, given the fact that you were in no way involved in the writing, preparation or submission of the manuscript, which was all done by your late husband prior to his demise. The estate, however, could be found liable, if the proof of theft that Ms. Lomax alleges does exist. Because you did follow through on getting the work published, as your late husband wished."

Brooke's throat tightened with dread. She folded her hands in her lap, glad she had Nate sitting beside her to offer support. She looked at the distinguished attorney. "What do you suggest I do?"

"I'd like to meet with Ms. Lomax and her lawyer, get a look at her proof, and if that holds up, see if we can't come to some kind of settlement before a lawsuit is filed and the matter becomes public."

Brooke relaxed slightly. "What about the university?"

"I'll talk to Phineas Rylander as soon as we know what the situation is."

"Thank you."

"It's no problem." The attorney stood and put his laptop computer back in the carrying case. "That's what we lawyers are here for. To help straighten out messes like this."

Brooke shook his hand, then waited while Nate walked him out.

She was standing at the window in Nate's private office, looking down at the Trinity River, when he returned. "Okay," he said, bracing his hands on his waist and pushing back the edges of his suit coat. "Let me have it with both barrels."

Why did he have to be so reasonable? Brooke wondered. It was charm like his that had gotten her into hot water in the first place.

"I get the fact that you like to manage things," she told him quietly, "but we need to be clear about something. You are *never* to jump in like that and take control of my life again."

NATE KNEW THE PRUDENT thing to do was simply to agree with Brooke. Unfortunately, he could not do that in good conscience. His integrity required he be honest with her. "If I see you making a mistake, hiding from the truth, I'm going to speak up."

"There's a difference between speaking up and telling me I'm wrong, and going out and hiring a lawyer for me."

Knowing he had to touch her or go crazy, Nate tucked his hand in hers and rubbed a thumb over the back of her hand. "I told you last night I would help you find someone to handle this for you."

Color highlighted her elegant cheeks. "I expected you to ask around and give me some names," she blurted. "Not actually set up an appointment with Percy Dearborn without speaking to me first." She paused, her silence filled with a mixture of disappointment and disillusionment. "I get that you were trying to help, but that was over the line, Nate."

He felt like he had when he was a kid and his parents were unhappy with him, despite the fact that he had done his level best to accomplish whatever it was that needed to be done.

And yet he knew the depth of his protectiveness would have been unwarranted, had he not been so interested in Brooke. "Point taken," he said finally, aware that he was rushing her and shouldn't be. "I should have consulted you first." Should have adopted a gentler, more patient approach.

Brooke peered up at him. "Why does my dilemma matter so much to you anyway?" she queried softly, searching his eyes.

Nate brushed a strand of hair from her cheek and tucked it behind her ear. "I didn't want to see you and Cole get hurt. I could tell from the look on your face that all you wanted to do was ignore the threat and wait for the trouble to blow over. And I know from personal experience how badly that always turns out."

Looking as beautiful as she did vulnerable, Brooke gave him a quizzical glance. Her encouragement prompted him to continue. "On some level I knew there was more going on with Seraphina and Miles Lawrence than she said, but I had a lot of reasons for not dealing with the situation the way I should have." Nate recited them wearily. "I was busy building my business. We were engaged. I loved her. I didn't want anything getting in the way of our marriage."

Brooke tightened her fingers around his. "Don't tell me you blame yourself for what Seraphina did," she murmured.

How could he not? It took two people to make a relationship succeed, to make it fail. Nate shrugged and admitted ruefully, "Had I paid attention to the signs, given her the attention she obviously needed, she might have never run off with Miles."

Brooke's eyes glittered as she jumped to his defense. "And maybe she would have anyway," she said. "Maybe the failing was hers and hers alone."

Wishing Brooke wasn't working for him, so he could go ahead and pursue her the no-holds-barred way he wanted to, Nate studied her. "Is that the way you feel about Seamus?"

She sighed. "I was a good wife. I loved him. I gave him everything I had and he cheated on me when he should have respected our marriage vows and been loyal to me and our son," she reflected sadly. "And now it's possible he cheated Iris Lomax, too, by stealing her work and passing it off as his own. Is it what Iris deserves, for carrying on with a married man? I don't know. The only thing I'm certain about is that I am not taking the blame for my late husband's lack of character. And you shouldn't blame yourself for what your ex did, either," Brooke told Nate pointedly. "Because the moral failing was hers and hers alone. Unless…you've cheated on someone, too?"

Ah, the test he had been expecting, given his undeserved reputation as a womanizer. "I would never do that," he told her quietly.

Their gazes meshed. "Neither would I," she said.

Nate smiled and took her other hand in his. "Then it seems we have that in common," he said, looking down at her.

Brooke smiled at him briefly, then withdrew her hands and stepped back. "Just don't try and boss me around or take over my life," she warned, all feisty, independent single mom and accomplished businesswoman. "Because I am perfectly capable of looking after myself."

BROOKE'S PARTING SHOT haunted Nate for the rest of his day. He knew she was a capable woman. He also knew she was in a weak position, legally and personally, and it was that vulnerability, the sense that she needed him as much as he needed her, that made him want to protect her.

The question was, how could he make her see that his concern was something to be appreciated instead of resented? That it was okay for a woman to accept help from the man in her life, and vice versa? And that was what he wanted to be, he realized. The man in her life.

Kissing her again would remind her of the chemistry they had felt. Maybe further develop intimacy and passion between them.

But that, too, was hard to accomplish when they had two chaperones on the premises every evening.

Nevertheless, Nate knew that where there was a will, there was a way.

In the meantime, he had told Brooke that he would retrieve the boys from summer camp and pick up some Texas barbecue on the way home, so he headed out.

"How was camp?" Nate asked, when the boys got in his Jaguar.

"Really cool," Cole answered, and proceeded to talk about the computer video game he was designing. Landry was working on a similar project. And they were still chattering about the problems and successes with their designs when they got home.

"Sounds like you're both learning a lot," Brooke observed over dinner.

Landry smiled at Brooke. He finished his mouthful of brisket and forked up some potato salad. "I really like the fencing lessons, too. It's a lot harder than it looks...."

"I'll bet." Brooke flashed an understanding, appreciative grin. As Landry basked in her approval, Nate saw how much the teen needed a maternal presence in his life again.

Almost as much as Nate himself needed this particular woman to stay in his life...

"I know what you're thinking," Brooke murmured, when he stayed behind to help her clean up after the boys went off to shoot hoops on the sport court at the rear of the property.

Glad for the time alone with her, he carried the dishes to the sink and gathered up the empty take-out containers. "And what is that?" he teased.

Brooke placed the leftovers in airtight bags and slid them into the fridge, then turned around to face him. Leaning against the fridge, she answered drily, "The same thing *I* think when I see Cole looking at you like you are some kind of superhero. It's not enough reason for us to get together."

Nate set aside what he was doing and slowly crossed the distance between them. He stopped in front of her and braced a forearm on either side of her slender shoulders.

He hadn't intended to make another move on her right here and now, but then again, he hadn't intended a lot of things when it came to Brooke Mitchell.

"Then how about this?" he offered softly, leaning in to kiss her again.

Chapter Seven

Brooke knew allowing Nate to put the moves on her wasn't the wisest course of action. But sometimes, she thought wistfully as his lips settled ever so nicely over hers, being cautious wasn't all it was cracked up to be.

Sometimes a gal had to just go with the dictates of fate.

And fate had put her right here, right now, with Nate.

So what if it wasn't meant to last? Or if they were drawn together solely by their mutual need for support, guidance and assistance?

They were here. Now. Together. They had maybe five minutes to enjoy the dreamy passion of their kiss, and the encapsulating warmth of his hard body pressed up against hers.

Five minutes to forget—even for one moment—that… Wait! Were those footsteps racing down the hall…toward them?

Apparently so, Brooke realized, since Nate heard them, too.

He broke off the kiss, stepped back.

She swung open the refrigerator door and ducked behind it, just in the nick of time.

The pounding footsteps hit the porcelain tile and swept

into the kitchen. "The ball's low on air," Cole announced, holding up an orange globe with black edging.

"Yeah. We figured you probably had an air pump somewhere," Landry added.

Brooke finished smoothing her hair and blotting her mouth. Composure restored as much as possible, she closed the fridge and stepped back. To her relief, Nate looked more relaxed than she felt.

He shot her a reassuring, we'll-pick-this-up-again-later glance that only she could see, then turned back to the boys. "The air pump is in the garage. Let's go out together so I can show you how it works."

NATE GOT THE BOYS SET UP, shot a few hoops with them, then headed back to the main house. Halfway there, he got a phone call from work, alerting him to a problem that needed to be addressed right away. It took an hour to work things out. No sooner had he hung up than Landry appeared at the library door. Dressed in a pair of jersey shorts, a T-shirt and flip-flops, his damp, spiky hair standing on end, he looked like he had just come out of the shower.

"Got a minute?" he asked.

Wondering if it was his imagination or if the teen had grown taller in the last few days, Nate nodded. "Come on in."

Landry shut the door behind him. "I was wondering if you still had pictures of my mom and you, when the two of you were together."

Good question, and one that caught Nate off guard. He gestured for him to have a seat. "I returned her stuff when our engagement ended."

Landry perched on the edge of the black leather sofa.

"So you don't have anything." His shoulders sagged in disappointment.

Nate spun around in his swivel chair, so they were facing each other. "If you're talking about old love letters or anything like that, no. But I might have some photos that escaped the postbreakup purge."

He turned back to his desk, disconnected from his company's network and opened up the drive that held all his personal information. Within it were files of photos that he'd scanned into memory, arranged chronologically.

He went back sixteen years, to the month he had first started dating Seraphina. The personal photos of the two of them were gone, but Landry's mom was in a number of his company photos. "Here she is at the second annual company picnic." Back then, Nate had employed only a dozen people, so it was easy to spot her.

Landry flattened his hands on the desktop and leaned in for a closer look. "Wow. She looks young."

And happy...as did Nate. He smiled, remembering that time in his life when it seemed he was going to get everything he wanted in short order, including the "happy family" of his dreams.

He scrolled through more photos. "And here she is at that year's 5k race to raise funds for cancer research."

Landry pulled up a chair close to Nate, so he could better view the screen. He propped his elbows on the desk and leaned in again. "Do you think she had any idea she would have cancer herself one day?"

"No. She just did that to help others."

Landry smiled fondly, reflecting. "She was good that way."

Nate found half a dozen more photos of him and Seraphina—all at company events, all with other people. He hadn't noticed it at the time, but as he studied their body language now, he could see what he had been blind to then. Subtly but surely, he and Seraphina had been growing apart as his success and the company grew.

Finally, they got to the last week he and Seraphina had officially been a couple. Nate clicked on the photo. "I think this is the last one I have," he said.

They had been with a group of friends at a New Year's Eve party at a swank hotel downtown. Dress was formal. Seraphina looked incredibly beautiful. And unhappy, even in her cardboard top hat, with a paper whistle in her hand.

Landry studied the numbers printed on the Happy New Year banner. "This was fifteen years ago," he said.

Nate nodded. "We broke up the following week."

Landry blinked. "You know, my birthday is in mid-August. Eight months later."

Nate swore to himself. He'd been so busy tripping down memory lane, he hadn't thought about Landry doing the math. He swallowed and aimed for reassuringly casual. "Yeah."

"So I could be *your* kid?" The boy's eyes widened.

Wasn't that the fifty-thousand-dollar question? "I don't know," Nate said finally, wishing he did. He forced himself to meet Landry's searching eyes. "It's…possible." There was no clue from the way Landry looked. He had his mother's hair and eye color. His features were an amalgam. His height he could have gotten from either Nate or Miles Lawrence.

Landry stood and began to prowl the room restlessly. "But you don't know for certain." His flip-flops slapped on the geometric patterned rug.

Nate wished he had the right to take him in a hug and comfort him the way he had seen his friends comfort their sons, the way his own father had never comforted him.

But he didn't. Because he knew that to push Landry into something else he wasn't ready for would be to lose the rapport they had managed to build thus far.

Aware he deserved an honest answer, Nate exhaled slowly. "No…I don't know for certain."

Hurt and confusion shone in Landry's blue-gray eyes. "Is that why you were so interested in becoming my guardian and adopting me?" He ran a hand across the peach fuzz on his face. "Because you think I'm yours?"

Nate reminded himself to get Landry a razor. He didn't even know if the boy had one. "I agreed to become your guardian and adopt you because it's what your mother wanted."

Landry's jaw thrust out pugnaciously. "What about what you and I want?"

Nate stood. He closed the distance between them in two strides and put his hand on Landry's shoulder. "This *is* what I want."

"Sure." Landry jerked away. "*If* I'm your kid." He stared at Nate, a muscle working in his jaw. "What if I'm not?"

Nate regarded him evenly. "You will be when the adoption is final."

Another tense silence ticked out. Landry stood as if braced for battle, still glaring. "You're telling me you don't want to find out?"

They were dealing with a time bomb here. Nate knew he could handle the results, whatever they were. He wasn't sure Landry could weather them half as well. And that being the case… Nate gestured noncommittally. "I don't see the point." It wouldn't change what happened in the end. Landry would still end up being adopted by him. Landry would be his son; he would be Landry's father.

"Well, I sure do." The teen threw up both hands in

barely suppressed fury. "I want a DNA test." The words were flat, final.

Nate struggled to calm him down. "Landry—"

"I have to know."

Nate could see that was so. In his place, he admitted to himself reluctantly, he would probably feel the same way. So he tackled the problem the way he did all others, head-on. "All right."

"So you'll arrange it?" Landry pressed, coming closer once more as he sought to extract a promise.

It was all Nate could do not to pull the kid into a hug. With a nod, he vowed, "First thing tomorrow."

BROOKE WAS LOADING clothes into the washer when Landry burst back into the caretaker's cottage. His face was a blotchy pink and white as he brushed past her, heading toward his bedroom. "Landry?" She dropped what she was doing and went after him. "What's wrong? What happened?"

"Ask Nate!" He slammed the door behind him.

Cole came out of the bathroom, smelling like soap and still drying his hair. "What's going on?" he asked in concern.

"I'm not sure," Brooke murmured, torn between going to Landry and talking to Nate first. Forewarned was forearmed. And right now she was leery of doing and saying the wrong thing and making an already bad situation worse. "Would you mind hanging here while I go talk to Nate?"

"No problem." Cole hesitated outside the shut bedroom door. "You think I should try?"

The door opened, and Landry appeared. He looked at Cole. "You can come in," he said tersely, glancing at Brooke as if she was an enemy. "That's it."

Okay. Now she *really* had to talk with Nate. "I'll be back in a few minutes, guys," she said. "You know where I'll be, so come and get me if you need me."

"Right, Mom." Cole's eyes were trained toward his friend.

The bedroom door shut.

Brooke slid her feet into her clogs and headed out across the lawn.

Nate was standing on the stone terrace that ran along the rear of the mansion. Hands gripping the balustrade, he was looking toward the cottage.

Slowly, he came to meet Brooke. She mounted the steps as quickly as possible. "What did he say?" Nate asked.

His usual self-assurance was gone.

Brooke's heartbeat accelerated as she closed the distance between them. "Nothing illuminating. What happened?"

Nate exhaled. Weary lines bracketed his eyes. "Landry wanted to see some photos of his mother and me. The last one was taken on New Year's Eve, right before we broke up. He read the banner, did the math. Figured out his paternity was somewhat in question."

Brooke caught her breath. "You didn't…"

"Lie to him?" Nate stiffened, letting her know she had struck a nerve. "No. I didn't. Which is why he now wants a DNA test."

Her eyes widened. "And you agreed?"

Nate's jaw set in that stubborn way she was beginning to know so well. "Landry wants to know the truth. I get that."

But did he get the rest of it? Brooke wondered, her years of parenting coming to the fore and giving her a broader view of the situation. "You understand," she told him, as gently as possible, "that however this turns out, you're in trouble."

Nate quirked a brow. "For telling the truth?"

Forcing herself to ignore the edge in his voice, she continued, "If Landry is your biological son, it means his birth certificate is a lie, and his mother lied to both of you all these years. And if he isn't, then…" Brooke lifted her hands helplessly. "That's got to hurt now, too."

Because it meant Nate and Landry would never have that biological connection every parent and child wanted, whether they admitted it or not.

Nate sighed and shoved a hand through his hair. "Obviously, it's not a situation I'd want." He turned gleaming blue eyes to hers. "But I'm not going to run from it or encourage Landry to do so, either. Whatever the situation turns out to be, it's best we deal with it now."

Another silence fell, this one even more packed with emotion. Nate studied her. "You don't agree?"

I think you're headed for a long, hard fall. And so is Landry. But aware she had already overstepped her bounds in giving her opinion, she shrugged. "It's not really up to me, is it?"

His mouth curved downward and he shook his head. "No, I guess it's not."

Another long, uncomfortable silence fell.

Hard to believe, Brooke thought, that just a couple of hours ago they had been standing in his kitchen making out like a couple on the threshold of taking the next big step….

Hard to believe she had put so much in jeopardy, so fast.

Which was why she had to take charge of her life once again. And control what she could of a situation that was fast becoming an emotional mess. "But there is something that is up to me. And that's our…attraction to each other."

Nate folded his arms across his broad chest and waited. With his black hair tousled, and a hint of beard lining his face, he looked wildly sexy.

"It can't continue." Brooke felt her throat tighten, but pushed on. "We can't let the kids see us kissing."

"I think they could handle it," Nate replied with a grin.

"They could handle seeing two random people kissing," Brooke countered, as her heart somersaulted inside her chest. "But you and me…?" Surreptitiously, she wiped her perspiring palms on the sides of her shorts. "I think it sends the wrong message."

"Which would be?"

She gulped, aware she was the one now on a road she never should have taken. "That it's okay to become casually involved with someone you're working for."

"First of all…" Nate's glance raked her appreciatively from head to toe. His voice dropped a husky notch. "There's nothing casual about the way I feel when I kiss you. And if you're honest with yourself, there's nothing casual about the way you feel, either."

Brooke's face heated. He had scored a point with that one. Wise or not, their kisses were hot!

"Second," he continued, looking deep into her eyes, "in another week or so you won't be working this job."

Which meant she wouldn't be here all the time. And then where would they stand? Would Nate still pursue her this intensely, or would she merely be out of sight, out of mind? The thought that she was about to hook up with another Casanova filled her with dread and made her want to pull back even more, to protect herself. "Exactly my point," she reiterated.

His shoulders tautened. "So what's the problem?"

Irritated at the continued need to spell out her objections for him, in great detail, Brooke retorted, "The problem is Landry is missing a mom and Cole is missing a dad. They like it when the four of us hang out together and have dinner and stuff, and when I'm not here that won't be happening anymore." Cole would miss it as much as she would. Probably Landry, too.

Nate regarded her, incredulous. "Who says?"

Brooke took a deep breath and let it out slowly. "You know what I mean."

He dropped his arms and moved in. "I know you're trying to put up boundaries that will keep us from getting any closer." He caught her by the arms and held her in place when she would have bolted. "It's not going to work." He lowered his gaze to her mouth, before returning it ever so slowly to her eyes. She stilled, fighting the riptide of desire churning through her. "Landry is bonding with you," Nate continued in a quiet, admiring voice. "And so am I. And Cole's important to me, too." He coaxed her closer still. "There's no getting away from that."

No getting away from how she felt whenever they were close like this.

Brooke paused and wet her lips. "I still don't want them to know that…"

"We've kissed?" He finished her sentence for her. "And that I want to make love to you?"

Brooke felt her stomach drop. "Just say what's on your mind, why don't you?" she muttered wryly.

Her attempt to deflect the emotions with a deadpan remark failed.

Nate only grew more serious. "I told you, Brooke. I believe in putting the truth out there, whatever it is. Ignoring feelings never accomplished anything."

Clearly, he wanted to kiss her again as much as she wanted to kiss him. And if it hadn't been for the two kids, the potential for hurt, Brooke knew she would have thrown caution to the wind. Fortunately, for all their sakes, she had a mission to fulfill.

"Honesty is always the best policy," Nate continued.

She thought about the hurt, confused look in Landry's eyes just now. And worse, what could be coming up. She splayed her hands across the solid warmth of Nate's chest, forcing distance between them. "You're wrong, Nate," she told him softly. "The best thing we can do is *protect* our kids. And make sure they don't have to deal with anything they shouldn't have to deal with. So I need your promise." She pushed free of his embrace. "No more kissing me when the boys are anywhere in the vicinity." She took a deep breath. "No more kissing me at all."

Nate's eyes darkened. "I agree to the first," he said, with the self-assured authority he probably used in board meetings. "Not to the latter."

Brooke blinked.

He regarded her with a mixture of resignation and amusement. "Yeah, I know you're used to calling the shots. You've made that perfectly clear." He flashed a wicked, challenging smile as he came closer once again, and chucked her beneath the chin. "But I like to call the shots, too. And what my gut is telling me is that this connection we feel is something special enough to pursue. And that, sweetheart, is exactly what I plan to do."

"EARTH TO BROOKE?" Holly Carson said, from the opposite end of the mansion's vast dining room at nine the next morning.

Brooke started. She hadn't been with it since she'd dropped Cole at camp and Nate and Landry had left for the doctor's office. She shook off her mental fog and headed toward the talented artist, who also happened to be the wife of Nate's business partner and good friend Travis Carson. "Sorry."

"You asked me to come here this morning to give you my opinion about using murals to break up the dining room into a more usable space, and all you've done is stare glumly out the window."

Brooke flashed an apologetic smile. "I'm sorry. I'm distracted."

"And no wonder." Holly looked around at the big, echoing space. "It's a huge job."

Brooke forced her mind back to business. "So what do you think?"

Holly paced back and forth, studying the light coming in through the tall windows. "That you're right. It would really help to put something on the wall at each end of the space, with a neutral-colored break in between."

They discussed possible themes, then walked toward the kitchen, where Holly's husband, Travis, and another business partner of Nate's, Dan Kingsland, were already taking measurements.

For the next fifteen minutes, they discussed how to replace the utilitarian, stainless steel work island in the center of the room with something warmer and more family friendly. Dan, an architect, was going to do the design. The custom-cabinetry arm of Travis's construction company would build and install the final product to match the existing wood cabinets. Marble countertops would be added—again by Travis's company—to further dress up the space.

They were just finishing when Nate walked in. All eyes turned to him.

"The DNA test go okay?" Travis asked.

Nate nodded. "We'll get the results in seven to ten days."

Holly held her sketch pad to her chest. With the comforting tone of a mother who had successfully weathered her own difficulties, she counseled, "Kids are remarkably resilient, even at a young age."

Dan spoke with the authority of a father of four. "They are also curious. Landry would have been asking these questions eventually, and putting two and two together. Best you go ahead and deal with it now and get it out of the way."

Everyone, Brooke noted, seemed to be in agreement with Nate. Except her.

"At least you've got time to prepare for whatever the results are," Travis said.

"Which is why—in the meantime—I want to do everything I can to get Landry moved into the main house, with me." Nate paused and looked straight at Brooke. "I want us to be a family in every sense before the results come in."

Chapter Eight

"This is going to be a computer room slash media center where we'll have everything you need to read, study and do homework," Nate told the boys after dinner the following day, as they toured a large, second-floor space in the mansion. "And next to it is going to be a video gaming room, where you can hang out and entertain friends."

Brooke noted that Cole smiled with all the enthusiasm Nate could have wished for—even though technically none of this was meant for her son, since he wouldn't be living here much longer.

"Sweet," Cole said.

Being careful not to touch the freshly painted walls, Landry stood with his hands stuffed in the pockets of his camp shorts, as usual. He had been remote and moody like this ever since the DNA tests were done.

Brooke and Nate had concurred it was best to give Landry his space for the first twenty-four hours. Now, they were beginning to worry. Hence Nate's rush to somehow get Landry involved in the design of his new home.

Nate continued down the hall to the next set of rooms, a bedroom and private bath suite. He looked at Landry. "What do you think about this for your bedroom?"

To Brooke's and Nate's frustration, there was no response either way.

"You can have whatever you want in here—just let Brooke know," Nate persisted.

"I'd be happy to help you pick out furniture and linens in whatever colors and styles you like," she offered amiably.

The positive attitude toward the future that Brooke knew Nate had hoped to see was nowhere in sight. Landry remained emotionally and physically aloof. He stepped away from the group, the look in his eyes far too cynical for his years. "Thanks for the offer, Nate, but—"

Uh-oh, Brooke thought, *here it comes....*

"—it's enough right now for me to sleep in the caretaker's cottage," Landry continued. "You've been really great, especially under the circumstances, but you don't need to do anything more. Especially since I might not be staying."

Nate tensed, and Brooke caught the flash of hurt on his face. Her heart went out to him, even as he recovered his composure.

"I thought we had settled that, Landry," he said.

"Until the DNA results come in—" Landry scowled with the might of all fourteen of his years "—nothing is settled." He turned to Cole, done with the revitalization tour of the mansion, and Nate's cheerful efforts to turn it into a more kid-friendly environment. "Want to go for a swim?"

Cole nodded, as if eager to get away from the animosity that had been simmering just below the surface for almost two days now. "Sure."

The two boys sauntered off in wary silence.

Nate and Brooke remained in the upstairs hallway. "Go ahead and say it," he said.

She looked at him, a question in her eyes.

"You think I'm being a little too pushy."

Well, duh, yes, of course. Avoiding the wet paint, Brooke started down the sweeping front staircase. She paused, her hand on the railing, and waited for Nate to catch up with her.

Like her, he was still in his work clothes, although he had taken off his suit coat and tie. And later unfastened the first two buttons on his shirt and rolled up his sleeves.

The sense of added formality helped—until Brooke found her gaze riveted on the strong column of his throat, and the dark hair springing out the open V on his starched shirt.

Curtailing the urge to explore both, she turned her gaze to the handsome planes of his face. Realizing she could spend all day—and all night—just looking at him, she chided wryly, "What happened to the plan to let Landry take his time, deciding this was where he wanted to be, before forging on with the details?"

Nate made a face—guilty as charged.

He sat down on the stairs, clasped her elbow and brought her down beside him. "I want Landry to realize I'm serious about adopting him, and plan to go ahead with it no matter what the DNA test reveals."

Once again, without warning, they were involved in an intimate conversation. Once again she felt her heart going out to him. Even if his actions were wrong, she knew his motivation came from the right place.

She watched him stretch his long legs over several stairs.

Wanting to be more comfortable, she did the same. "I admire your determination."

It was all she could do not to reach over and grip his hand.

Keeping his own hands to himself, he turned his head and met her gaze. "I hear an 'exception' in there," he noted, with a quiet smile that also indicated he wasn't about to change his mind.

Brooke brushed the hair out of her eyes and tried anyway. "I also know what it's like to be part of a family where decisions are made for you, your input disregarded." She paused to let her words sink in, and continued searching his face. "It's not a great way to live, Nate."

He turned slightly, so his spine was pressed against the railing, his bent knee pressed against her thigh. "Are we talking about your life with your parents?"

Aware of the steady warmth emanating between them, Brooke shook her head. Heart racing, she kept her gaze locked with his. "While I still had them, my folks were great. I'm speaking of my late husband." Wanting Nate to understand, she forced herself to talk about what she had always kept to herself, for fear of feeling disloyal. "It's what happens when you marry someone twenty years older than you, who thinks he has all the answers and you have none."

The understanding in Nate's expression encouraged her to go on confiding in him. And this time she did reach over and clasp his hand, tightening her fingers around his. "The only difference was, in my case, I believed Seamus was the sole authority on everything for a very long time. And that in turn led me to doubt everything I thought I knew about myself." Brooke paused. With effort, she withdrew her hand and stood. "I know you are used to running a corporation, that you built your business on your own. But you can't behave the same way in your relationship with Landry and expect him to want to be your son."

"DO YOU WANT THE BAD NEWS first or the good news?" Brooke asked Nate the following morning, after she had dropped the boys at computer camp and returned to the mansion.

Nate, who'd been about to leave for work himself, set his briefcase beside the front door. "The good."

"Both the boys are really excited about your plans for the rooms upstairs."

"That's great." Nate had been up half the night researching the latest electronic equipment, games and educational software for college-bound teens. "What's the bad?" He moved back to allow the construction crew to enter.

Brooke waited until the men walked past before she continued in a low, worried tone. "Landry told Cole that he had been thinking about running away before his greatgrandmother left him with you. He said he probably would have done so had Cole and I not showed up and allowed him to stay with us in the cottage. As long as we're here, Landry plans to stick around, but he won't guarantee anything once we leave."

"Angling to stay on?" Nate teased.

Brooke rolled her eyes. "Uh—no." She sobered. "Cole is really concerned about Landry taking off. And so am I. We don't want to see anything happen to him."

"Nor do I." Nate exhaled.

"Anyway, I thought you should know."

"Thanks for giving me the heads-up." He paused. "Although for the record, I think it's just talk. If Landry was going to bolt, he would have already done so. In any case, I don't think he would go very far from his greatgrandmother."

"Have you talked to him about going to see Jessalyn at her new quarters?"

"Twice. He's resistant." Nate sighed. "I'm hopeful if I keep asking every few days, he'll eventually change his mind."

"Me, too. I think it would help."

"Speaking of help... I don't know if I have articulated how grateful I am for all your help with Landry."

"You're paying me double time. That's thanks enough."

"Brooke—"

Her phone rang.

She checked the caller ID and frowned. "Do you mind if I get this? It's Percy Dearborn, the intellectual-property lawyer."

Nate gestured for her to do so, then walked off to the side to wait. When she had finished her conversation, Brooke ended the call.

Nate came back. "Everything okay?"

She only wished. "Apparently, the proof Iris Lomax is offering is flimsy at best. But the attorney wants me to go through Seamus's papers. See if I can find anything that will establish the work was definitively his. Otherwise, she's going to go ahead and file a lawsuit, and it will become public."

"Is it possible it's a scam?"

Brooke considered for a moment. "It could be. Or maybe she's just angry because he died in her arms and left her without anything, not even a mention in his will, and she finally sees a way to garner some inheritance for herself. It's hard to tell. All I really know is that this has to be done right away, so I'm going to have to ask you for the rest of the day off."

"You've got it. And Brooke—good luck."

"Hey, Nate, it's Cole. I'm sorry to bother you at the office, but, uh...Landry and I are in kind of a jam."

Please tell me you haven't done something stupid like try and run away, Nate thought, immediately wishing he had taken Brooke's warning more seriously.

Calmly, he stepped out of the meeting with his top managers, taking his cell phone down the hall to his private office. Resisting the parental urge to immediately start with the third degree, he asked matter-of-factly, "What can I do to help?"

"Well...Landry and I both forgot to get our permission slips signed for the field trip this afternoon."

Nate paused. "What field trip?"

"I guess we forgot to tell you. The camp is taking anyone who wants to go to a motion capture and virtual reality lab for kids at the University of Texas at Dallas this afternoon. And then out for pizza and a movie this evening. Only we can't go unless we have written permission, and I can't get ahold of Mom for some reason." Anxiety filled his voice. "And you can't sign for me, only Landry—I already asked. But you can fax in the permission slip. So if I can fax that to you, and you sign it and fax it right back, then Landry can go. But I can't unless we can find Mom before one o'clock." Cole heaved a big sigh.

"Let me give you my private fax number. Of course I'll sign."

"What about Mom?" Cole sounded glum.

She's at your house, going through boxes of your father's things, Nate thought. However, he knew revealing that would invite questions neither he nor Brooke were prepared to answer. "I'll track her down and take a copy of the permission slip over to her, and we'll get it faxed back in for you, too," Nate promised.

"Are you sure you have time?" Cole asked, sounding excited and upbeat again.

Nate looked at his watch; it was eleven-thirty. This part of parenting he could handle, no problem. "Positive. One way or another, Cole, I'll make sure you and Landry both get to go."

"Thanks, Nate." Cole's happiness was a palpable thing. "I knew we could count on you."

Nate smiled. Now, if only Landry felt the same way, they'd be all set.

BROOKE WAS IN THE MIDDLE of the living-room floor, surrounded by boxes and piles of papers and notebooks when the doorbell rang. She was half tempted not to answer it, but a glance out the window had her leaping to her feet.

Sure something was really wrong, since Nate was here unexpectedly, she headed for the door. "What's going on?" She took in his harried look and ushered him in.

"Sorry to interrupt. I've got some papers that need signing ASAP." Briefly, he explained.

Relieved it was only a paperwork snafu, Brooke relaxed.

"So if you have a fax...?" Nate smiled.

"Actually, I do." She paused to read the sheet, fill in the pertinent data and lifted a staying hand. "Let me go send these in and then I'll be right back."

Nate nodded.

Brooke disappeared down the hallway of her century-old bungalow.

While the beeps of a fax number being typed in sounded in the distance, Nate took a moment to look around.

Located in the residential enclave next to the Fort Worth university where her husband had taught, the house had both historic charm and modern appeal. It was cozy and stylish, warm and inviting—a lot like Brooke.

She returned, still clad in the trim lavender cotton skirt and sleeveless white blouse she'd had on earlier. But the panty hose and fancy sandals were gone. Barefoot and bare-legged, with her silky hair falling loosely around her shoulders, she looked gorgeous and slightly frazzled. The latter made him want to assist her all the more. "I phoned the camp office, just to make sure, and they're all set," Brooke reported with an efficient smile. "We pick them up there at eleven forty-five this evening."

Wishing he'd thought to call ahead and invite her to lunch, Nate lingered. "I can do that, if you like."

"Actually—" Brooke clapped a weary hand to the graceful slope of her neck "—I'd appreciate it."

Thinking there still might be a way for him to help, Nate nodded toward the stacks of materials. "Any luck with the search?"

Brooke's face fell. "Yes and no. I didn't find the proof I was looking for, but I did find this." She handed over a sheaf of papers bound together with elastic.

Their fingers brushed as the exchange was made.

On top was a cover letter from the publisher of Seamus's new volume of poetry. Nate noted the date. "This was sent three years ago."

"In response to another proposed manuscript," Brooke affirmed, looking all the more distressed.

Nate read aloud, "'Dear Seamus… It is with regret I inform you that The Poet's Press can not publish your new collection. The poems are much too dark and cynical. We want more works that capture the wonder and magic of falling in love again, not a detailed exposition of what it is to fall out of love and feel trapped in a marriage one regrets. We fear this collection would alienate the readers of your first three volumes, and damage sales of future works, as well. We advise you to go back to the themes that made your earlier works a success, and of course, we would like a first look at them when they are ready to be read….'"

Nate looked beneath the letter, at the manuscript. "Did you know about this?"

Brooke shook her head.

His concern for her well-being deepened. "Did you read any of this?"

She nodded. And then, without warning, burst into tears. Embarrassed, she tried to hide her face and move away.

Nate did the only thing he could—he pulled her into a hug. "Hey," he said, smoothing her hair with the flat of his hand. "It's okay."

"No." Her voice was muffled against his shoulder. "It's not. Nate, my husband loathed being married to me. He compared me to an anchor weighing him down, keeping him trapped in a sea of mediocrity."

"I'm sure it was an exaggeration. Poetic license..."

Brooke had lied to herself for years. Tried to give her late husband the benefit of the doubt. The poems she had read, the raw emotion in them, had opened her eyes. Wanting Nate to understand, she swallowed and explained, "For years I felt like a burden to Seamus. As if Cole and I were in the way." She shook her head in misery as the memories of unhappier times came flooding back. "I told myself it was because Seamus was an artist, and he was blocked— that he needed more time for his art...fewer demands from us... And I tried to give him that. But the reality is he never loved me. Never cared about me, the person."

The way I feel you caring about me...

Nate took her face in his palms. "That's impossible."

"No, it isn't. Nate..."

He smoothed a hand through her hair. "Listen to me, Brooke. You are one of the most lovable women I have ever met." He kissed her temple, then drew back, desire in his eyes. "You're beautiful and smart and amazing. If your husband didn't see that—" Nate rubbed the pad of his thumb across her lower lip "—then he was a fool." He flattened a hand against her spine and brought her closer still. "But I see it." He shifted her so her back was against the wall, his tall body pressed against hers.

Brooke struggled to keep her feelings in check, but it was an impossible task when he was holding her flush against him. The pandemonium inside her multiplied as he moved closer still, his sinewy chest molding to the softness of her breasts. Her skin registered the heat, and the hardness of his body compared to hers.

Nate flashed a slow, sexy smile as his head slanted slowly and deliberately over hers. "Wow, do I see it."

This time there was nothing tentative about his kiss. It was hot, persuasive, hungry. He was holding her tightly and it still wasn't enough. She wanted more of the slow, demanding caress of his lips, the feel of his hands sliding up and down her back. She wanted more of his kindness and understanding, and the womanly way he made her feel. She wanted to let go of the hurt and disappointment of the past, and live in the moment. And Nate seemed only too eager to comply.

As she encircled her arms about his neck and melted against him, she could feel the pounding of his heart matching hers, and the strength and power of his need. Once again they were completely caught up in the passionate tangling of their lips and tongues. And this time she made no attempt to put on the brakes. It had been two long years since she had been touched. Never before had she felt so cherished. Nate made her feel like living life to the ultimate. He made her want to take the risk. And though initially Brooke had feared he was as self-possessed and driven as her late husband, that despite his ease with people, he was too emotionally aloof to give and receive love, she realized she'd judged him unfairly. And as Nate continued to kiss and hold her, she realized he wasn't just prone to doing the honorable thing in whatever situation he found himself, he was a generous and affectionate man.

Kind enough to bring her out of her self-imposed chastity and back into a balanced life, where she had her son and her work—and mind-blowing passion....

Even if it was destined to be only a brief, impulsive affair.

Brooke knew she could handle it. Because she was still in full control of her emotions and knew exactly what this was.

She wouldn't make the mistake she had made before, confusing her need for comfort and support with falling in love.

She and Nate were friends who needed a little help getting through two unexpected personal crises—that was all. When their situations returned to normal, so would their lives....

Undoubtedly, Nate would go his merry way, she would go hers. With a memory of one hot-blooded lovemaking session going with them... But in the meantime, she intended to enjoy every second of pleasure and relief he had to offer.

NATE HADN'T PLANNED to take Brooke in his arms today. He had expected to come over, get her signature, see how things were going and be on his way. But remaining detached from her was proving impossible. He couldn't be with her and not want her. Not just as a parenting mentor or friend, but as a woman. His woman. And his need for exclusivity stunned him. He hadn't felt this intensely about a woman in...well, ever. And that fueled even more his need to possess her. He wanted to take her to bed and make wild passionate love to her, so thoroughly and completely they'd both remember it forever.

"The question is," he murmured as she kissed him back, moaning softly as his hands came around to slide sensuously over her breasts. He kissed her cheek, her temple, the shell of her ear, before returning ever so slowly to her lips. "Do *you* see how sexy you are?"

He dropped his hand down, pushing her skirt higher, to caress the insides of her thighs. Just that had her trembling with pleasure. "I'm beginning to," she murmured, between subsequent kisses.

"Good." He slid a hand beneath her knees and her back and lifted her in his arms. Headed in the direction of her bedroom and deposited her gently next to her four-poster bed. As her bare feet hit the carpet, he told her, "Because we're just getting started."

Brooke chuckled softly and slid her deliciously full lower lip out into a seductive pout. Splaying her hands across his chest, she gave him a look that let him know this afternoon was strictly for fun, nothing more. "Promises, promises…"

It sounded like a dare. Nate toed off his shoes, stripped off his shirt and pants. "Nothing I like more than a challenge," he murmured.

Nothing she liked more, he noticed as he stripped completely, than turning him on.

Her eyes widened at the proof of his desire. "Wow," she said.

Wow was right, Nate thought. He'd never been this aroused. "My turn." He planted one hand at the nape of her neck, the other at the base of her spine. Hauling her close, he dipped his head. Reveling in her soft gasp of desire, he delivered a long, soul-searching kiss. Her response was immediate. She swept her tongue into his mouth and brought him closer still. Nate drank in the sweet taste of her, luxuriating in the lilac fragrance of her hair and skin.

She groaned again as his hands moved beneath the hem of her blouse to her breasts. He cupped the full, soft weight through the lace of her bra. "Not fair," she murmured with an impatient sigh, "that I'm the only one still dressed...."

With her hair tumbling over her shoulders, her cheeks flushed, her lips damp and parted, she had never looked more beautiful. Or vulnerable. Nate's need to protect her expanded. "We can rectify that," he whispered, satisfaction roaring in his veins.

Seeing no need to rush through one of the most memorable days of his life, he took his time as he unbuttoned, unclasped and unzipped. He liked the way Brooke's chest rose and fell with each ragged intake of breath, the way she couldn't seem to take her eyes off him, any more than he could take his off her.

She trembled as he divested her of bra and bikini underwear, then bent and kissed her budding pink nipples, one by one. She clasped his shoulders and sighed contentedly as his mouth moved urgently over her soft curves.

He dropped to his knees, kissing the hollow of her stomach, stroking the insides of her soft thighs. He traced her navel with his tongue, then dropped lower still, to administer the most ardent of kisses. Overcome with pleasure, shuddering with sensation, she whispered, "Nate..."

She shifted position and her lips drifted over his skin, touching, exploring, until there was no more control, no more hesitation, and Nate drew her to the bed. Feeling how much Brooke wanted and needed him, he lay down with her on the lace-edged sheets. His own body throbbing, he used a light caress to convince her to part her legs for him again. Her head fell back as he found the sweet sensitive spot with the pad of his thumb, until she was rocking slightly, leaving no doubt about what they both needed to have.

Watching her face, and trembling with a depth of feeling he could no longer deny, Nate guided her legs around his waist. Savoring the intimacy and the wonder of it all, he plunged into her and began to thrust. Her body closed around him and cloaked him in warmth. What few boundaries existed between them evaporated. Amazingly, fittingly, they were one. As he took them to the limit and beyond, he knew in his heart nothing had ever felt so right.

BROOKE HAD NO SOONER come back down to earth than the guilt and uncertainty set in. She had never acted so selfishly in her life, prior to this. And as much as she wanted to romanticize what had just happened between her and Nate, she knew she had just made love with him for all the wrong reasons. As a salve to her bruised ego, and her even more wounded heart... The last thing she had wanted to do was hurt Nate. Or herself.

Reluctantly, she extricated herself from his warm and tender embrace, and sat up against the headboard. "I can't believe I just did that."

He rolled to his side, a paragon of rippling muscles and masculine satisfaction. Looking as if he wanted nothing more than to make her his all over again, he queried contentedly, "Made love on impulse in the middle of the afternoon?"

Brooke knew if she let him he would shatter whatever caution she had left. And she had too much responsibility to allow that to happen. Her pulse racing, she held the sheet to her breasts with one hand and pushed her hair away from her face with the other. For both their sakes, she had to be honest and let him know where they stood. He could deal with it.

She sighed and looked deep into his eyes with self-effacing candor. "I used you to make myself feel better."

Chapter Nine

For a second, Nate couldn't believe he had heard right. "You didn't use me," he said. "Any more than I used you. We came together because it was what we wanted."

Brooke rose, blanket wrapped around her, and went to her closet. When she emerged, she had on a calf-length terry robe. She looked beautiful and disheveled, and very much on edge. "Be that as it may," she told him softly, "I don't want us to do this again."

Determined to keep this from going south, Nate leveled his gaze on her and forced her to be specific. "You don't want us to spend time alone together?" Which had been great. "Get closer?" A feat that had been even more satisfying. He rose from the bed, slid on his shorts, then his slacks. "Make love?"

He knew from the darkening of her irises that he'd hit the mark.

Brooke lifted her chin, defiant. Her fingers tightened on the fabric of her robe. "I don't want our friendship—" She paused, fumbling with a hairbrush "—if that's what it is—"

"It is."

"—to morph into a romantic love that we both know will never last."

Nate watched, fascinated, as she restored order to her

silky hair. The pressure against his fly told him his desire for her wasn't going away anytime soon. And he knew the feeling was mutual. "And if our chemistry does last?" he interjected. "Then what?" What excuse would she use to run away from the best thing *he'd* ever felt, anyway?

Brooke perched on the edge of her bed. She dropped her brush into her lap, took his hand and drew him down beside her so they were sitting face-to-face. The contrite expression on her face told him she thought she had hurt his feelings. "Listen to me, Nate," she murmured. "You and I are together now because of the work I am doing for you, and because you need help bringing Landry all the way into your life."

Nate wouldn't deny that Brooke had filled his life with gentle understanding, tenderness and contentment, any more than he could deny the soft warmth of her fingers over his, or the fact she was the best thing to ever come into his life, hands down. "It's more than that," he argued gruffly. Without even trying, she understood what he needed and wanted. He'd *thought* he comprehended what she longed for in her life, too.

Her ambivalent expression said otherwise.

She swallowed, seemingly as reluctant to dis him as she was to make love with him again. "You're right," Brooke agreed. "My world has been turned upside down and I need the distraction, too. Heck—" she grinned crookedly "—I needed the ego boost. But once we get past these twin crises, our lives will return to normal, and we won't need each other anymore."

The hell they wouldn't, Nate thought, already aware of how lonely and empty his life would be without her and her son. And it wasn't just him. Landry would be devastated, too.

Brooke wet her lower lip. "And when we no longer need each other, we'll go our separate ways."

Nate tore his eyes from the soft curves of her breasts, visible in the V-neckline of her robe. "You're assuming a lot," he told her quietly.

Sadness crept into her eyes. "And with good reason, Nate. I've done this before. When I was a senior in college and my life was filled with uncertainty, I reached out to a man who seemed to have all the answers."

Seamus. Her lying, cheating, selfish jerk of a husband.

"I confused the friendship and the physical passion—and an even more pressing need for a complete family of my own again—with the kind of love that would last a lifetime. It didn't."

"But that doesn't mean what we are feeling—whatever this is—won't," Nate countered.

"Which is exactly the problem," Brooke argued, a vulnerable sheen in her eyes. "We don't really know what this is. All I know for certain is that had I not been in distress today…had you not shown up when you did…I wouldn't have reached out to you. We wouldn't have recklessly fallen into bed and made love. Because I don't do things like this, Nate." Her voice rose emphatically. "I don't have flings or affairs. For me, making love is a commitment." She swallowed, still holding his gaze. "Or it should be."

"I agree," Nate said. "And for the record, I don't sleep around, either."

Brooke shrugged, let go of his hand and stood. "Then we're on the same page."

Yes, Nate thought. *And no.* The time he had spent with Brooke and the boys had shown him everything he had been missing, not having a wife and children of his own. Maybe it was selfish of him to not want to let go of the makeshift family they had formed in the last week. He didn't care. He didn't want to give that up any more than he wanted to give her up. "I readily admit we jumped the gun a bit today, but what we just experienced was more than pure physical passion, or wrongheaded crisis management," he said.

She grinned at his subtle joke, but to his disappointment kept her defenses firmly in place. "How do you know?"

Because passion alone left you wanting to run the other way when your needs were met. Something more had you wanting to stay. This was something more, Nate thought. But not sure Brooke would accept his revelation as anything more than some cheesy line—the kind her late "love poet" husband had apparently been full of—Nate stuck to the facts.

"I won't stop wanting you," he told her firmly.

Her expression clouded. "If you did, it wouldn't be the first time it's happened to me," she said bitterly.

And once again Nate found himself paying for the sins of Seamus Mitchell.

"The point is—" Brooke picked up his discarded shirt and handed it to him "—it's not a position I want to put myself in. Not again. I like you, Nate. I do."

Wasn't that what Seraphina had said when they broke up? Nate wondered, shrugging on his shirt, then pulling on his socks and shoes.

"I want us to be friends," Brooke said, her expression determined, as she showed him to the door. "But friends and confidants are all we can be."

"YOU WANT TO TELL US WHAT the problem is?" Dan drawled at five o'clock Friday evening, as Nate, Travis and Dan gathered in the large mansion kitchen. "Or just leave us to guess?"

In no mood to play games, Nate demanded impatiently, "What are you talking about?"

Travis lifted a brow. "Well, either you don't like what Dan's architect and my company's construction crews have done to your kitchen, or you've got a problem elsewhere. And judging by Landry's and Cole's delight at the array of computer and electronic equipment that was just delivered and carted up to the second floor just now, it's not with either of the boys."

"They are happy," Nate acknowledged. At least for the moment, he added mentally. That too could change on a dime. "And the kitchen is great." Thanks to Brooke's collaboration with the guys, it no longer looked like a caterer's prep space, but a place where a family could hang out and cook together. The only problem was, the only woman he could envision there was not interested in being around long term....

"Then what is it?" Dan persisted. He exchanged knowing glances with Travis. "Or should we just say who...?"

Nate did not normally discuss his problems with women. However, these weren't the usual circumstances.

He walked over to the window—made sure Brooke was still outside talking to the furniture company guys, who had just delivered a whole houseful of new furniture—then walked back to his friends and admitted, "It's Brooke. I'm interested, but she just wants to be 'friends.'"

Dan and Travis both winced, easily understanding his pain.

"No chemistry on her part, huh?" Travis guessed.

Nate would understand, if that had been the case.

"Then you have to keep trying," Dan said. "Let her know you're serious."

"Build on the friendship and go from there," Travis advised. "It's what I did with Holly when we were ready for more."

And it had worked, Nate recalled. Holly and Travis were

spectacularly happy now, as were the rest of his married friends.

"Although you might want to delay the real pursuit until her work for you is done," Dan said.

"You didn't," Nate pointed out. Dan had fallen in love with Emily and proposed to her while she was still working as a personal chef for him and his kids....

"Not waiting made it harder to establish a relationship, not easier," Dan insisted.

"I'm not averse to challenge," Nate said.

"That we know." Travis grinned. "We're just saying be careful not to let your impatience get in the way of what you really want here."

Which was Brooke, Nate thought.

And not just, as she still thought, for the short term.

"So what do you think, Mom?" Cole asked late the next afternoon. "Did we or did we not do the most awesome job ever setting up the computer and game rooms?"

"You guys did a fantastic job," Brooke agreed, taking the tour of the two spaces with Cole and Landry. Her touches included the comfortable sectional sofas, shelving systems and computer workstations; Nate and the boys had selected and put together all the electronics. The end result was a state-of-the art study and social space, decorated in hardy fabrics and bright, teen-friendly colors.

"You are so lucky," Cole told Landry. He looked around with an admiring glance. "I only wish I could have a setup like this in our house. But my dad would never even let me have a video game system."

Out of the corner of her eye, Brooke saw Nate work to keep his own expression inscrutable. Embarrassed, she told her son, "I didn't know you wanted one." Cole had always acted as if Wii and PlayStation were for other kids.

He shrugged. "I figured you felt the same way as Dad did."

She hadn't. "I wish I'd known how you felt."

"You never disagreed with him on that kind of stuff. So it would have been pointless to ask."

Guilt hit hard. What else had Cole been afraid to talk to her about? "We can get one now," Brooke promised. "When we go back home." The live-in bonus she was getting on this job would pay for that and much more.

Cole grinned. "Way cool, Mom."

"No problem." Avoiding the concern she saw in Nate's eyes, Brooke flashed a smile. "About dinner…"

"Uh…" Cole looked at Landry.

Landry took over. "We were hoping we could invite some of our friends from computer camp to come over tonight and check it out."

"Maybe have some pizza," Cole added.

Brooke glanced at Nate. Although he hadn't said as much, she sensed he had been hoping for a quiet "family night." But when he took in the happy, hopeful faces of the kids, he shrugged and said, "Sounds good to me. Start making the calls."

By 8:00 p.m., they had ten boys gathered upstairs. Nate, who had been busy assisting with the fine-tuning of the game and computer setups, finally came down to the kitchen.

Despite the fact that he had been working with the boys for eleven hours straight, getting everything just the way they wanted it, Brooke thought Nate had never looked happier or more content.

He was such a *dad*.

Cole was right—Landry was indeed one lucky kid.

She was the one who was unlucky. Falling for the wrong

guy at the right time, then the right guy at the wrong time...

She knew Nate had been surprised by her emotional withdrawal the day before, but what choice had she had? Their decisions could affect two kids. They couldn't afford to be rash. As much as she wanted to, she couldn't take advantage of Nate's temporary vulnerability by letting him think he could only be a good father to Landry if she were in the picture, too. Because it just wasn't so. Nate and Landry would be fine, given a little time. Nate was a natural when it came to parenthood, even if he didn't quite see that yet.

And she couldn't let herself turn to him to help find her way out of the darkness she temporarily found herself in. Because the truth was, the situation with Iris Lomax and Seamus's publisher would get resolved. And once this crisis passed, she and Cole would be fine, too.

In the meantime, it didn't matter how tempted she was. It would be a mistake to lean on Nate, the way she had once leaned on her husband. She could get through this situation on her own. The last two years of widowhood had shown her that.

She needed to follow Nate's lead and pretend that their lovemaking had never happened. Even if doing so left her feeling more alone than she had ever imagined.

Brooke turned her attention back to the task at hand. "How is the food holding out up there?"

Nate lounged against the counter. "All the snacks you set out are pretty much gone. Same with the soft drinks."

As she passed by him, she was inundated with his brisk male scent. "The pizza should be here any minute."

"I'm sure they'll devour that, too." He watched her unwrap a stack of paper plates and set them on the counter, next to the napkins and ice-filled paper cups. "Listen,

I hope I didn't cause a problem for you—regarding the video-game system."

Brooke held up a hand. "I meant what I said up there. I do intend to get Cole one as soon as possible."

Nate nodded, his expression impassive.

Brooke felt compelled to explain, "I just didn't realize he had ever asked Seamus for one."

Nate's brow furrowed. "Your husband wouldn't have mentioned it to you?"

She shrugged self-consciously. "I doubt he felt it was worth his time. He wasn't interested in any nonintellectual pursuits. And he had no patience for doing anything with children of any age."

"I was under the impression he wanted a child when you married."

Comforted by Nate's steady male presence, Brooke explained, "It was more of an ego thing. Which isn't to say Seamus wasn't enormously proud of his son—he was. He made sure he took Cole to many a public event and introduced him around, which Cole loved. Seamus just never spent quality time with Cole, the way you have the past week."

Which was yet another reason why she was attracted to Nate.

It wasn't just his kindness and understanding attitude, it was his knack for integrating others into his life, even his capacity for love....

Whoever ended up living happily-ever-after with Nate was going to be one lucky woman....

"It's been my pleasure to get to know Cole," Nate continued sincerely. "You know that."

His voice sent ripples of desire up and down her spine. "I do."

Silence stretched between them.

She could feel his pull as strongly as the earth's gravity. Brooke swallowed, aware she was seconds from reaching out for him, telling him her decision to rebuff him had been a terrible mistake. "Nate..."

Footsteps sounded on the stairs. Seconds later, Cole came bursting into the room, joy radiating from every inch of him. He sprinted to Nate's side and wrapped his arms around him. "Nate! You gotta come upstairs and see this! Please!"

Nate returned Cole's brief, impromptu hug and ear-to-ear grin. Oblivious to Brooke's concern, he slung his arm around Cole's shoulders and off they went.

BROOKE MANAGED TO KEEP her distance from Nate the rest of the evening. It wasn't hard. Shortly after Cole had come down to get him, Landry had trotted down to retrieve her. Brooke had spent the remainder of the night alternately observing and officiating the teen tournament. When she wasn't doing that, she was replenishing the food and beverage tables—a feat that sounded easier than it had been, as all of them seemed to have huge appetites and stomachs that were bottomless pits.

Finally, at eleven-thirty, the last of the parents arrived to pick up their sons. Nate helped Cole and Landry restore order to the upstairs rooms, while Brooke went downstairs to work on the kitchen.

Finished, the boys appeared there. Nate trailed after them.

"Need help, Mom?" Cole asked.

Brooke looked at their faces. The excitement of the day had finally caught up with them. Both teens looked ready to collapse. "Why don't you guys head back to the cottage and hit the sack?"

Landry squinted at her, seeming to realize the kitchen

was another fifteen minutes or more from being squared away. "You sure?" he asked around a yawn.

Brooke nodded. She stepped between the boys, caught their shoulders and gave them each an affectionate squeeze. "Positive. Now go. Before you fall asleep on your feet and I have to carry you both to bed!"

Cole and Landry chuckled, but didn't argue. They seemed to finally realize how tired they were.

The boys departed.

Suddenly, it was just Nate and Brooke. "Surely there's something I can do," he said.

The idea of working side by side with him was appealing. Too appealing. Her pulse skittering as she thought about kissing him again, she turned away from his ruggedly sexy frame. "Thanks, but I can handle it." She had to get a grip here. Stop fantasizing and pretending life was simpler than it was.

She went back to loading serving platters in the dishwasher. "You can go—" She stopped just short of saying *Go on to bed*. And wary of the implications of that, swiftly amended it to a lame, "do...whatever...."

"Mmm-hmm."

There was a wealth of meaning in that presumptuous sound.

Perspiration broke out on the back of her neck, between her thighs, behind her knees, in the valley between her breasts.

Nate edged closer. He was standing behind her, so near she could feel the warmth of his breath on the top of her head.

Another ribbon of desire swept through her.

He waited.

Her head down, she kept busy cleaning.

"Why do I think I did something wrong?"

Brooke had to stand on tiptoe and reach across the counter to get the last platter. "I don't know what you mean."

When her fingers fell short of it, he leaned over, grasped it for her and set it in the sink.

Before she could pick it up, his fingers closed gently over her wrist, stilling the restless movement. "Stop cleaning for a minute," he urged softly, "and just talk to me."

Brooke forced herself to turn toward him. "My son looks at you with such hero worship in his eyes."

Nate acknowledged this with a modest dip of her head. "And that's a problem because…what? I'm not a hero?" he prodded drily.

That was the problem, he *was!*

And not just to the boys.

Telling herself she was not going to make the same mistake twice, Brooke frowned. "What's going to happen to Cole when this job ends, as it will in another week, and he doesn't see you anymore?"

Nate looked affronted. "He'll see me."

Brooke fought the urge to tear out her hair in frustration. "You know what I mean," she insisted.

"You're right," Nate said grimly. "It won't be the same."

So it wasn't just her, Brooke thought victoriously. Nate was thinking ahead, anticipating the difficulties and pitfalls, too.

Emboldened, she continued, "Landry's like a brother to him."

"And vice versa," Nate agreed.

"And that's great. But what happens if something damages their friendship or ours?"

Nate's lips thinned in obvious irritation. "It won't," he stated plainly.

"But if it does," she insisted.

He let out a long breath. "You're borrowing trouble."

Feeling on the verge of an emotion she couldn't control, Brooke moved away, grabbing the spray bottle of granite cleaner and a cloth. Aware of the way Nate was suddenly studying her, sizing her up, perhaps plotting his next move, she babbled nervously, "Which is funny, really, because I never see trouble coming. I always get blindsided."

Her parents' demise, her husband's infidelity and resultant death, the plagiarism claim…all had come with no warning.

Now she was seeing danger around every corner….

It was ironic, really. How much she wanted to take the risk and be with Nate. And how terribly, deeply afraid she was of doing just that.

If only she could be sure…. If only love came with guarantees.

But it didn't.

And she couldn't let her heart be stolen and smashed into pieces again.

Nate held out his arms to her. "Brooke…"

Tears of disappointment blurring her eyes, she rushed past him. "I can't, Nate! I can't…."

He closed the distance between them in two long strides and wrapped his arms around her. "You can take it one day—one moment—at a time," he whispered, holding her close, making her want to believe it was so. "We both will. It's the only choice we have."

Chapter Ten

Nate hadn't kissed her—hadn't even tried. So why was she feeling so let down? This was what she had wanted. Yet…being separated from him this way felt wrong, too, Brooke realized as she returned to the caretaker's cottage and went on to bed.

She slept fitfully. And dreamed of Nate over and over again. Which was why, when the guys brought up the amusement park idea early the next morning, she found herself forgoing work and accompanying them and Nate.

Naturally, no sooner had they walked through the gates than all three males headed straight for the scariest roller coaster. Billed as the tallest, fastest coaster in the Southwest, it was twenty-four stories tall and accelerated from 0 to 70 in four seconds. Just looking at it made Brooke feel ill.

"Come on, Mom, you can do it!" Cole tugged on her hand and urged her in the direction he wanted her to go.

"Look at the way you're latched in." Landry pointed to the sturdy over-the-shoulder-and-chest contraption that kept riders in place even when they were zooming through the loops upside down.

Nate caught Brooke's eye. He seemed to know her dilemma. She wanted to share in the fun with the rest of them, yet she was completely terrified. Prior to this, she had declared Cole not old enough for the most thrilling rides in the park. Now, given the way he'd grown in the last year, and the fact that he more than topped the height requirement for the ride, she had no such excuse.

"You'll be perfectly safe," Landry assured her.

Cole regarded her with hopeful eyes. "Please, Mom, don't let us down! Say yes!"

Brooke thought about all the similar experiences Cole had been denied over the years, because Seamus had not deemed them worthy of his time.

All her son wanted was to be a kid. Forget he'd lost a father. And enjoy the fact he'd found a spiritual "brother" in Landry, and a "surrogate dad" in Nate.

What was a little fear, if not to be conquered? If she was honest, she could use a little distraction, too. She lifted a palm to high-five each of the boys. "Let's do it!"

They hooted in delight and ran to get in the line, which didn't look all that long right now, unfortunately. "Landry and I want to sit together," Cole shouted over his shoulder as they joined the queue.

Brooke nodded and lifted a hand in assent, knowing that left her to sit with Nate, since the riders went two by two on this ride.

Nate sent her a reassuring sidelong glance as they strolled through the maze of metal bars. He clapped a companionable hand on her shoulder. "It'll be over before you know it."

"Not soon enough," Brooke muttered under her breath. "My knees already feel like Jell-O."

"You're a good sport to be doing this for the guys," he said, with an approving glance that made her feel all warm and tingly inside.

"That's me," Brooke joked nervously. "Always taking one for the team…"

As was Nate…

Their glances locked, and another thrill swept through Brooke.

Before long, Cole and Landry were climbing into their seats. Seconds later, Brooke found herself sitting down, too, with Nate beside her. As soon as they were securely latched in, behind the boys, Nate reached over and took her hand. Squeezed it hard. And then they were off.

"YOU DON'T LOOK SO GOOD, Mom," Cole told Brooke what seemed like a lifetime later. In reality, only a few completely harrowing minutes had passed, minutes she had been absolutely sure she would not survive.

"Yeah," Landry noted, "you're kind of green."

She felt as if she was about to throw up.

Nate studied her with compassionate eyes. And there was no doubt about it, Brooke admitted a little resentfully, given her wuss status in the day's events thus far. Nate's own color was great. He had the same flush of exhilaration staining his face that their boys had, the same euphoric laugh as they exited the ride.

In fact, Brooke realized, surveying him closely as she tried to get her land legs back, Nate looked good all over. In sneakers, knee-length shorts and a loose fitting, short-sleeve shirt that brought out the vibrant blue of his eyes, he was the epitome of a dad on a weekend outing with the kids. Only a whole lot sexier than the other dads around them. A lot sexier, in fact, than any dad she had ever seen.

The realization brought heat to her cheeks.

Nate's brow furrowed.

Obviously, he had misinterpreted the reason behind her sudden flush.

Nate wrapped a steadying arm about her shoulders, which only made her discomfort worse. He peered at her closely before turning to Cole. "I think your mom needs to sit down a second and catch her breath." Briefly, Nate shifted his glance to the teens. "Why don't you boys ride the tower? Unless—" Nate looked back at Brooke "—you want to do that one, too?"

Just the sight of the ride had all the blood draining from her head once again. "Thirty-two and a half stories straight up and down again, at a speed of forty-five miles an hour?" Weakly, she reiterated the information in the brochure.

Cole and Landry gave each other fist bumps. "It's got the best view of the park!" Landry claimed.

Brooke lifted a hand, begging for mercy. "I don't think so," she murmured, still feeling a little shaky. "You-all go ahead and have a great time!"

"I'll stay here with your mom," Nate volunteered.

Relieved, the boys raced off to get in line.

Nate led Brooke over to an empty bench with a clear view of the ride. Propping a solicitous hand on her shoulder, he lowered his face to hers and asked with a mixture of bemusement and quiet sympathy, "Can I get you anything?"

How about a kiss? A fierce, warm hug. The opportunity to rest my head on your broad shoulder and close my eyes and forget the terror I just felt.

Knowing it couldn't happen, shocked by the notion that she was even longing for such a thing, Brooke pushed the thought away.

"How about a heart that's not pounding so hard it's about to leap out of my chest?" she quipped.

He grinned, reassured, then tapped the park map she held clutched in her hands. "We could do the less intense rides for a while."

Brooke shook her head. Cole needed her to be strong and fearless.

So she would be.

"The boys want the maximum rush today. So let's make sure they do all the fastest, highest rides at least once," she stipulated firmly.

He smiled in admiration. "You going to be able to do any more?"

"Yep." One way or another, Brooke would conquer her fear. It would be easier with the indefatigable Nate by her side. "I'm warning you, though," she teased, her good humor returning as her system settled back into a normal rhythm, "I might squeeze your hand off in the process."

"That's okay." He flashed a very sexy smile that melted her insides. "I can take it."

And take it he did, Brooke noted as the day wore on.

The park had twelve thrill rides. The boys rode them all, and Brooke managed to do ten of them, which was a personal record for her. They saw a show, ate way too much food, and even spent time playing games in the arcade before staying for the fireworks that closed down the park.

The boys talked about their adventure all the way back to Nate's.

Still reliving every adrenaline-filled moment as they all got out of Nate's car, Cole grinned. "This was the best day ever."

Landry looked Nate square in the eye and said with heartfelt sincerity, "For me, too." He hesitated before extending his hand.

Nate swallowed up Landry's palm and shook it warmly.

Aware this was the first formal physical expression of acceptance between the two, initiated by Landry, Brooke got a lump in her throat.

"Thanks, Nate," the boy said huskily.

Nate looked as if he had just won the lottery. "Anytime," he promised thickly.

His eyes suspiciously moist, Cole shook hands with Nate, too.

"It was a great day," Brooke told Nate warmly, before they said good-night.

The only thing that would have made it more perfect, she noted as she and the two teens headed for the cottage, was if the four of them had been the actual "family" they'd felt like all day.

"I'VE BEEN THINKING," Landry said the next morning, over breakfast in the newly reconfigured kitchen. "Maybe I should visit my great-grandmother, after all. I mean, she might be kind of lonely or missing me or something."

Or in other words, Brooke thought, Landry yearned to see Jessalyn now, as much as the elderly woman had been wanting to see him. "I think that's a great idea," she enthused.

"Can you take me over to the retirement village after camp today?"

Brooke set plates of blueberry oatmeal pancakes in front of each boy. She lounged against the other side of the breakfast bar. "I'll have to clear it with Nate."

"Clear what with me?" he asked, walking in.

He circled the counter to help himself to some of the coffee in the pot while Brooke explained.

"So is it okay?" Landry asked.

Nate looked longingly at the golden cakes on the griddle. "Of course. In fact, I can take you if you want."

Landry looked at Brooke, half seeming to want her to intervene, half not.

She'd never been one to manipulate a situation, but this was for the best. She plated a breakfast for Nate, too. "Actually, Landry, it would be better if Nate drove you over, schedulewise." If the two of them were alone, they'd have a chance to build on the rapport they had already established, maybe feel even more like father and son....

"Can I go, too?" Cole asked, eager to be part of things.

Everyone turned to look at him.

Nate took his breakfast and sat down on a high stool at the island counter. The closest seat available was on the other side of Cole.

"Landry?" Nate leaned forward, tossing the ball back to him.

Landry grinned at Cole with brotherly affection. "Sounds good to me...."

And there went the solo bonding time, Brooke thought with a sigh.

But maybe this was good, too.

With Cole along, Landry was less likely to back out. And he needed to visit his great-grandmother.

Because Brooke was expecting a delivery, Nate drove the boys to camp that morning, as well. Since he was already in a suit and tie, she expected him to go on to the office from there. Instead, he came back to the mansion and walked upstairs, just as the truck that had brought the furniture for Landry's bedroom in the main house was driving away.

Brooke met him in the hall. "Everything okay?"

Nate glanced at the work in progress that would one day be his son's room.

"I wanted to thank you for bringing the boys here for breakfast this morning."

Glad he hadn't thought she was overstepping, Brooke went back to unwrapping linens. "The kitchen here is much nicer now than the one in the caretaker's cottage."

"That isn't why you did it."

It had been, however, the reason she had given the boys. She climbed up the ladder and slid the covering on the mattress of the elevated loft-style bed. Digging in his heels about only being there temporarily, Landry had never committed to any one particular style or color, so Brooke had had to rely on her intuition when selecting the decor. She was confident Landry would like it, however, once he moved out of the cottage and into this room. The large suite was the perfect place for him to call home, the furniture she had selected a harbinger of college years to come, with bookshelves on one end of the loft bed's base, a built-in desk on the other. A futon and easy chair in another corner provided space for Landry to hang out while listening to music or watching TV or talking on the phone.

"Yesterday was so nice…. I thought you might like to expand on that and spend time together," she said.

Nate came in to check out the dorm-style furniture system and decor. "Which is, I'm guessing, why you wanted me to pick him up from camp today."

Brooke climbed down the ladder, unfolded a set of organic cotton sheets. "His seeing his great-grandmother again is a big deal."

Nate steadied the ladder while she climbed up to finish making the bed. "As is his taking Cole with him."

Brooke smoothed out the soft warm blanket and boldly striped duvet. "It seems like everything is finally working out the way you had hoped."

Nate handed her the pillows. "Thanks in no small part to you."

Brooke arranged them artfully, then climbed back down to stand beside Nate once again. "Don't sell yourself short, Nate. You've got a natural affinity for kids." She looked around, pleased at the way the space was coming together, then turned back to him. "You're going to be...scratch that. You *already are* a great dad."

The corner of Nate's mouth lifted as he followed her out of the bedroom. "Coming from you, that's high praise."

"It was deserved," she admitted sincerely. "Being a parent is hard but rewarding work."

"You make it look easy," he said.

Brooke flashed a tremulous smile. "And we both know it's anything but," she murmured.

"True." Suddenly, the only sound in the entire mansion was the sound of the two of them breathing.

Their glances meshed. Another second passed. Once again, Brooke had the strong sensation Nate wanted to kiss her. Almost as much as she suddenly wanted to kiss him.... And just as swiftly, she knew she had been lying to herself. "We're not going to be able to do this, are we?" she asked, knowing she could avoid this reckoning if she only had the strength to move away. But she didn't. And Nate didn't want to move away, either. He'd already made that clear.

He made it clear again as he moved toward her. "We're not going to be able to do what?"

She lifted her hands in a humorous expression of defeat. "Remain just friends."

Nate's eyes darkened. "I can be patient."

"So can I," she declared.

But as they continued looking at each other, something changed. There was a smile in Nate's eyes and they went from mutually concerned parents who had once made love and shared a great weekend together, to a man and a woman sharing something deeper, more powerful.

Brooke hadn't allowed herself to feel anything like this in a long time, and the emotions were too overwhelming to resist. She reached for Nate. "Suppose I've changed my mind." *Suppose I'm tired of being alone, tired of denying myself what I really want, which is you.* She gulped, wondering when she had gotten so bad at negotiating. As two successful businesspeople, this should be their strong point. They ought to be able to come to some meeting of the minds. "Suppose—" she paused, looking deep into his eyes "—I don't want to wait."

"The first time we made love…"

The only time.

She'd told herself she was rebounding, that it had been nothing more than a way to assuage her injured pride, to prove she was worth something as a woman again.

Brooke saw now it had been so much more, a way back into a fully lived life.

A door to the future…their future?

Or just the here and now?

She didn't know, didn't care, as long as the incredible pleasure, the intense feeling of being alive she felt whenever she was with him, didn't stop.

Nate threaded his hands through her hair, holding her head. The unchecked longing on his face had her rising on tiptoe to kiss him.

"I wanted you then, too," she admitted passionately. "I just didn't want to admit how much."

He kissed her reverently. "You won't have to convince me again." Heat radiated from his body as he swept her into his arms and carried her down the hall to his bedroom.

He shut the door behind them. "I've wanted to be close to you, too, Brooke."

"Then make love to me, Nate," she said, her pulse pounding, as he slowly set her down. "Make love to me without a view toward tomorrow, or a glance back at yesterday." She wound her arms about his neck and kissed him persuasively. "Keep us in the here and now. Without rules or restrictions…"

Still kissing her, Nate drew her down onto the bed he'd been in too much of a rush that morning to make. When at last they broke apart, Brooke kicked off her sandals and lay back against the pillows. Nate shrugged out of his jacket, his tie. Unable to wait, he also kicked off his shoes and lay down beside her, looking unexpectedly vulnerable. "You're sure?"

Very. "I never do anything just for me," she whispered, lowering the wall around her heart a little more. She gave him a reason she thought he could accept. "I want you, just for me."

COMMON SENSE TOLD NATE to kiss Brooke until kissing was an end in itself. And then wait the traditional amount of time, until they knew each other thoroughly and they'd had a proper series of dates, before taking things to the next level again. He was old enough to know that was the safe way to proceed if he wanted to protect the investment he was making in their future together, especially if he wanted to convince her that what they had was much more than a fleeting sexual attraction. But when her hands skimmed over his entire body, there was no way to deny her. No way to stop the velvet caress of her lips pressing against his, any more than he could stop the burgeoning pressure against his fly. He wanted her, too.

And it wasn't just lust, as she wanted to think….

He needed her, needed this. Needed to discover the softness of her skin beneath her clothes, the warmth of her body, the jump in her pulse every time they connected. She was absolutely exquisite. Urging him on, trapping him with the sleek muscles of her long, slender thighs, she caressed him evocatively with her hands. She twisted beneath him, cupping his buttocks, molding her body to his, until they were both on fire.

The first time, he had seduced her. Now she was seducing him.

And still his hands rubbed down her back, claiming, exploring. The gentle curve of her hips, the swell of her breasts, the delicate skin between her thighs…

He followed the caress of his hands with the homage of his tongue, the adoration of his mouth. She arched her back and sucked in her breath. And then that, too, was too much.

He moved upward, claiming her mouth again, claiming her.

She encircled his neck with her arms and refused to let go. She wrapped her legs around his waist, giving herself over to him completely. And all the while she made soft sounds of surrender in the back of her throat that drove him wild.

He lifted her hips. And then they were one.

Soft as silk, hot as fire. Tight. Wet. Wanton.

Together, they rode the wave.

Faster, harder. Soft and slow. Slower, hotter, wetter still. And then she was his, really his. Not just for now, he determined, clasping her close. But as long as she would have him.

BROOKE LAY WRAPPED IN Nate's arms. In his bed.

The first time they'd made love they'd ended up in hers. Now they were in his.

Both times, it had felt right.

The only difference was that this time she wasn't as scared.

Now she was actually contemplating letting Nate become a part of her life. *One step at a time.* Wasn't that what she always told Cole? You can do anything if you break it down, and take it slowly?

On the floor beside them a humming began.

Recognizing the sound of a vibrating cell phone, Brooke lifted her head. Her phone was still set to ring. "That has to be for you."

Nate's eyes remained closed. "Let 'em leave a message."

She peered at him playfully, between her spread fingers. "Are you sure you're a CEO?"

The phone buzzed again.

The next thought occurred to both of them simultaneously. "What if it's…?"

"One of the kids." Nate let her go long enough to roll over and capture the offending electronic device.

He rolled back onto the pillows, lifting the screen where he could see it.

He hit a button, frowned, hit another button.

As their normal everyday life crept back in, Brooke found she needed reassurance. "Tell me that's not the kids with another field trip emergency."

"Actually, it's worse." The corners of Nate's mouth pulled down even more. "It's individual text messages— from my parents."

BROOKE SAT UP, holding the sheet against her bare breasts. Nate looked so distressed she had to ask, "Is everything all right with them?"

"I sent them an e-mail a few days ago and told them I was adopting Landry."

Brooke blinked. There were so many things wrong with that scenario she didn't know where to start. "And they're just now getting back to you?" she asked, aghast.

"They probably wanted to talk to each other, get on the same page, before they contacted me. And that wouldn't have been easy. I think I told you they live and work in different countries overseas."

What Nate hadn't discussed was the state of their union. Now, she had to wonder. "You didn't say…. Are they divorced?"

"No." Nate shrugged, as if that would be difficult to imagine, too. "They just live and work in different places," he explained. "It's been that way for the last, I don't know, ten or fifteen years."

"That must be hard."

"Honestly? I think they prefer it that way. Even when they worked in the same city they rarely saw each other. They're both married to their jobs."

"What was it like for you, when you were a kid?"

"I had nannies when I was younger. When I was in sixth grade, I switched to a residential private school, and I stayed at the school whenever they were out of town."

"Sounds…flexible." And as lonely, in certain ways, as her life as a foster child.

Funny, she'd thought she and Nate were so different. Now she saw that wasn't necessarily so. She swallowed the knot of building emotion in her throat.

Nate continued with a matter-of-fact shrug. "I understood they both had demanding jobs. And I never had any doubt that, despite the fact they weren't hands-on types in the parenting department, they loved me and wanted only the best for all of us."

Brooke took a deep breath and tried not to judge. It wasn't easy, given that this story was bringing out every protective, loving instinct in her and then some.

She traced the powerful outline of his shoulder with her fingertip and gently encouraged him to go on unburdening himself, the same way she had with him. "The best being?"

That rueful, cynically accepting smile came again. "Successful careers and professional lives for all of us, of course."

The Hutchinsons had certainly achieved that, from the sound of it, Brooke thought. Which brought them back to the text messages Nate's mom and dad had sent him. "So what did your parents say about your plan to adopt Landry?"

Nate peered at the screen. "My mother's text message says 'Nathaniel, if you want a child—and I'm not sure it's a good idea to go it alone given the tremendous business responsibilities you shoulder—then please get married and have one the old-fashioned way.'"

Brooke did her best not to wince. "And your dad?"

Nate read out loud, "'Is Landry your child? Because of course if he is, you have a duty to the boy. But if not, you have no business taking this on.'"

Nate showed the screen to her.

There were no loving overtures to soften the blow, just sanctimonious advice. Brooke's heart went out to Nate. "That's harsh."

He shrugged. "And direct. They're both CEO's.... So they tend to cut to the chase. I knew they wouldn't sugar-coat it, that they most likely would not approve of anything out of the ordinary on the personal front for me."

And yet he'd told them, anyway. Which meant part of him, the long-ago kid in him, still wanted their approval, even if he knew by now he would never get it. Not the way he wanted.

Brooke studied him. "What would have happened if you had e-mailed them that you were in love and getting married?" *If, for instance, you were ever to say that about us....*

"They would have offered formal congratulations and told me to get an ironclad prenup. After, of course, they did a thorough background check on not just my fiancée, but those around her."

Outrageous! Brooke rolled onto her stomach and rested her chin on her palm. "What did they think of Seraphina?" she asked curiously.

Nate frowned. "They saw her as a little too soft and sentimental to be a good executive wife, which was—in their estimation—what I needed for a successful climb up the career ladder."

Yet he had done it all by himself, Brooke noted proudly.

"So when the engagement ended?"

Nate tossed the phone aside and lay down again, facing her. His bare knee nudged hers beneath the covers. "They made no effort to disguise their relief," he continued, frankly. "They both felt I had avoided catastrophe."

Brooke studied his eyes for any clue to his feelings. "So to have Seraphina come back into your life, through her son…"

"Was not good news, not to them," Nate replied succinctly, then fell silent, brooding again.

There were mere inches between them. It felt like an ocean. Wanting to recapture some of their earlier closeness, Brooke reached out and covered his hand with hers. "What are you thinking?"

He gave her a rueful look, then ran a palm over his

face. "That I probably should have listened to my gut and not contacted my parents at all at this juncture. I should have waited until it was a fait accompli—when social pressure would have forced them to congratulate me, and welcome Landry to the family publicly. Knowing them, they'd find a way to make it all seem somehow noble and preordained."

Brooke's heart ached for him. She had an idea how much the lack of support from his parents must hurt. "It is noble and preordained, Nate. I've watched you with Landry. I know how right what you're doing is."

Although his expression lightened, a hint of sadness lingered in Nate's gaze. "Fortunately, my parents and I see each other so seldom now—once every year or two at most—that by the time we do get together again, Landry will officially be my son." He finished with his customary optimism.

Relieved that Nate had rebounded so quickly, Brooke lifted his hand and pressed a kiss to the back of his knuckles. "So they'll accept him and Landry will never have to know your parents disapproved."

The tension left Nate's body. He relaxed even more as she kissed his hand again. "That would be the plan."

Their eyes met. "You deserve better," she said quietly.

He took her arm and tugged her close. "I think I've finally got it." He bent his head and kissed her passionately "In you."

Chapter Eleven

"Why the frown?" Nate asked Brooke several hours later as he snuggled her closer, a wave of tenderness unlike anything he had ever felt radiating through him. She was so beautiful in her post-lovemaking dishabille. So beautiful all the time… It didn't matter whether she was in mom mode, on the job…or in his bed.

"I hate the thought of going back to work," she murmured, reluctantly glancing at her watch. "But with Holly Carson due here at one o'clock, to begin work on the dining-room mural, I've got to get going."

Nate had meetings, too. He rose and began to dress. "About this evening. I'll pick up the kids at camp and take them to the retirement village to see Jessalyn."

"I promised Landry I'd stop by to say hello to his great-grandmother, too. He wants her to get to know me."

Nate understood why. Brooke was one special woman. She'd already made a huge difference in Landry's life, by coaxing him out of his shell. "Then why don't we go over together to pick them up after the visit. Around seven o'clock?"

Surprise registered in Brooke's eyes. "You're not going to stay for the visit?"

Nate would have, had he been invited. "Landry thought it might go better with just him and Cole there. But he wanted me to stop in and say hello at the end of their time together."

"Then let's go together," Brooke said.

"Maybe stop for dinner out afterward?" Nate suggested, aware how much the four of them were beginning to feel like family.

Brooke smiled in a way that warmed his heart. "Sounds like a plan."

The rest of the day flew by. Nate picked up the guys as scheduled, at five o'clock, when camp ended. As usual, Landry and Cole spent the entire time talking, while Nate drove. But now he was occasionally included in the conversation about digital imaging and computer conversions.

"You sure you don't want me to go in?" Nate asked, pulling up in front of the entrance to the retirement home.

Landry nodded. "We can handle it. But—" he paused, sounding as if his heart was in his throat "—thanks for offering, Nate." Gaze averted, the boy got out of the car.

Cole followed. With their heads close together, they strolled toward the entrance. Nate thought—but couldn't be sure—that he saw Landry wipe a tear from the corner of his eye.

No doubt about it. This was a big day...for all of them.

"Everything okay?" Brooke asked, when Nate swung by the mansion to pick her up. He looked distracted, and concerned in a way he hadn't been when they had parted earlier that afternoon.

For a second she thought he wouldn't answer. Finally, he said, "I hope Landry's visit with Jessalyn is going well."

Brooke grinned, hearing the worry in his voice. "You sound like such a dad," she teased, and it was so good to see and hear. "Worrying—often unnecessarily—is what we parents do best," she explained when he shot her a sidelong glance.

He grinned as they walked toward his Jaguar. "Is that what this is?"

Brooke let her shoulder brush him in a playful nudge. "Doesn't feel familiar, huh?"

He wrapped his arm about her shoulder and pulled her close to his side. "It's beginning to," he whispered in her ear.

When they reached his sedan, he continued around to the passenger side. Trying not to make too much of the fact that he was opening her door for her, the way he would have had they been on an actual date, Brooke slid into the car, settled into the leather seat and smoothed her skirt over her knees. "I'm sure Landry and Cole are both doing fine." She paused to look up at him. "Otherwise, we would have heard. Cole would have called me on his cell phone."

Nate came around to the driver's side and slipped behind the wheel. "I wasn't aware he had a phone of his own."

"He doesn't use it a lot. He's not at the age where he spends a lot of time talking on the phone. But I feel better knowing he has it, in case of an emergency, or if anything unexpected comes up."

"I should probably get Landry one." Nate frowned, as if he felt he had failed. "I hadn't thought of that."

"I'm sure he'd appreciate it." Brooke opened up her purse and removed her notebook.

"I'll talk to him about it this evening," Nate vowed.

"In the meantime, I'd like to update you on where we stand with the makeover." She consulted her notes.

"So all you have left to do is add accessories and art-work and finish the formal dining room," Nate concluded, when her recitation was complete.

Brooke nodded. "With the exception of the mural,

which is going to take a few weeks, I'll be done by Friday evening. Which is good, because I start another job next Wednesday, and I need a couple of days off to handle things I've let slide at home."

Nate parked in front of the assisted-living center. "You're welcome to stay in the caretaker's cottage as long as you like," he offered as he cut the motor.

"Thank you, but it's time Cole and I head home. Especially since…"

He guessed correctly where the conversation was headed. "We've become lovers."

Brooke thrilled to hear him say that out loud. Still, Nate was a man with a reputation for having dated a lot of women. She released the latch on her shoulder harness and turned toward him. Suddenly, her heart was pounding. Her palms were damp. "*Is* that what we are?"

With his marine-blue eyes glittering warmly, he put his hand on hers and murmured, "I guess now is as good a time as any to make my pitch." He paused, looking sexy and unutterably masculine. She felt another lightning bolt surge of attraction. "I want us to come out of the shadows. Make it official. And start being seen together publicly."

"Are we talking about dating?"

His confident smile widened. "Call it whatever you want. As long as we're exclusive."

It was a tempting invitation. If their lives hadn't been so complicated, she would have jumped on it. As it was, it felt as if they were moving too fast. And it scared her. "That's a little more than just dating."

He nodded, accepting her assessment. His eyes swept the length of her, then returned with laser accuracy to her face. "And I hope you want that, too."

Despite what she had tried to tell herself earlier, Brooke had to admit she wouldn't have made love with Nate if her feelings for him hadn't been serious. The question was, would he have gone after her if he hadn't needed her to help him connect with his "son"? The last thing she wanted either of them to do was mistake need for love. And there was no doubt Nate—and Landry—had needed her the last couple of weeks. Just as she and Cole had benefited immensely from having Nate and Landry in their lives.

"Aren't we skipping a few steps?" she asked gently, as her customary common sense reasserted itself. She didn't want to make the same mistake she had made with Seamus. He'd been a serial dater, too, with a reputation for never being satisfied with any one woman until Brooke came along. And look how that had worked out….

She knew she wouldn't be able to bear it if Nate ever looked at her the way her late husband had—with sadness and disappointment, and then later, with avoidance and detachment.

She couldn't bear another mistake in the marriage department. She doubted Nate wanted another failed romantic relationship, either.

"I know what I want," he said quietly, with the drive and focus she was beginning to know so well. "And that's you." He paused, his emotional armor going up once again. "The question is—what do you want?"

"Time," Brooke answered honestly. *To make sure our feelings are real and lasting.* She swallowed painfully. "And enough space to figure this all out."

It wasn't the answer Nate was looking for, but it left the window for more wide open, and that was better than all-out rejection. He forced himself to sacrifice his own timetable and desires in favor of hers. "Take all the time you need," he told her gently.

Brooke regarded him with wonder in her golden-brown eyes. "You mean that."

Although he had once sworn he would never open his heart to another woman who didn't feel everything he did, Nate was suddenly willing to wait as long as it took. Which was another sign of how important Brooke was to him. "I do," he told her sincerely.

Her smile lit up his day. Visibly relieved, she squeezed his hand. Together, they got out of the car and went inside to find their sons.

Cole and Landry were in the visitors room, a large light and airy space filled with comfortable tables and chairs. Jessalyn was holding court with the two young men, chatting away and laughing.

She looked radiant, and much more energetic than the last time Nate and Brooke had seen her. He couldn't help but note that Landry appeared much healthier and happier, too.

"Thank you for bringing the boys to see me," Jessalyn said as Nate approached.

"It was my pleasure."

"We told Gran that we'd visit again on Saturday morning," Landry said. "It's okay, isn't it?"

Nate nodded. He had been hoping Landry and Jessalyn would make up. "It's more than okay."

Nate and Brooke stayed to visit for a while, and then all four of them headed out to the car. Since it was nearly 8:00 p.m., the boys were ravenous. After a brief consultation, they headed for P. F. Chang's.

"I'm glad you visited your great-grandmother," Nate said, after they had all studied the menu and placed their orders.

"I thought seeing her in an old people's home would be awful," Landry admitted with a rueful twist of his lips.

"That she'd be just sitting around waiting to die. But it was actually pretty nice. I can see that she's better off with all the nurses, and people her own age and stuff. Anyway—" he ducked his head "—I guess I don't have to feel like I deserted her anymore."

Nate had assumed—wrongly, he now knew—that it was the other way around, that it was Landry who had felt abandoned. "I imagine it comforted your great-grandmother to see you looking so good, too," he soothed.

Landry nodded. "She thinks it's clear I'm where I'm supposed to be now."

The question was, what did Landry think? Nate wondered.

The teen's brow furrowed. "Did you hear anything about the DNA test yet?"

"We probably won't learn anything until early next week." Nate wasn't about to protest any turn of events that would buy him more time to convince Landry that he belonged with him.

The teen fiddled with the chopsticks next to his plate. "What about your lawyer and that court thing we've got to do?"

"Ms. Tanous will file the papers as soon as we tell her we're ready."

Landry nodded, taking it all in.

Cole looked uneasy, as if he felt for his friend.

Brooke appeared about to intervene, but then Landry leaned forward and asked, "Do you think I'm more like you, Nate? Or Lawrence? 'Cause I've been thinking I'm a lot like you, in that I like to make decisions and be in charge of stuff."

Surprised and pleased by the comparison, Nate smiled. "You want to run your own company one day?"

"Maybe," he acknowledged shyly.

Cole chuckled. "I can totally see you calling all the shots. You're bossy, man."

Landry grinned and elbowed him.

"Always telling me what to do," Cole added.

The two boys pretended to fight over the last dumpling. "That's cause I'm older."

"By one year!" Cole protested.

Landry let him have the dumpling, and ate a spring roll with spicy orange sauce instead. "One year's a lot, especially between middle and high school."

His mouth still full, Cole conceded the point by mugging comically.

"So anyway—" Landry leaned toward Nate and continued his quest for information "—am I more like my dad or you in terms of personality? 'Cause I'm not really a funny guy. I like to laugh, but I'm never the one coming up with the jokes."

"Me, either," Nate said. He usually left that to people with true comic ability.

"I mean, I know I look like my mom," Landry continued earnestly. "I've got her hair and eye color and all that."

"Yes, you do," Nate said. Landry had all of Seraphina's good qualities.

"So that doesn't really tell us anything. It'd be easier, I guess, if I had any real memories of Lawrence, but all I've got are a couple of pictures my mom gave me, from when they were still together." Landry reached into his back pocket, withdrew his wallet. He brought out two tattered color photos of Lawrence and Seraphina. They had their arms around each other in both photos, and appeared to be laughing and having a good time. "It just feels weird, not to know more about him," the boy admitted.

Nate wanted to say it wasn't important, but clearly it was to Landry. The teenager was searching for connection. It was only fair, Nate thought, that he do what he could to ease the pain. "I'll see what I can dig up for you," he promised.

A SEARCH ON YouTube that night turned up nothing on Lawrence. Ditto the Google, Yahoo and Safari Internet search engines. Frustrated, Nate went on to bed. The next day, over a working lunch, he talked to the guys about it.

"You could have Laura Tillman's private detective agency see what they could find, if you really want to go that route," Travis advised.

Nate trusted the guys, who were all great dads in their own right. "You think it's a mistake to be looking backward?" he asked.

Dan, the veteran parent of teenagers, shrugged, and predicted, "If the DNA results come back that way, you won't have a choice."

Nate knew Dan had shepherded his own kids through their fair share of biological-parent-induced hurt. It had been excruciating—and unfair.

"In the meantime, maybe you should concentrate on answering Landry's questions, while keeping him focused on his future with you," Jack said, with his customary protectiveness toward family.

"You're what he needs. And the sooner he realizes that, the better," Grady agreed.

Nate relaxed. "I think he already is." He related everything else that had happened in the previous few days.

"We should celebrate," Grady said.

"And I know just the way," Nate replied. Now all he had to do was talk Brooke into it.

"YOU WANT TO HAVE A PARTY here on Saturday?" Brooke asked, when she and Nate went in to look at the mural sketched on the dining-room wall.

Holly wanted Nate's approval before she actually started painting.

Nate studied the historical pictorial of Fort Worth, from the early days to the present, ending with the current skyline and the skyscraper that housed One Trinity River Place, home to Nate's business.

He gave the drawing his seal of approval, then turned back to Brooke. "It'll be sort of a home makeover slash Father's Day celebration with all the guys and their families. And of course, I want you and Cole to be here, too."

The enthusiasm he expected to see on Brooke's face was nowhere to be found. "It might be kind of awkward, given the fact that Cole's dad won't be here."

Nate bit back an oath. How could he have made such a blunder? Then again, considering his own family-challenged upbringing, how could he not? Nate exhaled slowly, wondering how to get out of this. "I'm sorry…. I didn't think about that." The last thing he wanted to do was resurrect Cole's grief.

Brooke paused, as if having second thoughts. "The truth is—we never did much to celebrate that particular holiday. It wasn't one Seamus put much stock in. Let me ask Cole, see how he feels." She slipped off to do so before Nate could protest.

He went back to studying the mural, then walked through the entire first floor of the mansion. Soft, earthtoned hues were on all the walls. Warm rugs livened up the wide plank floors. Comfortable furniture and fun, familyoriented accessories abounded. There were flowers in the front hall. A bowl of fresh fruit on the kitchen counter. And little touches that said Brooke everywhere he looked.

She returned, a jubilant expression on her face. "Cole wants to attend the party, and so does Landry."

"Even knowing we plan to celebrate Father's Day?" Nate asked.

She shrugged, evidently as surprised as he was. "Especially knowing that, they both said. They think it's awesome you're going to be a dad, too."

Contentment flowed through Nate. "So Landry is finally getting used to the idea of me adopting him?"

Brooke nodded in approval. "Seeing Jessalyn happy in her new place seems to have given him permission to move on, too."

"Then I guess there's just one more question to be asked. Will you stay through the weekend and cohost the party with me?"

Chapter Twelve

"If it was just me," Brooke said, "I'd have no problem saying yes. But I have Cole and you have Landry to consider."

Once again, she had the strong intuition that Nate wanted to kiss her. Senses reeling, she stepped back.

He shoved his hands into his back pockets and rocked toward her. His expression was as steady and resolute as his voice. "I think they'd be okay with it."

"More than okay if things work out," Brooke conceded. She shifted her attention away from his washboard abs, what she knew was hidden behind his fly. "The problem is—" she forced her attention upward, to the handsome contours of Nate's face "—what if they don't?"

"Borrowing trouble?"

She shot him a get-with-the-program-before-we're-both-in-big-trouble look. "Being realistic. I'm getting ready to move back to my place. And you're coming up with ways to keep me—and Cole—here at least one more day." And while it was flattering, unexpected, and oh so romantic, it was also completely impractical.

Unless, of course, they wanted everyone, even the boys, to know they had a thing for each other, and she didn't... not just yet.

"Can you blame me?" Nate held her gaze with his

mesmerizing blue eyes, making her feel all hot and bothered inside. Slowly, a smile bloomed on his lips. "Life has been so much better since you arrived."

For me, too. "It's still not a prudent move to make." And she had let the fantasy of what could be guide her once before, into a hasty marriage that had fallen far short of expectation. For all their sakes, she didn't want to make the same mistake again.

"You and I are going to work out for the long haul, Brooke."

She so wanted to believe it. As if he knew that, Nate bent his head and kissed her sweetly. Longing swept through her, along with the intense feelings she had for him. She moaned, knowing that if they kept this up she wouldn't sleep all night, but lie awake wanting him. And she couldn't have that, either. Not when she had so many responsibilities to fulfill. She pressed her palms to his chest, wishing, at least for now, it was just the two of them. "Nate…"

He kissed her again, slowly, lingeringly. Then he swept his fingers through her hair and gazed deep into her eyes. "Just tell me you'll think about it," he urged softly, scoring his thumb across her lower lip with a tenderness that almost undid her completely.

"All right. But that's all I'm doing right now," she told him sternly. "Mulling it over."

He smiled and kissed her again, feeling victorious. "Good enough."

Aware that it was getting late, Brooke said good-night to Nate and went down to the caretaker's cottage.

Cole and Landry were where she had left them a few minutes before. Both were huddled on the couch in front of Cole's laptop computer, looking at the photos of their visit to the amusement park the previous weekend.

"I thought you guys were going to hit the shower," Brooke murmured.

"In a minute, Mom." Cole waved her over to join them. "Isn't this a great picture of Nate?"

Brooke perched on the back of the sofa behind them and studied the photo on-screen. Nate was standing in front of the last roller coaster they had ridden that day, his arms around Landry and Cole. All three of them were a little sunburned and windblown. The happiness they had been feeling was palpable. "I remember taking that one," she murmured.

"Here's one of you and us." Landry scrolled to the next image.

Brooke had been clowning around with both kids, hands framing her face, as if in a silent movie scream of fake terror as she lingered in front of the entrance to a kiddie ride that wouldn't have scared a six-year-old. Landry and Cole were both laughing and grinning from ear to ear.

"That was a really good day," Landry said softly. "One of the best I've ever had."

"For me, too," Cole murmured.

"It was for all of us." Brooke placed a comforting hand on a shoulder of each boy.

She would hold the memory close for a long time, and sensed they would, too.

The guys turned to her with beseeching grins. "Which brings us to our next request," Landry drawled. "Could you do us one more tiny little favor?"

FRIDAY MORNING, Brooke and the boys overslept. By the time Nate realized everyone in the caretaker's cottage was still asleep, and hastily woke them, it was a mad rush to get ready for camp and hurry out the door.

His calls to Brooke during the day went straight to voice

mail. Ditto hers to him. He had a stop to make on the way home from work, and it was seven o'clock before he pulled in the driveway.

To his surprise, Brooke was just arriving, too.

He got out of the car and headed for hers. In the rear seat, both boys waved and then ducked down. As he neared, he saw they were both zipping up the backpacks they'd taken to camp. The expressions on their faces were choirboy innocent as they piled out of the car.

"Hi, Nate." Cole didn't quite meet his eyes.

Landry's gaze focused on the ultracasual fist bump he gave Nate. "Hey, dude. What's happening?"

Exactly what I'd like to know, Nate thought, as Brooke got out from behind the steering wheel, her cheeks a lot more pink than usual, too. "Sorry I missed all your calls today," she said. Then, realizing they had company, and catching herself, she added, "I assume you wanted to talk about the plans for the party here tomorrow."

"I do." But that wasn't why Nate had called her. He had dialed her number because he wanted to hear her voice. The intense need for connection was new to him. And yet satisfying, too.

"I guess you-all stopped and had dinner on the way home from camp," Nate said, disappointed they wouldn't all be eating together, as had become the custom.

"Uh…actually, no, we didn't." Brooke abruptly rummaged through her purse and came up with nothing, before zipping it closed again. "I just… I had a few errands to run and the boys graciously agreed to go with me," she murmured, still averting her gaze.

Was she lying to him? Nate wondered. Or at the very least, not telling him something?

He hadn't had a woman *not* look at him quite that

way since Seraphina had been ducking out on him with Lawrence, behind the scenes....

"But I imagine the boys are hungry." Brooke rambled on, as even more color flooded her high, sculpted cheeks.

"Very hungry," they chimed in.

"You want to go out?" Nate asked, more than happy to treat them all.

Shrugs all around. Again, to Nate's frustration, something wordless—and private—passed between Brooke and the boys. "Actually, we've got some stuff to do," Cole murmured finally, taking the lead. "But—" he looked at his mom, silently pleading "—if you and Nate want to go out and get something and bring it back, that would be good."

Brooke appeared to understand whatever Cole was telling her. "No problem," she said. "Nate, we'll go together. And let's make it a steak-house night." She named a place a good thirty minutes away.

Nate countered, "We could go to Morty's—it's a lot closer. If the guys are hungry."

The boys looked at Brooke. "Uh...we can wait," Cole said.

"Yeah, we'll have a granola bar or something in the meantime." Landry stuffed his hands into the pockets of his khaki shorts.

Brooke's usual admonishment not to eat too much right before dinner never came.

She smiled and, grasping Nate's elbow, guided him in the direction she wanted him to go.

"So what's going on?" Nate asked, as he and Brooke got in the car and headed for her favorite steak place, on the other side of town.

She flashed him a look of pure confusion.

Nate didn't buy her naivete for a moment. Drolly, he explained, "I'd say the kids were matchmaking, but they don't know we're together. So there has to be another reason they want us both out of the cottage for a good long while."

She took a deep breath, her soft breasts rising and falling beneath her tailored cotton blouse. She made a show of tugging her business-casual skirt down to her knees. "Look. Obviously the boys are behaving a bit melodramatic tonight."

"Because?"

"Because they're kids and they're excited about this project they're working on."

"For camp?" Nate persisted.

Brooke lifted a silencing palm. She wrinkled her nose into a comical expression. Chuckling, she said, "I can't tell you anything else so you need to stop asking questions."

While they waited at the traffic light, Nate slanted a glance at her trim ankles and fantastically shaped calves. "Obviously you know what Cole and Landry are up to."

"Yes." Brooke watched the red turn to green. She gestured, indicating it was safe for him to go. "I do."

Nate doubled-checked the road, then went through the intersection. As soon as it was safe, he pulled over and put the car in Park.

In the soft light of a summer evening, her classically beautiful features were more pronounced. In deference to the heat of the June day, she'd swept her glossy hair into a clip at the back of her head. Tendrils escaped to frame her face and neck.

Nate draped his arm along the seat, behind her head. "Then why can't I know?" He hated being excluded. It reminded him of his youth.

Brooke released her seat belt and scooted toward him.

She kissed him until all he could think and feel and want was her.

"I promise you," she murmured eventually, pressing closer, "if you do as I ask and let the boys do what they need to do tonight, they'll be happy campers and so will we."

That sounded even more mysterious. But in a good way.

He relaxed as Brooke slipped back into her seat and refastened her safety belt. He couldn't resist the merry look in her golden-brown eyes. He turned to her with a wink. "Okay, then. Your wish is my command."

"THAT WAS A GREAT dinner!" Cole exclaimed an hour and a half later, when four steaks, nearly a dozen yeast rolls with butter, and a round of salads and desserts had been consumed. He grinned with thirteen-year-old exuberance. "Thanks, Nate."

Landry patted his full belly, looking equally content. "Yeah, thanks."

It still amazed Nate how much these guys could eat. They were true bottomless pits. They took so much pleasure in eating that it was a privilege supplying them with food. Particularly when Nate contrasted this evening's meal with Landry's first dinner at the mansion, twelve days before.

Aware that he wasn't the only one harboring a secret that evening, Nate rose leisurely from his seat. "It's not the only thing I have for you guys tonight."

Although the boys hadn't revealed what they had been working on earlier, their brows lifted in interest.

Nate walked over to his briefcase and withdrew two BlackBerry Smartphones. He carried them over to the boys and wordlessly handed one to each, along with the instruction manuals. The teens stared at him, not understanding. "They're all programmed and ready to go," Nate said.

Cole's jaw dropped. The cell phone he carried now was a basic model, with very limited capability. Landry didn't have a phone at all.

"Of course, you can use them to make calls," Nate told them proudly. "But you can also check your e-mail, text message, browse the Web, use the GPS, take and store photos, even transfer programs and watch them. I've already put in your mother's cell phone and home numbers, and all of mine. The manuals will tell you how to add those of your friends."

The boys continued staring at their phones in sheer amazement.

"Wow," Cole said finally.

"I can't believe I've got something like this," Landry murmured, his eyes glimmering with moisture.

Afraid if he looked directly at Landry, he'd tear up, too, Nate turned and caught a glimpse of Brooke's inexplicably shocked expression, and went back to his briefcase. "And I have one other thing," he told the boys, knowing this would mean even more, at least to Landry. "I was able to get some old footage from one of the comedy clubs in town. Apparently, they tape all their open-mike nights and hold on to the video, just in case someone later becomes really famous. They had a couple of the routines Miles Lawrence did. I thought you might like to watch them."

AT THE BOYS' INSISTENCE, all four of them trooped up to the media room. The videos were slipped into the DVD player. They all sat down to watch.

Miles Lawrence was tall—like Nate and Landry. Handsome in a slightly disheveled, ne'er-do-well frat boy way—and hysterically funny. They were all chuckling as they watched, even Nate.

As he watched the routine about unrequited love, it was clear Landry felt comforted. When the last bit ended, he sat there a moment, silent, then murmured, "I guess I see why my mom fell so hard for him."

Then, realizing the impact of his words, he froze in horror and turned to Nate. "Oh, man, I—"

"I know what you mean," Nate said kindly. "Miles was a funny guy. And I think your mom loved him very much."

"It just wasn't a love that was returned," Landry reflected with a swiftness that indicated he had spent a fair amount of time thinking about this. "'Cause otherwise Miles would have married her, don't you think?"

For a moment, Brooke noted, Nate looked as if he was going to play that down. Then his expression changed to the one of forthright honesty she knew so well, and he said, "I think you're right—Miles didn't love your mother enough for a marriage to succeed—so they're probably lucky they didn't go down that road. But I also think, had he had an opportunity to get to know you—and realize what a gift it is to have a son—he would have done right by you, even if he and your mom never married. I think he would have been a *great* dad to you, Landry."

Brooke knew Nate sure wanted to be…and in so many ways, already was.

Once again Landry's eyes teared up. He nodded, seeming so choked up he was unable to get any words out. Then he turned back to the TV and mumbled to Cole, "Let's watch it one more time, okay?"

"As many times as you want," Cole said.

Figuring now was as good a time as any to say what she needed to Nate—alone—Brooke sent him a look and inclined her head toward the hall. They walked out together.

Nate peered at her closely. "You okay?" he murmured.

Yes, Brooke thought. *And no.* "Let's walk out by the pool," she said instead.

He followed her down the stairs, out the back door, across the yard. "What is it?" he asked, when they finally reached the lagoon-style swimming area.

I think I'm falling in love with you....

But knowing now wasn't the time to make that admission, Brooke forced herself to return to the issue at hand. "I was going to read you the riot act about the Smartphone."

Nate looked stunned by the slight censure in her tone, then apologetic. He ran a palm across his jaw. "I gather I should have asked first."

Heck yes, he should have! "Nate, I know you meant well, but I can't give Cole gifts like that."

Nate shrugged, still not seeing the problem. He angled a thumb at his chest. "But I can."

Brooke's eyes were drawn to the smooth skin and curly tufts of black hair springing out of the open V of his shirt. Light-headed from the memories and images bombarding her, she drew a breath and stepped back. "I'm not even sure he should have anything that elaborate."

Nate studied her, some of the light exiting his blue eyes. "From me or in general?" he wondered aloud.

Brooke knew she was hurting his feelings, but it couldn't be helped. "Both," she answered bluntly.

"I'm sorry. I wanted Landry to have a phone."

Naturally, a well-to-do Nate wanted Landry to have the very best.

"And I didn't want to give him a gift and hand Cole nothing."

Brooke appreciated Nate's thoughtfulness, even if he still didn't see the emotional implications of his actions. "Landry is your son."

"That's the thing, Brooke. Cole feels like my son, too."

What could she say to that? She loved the way Nate treated Cole. Brooke's heart skipped a beat. "I'm fond of Landry, too."

Hope shone on Nate's face. "Then it's okay?"

She rolled her eyes in exasperation. "No! It's not! In the future, if you're going to do something like this, or you're even tempted to do so, you need to run it by me first."

"Fair enough."

Silence descended.

"Something else is on your mind."

"What you did just now for Landry—getting that recording for him, saying what you did about Miles—was really decent."

"Even if it wasn't one hundred percent true." Nate looked conflicted. "I misled him there at the end, when I said Lawrence would have appreciated him."

Brooke edged closer and slipped her hand in his. "Then why did you do it?"

Nate squeezed her fingers as he admitted in a low, troubled voice, "Because I couldn't stand to see him hurt." He paused, as if struggling with his conscience. "It's what I hope would have happened…."

"But you don't know for sure," Brooke interjected.

He turned to her, a beseeching look in his eyes. "I never understood why you would lie to protect your son. Until now." His lips compressed. "Because that's what I just did."

Afraid the boys might come out and see the clandestine show of affection, Brooke stepped back. "There are worse things."

Nate tore his eyes from the underwater lights and shimmering blue of the swimming pool amid the darkening night. "Are there?"

Unable to seek solace from his arms, Brooke let the warmth of the summer evening surround her. "Our boys may look like almost-adults," she told him softly, "but at heart they're still just kids in a lot of ways."

Kids who needed parents, Brooke thought. And Nate was turning out to be one fine one indeed.

"Mom?" Cole asked Saturday morning over breakfast, while Nate gave them a tutorial on their new phones. "Is it okay with you if Landry goes to the book publication party for Dad?"

Brooke looked up from the to-do list she was writing for their own casual party later that day. "Well, I—" she began.

"The other professors at the university won't mind, will they?" Cole persisted. "I want Landry to see who my dad was, too."

To her relief, Nate's expression remained blessedly inscrutable.

Which left the ball firmly in her court. How should she answer this? "Of course Landry can come—if they have the party," Brooke said finally.

Cole's brow furrowed. "Why *wouldn't* they have it?"

Time to fib, Brooke thought, her own conscience prickling. "There was some sort of scheduling problem they were trying to work out, last I heard." *Based on whether they could figure out if there was any validity to the plagiarism claim.*

"So you don't know if they are going to have it or not?" Cole pressed.

Brooke was finally able to answer honestly. She looked him in the eye. "I'm still waiting to hear."

"Well, whenever they do have it, I want to go," Cole stated firmly. "And I want Landry to come with us, too."

"So noted." Brooke wasn't about to engage in an argument about the hypothetical. Ignoring Nate's under-the-radar look—which seemed to indicate she had done something wrong—she continued, "In the meantime, I've got a ton of grocery shopping to do." She smiled brightly. "Who wants to come with me?"

Cole and Landry exchanged looks. "Uh, we've got that project to work on," Cole said. "We didn't finish it yet."

Nate lifted a brow, perplexed. "What project?"

The boys again traded glances, and shrugged. "Just something we're working on," Landry said vaguely.

"So can we opt out?" Cole asked.

Knowing exactly what they were up to, she smiled and nodded, then turned to Nate. "Can you come with me, then?"

He stood agreeably. Still curious, but cool enough not to ask. "You bet."

Brooke grabbed her list and her purse. She turned to the boys, who were already half out the door, their Smart-phones in hand. "Just be warned that when I get back I will be enlisting your help."

They nodded in agreement and waved her off.

"Alone at last," Nate teased as they hit the driveway.

He made it sound so sexy! If only it could have been that way. But with a party set to start in a matter of hours, that wasn't an option. She peered at him playfully. "I didn't plan this."

He wrinkled his nose. "I wish you had."

So, thought Brooke wistfully as they set off to complete their chores, did she.

"I DON'T KNOW WHAT'S better," Grady McCabe said hours later, as he and the other guys finished the tour of Nate's redecorated home. "The changes Brooke brought to the living quarters or the change she brought to you."

Nate stopped at the cooler they'd put on the patio, and handed out beers. "My happiness shows, hmm?"

"Landry looks pretty content, too." Dan nodded at the badminton net set up on the sport court. Cole and Landry were dividing the other kids into teams.

"He's a great kid," Nate said proudly.

"That he is," Dan said. The others all nodded in agreement.

"So what's the deal with Brooke?" Jack asked, deadpan. "You-all out of the closet yet?"

Chuckles abounded.

"No." Nate elbowed the guys closest to him and kept his voice purposefully low. "She thinks all the kids need to know right now is that the two of us have developed a very casual platonic friendship."

Travis grunted. "Which might be fine if the kids weren't very bright, but…"

"You're right—they're sharp as a tack," Nate agreed. "And I'm afraid they're going to pick up on something." A look, a touch, the most inane comment… He shook his head in frustration. "But she still won't budge."

"Why not?" Dan helped himself to guacamole and chips. "From what I've noticed—and from what she's told Emily—it looks like she really has a thing for you."

Nate had only to think about the passionate way Brooke made love with him to realize the validity of that. "She does. And I have a thing for her that goes beyond anything I've ever felt."

The guys, having all been there themselves with their wives, grinned. "So what's the problem?" Grady teased.

That much, at least, was easy, Nate thought. "Deep down, Brooke doesn't trust romantic love. She sees it as a fleeting, ephemeral thing."

Travis shrugged. "It probably was, in her marriage. It won't be the same for the two of you. Especially if you're this serious."

He was. Frustrated, Nate took a swig of his beer and glanced over at Brooke as she and the other women emerged from their tour of the house. With sunlight glinting off her hair, and her eyes bright with laughter, she was more beautiful than ever. "I want to tell the world." Nate worked to contain his disappointment when the women stopped to talk once again. "But she's not ready yet."

"It'll happen," Grady predicted with the legendary McCabe knowledge of male-female dynamics. He studied Brooke, and the way she looked so completely at home on Nate's turf, then turned back to his pal. "Maybe sooner than you think…"

Nate sure as heck hoped so. He was a patient man, but only to a point.

Chapter Thirteen

On Sunday morning, Brooke met Nate as he headed for the caretaker's cottage. Swiftly, she moved to block his path, then adopted the stance of a baseball outfielder protecting a base. "You can't go in there."

Nate chuckled at her playful gesture and flashed a perplexed smile. He stopped and folded his arms across his chest. "You want to tell me why?" He cocked his head. "Or am I supposed to guess?"

Brooke looped her arm through his, guided him into a one-hundred-eighty-degree turn and steered him toward the swimming pool, where she sank down on the foot of a chaise. He took the one next to her.

"Since it's our last morning here, Landry and Cole thought they should do something special." She slipped off her flip-flops and flexed her bare toes on the sun-warmed concrete. Her hot-pink nail polish glinted in the sunshine. "So they're cooking breakfast for all of us."

"Wow." Like her, Nate couldn't help but be impressed.

It was unusual. Teenage boys generally spent most of their time in the kitchen either eating or asking to be fed. They were also loath to do chores of any kind. Yet there they were, working like a well-oiled team toward a common goal. Miracles, it seemed, would never cease, at least where the four of them were concerned.

"They said they'd call us when it's ready," Brooke continued.

His lips compressed into a thoughtful line, as if he sensed there was more to this than she was saying thus far. "Can't wait."

Fearing if she continued looking into his eyes, she would give away the real reason behind the "family fete," Brooke turned her glance away. She wondered what Nate's reaction was going to be when he saw the entire surprise Cole and Landry had dreamed up Thursday evening, and spent most of the weekend working on behind closed doors.

Nate stood and moved restlessly to the edge of the pool. For a while he looked down at the shimmering water, then turned and strolled back. "I can't believe you have been here for almost two weeks." He stopped just short of her, towering over her.

Brooke flushed. "Time flies when you're having fun."

Nate reached for her hand and pulled her to her feet. "And it has been fun," he murmured softly, still looking down at her.

She could tell he was thinking about kissing her.

She knew, because she was thinking about kissing him.

The door to the cottage banged open, prompting them to move surreptitiously apart.

"Mom! Nate!" Cole shouted, clearly oblivious to the impulsive show of affection that would have "outed" them to the boys, had temptation gotten the best of them yet again.

"Come on!" Landry added. "It's going to get cold!"

Nate shrugged. He still looked as if he wanted to kiss her. "You heard the chefs."

Feeling hot and bothered all over, Brooke pivoted and strolled with Nate toward the cottage.

Inside, the table had been set. Glasses of juice and steaming cups of coffee sat beside their plates. Buttered toast, slightly charred eggs and undercooked bacon completed the repast. In the center of the awkwardly laid table was a bouquet of flowers that had been picked from the beds along the front of the house. That touch, Brooke figured, had been more for her than Nate.

Nate nodded approvingly at the kids' efforts, and helped Brooke into her chair. "Looks great, guys."

The boys grinned from ear to ear, knowing—as did Brooke—that the biggest revelation was yet to come.

The three of them sat down in turn. "So anyway...we were thinking—" Cole began his pitch, catching her off guard, too "—there's really no reason Mom and I need to rush off today, it being the weekend and all...."

Landry continued, "So maybe the four of us could just hang out together this morning and go see a movie or something this afternoon."

Brooke lifted a brow. She had an idea where this campaign was going.

"That's a great idea!" Nate enthused. "Brooke?"

Emotion warred with common sense. Her feelings for Nate won. "That's fine, but we really have to get our stuff together and go home after that, Cole," she warned. It was going to be hard enough to leave as it was.

Nate understood the difficulty they were facing. He turned to the boys compassionately. "It's not as if we won't see each other after that," he said. "We'll see each other all the time. In fact, I'd like to continue carpooling to camp for the rest of the summer."

"It's a little out of the way," Brooke noted.

Nate eyed her expectantly. "The extra drive time will give us all time to talk."

"Sounds good to me!" Cole exclaimed.

"Me, too!" Landry said.

To Brooke, as well, if she was honest. She just wished she didn't harbor so many fears about getting in too deep.... She blew out an exasperated breath. "Make that me, three...."

The boys grinned victoriously, then turned back to Nate. "What movie do you want to see?" Landry asked, hero worship glowing on his young face.

"Depends on what's showing," Nate said.

Cole pulled out his new BlackBerry. "I'll look it up on the Internet."

Options were discussed throughout the rest of the meal. They finally decided to see an action-adventure film starring a group of teenagers.

The meal over, their plans set, Nate stood. "I'll do the dishes this morning."

The boys rushed to intervene. "You can't do that," they said in unison.

Nate grimaced in confusion. "Why not?"

More furtive looks were exchanged. "Wait here!" They told him, then disappeared into their respective bedrooms.

"Why don't you take a seat on the couch?" Brooke suggested, knowing what was next.

More baffled than ever, Nate let her lead him there.

The boys burst back out, hands behind their back. Expressions jubilant, they thrust two presents at him. "Happy Father's Day!"

For the briefest of seconds, Brooke thought Nate was going to lose it. She was close herself, with her throat closing up and sentimental tears welling in her eyes. Wary of doing anything that would detract from the pure sweetness of this moment for any of them, she sucked in a breath and worked valiantly to put her own emotions on hold.

Fortunately, the three males were so wrapped up in their gift giving and receiving they were oblivious to her reaction. Silence reigned as the two boys focused solely on the recipient of their admiration and affection. And in that moment, Nate looked like the proud and grateful father *both* kids needed him to be. Even Cole…

Nate shook his head, cleared his throat. "I'm…overwhelmed," he managed to say finally.

So were the boys, Brooke noted happily. Everything was working out so well.

Predictably, the older, streetwise Landry was the first to get it together. He discreetly rubbed a hand beneath his eye. "You can't be overwhelmed until you open it," he chided Nate.

Beside him, Cole was surreptitiously blotting his eyes, too. "Mine first," he said. When Landry looked less than pleased, Cole added, "We're saving the best for last!"

Landry's face split into a wide grin. "True."

Nate tore into the wrapping appreciatively. The top of the gift box bore the words Parent Survival Kit.

"I figured you might need it, you being new at this stuff and all," Cole teased.

Chuckling, Nate opened the box. Inside were all the essentials. *A Father's Guide to Understanding his Teenage Son*—written in guyspeak, by a famous comedian they all admired. Next up was a detailed playlist of all the essential tunes, and can't-miss movies and TV shows, meticulously compiled by both boys. And an invitation to join them in the enjoyment of said entertainment anytime. Earplugs, for when he couldn't stand the noise. A schedule for the Texas Rangers baseball games, with an IOU for tickets to the game of his choice. And last but not least, a how-to guide and promise of further hands-on tutorials designed to bring him up to speed on his interactive-video-game-playing skills so he would be better able to compete in family tournaments.

"Right now, we kind of feel like we're taking advantage of you," Cole teased.

Nate shook his head, visibly pleased. "This is great. Thank you."

Cole and Landry bumped fists. "It's officially from me, but we came up with all the stuff together."

They were so much like brothers, Brooke thought. Always giving exactly what the other needed...

"But this one is just from me," Landry said, handing over the second present.

Nate sent him a grateful look and opened it.

Inside was a photo of Landry and Nate, taken at the amusement park. They were standing with their arms around each other, exuding happiness. The personally engraved message on the sterling silver frame said, "Happy Father's Day, to the Best Dad Ever."

NATE HAD NEVER BEEN the kind of guy who cried happy tears. Damned if he wasn't tempted to change that, here and now. Deciding to put better use to the emotion, he stood, grabbed both boys and pulled them into a fierce group hug. Throat tight, he held them there, putting all the love he felt for them—and he did love both of the boys—into the single gesture. They hugged him back just as fiercely.

Brooke, overcome, started to walk away.

Not about to let her miss out on what was turning into a very satisfying exchange, Nate grabbed her, too, and pulled her into the middle. As she joined in the embrace, the sound that came out of her mouth was half laugh, half sob.

It brought the boys up short. "Mom!" Cole demanded, shocked. "Are you crying?"

"Of course not," she fibbed tearfully.

Cole shook his head, ignoring the fact he and Landry had been all choked up just seconds earlier. "You're not supposed to cry! This is a happy occasion!"

"I know." Brooke patted her cheeks with her splayed fingertips. "I can't help it!" she complained, her chin quivering. "You-all are just so sweet."

Cole and Landry groaned as if in terrible pain.

Brooke teared up even more….

Nate wasn't sure what this was about. More than the sentimentality of the occasion and the gifts, certainly… He touched both boys on the shoulder. "Why don't you give your mom a moment?" he suggested.

Appearing all too glad to be away from the show of unchecked emotion before they got sucked in, too, they acquiesced. "We'll be over at the main house, playing video games," Landry said.

"Good idea," Nate told him, while Brooke continued to cry.

Nate waited until the boys had crossed the lawn and disappeared into the house, then went back into the cottage and pulled Brooke into his arms. "Hey, now," he said, patting her back. "It's okay."

"More than okay." She buried her head in his shoulder. Her voice was muffled against his shirt. "That's the problem."

Nate led her to the kitchen and guided her into the walk-in pantry, so that even if the boys slammed back into the house unexpectantly, he and Brooke would have a chance to move apart before being seen. He steadied her with a gentle hand on her waist. "You're going to have to explain that one."

She stood close to him and tilted her face up to his. "Cole adores you so much."

He pressed a tender hand to her cheek, then smoothed it through her hair. "I love him, too."

She went very still. With a conflicted look in her eyes, she searched his face. "You do, don't you?"

Nate wondered if she was feeling as deprived of intimacy and affection as he was. "Yes. Cole's a great kid. He got into my heart in no time." *Same as you...* But sensing she wasn't ready to hear that just yet, he said only, "Same as Landry."

Brooke extricated herself from his possessive grasp and stepped aside. "I worry—"

He came closer and pressed a finger to her lips. "Stop."

Her shoulders stiff, she continued anyway "—what will happen if you and I—"

Nate wouldn't consider the possibility that what they shared might end. He wrapped his arms around her yet again. Holding her close, he promised, "I'm going to be there for him, whenever...however he needs me, Brooke." The raw vulnerability in her face gave him the courage to add, "I'm going to do the same thing for you. And for Landry."

She regarded him soberly. "You mean that, don't you?"

Hell yes. Nate nodded. "You've got my word." He bent to kiss her, and she wound her arms about his neck and melted against him in sweet surrender.

Knowing it was either stop now or continue kissing her and end up making love to her under far less than ideal circumstances, he paused and drew back. That would happen soon, at the appropriate time. But for now, it was important that she had confided in him. It meant a lot that he could confide at least part of what he was thinking and feeling in turn.

Certain they could build on that foundation, he smiled and took her hand. "Let's go find the boys."

SUNDAY EVENING, Cole roamed the house like a prisoner in a cell. It was still Father's Day, but the father figure most recently in his life was nowhere close. "You said we'd be happy coming back home," he told Brooke disconsolately.

Normally, we would be, Brooke thought morosely as she sorted through two weeks' worth of mail.

Of course, normally she wasn't involved in an openended love affair where the possibility of love hadn't even been broached…. And yet despite that, she had never felt happier than when she was with Nate.

Cole folded his arms across his chest. "Well, I'm not happy at all, Mom! I miss Nate and Landry!"

I miss them, too. More than I thought I would. But that didn't mean she should allow herself to rely on Nate and Landry to make her and Cole happy 24/7. That was her job, Brooke reminded herself sternly.

Still scowling, her son shoved his hands through his hair. "I wish we could have just stayed there."

Forced by circumstance to play the role of spoilsport, Brooke ignored her own yearning. "You know why we couldn't do that."

He snorted. "Because your job there is done, except for the dining-room mural, and we don't need to be on-site for that to happen. You just have to be available to troubleshoot if a problem comes up."

Brooke thought her repeated explanation had fallen on

deaf ears, she'd had to say it so many times. Pleased that it hadn't, she reminded him kindly, "You're going to see Landry and Nate tomorrow. I'm taking both of you boys to camp in the morning, and Nate is picking you up tomorrow evening." So it wasn't as if they had to cut off all contact, because that would have been way too tough for both kids. And herself, if she was completely honest.

Cole perked up. "Can they stay for dinner with us tomorrow night? You know Nate can't cook," he cajoled.

Knowing they had to stop acting as if they were a family, and get back to the reality of leading separate lives, at least part of the time, Brooke responded, "He's also very good at going to restaurants or picking up take-out meals."

Cole marched over to the computer, switched it on and regarded her glumly. "It's not the same thing as the four of us sitting down together."

Brooke missed the camaraderie, too. That wasn't the point. They'd had independent lives before they met; for all their sakes, they needed to set some boundaries and maintain them. "Cole, I know we felt like a family when we were there," she started awkwardly. *And that's my fault. I fell for the fantasy, hook, line and sinker.*

Hurt glimmered in Cole's eyes. "We *are* a family, Mom," he interrupted, a crestfallen expression on his face. "Or at least we could be if you weren't so stubborn!"

Maybe someday, Brooke thought wistfully. But only if she and Nate were in love. And although they had made love, and flirted with the idea of it, neither of them had begun to make that kind of no-holds-barred commitment. Until they did, she couldn't let Cole think more was possible. He'd already been disappointed enough in the personal realm.

Forcing herself to be practical yet again, when all she really wanted to do was be wildly impractical and impulsive, she counseled, "I know the last two weeks were fun, but right now we each need space to get back to our normal lives."

Cole scowled and stormed out of the room. "I don't want my normal life—I want a dad and a brother. I want Nate and Landry!"

HER SON'S WORDS still ringing in her ears, Brooke gave up sorting through the mail and went to take a shower. She wished she could give Cole what he wanted. But his reaction to leaving the mansion after just two weeks of interacting daily with Landry and Nate filled her with fear. She had a responsibility to prevent her son from being hurt by unrealistic expectations, as well as a duty to let Nate—who might be dealing with the same thing with Landry—know what was going on.

"I'm glad you called," Nate told her when he showed up on her doorstep at noon the following day.

Ignoring his warm, deliberate gaze and blatantly sensual manner, she stiffened her resolve and ushered him inside. "I wanted to talk to you when the boys weren't present." She had promised herself she was going to get their life back on track and return everything to normal. Actively taking steps to do so already made her feel stronger. "Since they're both at camp for the day, this was the perfect time." Mindful of his busy schedule, she led Nate into the living room.

He took off his suit jacket, draped it over the back of a wing chair and loosened the knot on his tie. "I wanted to talk to you, too. Landry moved into the main house last night after you left."

The announcement filled her with happiness. Brooke tore her eyes from the exposed column of Nate's throat, aware he'd been with her for less than a minute and her pulse was already pounding at his nearness. "That's great!" she said.

He grinned like a proud dad emerging from the delivery room. The words spilled out joyously. "I offered to move into the caretaker's cottage with him...since Landry was already comfortable there. But he said he thought it was time he started acting like he was my son—for real—and not just some guest."

Brooke wrapped Nate in a congratulatory hug, then stepped back, still smiling as she looked up at him. "That is big," she said warmly. "I am so happy for you."

He dipped his head in acknowledgment, then sobered. "The only problem is he misses you and Cole."

Empathy united them once again. "Cole feels the same way," she admitted.

Nate studied her through hooded eyes, leaving Brooke feeling as if they were suddenly on the verge of something even more compelling...and emotionally risky...

Her heart began to pound.

He curved a hand over her cheek and temple, and pushed away her hair. "Unless I'm wrong," he confessed, gazing reverently into her eyes, "I think we all miss each other."

Emotion welled inside Brooke, along with a longing unlike anything she had ever felt. Unable to help herself, she looked straight into his eyes and whispered, "You're not wrong. You're not wrong at all." And then she did what she had wanted to do ever since he walked in. She put aside what she knew she should do and leaned in to kiss him.

NATE HADN'T COME OVER to make love, but now that Brooke had issued the invitation, he was all for it. Filled with longing and the primal need to possess, he gathered her close. Cupping her face in his hands, he tilted her chin for better access. One kiss melted into another. She returned his passion, straining against him, her body undulating softly. Sensations hammered him. The hot heavy pressure in his groin nestled against her closed thighs. Knowing he had to find a way to be closer to her, to find the fulfillment they both sought, Nate lifted his head. "Your bedroom okay?"

She wreathed her arms about his neck and gazed up at him. "More than okay."

Nate needed no further persuasion. He swept her up into his arms and carried her down the hall to the master suite. He set her down next to her bed, then lowered his head to hers once again. Her lips parted and he swept his tongue inside her mouth, tasting the sweetness, and assuaging the desperate hunger inside him.

They undressed in a haze of longing. When they had finished, she looked up at him, her eyes glowing with love. And Nate knew his search was over. He had found the woman—the only woman—for him, at long last.

She guided him onto the lace-edged sheets that adorned her bed.

They kissed again, their caresses melting one into another. Brooke's body ignited in a flame of sensation. And she knew what she had been trying to deny for days now. There was no guarantee what the future held, and there never had been. The chance to be with Nate like this might be as fleeting as she feared in the darkest recesses of her soul. But if she didn't take advantage of it, right now, she would regret for the rest of her life not making love with him. And she didn't want any regrets where he was concerned. She wanted only love and sweet, wonderful memories that would sustain her when life was not so great, yet again….

Nate's hands skimmed lower, slipping between her

thighs. He explored her intimately, his questing caress sending her arching up into the warmth of his fingertips. He was hard all over, and lower still, below the waist, as aroused as she. She let her palm close around him, wanting to draw out the experience as sensually as possible, knowing she had never needed or wanted him more than at that moment.

"I don't want to be without you," he whispered, between deep, demanding kisses.

"I don't want to be without you, either," she confessed, as their bodies melded in boneless pleasure. Hers felt as if it were on fire from the inside out. Unable to wait any longer, she grasped his hips and guided him, so he was positioned precisely where he should be. Surrendering with a fierce, unquenchable ache, she murmured, "I want you. Now, Nate!"

"I want you, too." He kissed her again, commanding everything she had to give, then pushed her thighs apart with his knees. He stroked her gently and that was all it took. Brooke arched up from the bed, already falling apart, as he surged inside her. Overwhelmed with sensation, with the feelings welling in her heart, she let every part of her love every part of him, until at last they were soaring, flying free.

It was only hours later, as Nate dressed again and prepared to leave, that he noticed the message from his physician's office on his phone, asking him to call in immediately.

Chapter Fourteen

"You found out the results of the DNA test, didn't you?" Landry guessed, apprehension tautening the lines of his young face.

It was all Nate could do not to look at Brooke. He had asked her to be with him when he told Landry. In turn, Landry had asked that Cole be present. It seemed that everyone needed reinforcements for this "talk." And right now, Cole looked as tense and pale and out of his mind with worry as Landry.

Nate squared his shoulders and said the words he had hoped never to utter. "Our DNA did not match. You and I are definitely not father and son."

Landry's gangly shoulders sagged. "So Miles Lawrence is my dad, after all."

Although there was no way to say definitely, since Lawrence was deceased, Nate took it on faith. "It would appear so."

"Are they sure?" Landry leaned forward urgently in his seat, clasped hands dangling in front of him. The desperation to belong gleamed in his eyes. "I mean, I'm way more like you than I am him, at least what I know of him."

"It doesn't matter what the genetics are." Nate worked to quell his own disappointment. Strength and conviction were what was needed here. "I told you that before." He looked Landry in the eye. "I still want to be your dad. I want you to be my son."

The teen raked both his hands through his hair, despair pouring out of him. "It's not going to be the same," he muttered.

Nate clamped a paternal hand on his shoulder. "It'll be exactly the same," he assured him.

"How can you say that?" Landry demanded, jerking away.

Vaguely aware of the distraught looks on both Brooke's and Cole's faces, Nate followed him. "Because nothing of importance will change. The adoption is still going to go through."

Landry shook off both touch and reassurance once again. Refusing to look anyone in the eye, he pivoted. "I'm going outside." He dashed away and slammed out of Brooke's home.

Cole headed for the back door, too. "I'll talk to him," he threw the words over his shoulder.

Nate wasn't sure what Cole could say. Brooke looked as if she didn't know what to do or say, either. She was about to try when the doorbell rang. A glance through one of the transom windows beside the portal caused the color to leave her face. From where he stood, Nate couldn't see the visitor. "Who is it?"

"Professor Rylander."

Obviously, Nate thought, the English lit department had news, too.

Brooke looked to Nate to run interference. "The boys can't know he's here. I'll talk to him outside."

"I'll take care of it," Nate promised.

Trembling slightly, she opened the front door and eased out onto the porch, shutting the door behind her. While she was doing that, Nate noticed a United States Postal

Service truck pull up at the curb. A mailwoman got out, clipboard in hand, and headed up the walk. The uniformed courier stopped in front of Brooke, passed her a card for signature. She waited for Brooke to comply, then handed over a letter.

Phineas Rylander seemed to be urging Brooke to open it. She did, and paled even more.

Nate was torn between his role as sentry and that of protector.

Decision made, he started toward the front door. Only to have Brooke open it and slip through, certified letter in hand.

"What's going on?" he asked in concern.

"Professor Rylander wanted to let me know that the book party was canceled."

"How come?" Cole walked in to join them.

Landry was still outside, sitting on the back patio.

Brooke hesitated.

Cole's glance fell to the publisher's logo on the envelope in her hand. And suddenly, Nate realized, the do-or-die moment Brooke had been dreading was upon them.

IT WAS NOW OR NEVER, Brooke thought. Yet even as she opened her mouth to explain to Cole what was going on, she was torn with indecision. Should she destroy what little illusion her son had left? Or continue covering for Seamus to protect Cole, and wait until her son was much older to let him know the whole story? She had only seconds to decide. And in the end, she knew what she had to do.

Brooke looked her son in the eye and stuck to the facts she felt she could reveal to him at this time. "The publisher has decided not to go ahead with your father's last book."

Cole's brow furrowed in confusion. "How come?"

Her chest tightened. She knew what Nate would want her to do here. She knew he wouldn't respect her if she didn't come clean. But she wouldn't live up to his high standard of parenting. She still couldn't adhere to—or even agree with—his standard of parenting. "I'm not sure," Brooke fibbed finally. "But the publisher also told the university of their decision, so the party in your dad's honor has been canceled, too."

Cole's face crumpled. "This doesn't make sense!" he cried. "People love all that mushy stuff."

Brooke recalled taking Cole to a book signing when he was six. Seamus had been surrounded by fawning women and students who idolized him. But that had been when Seamus still had a seductively cheery outlook on life. "Well, that was part of the problem, honey. This new collection of poems was very dark, and there just…" She swallowed, aware she was about to tell an even bigger fib. "There isn't a market for it. Not the kind that's needed."

"Well, at least we've got the advance copy," Cole said. "In case we want to look at it someday."

Actually, Brooke thought, they didn't, as she had given that to the intellectual-property lawyer she'd hired to represent their interests. Unable to tell Cole any of that right now, however, she changed the subject to a matter even more pressing. "How's Landry?"

Cole's expression darkened. "Bummed."

Her heart swelled. "Can we do anything for him?" she asked.

Her son shook his head and averted his gaze to the backyard, where Landry was still hanging out, alone. "I think we're going to walk down to the park for a while, if it's okay."

Brooke looked at Nate for a decision.

He shrugged, then turned back to Cole. "Okay by me, if it'll help. You got your cell phone?"

Cole patted his pocket.

"Call if you need anything," Brooke advised.

"Okay." Cole went back outside, spoke to Landry. The taller teen stood, and together they headed out the back gate.

Feeling as if she had dodged yet another bullet, Brooke let out a long, slow breath. "What didn't you tell Cole?" Nate asked.

The simple question evoked a flood of guilt. Not trusting herself to speak, she handed over the letter.

Nate read it for himself. "…due to the fact that it cannot be established that Seamus Mitchell is the sole author and owner of this Work…and is at risk of legal claim, suit and/or action…Publisher is giving notice of its intention to cancel publication of the work. All advance monies paid to the Author's Estate are to be returned to the Publisher, within six months of this notification…as per the terms of the contract…." He put down the letter. "Is Iris Lomax going to sue?"

"So far all she has done is threaten. She's met with the university and their intellectual-property lawyers. And while they can't prove Seamus authored any of the poetry, even partially, any more than I can, they don't feel she has produced enough evidence of her own to actually prevail in civil court." Brooke sighed. "But just the publicity of the claim would be devastating to all concerned. Hence, the publisher's and the university's immediate move to permanently distance themselves from Seamus and anything he may or may not have done."

"Even so…" Nate shook his head, clearly worried. "You have to let Cole know what's going on."

As if it were only that easy, Brooke thought bitterly,

wishing she could have depended on Nate to support her in this very important regard. She threw up her arms in frustration. "I can't tell Cole his father is suspected of plagiarizing the work of a young woman he was having an affair with!"

Nate challenged her with the lift of his brow. "Better to let him find out some other way?"

The sarcasm stung. "I'll talk to my lawyer, have him come to some kind of settlement with Iris Lomax to keep her quiet."

Nate gave her a long look, his expression grave. "We have to be realistic here. Too many people know about it now for it to stay quiet indefinitely. If the Dallas or Fort Worth papers, or even faculty at one of the competing universities in the area learn of this, the news will be public. You can't let Cole find out that way. You owe it to him to be honest with him."

Brooke knew they were at a turning point. Nate would either understand her point of view or he wouldn't. "My goal here is to protect him. To keep Cole from becoming disenchanted."

Nate shook his head in silent censure. "By lying to him, directly and by omission."

Brooke's knees felt as shaky as her moral center. "Whose side are you on?" she cried, upset.

"Yours."

She regarded Nate stonily, feeling as if her heart were encased in a block of ice. "It doesn't sound that way."

Nate picked up the paper and waved it impatiently. "If Cole finds out any of this, and realizes you knew and didn't tell him, he is going to be completely devastated. He's going to question whether or not he can ever trust you again."

Nate wasn't telling her anything she hadn't already

thought about—many times. Brooke knew this had the potential to destroy her relationship with her son. She didn't need Nate questioning her beliefs, making her doubt herself, the same way Seamus had done, time and time again. "I don't see that it helped Landry to know the truth," she countered, resolute.

Nate's eyes turned grim. "If you're referencing the DNA test—"

Brooke's lower lip trembled as she forced herself to assert, "Landry would have been better off if you had just denied that it was possible you could be his father."

Nate braced his hands on his waist. "I didn't have a choice once he saw that photo and realized that his mother was still engaged to me eight months before he was born."

Brooke lifted her chin. "You could have made something up, or... I don't know..."

Nate's jaw clenched. "I couldn't do that to him."

"He's suffering."

"We both are," Nate declared flatly. "But we'll get over it, because we dealt with each other and the situation honestly."

Brooke had never considered Nate a cockeyed optimist, until now. "And if you don't? If Landry remains distraught and confused...then what?"

"We'll figure out a way to make things better."

Silence fell between them, every bit as devastating as their words.

Brooke held up a hand. "I can't talk about this anymore."

He clamped a hand on her shoulder. "We have to."

She shrugged free, feeling as if her heart was breaking. "This is my decision to make, Nate," she reminded him, hanging on to her composure by a thread. "Your only job as my friend—" *and lover* "—is to back off and support whatever I decide."

"Listen to me, Brooke. I know what it is to be so devastated by just the thought of betrayal that you can't deal, because I did that with Seraphina. But burying your head in the sand and pretending a situation doesn't exist doesn't help anything. It only makes things worse." He looked her square in the eye. "As painful as it is, you have to start facing reality here and help Cole deal with his father's frailties."

Her spirits sank even lower. "That sounds like an ultimatum."

Nate stared at her, a force not to be denied. "I can't just stand by and do nothing while you put yourself and Cole in harm's way."

Brooke braced herself for the worst, even as she stipulated angrily, "You can't tell Cole, either."

Nate exhaled in displeasure. "I wouldn't have to. Your son is a smart kid. As time goes on, he'll figure it all out. And like I said…if it comes to that, he'll never trust you again."

Brooke's lower lip trembled. "You're supposed to back me up!"

But to her dismay, he refused. He moved toward her, his arms held out beseechingly. "If we're going to have a relationship that endures, we have to be able to talk about things and work them out, even when we disagree."

Brooke evaded his embrace and stalked past him. "What you really mean is that I have to do things your way." She whirled around to face him once again. "I've already been in a marriage like that. Where my husband belittled my opinions and made all the major decisions for us, and I had no choice but to follow. I won't do that again, either."

Nate rocked back on his heels. "You're deliberately misinterpreting."

She stomped closer. "And you're deliberately under-playing the significance of this argument! I can't be with someone who won't do everything in his power to protect my son."

Nate looked even more irritated. "And I can't be with someone who would willingly lie to her son, or mine."

There it was, the ultimatum she had been expecting all along. The one that told her…once again…she just wasn't good enough to hold the love and attention of the man she wanted.

Brooke worked to keep her emotions under wraps. "So it's over?" she asked with icy control.

Nate shrugged, no longer the hot-blooded lover she de-sired and once again the accomplished CEO who always walked off alone. "It has to be," he told her, in that crisp businesslike voice she knew so well. He exhaled in silent censure, shook his head, then once again met her eyes. "Thank God we didn't tell the kids there was ever anything going on in the first place."

Bitterness welled inside her. Brooke looked at Nate, feeling more disillusioned than ever before. "I can't argue with that."

Refusing to cry in front of him, she rushed toward the front door. "I'm going to go check on the boys." Once past Nate, she practically sprinted down the block.

He was right behind her, his long strides eating up the sidewalk. Brooke rushed on. She got to the small two-acre park in the middle of her subdivision. Two toddlers were playing on the swings with their mothers. A group of boys was playing pickup basketball. There was no sign of Cole or Landry.

Nate caught up with her, his strides as unhurried as

hers had been rushed. Hands clamped on his waist, pushing back the edges of his suit coat, he gazed around. "Is this where they're supposed to be?" he growled in frustration.

Brooke nodded, scanning the area, to no avail.

"Anywhere else they might have gone?"

Beginning to feel a little panicky, Brooke forced herself to concentrate. "I don't know. You ask the boys and I'll ask the two moms."

Nate and Brooke went their separate ways. When they returned to each other, her news was bad. Judging by the grim expression on Nate's face, so was his. "They were here, but they didn't play ball," he reported. "They went down to the corner and hopped on a city bus instead."

NATE DIALED LANDRY'S mobile-phone number. Brooke dialed Cole's. Neither answered. Frantic, Brooke checked her cell-phone messages, while Nate walked off to do the same.

She had one from the IP attorney, asking her to call. Apparently he'd heard about the book cancellation and the university's position, too. The second was an emotional entreaty from Cole. "You have to stop treating me like a kid, Mom, and start telling me what's really going on! 'Cause until you do—" his voice broke slightly before becoming defiant once again "—I'm not coming home!" *Click.*

Nate walked back toward Brooke. Trembling, she handed him her phone and had him listen to Cole's message.

He handed her his.

Landry's disconsolate voice sounded in her ear. "Look, Nate, I know you're trying to do the right thing here. You always do the right thing. But the truth is I'm not your kid. And that has to matter a lot more than you say. I know it does. So…you're off the hook," Landry choked out. "I'm outta here." *Click*.

"I can't believe this." Heart pounding, Brooke clutched the cell phone. "They've run away."

Nate put his emotions aside and focused on the problem. "They can't have gotten very far."

Maybe not, but… Brooke swallowed as a hundred horror stories crossed her mind. "You don't have to get very far from home for something bad to happen, Nate."

He grimaced and wrapped a reassuring arm around her shoulders. Determination lit his eyes. "We'll find them."

Brooke only wished she felt as sure. "How?" she asked, once again on the verge of breaking down.

Nate tightened his grip on her protectively before releasing her altogether. Heading back toward her house, he said, "Those phones I gave them are equipped with GPS. I didn't activate the feature. I didn't think we'd need to, but I'm sure as soon as the service provider turns it on, we'll know exactly where they are. Unfortunately, I'm going to have to go over to one of the stores in person to get that done."

At least they had a plan. Brooke was prepared to do her part, too. She pulled herself together, as she too raced toward her home, where their vehicles were parked. "While you do that, I'm going to start driving around the neighborhood, looking for them."

"Call me if you find them," he said, as he climbed into his Jaguar.

"I will," Brooke promised, before running inside to get her purse and car keys. "And you do the same."

Brooke checked out all Cole's favorite haunts. The burger place a mile and a half from home. The video store and the park. The strip mall and, farther away, the bigger retail shopping mall where they had gone to get clothes and haircuts.

While she searched, she called Cole on his cell phone every five or ten minutes, leaving another message, pleading with him to let her know where he was so they could talk this over. She also called a few of his close school friends. No one had heard from him.

As for Landry... He had no one she knew of to turn to...except... And suddenly, Brooke knew. She picked up her phone and dialed again. And found the answer she had been looking for.

NATE AND BROOKE MET UP in the parking lot of the retirement center. "Thank God they're safe," she said, aware she had never been happier to see him or be with him in her life. She needed Nate's love and support, and right now, even though she supposed they were still technically broken up, she could feel both exuding from him in waves.

Nate again wrapped a comforting arm around her shoulders.

Once again, Brooke noted, almost by default they were parenting their two boys together. But was it anything more than that? Could it ever be again? She didn't know the answer. The inscrutable expression on his handsome face gave her no clue. "Do any of them know that we're aware the boys are here?" Nate asked quietly.

Hoping the two of them still had a chance to make things right with each other, as well as their two sons, Brooke relinquished control and leaned on Nate's strength. "I asked the staff not to say anything to the boys or Jessalyn, just to keep them here until we arrived."

As they neared the entrance to the building, Nate dropped his arm and moved away from her. "Guess we should have come here first," he murmured, the brooding, serious CEO look back on his face.

Brooke's shoulders slumped. "Guess we should have done a lot of things." Treated Cole like the grown-up he was turning into, let him in on the problems, no matter how painful the process.

Without warning, Nate reached over and clasped her hand, one friend to another. He looked her in the eye. "We'll get through this."

With him by her side, Brooke felt they just might.

They walked into the center, signed in at the reception desk and then headed back to Jessalyn's private suite, where the boys were holding court with Landry's great-grandmother.

As Brooke and Nate walked in, both boys started guiltily, then just as quickly turned defiant. Cole clamped his arms across his chest and thrust his chin out stubbornly. "I'm not going home until you tell me the truth."

Jessalyn reached for her cane. "Perhaps I should let you-all talk alone," she said.

Landry held on to her arm. "No, Gran. Stay."

"He's right," Nate told her kindly. "You're family. And this is a family matter."

"I told Landry and Cole both they should not have run away," Jessalyn said, pausing to give her teenage callers a stern look. "As difficult as it can sometimes be, there are better ways to make a point."

"And the point of all this, for me, anyway—" Landry locked eyes with Nate "—is I am not your kid."

THIS WAS IT, Nate thought. His big chance to step up to the plate and figure out how to be the kind of father Landry deserved. There was no time to lean on Brooke to help bail him out, or to go to the guys for advice. It was his chance to be there emotionally for *his kid*—the way his parents had never been for him. And Landry was his kid. Nate had never been more sure of that. The question was how to convey it to him, to make him believe....

Nate pulled up a chair and sank into it so he and Landry were sitting face-to-face.

It was time, Nate thought, to dig deep—deeper than he had ever gone before—and speak straight from his gut. Because he was never going to get in the game the way he wanted to be, if he didn't risk his whole heart.

"While I don't agree with your actions today—and for the record, if you ever pull a stunt like this again, you're going to be grounded within an inch of your life." He shot a warning look in Landry's direction. "But that being said... your actions did serve a purpose. And that was to get my attention."

Nate held up a staying hand when Landry started to object. "Let me get this off my chest, okay?" He sighed. "The truth is, you were right—the DNA test *does* matter. I wanted us to be linked that way. In fact, I felt sure we were, because over the last few weeks I feel like we've truly become father and son. So it sure would have been nice to know we shared the same chromosomes." He paused for a long moment. "But even though the test didn't turn out the way we'd hoped, it will not ever change the way I feel about you."

"How can you say that?" Landry lamented, tears welling in his eyes.

"Because I love you, Landry. You are my family," Nate said emphatically. "We're father and son in every way that matters. And to make it real—to make it lasting—all we have to do is take the next step and make it legal." He paused, his heart in his throat. "So what do you say? I want to be your father from now on. But the question is do you want to be my son?"

Chapter Fifteen

Brooke could not stop crying and Landry hadn't even answered yet.

Nate was the best man—the best dad—she had ever had the privilege to know. Landry was one lucky kid. The question was, did he know it yet? Judging from the unchecked tears pouring down his face—and Nate's—they were both beginning to grasp the importance of this link they shared.

"Well, heck," Landry mumbled, crying openly now, "if you put it that way." The lanky teen stood and threw himself into Nate's arms. The lump in Brooke's throat grew, along with the joy in her heart.

"I'll call Ms. Tanous and get the legal stuff going first thing tomorrow morning," Nate said thickly, holding the boy tightly.

Landry nodded, and continued to weep, in joy and relief, while Cole watched with tearful longing.

Nate finally clapped Landry on the back. Dabbing their eyes, appearing a little embarrassed, the two stepped apart. Cole sat there, waiting. Obviously happy for his friend, yet more bereft than ever for himself. And Brooke knew it was time she stepped up to the challenge, too. In a way she had been avoiding.

She brought a chair over and sat opposite Cole, the way

Nate had done with Landry. Gently, she reached out and took her son's hand. She hated the resistance she felt from him, but she understood, and knew she deserved it. "You're right to be upset with me, Cole. I haven't been honest with you about what is going on, either."

"Why not?" he challenged, clearly angry now.

Brooke gulped and kept her gaze on him steady. "Because I was trying to protect you," she explained gently.

Cole's lip thrust out mutinously. "From what?" he demanded.

"The truth."

Silence fell between them. "This has something to do with that Iris Lomax person, doesn't it?" Cole asked emotionally.

It was Brooke's turn to be taken aback. "What do you know about that?"

"She was Dad's teaching assistant. She used to come over to the house sometimes when you weren't there." Cole explained. "They were writing poetry together—the poetry that was in Dad's new book."

Poetry that had detailed the suffocating confinement of marriage...countered by the joyous rebirth of passion. Her heart sank. Unsure whether she felt more humiliated or foolish, she asked, "You're sure they were doing it together?"

Cole shrugged, looking unbearably young again. "Well...from what I overheard...Ms. Lomax was coming up with most of the stuff, but Dad was the one who was saying it was either okay or not." Cole frowned. "You know how picky he was about words and stuff."

Yes, Brooke had known. Up to now, she had only thought that impacted Cole because his father had been too impatient and overbearingly critical to help his son with his homework. Had she been more attuned to what was going on, she surely would have seen Cole was upset about much more than that with his dad, in the months leading up to Seamus's untimely death. Instead, she had naively chalked it up to father-son angst.

Aware that Cole was waiting for her to explain, she forged on. "Well, that's been part of the problem that I didn't want you to know about. Ms. Lomax claims that your father stole that work from her. She says he wasn't the author of the poetry, that she was. As a result, the publisher had no choice but to stop publication of the book." Brooke exhaled softly. "If your dad was still here with us, it would be different. Because he isn't here to defend himself or explain whatever the writing process was that he and Ms. Lomax used, they can't be sure he didn't plagiarize her writing."

A cynical expression crossed Cole's face. He sat back in his chair with a disillusioned but accepting sigh. "I think he did, Mom. At least a little bit."

Given the extent of Seamus's writer's block, so did Brooke. "I've been thinking we may want to turn the rights for the material over to Iris Lomax, let her publish it under her name, or her name and Dad's," Brooke said.

"I think we ought to just give the stuff to her, Mom, and leave Dad out of it," Cole said.

"I think you're right," Brooke agreed. It would make so many of their problems go away. "Morally, it's the right thing to do." And legally, and financially... "Anyway, that is why the university canceled the party—because there is no new book to celebrate," she finished.

Cole looked her in the eye. Something still seemed to be troubling him, she noted, and the continued wariness in his expression made her heart sink. He was still looking at her as if he thought she had betrayed him on some level. Obviously, they hadn't aired all their troubles yet. She waited for him to tell her what was on his mind.

Finally, Cole blurted, "Did Dad have an affair with Ms. Lomax?"

Another stab to the heart. Not for the infidelity—Brooke had long ago come to terms with that—but for the fact that her son had to suffer the pain of the betrayal, too. Careful only to deal with what her son was old enough to handle, she asked, "Do you even know what that is?" She hadn't covered it in her sex talk with him, and neither had the school….

Cole rolled his eyes, then sighed. "Mom, I'm thirteen, not ten! Yes, I know what that is! It's when two people who aren't married sleep together and stuff."

Brooke's defenses went up. Apparently she wasn't as good at this truth-telling as Nate was yet. She studied her son. "Why would you think they had an affair?" It broke her heart that she and Cole were forced to have this conversation.

He shoved his chair back several inches and stared at her with adolescent angst, commanding her to treat him like the adult he deemed himself to be. "Because that night at the hospital, when I went there to see Dad in the CCU, I heard some of the nurses talking about how horrible it was that he'd been with that grad student when he died, instead of his wife. It sounded like…" Cole choked.

"He and that Iris lady were in bed," Landry interjected for him.

Cole sent him a grateful glance, then turned back to his mom.

She didn't know what to say.

Cole continued, more composed now. He seemed determined to get this all out. "And that wasn't really a big surprise, because he was always flirting with Iris Lomax when she came to the house." He gulped. "And I saw him kissing her a few times." Bitterness mingled with the confusion and hurt on Cole's young face. "He told me not to tell you, and I didn't because I didn't want to hurt you, but…it made me mad, seeing him do that with her. It wasn't right for him to cheat on you like that…."

No, it hadn't been.

The worse thing, Brooke thought with a stab of guilt that went soul-deep, was that Cole had been forced to carry this burden alone for several years. Her own body sagged miserably before she reached out to touch his arm. "You should have told me what you'd seen."

Visibly confused, he shrank from her touch. "I couldn't. I didn't want to hurt *you*."

And yet, Brooke thought, even more miserably, they had both done that anyway, despite their best intentions.

Cole sized her up. "But you were already hurt, weren't you?"

"Yes," Brooke noted sadly. "As were you."

Cole waited. Brooke knew she had to say something that would help her son put this all in perspective. But what? She turned to Nate. He gave her an encouraging glance, and suddenly she knew what she had to do was put it all out there, and let the chips fall where they may.

"Yes, your father had an affair with Ms. Lomax. I didn't know about it until the night he died, and I found out then by accident, same as you." She took a deep breath and forced herself to go on. "I had hoped you would never learn about it. I didn't want you to think less of your father…." *But instead you ended up thinking less of me.* Brooke felt like a total failure as a mother. "So I covered for him."

This, Cole already knew.

His jaw clenched. "Were you ever going to tell me?"

The fifty-million-dollar question. Once again, she forced

herself to dig deep and answer honestly. "I don't know. But I should have told you at least the part you could handle at the time. Because if I had done that it would have opened the door for you to confess to me all you had seen and heard." She sighed with regret. "You wouldn't have had to carry these secrets for all these years, and neither would I. And that would have been better for both of us, I think."

Cole relaxed, at ease once again. He regarded her with forgiveness in his eyes. "Yeah," he told her gravely, "it would have."

Brooke reached across and clasped both his hands in hers. "I'm sorry I made a mistake." She squeezed his palms with all the mother love she had to offer and looked him straight in the eye. "I promise you I won't do it again. If something bad happens, I'll tell you right away. And I want you to do the same with me."

Cole's eyes welled, even as the love poured out of him. "I will…I promise," he said thickly.

Her own eyes misting over, even as relief poured through her, Brooke stood and held out her arms. Cole went into them, and they hugged each other fiercely.

Finally, Cole stepped back. "There's only one more thing we want to know," he told his mother bluntly. He turned and looked at Landry.

Whatever the two young men were thinking, Brooke noted, they were totally on the same page.

Landry nodded, and Cole pivoted back to Brooke and Nate. He took a deep breath and said, "Me and Landry want to know what's going on with the two of you."

Cole paused a beat, and wordlessly, Landry urged him on, as only an older brother could. Then Cole demanded even more bluntly, "Do you love Nate, Mom? And does Nate love you?"

OUT OF THE MOUTHS of teens, Brooke thought, as her heart kicked inside her chest.

Did they love each other? Brooke knew how she felt, notwithstanding their recent disagreement. But how did he feel? Was it enough? Should they even be discussing this? Especially now, when so much had already been disclosed.

With a mixture of relief and apprehension, she realized that Nate apparently thought so. His posture CEO-confident, he closed the distance between them and took her hand. She searched his eyes, still not knowing what lay ahead, almost afraid to wish….

His expression inscrutable, Nate spoke to Cole, Landry and Jessalyn. "It's a good question. And I'm going to answer it, but I need a moment to speak with your mother privately first."

Jessalyn smiled, a matchmaker's gleam in her eyes.

Cole's glance narrowed speculatively, as did Landry's.

The next thing Brooke knew, Nate had placed a cordial hand beneath her elbow. Gallantly, he escorted her from the room and down the hall, past the groups gathered in the solarium, to the deserted patio outside. As she swung around to face him, her heart rate kicked up another notch. Never had she hoped for so much.

"First, I owe you an apology," Nate said.

Was that all this was? A chance to clear the air before going back to tell everyone that although they had briefly tested the waters, they were going to be "just friends"?

Brooke knew only that she didn't want to squander what chance of happiness she had left. Still holding Nate's steady gaze, she swallowed the knot of emotion in her throat. "I owe you one, too."

A corner of his mouth kicked up ruefully. "You knew

the whole DNA thing was more emotionally complicated than I was willing to let it be."

She nodded. "And you knew I should have leveled with Cole all along, that pain is as much a part of life as joy. And as much as we want to, we can't shield our children from pain." Feeling as if her whole soul had been laid bare, Brooke joked nervously, "Put our two methods together and we would almost be the perfect parent."

Nate chuckled, and she continued self-effacingly, "Minus another half-million mistakes along the way."

He sobered, suddenly looking as if his whole future was on the line, too. "I'm beginning to think it might be okay to let this idea of perfectionism go, at least when it comes to families and relationships."

Praying this wasn't a prelude to his giving up on them, Brooke went very still. She swallowed. "What are you saying?"

"My family was run like a business commodity when I was growing up."

Brooke knew Nate was insecure in his ability to connect with family the way loved ones should. He wasn't the only one who had come up missing. "I never had a dad." Never knew what a male role model in the home should be...until she'd seen Nate in action.

He compressed his lips together ruefully. "When it comes to relationships—the idea of marriage...kids—I don't have a clue what I'm doing."

At last, something in common, something to build on again. She took in a nervous breath, stepped closer and splayed her hands across the solid warmth of his chest. "Here's a secret. A lot of times I don't, either."

His hands settled around her waist. "But I know one thing, Brooke."

Beneath her fingertips, his heart was beating very hard and fast. Almost as quickly as her own, in fact.

"My life is better and a heck of a lot more satisfying with you in it."

Hope rushed through her, followed swiftly by an overwhelming tide of emotion. "My life is better, too," she whispered, misting up. "Way better, as Cole and Landry would say."

Nate nodded, ever so solemn and truthful and determined. "And that's why we have to throw in the towel, surrender our pride and admit we both lost the battle to keep it casual days ago," he finished in a rusty-sounding voice.

Brooke took a deep breath, braced herself. More nervous than ever, she asked, "You want to tell the boys we're dating?" She realized she was finally sure enough of her own feelings to take that leap.

"No," Nate said, in the flat decisive voice that said his mind was already made up. "We should have done that a while ago. Since we didn't..." He paused and searched her eyes. "Cole and Landry have been very clear that they want more than that from us. They want us to be a family."

Brooke's heart sank as the declaration she had been hoping to hear fell short. "I know that," she replied quietly. *I want that, too.* "But we can't continue to join forces just to fulfill some sort of fantasy the boys have of what their life would be like if we all stay together. Especially when we just promised them they would have the whole truth from both of us from here on out." Although what that was, on Nate's part, she *still* didn't know.

His grip on her tightened. "And it's a vow I mean to deliver on," he said in a tone that made her feel safe and protected.

The pulse in his throat was throbbing.

"Which is why I have to tell you what I should have told you days ago." Nate paused again and looked deep into her eyes, his expression raw, and filled with the longing she harbored deep inside. "I don't just want you or need you or want to spend every waking minute with you." He paused, then continued thickly, "Although for the record, all of that is true."

"For me, too." Brooke's own voice broke slightly.

Nate flashed a crooked smile. "That's good to hear," he told her reverently. "Because I love you, Brooke, with everything I am and everything I have. I love you more than I've ever loved anyone in my life."

Relief filtered through her, followed swiftly by joy. She threw her arms around his neck, brought him close and whispered tenderly, "Oh, Nate!" She was thrilled to realize she was finally getting everything she had ever dreamed. "I love you, too," she cried, trembling. She drew back and looked deep into his eyes. "So very much."

He gathered her even closer, bent his head and kissed her with the promise of all the days and nights to come.

Finally, he bussed her on the forehead and declared with typical CEO efficiency, "Then there is only one thing for us to do."

Epilogue

One year later...

"What did you say to the boys?" Brooke emerged from the bedroom dressed in a knee-length white silk dress. She watched as Landry and Cole raced away from the caretaker's cottage, showing the same energy and excitement with which they had dashed in.

"My credo, since I met you." Nate strode toward her, looking resplendent in his own light summer suit and tie. He took her hands in his and leaned forward to tenderly kiss her lips. "Slow and steady wins the race every time."

Brooke tingled from the caress. Holding on to Nate, she gazed up at him affectionately. The last year had been the happiest of her life, and the future looked even brighter. "Did they listen?"

His eyes sparkled with merriment. "Let's just say they're still intent on making a few 'miracles' of their own, via a surprise or two."

Curiosity mingled with the overwhelming excitement deep inside her. "Of which you know...?"

"Nothing," he confirmed, wrapping his arms around her. "I'll be as amazed by whatever they've dreamed up for us as you will be."

Brooke cuddled close and laid her cheek against his shoulder. Suffused with his warm, hard strength, she murmured, "The two of them are so sweet, to be putting on a small, private wedding for us."

It *was* an amazing gift, Nate thought.

All he and Brooke had had to do was okay the budget for the celebration and put them in touch with Jack's wife, wedding planner Caroline Mayer Gaines. The rest had been done, to the astonishment of all their friends, primarily by the two teenage boys. Now, he and Brooke—who had no superstitions about seeing each other prior to the ceremony—were sequestered together, awaiting their cue that it was time to get the show on the road.

Nate watched as Brooke went over to her jewelry case and removed the diamond necklace and earrings he had gifted her with the previous Christmas.

He helped her with the clasp of her necklace, while they continued talking about the wedding.

"Although as far as Cole and Landry are concerned," she reminded him with a teasing look, "we gave them no choice."

That was true, Nate thought. Both boys had vehemently vetoed Nate and Brooke's original plan to have their wedding ceremony in a judge's chamber, just down the hall from the courtroom where the adoption of both boys had become official that very morning. Now, Cole was officially Nate's son, and Landry was legally the son of Brooke as well as Nate. With Brooke and Nate's wedding, the circle would be complete and everyone would at long last have the loving family they had wanted.

"The kids wanted us to have a honeymoon. And we wanted to have the adoption on the first anniversary of the day we all met."

Brooke smiled and nodded. "It's all working out."

Cole raced back in. "Hey, Mom, you look great! You, too, Nate! Jessalyn and her friends from the retirement center have arrived!"

Landry was right behind him. "The rest of your friends and the judge are all here, too. So as soon as the sound team is done setting up, we're ready to go."

"Any clue what the music is going to be?"

Cole and Landry looked at each other and grinned. Cole said, "We figure when you hear it, you'll recognize it," he replied. "Nate, you will lead the way down the aisle. Landry is your witness, so he'll follow you. I'll go next, since I'm the official witness for Mom, and Mom…you're the bride—and the main attraction—so you'll go last."

Cole and Landry slipped outside.

A moment later, they came back in. Cole handed Brooke a beribboned bouquet of Texas wildflowers.

The strains of the famous Goo Goo Dolls song, "Let Love In"—a favorite of both Brooke and Nate—started up. The teens passed Brooke and Nate each a pair of dark sunglasses. "You're going to want these." They grinned, sliding on their own shades, then led the way out of the caretaker's cottage, onto the lawn. And together, the four of them danced and celebrated their way toward the guests….

"THIS IS ONE FANTASTIC wedding," Grady McCabe mused, several hours later, as the party wound on.

Dan grinned. "Foosball and Ping-Pong." He looked toward the sport court, where a tournament for the young people was set up and a wildly good time was being had by all.

Jack sipped champagne. "A wedding cake in the shape of your mansion. And a groom's cake that looks like the caretaker's cottage."

Nate shrugged. "A great sentimental choice by the boys, since this is where it all happened." Where he and Brooke fell in love, and Landry and Cole bonded. Where he'd become a father for the first—and second—time. And they all became the family they wanted and needed.

Travis slapped him on the shoulder as a radiant Brooke headed toward them. "Looks like you've got it all, Nate."

Nate's glance encompassed the loved ones of his four best friends, then turned back to them. Two years ago, they'd all been single. Now, they were all happily married. "We all do."

The guys murmured in agreement.

Brooke slipped her arm through Nate's. "The dancing is about to start."

Nate knew the kids had picked out the music for this, too. "Any idea what our song is going to be this time?"

"All I know is it's a slow tune. And very romantic. At least in their view."

"That's all I need to know." Nate winked at Brooke, then turned to the guys. "Excuse us, fellas. I've got a date to dance with the love of my life."

* * * * *

LET'S TALK
Romance

For exclusive extracts, competitions
and special offers, find us online:

f facebook.com/millsandboon

◎ @millsandboonuk

𝕏 @millsandboon

Or get in touch on 0844 844 1351*

For all the latest titles coming soon, visit
millsandboon.co.uk/nextmonth